COMA

a Novel
by
Robin Cook

A SIGNET BOOK

SIGNET
Published by the Penguin Group
Penguin Books USA Inc., 375 Hudson Street,
New York, New York 10014, U.S.A.
Penguin Books Ltd, 27 Wrights Lane,
London W8 5TZ, England
Penguin Books Australia Ltd, Ringwood,
Victoria, Australia
Penguin Books Canada Ltd, 10 Alcorn Avenue,
Toronto, Ontario, Canada M4V 3B2
Penguin Books (N.Z.) Ltd, 182–190 Wairau Road,
Auckland 10, New Zealand

Penguin Books Ltd, Registered Offices:
Harmondsworth, Middlesex, England

This is an authorized reprint of a hardcover edition published by
Little, Brown and Company. Published simultaneously in Canada by
Little, Brown and Company (Canada) Limited.

First Signet Printing, December, 1977
46 45 44 43 42 41 40 39

 REGISTERED TRADEMARK—MARCA REGISTRADA

Printed in the United States of America

*In memory of my father,
recognition of my mother,
and thanks to Sharron.*

COMA

PROLOGUE
February 14, 1976

Nancy Greenly lay on the operating table on her back, staring up at the large kettledrum-shaped lights in operating room No. 8, trying to be calm. She had had several pre-op injections, which she was told would make her sleepy and happy. She was neither. Nancy was more nervous and apprehensive than before the shots. Worst of all, she felt totally, completely, and absolutely defenseless. In all her twenty-three years, she had never before felt so embarrassed and so vulnerable. Covering her was a white linen bed sheet. The edge was frayed, and there was a small tear at the corner. That bothered her, and she didn't know why. Under the sheet, she had on one of those hospital gowns which tie behind the neck and descend only to mid-thigh. The back was open. Other than that, there was only the sanitary napkin, which she knew was already soaked with her own blood. She hated and feared the hospital at that moment and wanted to scream, to run out of the room and down the corridor. But she didn't. She feared the bleeding that she had been experiencing more than the cruel detached environment of the hospital; both made her acutely aware of her mortality, and that was something she rarely liked to face.

At 7:11 on the morning of February 14, 1976, the eastern sky over Boston was a chalky gray, and the bumper-to-bumper cars coming into the city had their headlights on. The temperature was thirty-eight degrees, and the people in the streets walked quickly on their separate tracks. There were no voices, just the sound of the machines and the wind.

Within the Boston Memorial Hospital, things were different. The stark fluorescent lights illuminated every square inch of the OR area. The bustle of activity and excited voices lent credence to the dictum that surgery started at 7:30 sharp. That meant the scalpels actually cut the skin at 7:30; the patient fetching, the prep, the scrub, and the induction under anesthesia had to be all completed before 7:30.

As a consequence, at 7:11, the activity in the OR area was in full swing, including room number 8. There was nothing special about No. 8. It was a typical OR in the Memorial. The walls were a neutral-colored tile; the floors were a speckled vinyl. At 7:30, February 14, 1976, a D&C—dilation and curettage, a routine gynecological procedure—was scheduled in room No. 8. The patient was Nancy Greenly; the anesthesiologist was Dr. Robert Billing, a second-year anesthesiology resident; the scrub nurse was Ruth Jenkins; the circulating nurse was Gloria D'Mateo. The surgeon was George Major—the new, young partner of one of the older, established OB-GYN men—and he was in the dressing room donning his surgical scrub suit, while the others were hard at work.

Nancy Greenly had been bleeding for eleven days. At first she passed it off as a normal period, despite the fact that it was several weeks early. There had been no premenstrual discomfort, maybe a vague cramp on the morning the first spotting occurred. But after that it had been a painless affair, waxing and waning. Each night she hoped to have seen the last of it but had awakened to find the tampon soaked. The telephone conversations, first with Dr. Major's nurse, then with the doctor himself, had allayed her fears for progressively shorter and shorter durations. And it was a bother, a gigantic nuisance, and as it was with such things, it had come at a most inopportune time. She thought about Kim Devereau coming up to spend his spring break from Duke Law School with her in Boston. Her roommate had fortuitously made plans to spend that week skiing at Killington. Everything seemed to have been falling into beautiful, romantic place, everything except the bleeding. There was no way Nancy could blithely dismiss it. She was a delicately angular and attractive girl with an aristocratic appearance. About her person she was fastidious. If her hair was the slightest bit dirty she felt uneasy. So the continued bleeding made her feel messy, unattractive, out of control. Eventually it began to frighten her.

Nancy remembered lying on the couch with her feet up on the arm, reading the editorial page of the *Globe* while Kim was in the kitchen making drinks. She had become aware of a strange sensation in her vagina. It was different from anything she had ever felt before. It felt as if she was being inflated by a warm soft mass. There had been absolutely no pain or discomfort. At first she was perplexed as to the origin of the sensation, but then she felt a warmth on her inner thighs and a tickling trickle of fluid run down into the recess of her buttocks. Without undue anxiety, she recognized that she was bleeding, bleeding very fast. Casually, without moving her body, she had turned her head toward the kitchen and called out, "Kim, would you do me a favor and call an ambulance?"

"What's wrong?" asked Kim, hurrying to her.

"I'm bleeding very fast," said Nancy calmly, "but it's nothing to get alarmed about. An extra-heavy period, I guess. I just should go to the hospital right away. So please call the ambulance."

The ambulance ride had been uneventful, without sirens or drama. She had to wait longer than she thought reasonable in the holding area of the emergency room. Dr. Major had appeared and for the first time awakened a feeling of gladness in Nancy. She had always detested the routine vaginal exams to which she had submitted and had associated the face, the bearing, and the smell of Dr. Major with them. But when he appeared in the emergency room, she felt glad to see him, to the point of suppressing tears.

The vaginal examination in the emergency room had been, without doubt, the worst she had ever experienced. A flimsy curtain, which was constantly being whisked back and forth, was the sole barrier between the throng in the emergency room and Nancy's flayed self-respect. Blood pressure was taken every few minutes; blood was drawn; she had to change from her clothes into the hospital gown; and each time something was done the curtain flashed aside and Nancy was confronted with an array of faces in white clothes, children with cuts, and old, tired people. And there was the bedpan sitting there right in the open for everyone to gape at. It contained a large, semiformed dark red blood clot. Meanwhile Dr.

Major was down there between her legs touching her and talking to the nurse about another case. Nancy closed her eyes as tightly as she could and cried silently.

But it was all to be over shortly, or so Dr. Major had promised. In great detail he had told Nancy about the lining of her uterus and how it changes during the normal cycle and what happens when it doesn't change. There was something about the blood vessels and the need for an egg to be released from the ovary. The definitive cure was a dilation and curettage. Nancy had agreed without question and asked that her parents not be notified. She could do that herself after the fact. She was sure her mother would think she had had to have an abortion.

Now, as Nancy gazed up at the large overhead operating room light, the only thought that made her the slightest bit happy was the fact that the whole goddamned nightmare was going to be over within the hour, and her life would return to normal. The activity in the operating room was so totally foreign to her that she avoided looking at anyone or anything, save for the light above.

"Are you comfortable?"

Nancy glanced to the right. Deep brown eyes regarded her from between the synthetic fibers of the surgical hood. Gloria D'Mateo was folding the draw sheet around Nancy's right arm, securing it to her side and immobilizing her further.

"Yes," answered Nancy with a certain detachment. Actually she was as uncomfortable as hell. The operating table was as hard as her cheap Formica kitchen table. But the Phenergan and Demerol she had been given were beginning to exert their effects somewhere within the depths of her cerebrum. Nancy was far more awake than she would have liked; but at the same time she was beginning to feel a detachment and dissociation from her surroundings. The atropine she had been given was having an effect as well, making her throat and mouth feel dry and her tongue sticky.

Dr. Robert Billing was engrossed with his machine. It was a tangle of stainless steel, upright manometers, and a few colorful cylinders of compressed gas. A brown bottle of halothane stood on top of the machine. On the label was written: "2-bromo-2-chloro-1,1,1-tri-fluoroethane $(C_2HBrClF_3)$." An almost perfect anesthetic agent. "Almost" because every so often it seemed to destroy the patient's liver. But that rarely

4

happened, and halothane's other characteristics far over-shadowed the potential for liver damage. Dr. Billing was crazy about the stuff. Somewhere in his imagination he pictured himself developing halothane, introducing it to the medical community in the lead article of the *New England Journal of Medicine,* and then walking up to receive his Nobel prize in the same tuxedo he had worn when he was married.

Dr. Billing was a damned good anesthesiology resident, and he knew it. In fact, he thought most everyone knew it. He was convinced he knew as much anesthesiology as most of the attendings, more than some. And he was careful, very careful. He had had no serious complications as a resident, and that was indeed rare.

Like a 747 pilot, he had made himself a checklist, and religiously he adhered to a policy of checking off each step of the induction procedure. This meant having Xeroxed off a thousand of the checklists and bringing a copy along with the other equipment at the start of each operation. By 7:15, the anesthesiologist was right on schedule at step number 12: that meant hooking up the rubber scubalike tubing to the machine. One end went into the ventilating bag, whose four-to five-liter capacity afforded him an opportunity to inflate forcibly the patient's lungs at any time during the procedure. The other end went to the soda-lime canister in which the patient's expired carbon dioxide would be absorbed. Step number 13 on his list was to make sure the unidirectional check valves in the breathing lines were lined up in the right direction. Step number 14 was to connect the anesthesia machine to the compressed air, nitrous oxide, and oxygen sources on the wall of the OR room. The anesthesia machine had emergency oxygen cylinders hanging from the side, and Dr. Billing checked the gauge pressures on both cylinders. They were fully charged. Dr. Billing felt fine.

"I'm going to place some electrodes on your chest so we can monitor your heart," said Gloria D'Mateo while pulling down the sheet and pulling up the hospital gown, exposing Nancy's midriff to the sterile air. The gown just barely covered Nancy's nipples. "This will feel cold for a sec," added Gloria D'Mateo as she squeezed a bit of colorless jelly onto three locations on Nancy's exposed lower chest.

Nancy wanted to say something, but she couldn't deal

rapidly enough with her ambivalent attitudes about what she was experiencing. She was grateful, because it was going to help her, or so she had been assured; she was furious because she felt so exposed, literally and figuratively.

"You're going to feel a little stick now," said Dr. Billing, slapping the back of Nancy's left hand to make the veins stand out. He had placed a piece of rubber tubing tightly around Nancy's wrist, and she could feel her heart beat in the tips of her fingers. It was all happening too fast for Nancy to assimilate.

"Good morning, Miss Greenly," said an ebullient Dr. Major as he whisked through the OR door. "I hope you had a good night's sleep. We'll get this affair over with in a few minutes and have you back to your bed for a restful sleep."

Before Nancy could respond, the nerves from the tissues on the back of her hand became alive with urgent messages for her pain center. After the initial thrust, the intensity of the pain increased to a point and then dissipated. The snug rubber tourniquet disappeared, and blood surged into Nancy's hand. She felt tears well up from within her head.

"I.V.," said Dr. Billing to no one, as he made a black check next to number 16 on his list.

"You'll be going to sleep shortly, Nancy," continued Dr. Major. "Isn't that right, Dr. Billing? Nancy, you're a lucky girl today. Dr. Billing is number one." Dr. Major called all his patients girls no matter what age they were. It was one of those condescending mannerisms he had adopted unquestioningly from his older partner.

"That's correct," said Dr. Billing, placing a rubber face mask on the anesthesia tubing. "Number eight tube, Gloria, please. And you, Dr. Major, can scrub; we'll be ready at seven-thirty sharp."

"OK," said Dr. Major, heading for the door. Pausing, he turned to Ruth Jenkins, who was setting up the Mayo stand with instruments. "I want my own dilators and curettes, Ruth. Last time you gave me that medieval rubbish that belongs to the house." He was gone before the nurse could answer.

Somewhere behind her, Nancy could hear the sonarlike beep of the cardiac monitor. It was her own heart rhythm resounding in the room.

"All right, Nancy," said Gloria. "I want you to slide down

the table a bit and put your legs up here in the stirrups."
Gloria grasped Nancy's legs in turn under the knees and
lifted them up into the stainless steel stirrups. The sheet slid
between Nancy's legs, exposing them from mid-thigh down.
The lower part of the table fell away, and the sheet slid to
the floor. Nancy closed her eyes and tried not to picture
herself spread-eagled on the table. Gloria picked up the sheet
and haphazardly put it on Nancy's abdomen so that it draped
between her legs, covering her bloodied and recently shaved
perineum.

Nancy wanted to be calm, but she was getting more and
more anxious. She wanted to be grateful, but the tide was
swinging more and more in the direction of undirected anger
and emotion.

"I'm not sure I want to go through with this," said Nancy,
looking at Dr. Billing.

"Everything is just fine," said Dr. Billing in an artificially
concerned tone of voice, while checking off number 18 on
his list. "You'll be asleep in a jiffy," he added, while holding
up a syringe and tapping it so that the bubbles all fled upward
to the room air. "I'm going to give you some Pentothal right
away. Don't you feel sleepy now?"

"No," said Nancy.

"Well, you should have told me," said Dr. Billing.

"I don't know how I'm supposed to feel," returned Nancy.

"It's all right now," said Dr. Billing, pulling his anesthesia
machine close to Nancy's head. With well-rehearsed adept-
ness, he attached his Pentothal syringe to the three-way valve
on the I.V. line. "Now I want you to count to fifty for me,
Nancy." He expected that Nancy would never get past fifteen.
In fact, it gave Dr. Billing a certain sense of satisfaction to
watch the patient go to sleep. It represented repetitive proof
for him of the validity of the scientific method. Besides, it
made him feel powerful; it was as if he had command of the
patient's brain. Nancy was a strong-willed individual, however, and although she wanted to go to sleep, her brain involuntarily fought against the drug. She was still audibly
counting when Dr. Billing gave an additional dose of Pentothal. She said twenty-seven before the two grams of the
drug succeeded in inducing sleep. Nancy Greenly fell asleep
at 7:24 on February 14, 1976, for the last time.

Dr. Billing had no idea this healthy young woman was

going to be his first major complication. He was confident that everything was under control. The list was almost complete. He had Nancy breathe a mixture of halothane, nitrous oxide, and oxygen through a mask. Then he injected 2 cc's of a 0.2 percent succinylcholine chloride solution into Nancy's I.V. to effect a paralysis of all her skeletal muscles. This would make the placement of the endotracheal tube in the trachea easier. It would also allow Dr. Major to perform a bimanual exam, to rule out ovarian pathology.

The effect of the succinylcholine was seen almost immediately. At first there were minute fasciculations of the muscles of the face, then the abdomen. As the bloodstream sped the drug throughout the body, the motor and end plates of the muscles became depolarized, and total paralysis of the skeletal muscles occurred. Smooth muscles, like the heart, were unaffected, and the beep from the monitor continued without a waver.

Nancy's tongue was paralyzed and it fell back, blocking her airway. But that didn't matter. The muscles of the thorax and abdomen were paralyzed as well, and any attempt at breathing ceased. Although chemically different from the curare of the Amazon savages, the drug had the same effect, and Nancy would have died in five minutes. But at this point nothing was wrong. Dr. Billing was in total control. The effect was expected and desirable. Outwardly calm, inwardly very tense, Dr. Billing put down the breathing mask and reached for the laryngoscope, step number 22 on his list. With the tip of the blade, he pulled the tongue forward and maneuvered past the white epiglottis, while he visualized the entrance to the trachea. The vocal cords were ajar, paralyzed with the rest of the skeletal muscles.

Swiftly Dr. Billing squirted some topical anesthetic into the trachea, followed by the endotracheal tube. The laryngoscope made a characteristic metallic snap as Dr. Billing folded the blade onto the handle. With the help of a small syringe, he inflated the cuff on the endotracheal tube, providing a seal. Quickly he attached the tip of the rubber hose, without the face mask, to the open end of the endotracheal tube. As he compressed the ventilating bag, Nancy's chest rose in a symmetrical fashion. Dr. Billing listened to Nancy's chest with his stethoscope and was pleased. The entubation had been as characteristically smooth as expected. He was in total control of the patient's respiratory state. He adjusted his flow meters and set the combination of halothane, nitrous oxide, and oxygen he wanted. A few pieces of tape secured the endotracheal tube. A twist of the finger adjusted the I.V. rate. Dr. Billing's own heart began to slow down. He never showed it, but he always got very tense during the entubation procedure. With the patient paralyzed one has to work fast, and do it right.

With a nod, Dr. Billing indicated that Gloria D'Mateo could begin the prep of Nancy's shaved perineum. Meanwhile Dr. Billing began to make himself comfortable for the case. His job was now reduced to close observation of the patient's vital signs: heart rate and rhythm, blood pressure, and temperature. As long as the patient was paralyzed, he had to compress the ventilating bag, to breathe the patient. The succinylcholine would wear off in eight to ten minutes; then the patient could breathe herself, and the anesthesiologist could relax. Nancy's blood pressure stayed at 105/70. The pulse had steadily fallen from the anxiety state prior to anesthesia to a comfortable seventy-two beats per minute. Dr. Billing was happy, and he looked forward to a coffee break in about forty minutes.

The case went smoothly. Dr. Major did his bimanual examination and asked for some more relaxation. This meant that Nancy's blood had detoxified the succinylcholine given during the entubation. Dr. Billing was happy to give another 2 cc. He dutifully recorded this in his anesthesia record. The result was immediate, and Dr. Major thanked Dr. Billing and informed the crew that the ovaries felt like little smooth, normal plums. He always said that when he felt normal ovaries. The dilation of the cervix went without a hitch. Nancy had a normally antero-flexed uterus, and the curve on the dilators was a perfect match. A few blood clots were sucked out from the vaginal vault with the suction machine. Dr. Major carefully curetted the inside of the uterus, noting the consistency of the endometrial tissue. As Dr. Major passed the second curette, Dr. Billing noted a slight change in the rhythm of the cardiac monitor. He watched the electronic blip trace across the oscilloscope screen. The pulse fell to about sixty. Instinctively he inflated the blood pressure cuff and listened intently for the familiar far-away deep sound of the blood surging through the collapsed artery. As the air pressure drained off more, he heard the rebound sound indicating the diastolic pressure. The blood pressure was 90/60. This was not terribly low, but it puzzled his analytical brain. Could Nancy be getting some vagal feedback from her uterus, he wondered. He doubted it, but just the same he took the stethoscope from his ears.

"Dr. Major, could you hold on for just a minute? The blood pressure has sagged a little. How much blood loss do you estimate?"

"Couldn't be more than 500 cc," said Dr. Major, looking up from between Nancy's legs.

"That's funny," said Dr. Billing, replacing the stethoscope in his ears. He inflated the cuff again. Blood pressure was 90/58. He looked at the monitor: pulse sixty.

"What's the pressure?" asked Dr. Major.

"Ninety over sixty, with a pulse of sixty," said Dr. Billing, taking the stethoscope from his ears and rechecking the flow valves on the anesthesia machine.

"What the hell's wrong with that, for Christ's sake?" snapped Dr. Major, showing some early surgical irritation.

"Nothing," agreed Dr. Billing, "but it's a change. She had been so steady."

"Well, her color is fantastic. Down here, she's as red as a cherry," said Dr. Major, laughing at his own joke. No one else laughed.

Dr. Billing looked at the clock. It was 7:48. "OK, go ahead. I'll tell you if she changes any more," said Dr. Billing, while giving the breathing bag a healthy squeeze to inflate Nancy's lungs maximally. Something was bothering Dr. Billing; something was keying-off his sixth sense, activating his adrenals and pushing up his own heart rate. He watched the breathing bag sag and remain still. He compressed it again, mentally recording the degree of resistance afforded by Nancy's bronchial tubes and lungs. She was very easy to breathe. He watched the bag again. No motion, no respiratory effect on Nancy's part, despite the fact that the second dose of the succinylcholine should have been metabolized by then.

The blood pressure came up slightly, then went down again: 80/58. The monotonous beep of the monitor skipped once. Dr. Billing's eyes shot to the oscilloscope screen. The rhythm picked up again.

"I'll be finished here in five minutes," said Dr. Major for

Dr. Billing's benefit. With a sense of relief, Dr. Billing reached over and turned down both the nitrous oxide and the halothane flow, while turning up the oxygen. He wanted to lighten Nancy's level of anesthesia. The blood pressure came up to 90/60, and Dr. Billing felt a little better. He even allowed himself the luxury of running the back of his hand across his forehead to scatter the beads of perspiration that had appeared as evidence of his increasing anxiety. He glanced at the soda-lime CO_2 absorber. It appeared normal. Time was 7:56. With his right hand he reached up and lifted Nancy's eyelids. They moved with no resistance and the pupils were maximally dilated. The fear returned to Dr. Billing in a rush. Something was wrong . . . something was very wrong.

**Monday
February 23
7:15 A.M.**

Several small flakes of snow danced down Longwood Avenue in the half-light of February 23, 1976. The temperature was a crisp twenty degrees and the delicate crystalline structures fluttering earthward were intact even after striking the pavement. The sun was obscured by a low cover of thick gray clouds which shrouded the waking city. More and more clouds were swept in by the sea breeze, enveloping the tops of the taller buildings in a mist, making it become paradoxically darker as dawn spread its frail fingers over Boston. It was not supposed to snow, yet a few flakes had crystallized over Cohasset and had blown all the way into the city. The few that reached Longwood Avenue and were blown right on Avenue Louis Pasteur were the survivors until a sudden down-draft slammed them against a third-story window of the medical school dorm. They would have slid off had it not been for the layer of greasy Boston grime on the pane. Instead they stuck there while the glass slowly transmitted the heat from within, and their delicate bodies dissolved and mingled with the dirt.

Within her room Susan Wheeler was totally unaware of the drama on the window pane. Her mind was preoccupied with extracting itself from the clutches of a meaningless, disturbing dream after a restless, near-sleepless night. February 23 was going to be a difficult day at best and possibly a disaster. Medical school is made up of a thousand minor crises occasionally interrupted by truly epochal upheavals. February 23 was in the latter category for Susan Wheeler. Five days earlier she had completed the first two years of medical school, the basic science part taught in the lecture halls and science labs with books and other inanimate objects. Susan Wheeler had done very well because she could handle the classroom, the lab, and the papers. Her class notes were renowned and people always wanted to borrow them. At first she lent them indiscriminately. Later, as she began to perceive the realities of the competitive system which she thought she had left behind in Radcliffe, she changed her tactics. She lent her notes only to a small group of people who were her friends, or at least were people from whom she could borrow notes if she had had to miss a class. But she rarely missed a class.

A number of people chided Susan playfully about her marvelous attendance record. She always responded by saying she needed all the help she could get. Of course that was not the reason. Having entered a profession dominated by males, in which essentially all the professors and instructors were males, Susan Wheeler could not skip a class without being missed. Despite the fact that Susan looked on her mentors in a neutral sexless way as her professional superiors, they did not return the view in kind. The fact of the matter was that Susan Wheeler was a very attractive twenty-three-year-old female.

Her hair was the color of winter wheat and very wispy. Since it was long and fine it drove her batty in the wind unless she had it pulled back and clasped with a barrette at the back of her head. From there it fell in a sheen to the lower edges of her shoulder blades. Her face was broad with high cheekbones, and her eyes, set well back in their sockets, were a mixture of blue and green with flecks of brown so that the chromatic effect changed with different light sources. Her teeth were ultra white and perfectly straight, the result of fifty percent nature and fifty percent suburbanite orthodontist.

All in all Susan Wheeler appeared like the girl of the Pepsi-Cola people's dreams. At twenty-three years old she was young, healthy, and sexy with that American, Californian style that made eyes turn and hypothalamuses awaken. And on top of it all, perhaps in spite of it all, Susan Wheeler was very sharp. Her grammar school IQ ratings had hovered around the 140 range and were a source of infinite delight to her socially committed parents. Her school record was a monotonous series of A's with numerous other evidences of achievement. Susan liked school and learning and reveled in using her brain. She read voraciously. Radcliffe had been perfect for her. She did well but she earned her grades. She had majored in chemistry but had taken as much literature as possible. She had no trouble getting into medical school.

But being attractive as Susan was had certain definite drawbacks. One was the difficulty of missing class without being noticed. Whenever questions were asked, she was among those unfortunate few who served to demonstrate the stupidity of the students or the brilliance of the professors. Another drawback was that people formed opinions about Susan, with very little information. She so resembled models glaring out from advertisements that people continuously confused her with those frequently mindless girls.

There were advantages, though, to being bright and beautiful, and Susan was slowly beginning to realize that it was reasonable to exploit them to a degree. If she needed a further explanation regarding some complicated topic, she only had to ask once. Instructors and professors alike would hasten to help Susan understand a fine point of endocrinology or a subtle point of anatomy.

Socially, Susan did not date as much as people imagined she would. The explanation for this paradox was severalfold. First, Susan preferred reading in her room to a boring date, and with her intelligence, Susan found quite a few men boring. Second, few men actually asked Susan out, just because Susan's combination of beauty and brains was a bit intimidating. Susan spent many Saturday nights engrossed in novels, some literary, some otherwise.

Starting February 23, Susan feared her comfortable world was going to be blown up. The familiar lecture routine was over. Susan Wheeler and one hundred and twenty-two of her classmates were being rudely weaned from the security of the inanimate and tossed into the arena of the clinical years. All the confidence in one's abilities formed during the basic science years were hardly proof against the uncertainties of actual patient care.

Susan Wheeler had no illusions concerning the fact that she knew nothing about actually being a doctor, about taking care of real live patients. Inwardly she doubted that she ever would. It wasn't something she could read about and assimilate intellectually. The idea of trial by fire was diametrically opposed to her basic methodology. Yet on February 23 she was going to have to deal with patients some way, somehow. It was this crisis of confidence that made sleep difficult for her and filled the night with bizarre, disturbing dreams in which she found herself wandering through foreign mazes searching for horrible goals. Susan had no idea how closely her dreams would approximate her experience during the next few days.

At 7:15 the mechanical click of the clock radio broke her dream's feedback circuit and Susan's brain awakened to full consciousness. She turned off the radio before the transistors had a chance to fill the room with raucous folk music. Normally she relied on the music to wake her. But on this particular morning she needed little assistance. She was too keyed up.

Susan put her feet onto the floor and sat on the edge of the bed. The floor was cold and uninviting. Her hair descended from her head haphazardly, leaving only a two-to-three-inch gap through which to regard her room. It wasn't much of a room, about twelve by fourteen feet, with two multipaned windows at the end. The windows gave out onto another brick building and a parking lot so that Susan rarely looked out. The paint was reasonably fresh because she had painted the room herself about two years previously. The color was a pleasing pastel yellow which accented perfectly the Marimekko Printex fabric she had used to make the curtains. Their colors were several shades of electric green, separated by dark blue. On the walls hung a variety of colorful posters, framed with stainless steel, advertising past cultural events.

The furniture was medical school issue. There was an old-fashioned single bed, which was too soft, and difficult for entertaining. There was a worn, overstuffed easy chair, which Susan never used save for depositing dirty laundry. Susan liked to read on the bed and study at the desk so that the easy chair really wasn't "critical," in her words. The desk was oak and ordinary except for the pattern of initials and scratches carved in the top. In its right corner, Susan had even found a few obscene words associated with the word *biochem.* A physical diagnosis book was open on the desk. During the last three days she had totally reread it, but the text had failed to buoy her sagging confidence.

"Shit," she said out loud, with little inflection. The remark was directed at no one and at nothing. It was a basal response as she comprehended that February 23 had indeed arrived. Susan liked to swear and she did it a lot, but mostly to herself. Since such language contrasted sharply with her wholesome image, the effect was truly remarkable. She had found it a useful and entertaining tool.

Having pulled herself from the warmth of her covers with such dispatch, Susan realized that she had an extra fifteen minutes to spare. That was the usual duration of her ritual of repeatedly turning off her radio alarm before actually making it into the bathroom. Her ambivalence toward starting this day made her squander the time by just sitting and staring ahead, wishing that she had gone to law school or graduate school in literature . . . anything besides medical school.

The coldness of the bare waxed floor worked its way into Susan's feet. As she sat there, her circulatory system dissipated her body heat into the cold room, making her nipples rise up from the summits of her shapely breasts. Goose pimples appeared from nowhere along the insides of her naked thighs. She wore only a thin worn-out flannel nightgown she had gotten for Christmas when she was in the fifth grade. She still wore it to bed almost every night, at least when she was sleeping alone. Somehow she loved that nightgown. Amid the furious pace of change in her life, it seemed to afford a sanctuary of consistency. Besides, it had always been her father's favorite.

Susan had enjoyed pleasing her father from a very early

age. Her first remembrance of him was his smell: a mixture of the outdoors and deodorant soap covering a distinctive odor she later realized was male. He had always been good to her, and she knew that she was his favorite. That secret she never shared with anyone, especially not with her two younger brothers. It had always been a source of confidence for her as she faced the usual hurdles of childhood and adolescence.

Susan's father was a strong-willed individual, a dominant but generous and gentle man who ran his family and his insurance business like an enlightened despot. A charming man whose brood acknowledged him as the last word on any subject. It wasn't that Susan's mother was a weak-willed individual. It was just that she had met more than her match in the man she married. For much of her life Susan accepted this situation as the invariable norm. Eventually, however, it began to cause her some inner confusion. Susan was very much like her father, and her father encouraged her development in that direction. Then Susan began to realize she could not be like her father and expect one day to have a home of her own like the one in which she was reared. For a time she wanted desperately to be like her mother, and consciously tried. But it was to no avail. Her personality showed more and more her father's traits, and in high school she was literally forced into a leadership role. Susan was voted president of her graduating class at a time in her life when she thought that she would have preferred to be more in the background.

Susan's father was never particularly demanding, and certainly never pushy. He remained a source of confidence and encouragement for Susan to do whatever she wanted, without considering her sex. After Susan had entered medical school and became familiar with some of her female classmates, she realized that many of them had emerged from a similar paternalistic background. In fact when she met some of their parents, the fathers seemed to be vaguely familiar, as if she had actually known them in the past.

A resonant thumping issued from the radiator beneath the window, heralding the coming of heat. A tiny bit of steam hissed from the overflow valve. The radiator's stirring reminded Susan of the coldness of the room. Stiffly she stood up, stretched, and closed the window. It had been open only about a half-inch. Susan lifted the nightgown over her head and regarded her naked body in the mirror on the bathroom door. Mirrors held a strange attraction for her. It was almost impossible for her to pass a mirror without at least a quick reassuring look.

"Maybe you should be a dancer, Susan Wheeler," she said rising up onto her tiptoes and stretching her arms straight up, "and give up this idea of becoming a fucking doctor." Like a balloon being deflated, she let herself sag until she was slumped over. She was still looking at herself in the mirror. "I wish I could do that," she added more quietly. Susan was proud of her body. It was soft and supple, yet strong and well tuned. She could have been a dancer. She had good balance and she was filled with a sense of rhythm and movement. She envied Carla Curtis, a friend from Radcliffe who had gone into dance after college and was somewhere in the New York world. But Susan knew she could not actually go into dance despite her fantasy about it. She needed a vocation which would constantly exercise her brain. Susan made a horrible grimace and stuck her tongue out at the girl in the mirror, who did the same. Then Susan went into the bathroom.

In the bathroom she turned on the shower. It took four or five minutes to get hot. She looked at her face in the bathroom mirror, after shaking her hair from her line of sight. If only her nose had been made a little more narrow, she thought that she would be quite attractive. Then she started her bathroom routine with one lavender tablet of Ortho-Novum. Among her other characteristics, Susan Wheeler was a practical woman; strong-willed and practical.

**Monday
February 23
7:30 A.M.**

The Boston Memorial Hospital is certainly not an architectural landmark, despite the disproportionately large number of architects in the Boston area. The central building is attractive and interesting. It was constructed over a century ago with brownstone blocks carefully fitted together with skill and feeling. But the structure is inconveniently small and only two stories tall. Besides, it was designed with large, general wards, now outmoded. Hence its present-day practicality is minuscule. Only the ooze of medical history which permeates its halls keeps the wreckers and the planners at bay.

The innumerable larger buildings are studies in American gothic. Extending off at obtuse angles, millions upon millions of bricks join together to hold up dirty windows and flat monotonous roofs. The buildings were added in spurts, responding to the purported need for beds or the availability of funds. There is no doubt that it is an ugly combination of buildings, except perhaps for a few smaller research buildings. Those had architects and money to burn.

But very few people ever noticed the appearance of the buildings. The whole is larger than the sum of its parts; perception is too clouded by innumerable layers of emotional response. The buildings are not buildings by themselves. They are the famed Boston Memorial Hospital, containing all the mystery and wizardry of modern medicine. Fear and excitement intermingle in an ambivalent dialogue as lay people approach the structure. And for the professional individual, it is the mecca: the pinnacle of academic medicine.

The setting for the hospital adds very little. On one side a maze of railroad tracks leading to North Station and a bewildering array of elevated highways forms an enormous sculpture of rusting steel. On the other side is a modern housing project for low income families. Somehow that goal got mixed up in the renowned corruptness of the Boston government. The apartment buildings look like housing for the underprivileged because of their lack of outward design. But the rents are out of sight and only the rich and privileged live there. In front of the hospital is a stagnant corner of Boston Harbor with water like black coffee, sweetened with sewer gas. Separating the hospital and the water is a cement playground filled with discarded newspapers.

By seven-thirty this Monday morning all the operating rooms at the Memorial hummed with activity. Within a five-minute interval, twenty-one scalpels sliced through unresisting human skin as the scheduled operations commenced. The fate of a sizable number of people depended on what was done or not done, what was found or not found in the twenty-one tiled rooms. A furious pace was set which would not slow down until two or three in the afternoon. By eight or nine o'clock in the evening only two rooms would still be functioning, and they often continued until the seven-thirty rush the following morning.

In sharp contrast to the bustle in the OR area, the surgical lounge presented a luxuriant hush. Only two people were there, because the coffee break pattern did not begin until after nine. By the sink was a sickly-looking man appearing much older than his sixty-two years. He was busy trying to clean the sink without moving the twenty-odd coffee cups left there half-filled with water by their owners. Walters was his name, although few knew if it was his first or last name. His whole name was Chester P. Walters. No one at all knew what the P stood for, not even Walters himself. He'd been an employee of the Memorial OR since he was sixteen, and no one had the temerity to fire him despite the fact that he did almost nothing. He wasn't well, he'd say, and, indeed, he did not look well. His skin was a pasty white and every few minutes he'd cough. His cough rattled with phlegm deep within his bronchial tubes, but he never coughed hard enough to get it up and out. It was as if he was content to merely keep his tubes grossly patent without disturbing the cigarette he had constantly in the right corner of his mouth. Half the time he had to have his head cocked over to the left so that the smoke would not burn his eyes.

The other occupant of the surgical lounge was an intermediate surgical resident, Mark H. Bellows. The H stood for Halpern, his mother's maiden name. Mark Bellows was busy writing on a yellow legal tablet. Walters's coughing as well as Walters's cigarette definitely bugged Bellows, and Bellows would look up each time Walters started yet another coughing sequence. To Bellows it was incomprehensible how an individual could do so much bodily damage to himself and still keep it up. Bellows did not smoke; Bellows had never smoked. It was equally incomprehensible to Bellows how Walters managed to stay around the OR despite his appearance, personality, and the fact that he didn't do a damn thing. Surgery at the Memorial was the apogee, the zenith of the art of modern surgery, and being on its staff offered Nirvana, as far as Bellows was concerned. Bellows had striven hard and long for his appointment as a resident. Yet here, smack in the middle of all this excellence, was, as Bellows put it to his fellow residents, this ghoul. It seemed too ridiculously inconsistent.

Under normal circumstances Mark Bellows would have been inside one of the twenty-one operating rooms contributing to or directing one of the acts of mayhem. But on February 23 he was adding five medical students to his burgeoning list of responsibilities. Bellows was currently assigned to Beard 5, meaning the fifth floor of the Beard Building. It was a good general surgical rotation, maybe the best. As the intermediate resident of Beard 5, Bellows was also in charge of the surgical intensive care unit physically adjacent to the ORs.

Bellows reached for the table next to his chair and grasped a coffee mug without looking up from his work. He sipped the hot coffee loudly before abruptly replacing the cup with a minor clatter. He'd thought of another "attending" who would be good at lecturing to the students, and he quickly penciled the name onto the tablet. In front of him on a low table lay a piece of Surgical Department stationery. He picked it up and studied the names of the five students: George Niles, Harvey Goldberg, Susan Wheeler, Geoffrey Fairweather

III, and Paul Carpin. Only two of the names made any impression. The Fairweather name made him smile and conjure up the image of a spoiled, slender fellow with glasses, Brooks Brothers shirts, and a long New England genealogy. The other name, Susan Wheeler, caught his eye purely because Bellows liked women in a general way. He also thought that women liked him in return; after all, he was athletic and a doctor. Bellows was not very subtle in his social concepts; he was rather naive, like most of his fellow doctors. Looking at the name Susan Wheeler, he reflected that having one female student might make the next month a little bit less of a pain in the ass. His mind didn't struggle to find a mental image for the name Susan Wheeler. The part of his brain concerned with stereotypes told him it wasn't worth it.

Mark Bellows had been at the Memorial for two and one half years. Things had been going well, and he was reasonably sure of finishing the program. In fact, it had begun to look as if he might have a fighting chance for the chief resident position if everything went smoothly. Having been selected while he was an intermediate resident to get a group of medical students was certainly auspicious, although a bother. It had been an unexpected turn and was the immediate result of Hugh Casey coming down with hepatitis. Hugh Casey was one of the senior residents whose job included teaching two groups of medical students during the course of the year. The hepatitis came on only three weeks earlier. Right after that Bellows had received the message to come to Dr. Howard Stark's office. Bellows had never associated the message with Casey's illness. In fact, with the usual paranoia following a request to come to the Chief of the Department of Surgery's office, Bellows had mentally tried to relive all his latest blunders so as to be prepared for the tirade he expected. But contrary to his usual self, Stark had been very pleasant and had actually commended Bellows on his performance related to a recent Whipple procedure Bellows had done. After the unanticipated honeyed words, Stark had asked if Bellows would be interested in taking the medical students scheduled to be with Casey. Truthfully, Bellows would have preferred to pass up the chance while being on the Beard 5 rotation, except that one did not pass up a request by Stark even if it were carefully couched in the form of an offer. It would have been professional suicide for Bellows to have done so and he knew it. Bellows comprehended the vengeance of the affronted surgical personality, so he had agreed with the proper amount of alacrity.

With a straightedge Bellows filled the front page of his yellow legal tablet with little squares about an inch on a side. He then proceeded to fill in the dates of the subsequent thirty or so days the medical students were scheduled to be under his tutelage. Within each square he blocked off morning and afternoon. Each morning he planned to give a lecture; each afternoon he was going to enlist one of the attendings to give a lecture. Bellows wanted to schedule all the topics in advance to avoid duplication.

Bellows was twenty-nine years old, having just celebrated a birthday the week before. However, it was relatively hard to guess his age. His skin was smooth for a man and he was in excellent physical shape. Almost without fail he jogged two to three miles per day. The only outward evidence of the fact that he was almost thirty was the thinning area on the crown of his head and the slightly receding hairline at the temples. Bellows had blue eyes and an almost imperceptible salting of gray over his ears. He had a friendly face, and he was endowed with the enviable quality of making people feel comfortable. Most everyone liked Mark Bellows.

Two interns were also assigned to the Beard 5 rotation. Under the new terminology they were called first-year residents, but Bellows and most of the other residents still called them interns. They were Daniel Cartwright from Johns Hopkins and Robert Reid from Yale. They had been interns since July and hence had come a long way. But in February they were both experiencing the familiar intern depression. Enough of the year had passed to blunt the uniqueness of their roles as well as the terror of the responsibility, and yet so much remained before the year would be over and they would earn relief from the burden of every other night on call. Hence they demanded a certain amount of attention from Bellows. Cartwright was presently assigned to the intensive care unit, while Reid was on Beard 5. Bellows decided he would also use them for the medical students. Cartwright was a bit more outgoing and would probably be more helpful. Reid was black and had recently begun to attribute being called and harassed so much to his color and not his role as an intern. That was just another symptom of the February blues, but Bellows decided that Cartwright would be more helpful.

"Terrible weather," said Walters, presumably to Bellows but in an offhand undirected way. That was what Walters always said because to him the weather was always terrible. The only conditions which made him feel comfortable were seventy-six degrees and thirty percent humidity. That temperature and water content apparently agreed with the ailing bronchial tubes in the depths of Walters's lungs. Boston weather rarely fulfilled such narrow limits, so to Walters the weather was always terrible.

"Yeah," said Bellows in a noncommittal sort of way while he directed his attention outside. Most people would have agreed with Walters at that point. The sky was darkened by racing gray clouds. But Bellows wasn't thinking about the weather. Rather suddenly he was pleased about the pending five medical students. He decided that they probably would help him in his standing in the program. And if that were the case, then the time investment was more than worthwhile. Bellows was Machiavellianly practical in the final analysis; he had to have been to have got a position at the Memorial. The competition was fierce.

"Actually, Walters, this is my favorite kind of weather," said Bellows, getting up from the lounge chair, indecently teasing the coughing Walters. Walters's cigarette twitched in the corner of his mouth as he looked up at Bellows. But before he could say anything Bellows was through the door, on his way to meet his five medical students. He was convinced he could turn the burden into an asset.

**Monday
February 23
9:00 A.M.**

Susan Wheeler got a ride in Geoffrey Fairweather's Jaguar from the dorm to the hospital. It was an older vintage model, an X150, and only three of them could squeeze into it. Paul Carpin was good friends with Fairweather so he was the other lucky one. George Niles and Harvey Goldberg had to bear the brunt of the rush hour Boston MBTA in order to get to the Memorial for the nine o'clock meeting with Mark Bellows.

Once the Jaguar started, which was a minor ordeal typically associated with English motor cars, it covered the four miles in good time. Wheeler, Fairweather and Carpin walked into the main entrance of the Memorial at 8:45. The two others, having expected a miracle of modern transport to carry them the same distance in thirty minutes, arrived at 8:55. It had taken about one hour. The meeting with Bellows was to take place in the lounge of Beard 5 ward. No one knew where the hell they were going. They all trusted to fate to lead them to the proper place as long as they walked into the Memorial itself. Medical students tend to be rather passive, especially after the first two years of sitting in lecture halls daily from nine until five. The two groups met up partly by chance, partly by design, at the main elevators. Wheeler, Fairweather, and Carpin had tried to get to Beard 5 by going up the Thompson Building elevators directly opposite the main entrance. Having been built in haphazard spurts, the Memorial was labyrinthine.

"I'm not sure I'm going to like this place," said George Niles rather quietly to Susan Wheeler as the group squeezed onto the crowded elevator amid the morning rush. Susan was well aware of the meaning behind Niles's simple statement. When you don't want to go somewhere and then have trouble finding it, it's like adding insult to injury. Besides, all five medical students were in an acute crisis of confidence. They all knew the Memorial was the most renowned teaching hospital and for that reason wanted to be there. But at the same time they felt diametrically opposed to the concept of actually being a doctor, to actually being able to handle some judgmental decision. Their white coats ostensibly associated them with the medical community and yet their ability to handle even the most simple patient-related matter was nonexistent. The stethoscopes which dangled conspicuously from their left side pockets had been used only on each other and a few hand-picked patients. Their memory of the complicated biochemical steps in the degradation of glucose within the cell afforded little support and even less practical information.

Yet they were medical students from one of the best medical schools in the country and that should count for something. They all shared this delusion as the elevator lifted them floor by floor to Beard 5. The doors opened for a doctor in a scrub suit to get out on Beard 2. The five medical students caught a glimpse of the OR holding area in full swing.

Emerging on the fifth floor, the medical students spun on their heels, not sure of which direction to take. Susan took the lead by walking down the corridor to the nurses' station. Like the OR area below, the nurses' station on Beard 5 was a beehive of activity. The ward clerk had his right ear glued to the telephone getting A.M. stat blood-work reports. The head nurse, Terry Linquivist, was checking the OR schedule to be sure the pre-op meds had been given to those patients who would be called within the next hour or so. The other six nurses and three LPNs were in all stages of endeavor trying either to get those patients to surgery who had been called or to take care of those patients whose surgery was already part of the past.

Susan Wheeler approached this area of directed activity with an outward show of aplomb, carefully concealing her inner uncertainties. The ward clerk seemed the most accessible.

"Excuse me, but could you tell me . . . ," began Susan.

The ward clerk raised his left hand toward Susan. "Tell

me that hematocrit again. There's pandemonium here," he shouted into the telephone he held between his head and cocked-up shoulder. He wrote on a pad in front of him. "And the patient had a BUN ordered too!" He looked up at Susan, shaking his head about the person he was talking to on the phone. Before she could say anything, his eyes went back to the patient's chart he had out. "Of course I'm sure a BUN was ordered." He frantically looked through the chart to find the order sheet. "I filled out the lab request myself." He checked in the order sheet. "Look, Dr. Needem is going to be bananas if there's no BUN. . . . What? . . . Well if you don't have enough serum get your ass up here and get some more. The patient is scheduled for eleven. And what about Berman; you got his lab work now? Of course I want it!"

The clerk looked up at Susan, keeping the phone pressed between his ear and his shoulder. "What can I do for you?" he asked Susan rapidly.

"We're medical students and I wondered if . . ."

"You'd better talk to Miss Linquivist," said the clerk suddenly as he looked down at his paper and began madly scribbling figures. He paused long enough to extend his pencil toward Terry Linquivist for Susan's benefit.

Susan looked over at Terry Linquivist. She noted that the nurse was probably about four or five years her senior. She was attractive in a wholesome sort of way, but definitely overweight according to Susan's taste. She seemed no less busy than the clerk but Susan was not about to argue. With a quick glance at the rest of her group, who were more than willing to let Susan take the initiative, Susan walked up to Miss Linquivist.

"Excuse me," said Susan in a polite tone, "we are medical students assigned to . . ."

"Oh no," interrupted Terry Linquivist, looking up and then rapidly putting the back of her right hand to her forehead as if she were in the throes of a migraine attack. "Just what I need," said Linquivist to the wall, carefully emphasizing each word. "On one of the busiest days of the year, I get a new batch of medical students." She turned to Susan and eyed her with an obvious air of exasperation. "Please don't bother me now."

"I don't intend to bother you at all," said Susan defensively.

"I was just hoping you could tell me where the Beard 5 lounge is."

"Through those doors opposite the main desk," said Terry Linquivist, mellowing slightly.

As Susan turned and moved toward her group, Terry Linquivist called out to one of the other nurses. "You're not going to believe it, Nance, but today is going to be one of those days. Guess what we just got? . . . We got ourselves a new group of green med students."

Susan's ears, sensitized as they were, could pick out a few sighs and groans from the Beard 5 team.

Susan moved around the clerk's desk. He was still on the phone and still writing. She walked toward the two plain white doors opposite the desk. The others fell in beside her.

"Some welcoming committee," said Carpin.

"Yeah, real red carpet treatment," said Fairweather. Despite problems of confidence, medical students still thought of themselves as very important people.

"Ah . . . a couple of days and the nurses will be eating out of your hand," said Goldberg smugly. Susan turned and flashed a disdainful glare at Goldberg, who missed it altogether. Goldberg missed most subtle social interpersonal communications. Even some that weren't very subtle.

Susan pushed through the swinging doors. The room was a jumble of old books, mostly outdated *PDR's (Physician's Desk Reference)*, scratch paper, dirty coffee cups, and an assortment of disposable needles and I.V. paraphernalia. There was a counter, desk height, that ran along the length of the wall on the left. A large commercial-type coffee maker was in the middle. At the far end was a curtainless window covered on the outside with Boston grime. Only a meager amount of February morning light penetrated the glass and fell in a pale patch on the aging linoleum floor. The illumination in the room depended entirely on an ample bank of fluorescent lights in the ceiling. The right wall had a bulletin board filled with messages, reminders, and announcements. Next was a blackboard, which had a fine covering of chalk dust. In the center of the room was a group of classroom chairs with a small desk piece on each right arm. One of them was pulled in front of the blackboard for Bellows. He was sitting with his yellow legal tablet in front of him. As the medical students filed in, he lifted his left hand and studied his watch. The maneuver was for the benefit of the students, and they recognized the gesture immediately. Especially Goldberg, who was extremely sensitive about nuances which might have an effect on his grade average.

No one said anything for several minutes. Bellows was silent for effect. He'd had no experience with medical students but from his own background he felt obliged to be authoritarian. The medical students were silent because they already felt ill at ease and a bit paranoid.

"It is nine-twenty," said Bellows eyeing each student in turn. "This meeting was supposed to take place at nine, not nine-twenty." No one contracted a single facial muscle lest Bellows's attention be drawn to him. "I think we'd better start out on the right foot," continued Bellows with authority. He got up laboriously and picked up a piece of chalk. "There's one thing about surgery, especially here at the Memorial. Things happen on time. You people better take that to heart, or, believe me, your experience here is going to be . . ." Bellows searched for the proper word while he tapped the chalk on the blackboard. He looked at Susan Wheeler, whose appearance added to his momentary confusion. He glanced out of the window, ". . . a long cold winter."

Bellows looked back at the students and began a semiprepared introductory talk. He examined the faces of the students as he talked. He was sure he recognized Fairweather. The very narrow amber-colored horn-rimmed glasses fit into Bellows's preconception. And Goldberg: Bellows was reasonably confident he could pick him out. The other two males were nondescript entities at that point to Bellows. He hazarded another glance at Susan and felt the same instantaneous confusion. He had not been prepared for the attractiveness of the girl. She was wearing dark blue slacks which seemed to cling disturbingly snugly about her thighs. Above, she had on a lighter blue Oxford cloth shirt, accented by a darker blue and red silk scarf tied around her neck. Her medical student white coat was casually opened. Her ample breasts defiantly advertised her sex, and Bellows was not at all ready to deal with this concept in light of the plans he had formulated for dealing with the students. With some effort he avoided looking at Susan for the time being.

"You'll be assigned to Beard 5 for only one month of your three month surgical rotation here at the Memorial," said

Bellows, shifting into a familiar monotone associated with medical pedagogy. "In some ways this is an advantage and in others a disadvantage, like so many things in life."

Carpin chuckled at this feeble attempt at philosophy, but noticing that he was alone, he shut up quickly.

Bellows fixed his gaze on Carpin and continued, "Beard 5 rotation includes the surgical intensive care unit. Hence you will be subjected to an intensive teaching experience. That's the good part. The disadvantage is that it occurs so early in your clinical exposure. I understand this is your first clinical rotation. Is that correct?"

Carpin looked from side to side to make sure that this last question was directed at him. "We . . ." His voice faltered, and he cleared his throat. "That's right," he managed to say with some difficulty.

"The intensive care unit," continued Bellows, "is an area where you all have the most to learn, but it represents the most critical area for patient care. All the orders that you write on any patient must be countersigned by myself or one of the two interns on the service, whom you will meet presently. If you write orders in the ICU they have to be countersigned the moment you write them. Orders for patients on the ward can be countersigned en masse at various times during the day. Is that clear?"

Bellows looked at each student, including Susan, who returned his gaze without altering her neutral expression. Susan's immediate impression of Bellows was not particularly favorable. His manner seemed artificial and his opening mini-lecture on punctuality seemed a little unnecessary so early in the course of events. The monotone of his remarks combined with the pitiful stab at philosophy tended to support the image Susan had begun to construct of the surgical personality from previous conversations and her reading . . . unstable, egotistical, sensitive to criticism, and above all, dull. Susan did not notice that Mark Bellows was male. Such a thought did not even register in her mind.

"Now," said Bellows in his artificial monotone, "I'll have some schedules Xeroxed for you which will outline the basic calendar we'll follow while you are assigned to Beard 5. The patients on the ward and in the ICU will be divided among you, and you are to work directly with the intern on the case. As for admissions, I want you to set up your own schedule for equitably dividing them. One of you will do a full workup on each admission. As for night call, I want at least one of you to stay here. That means you'll be on only one in five nights and that's not overburdening you. In fact, that is less than usual. If others want to stay in the evenings, that's fine, but at least one of you stays here all night. Get together some time today and give me a schedule of who will be on when.

"Rounds will begin each morning in the ICU at six-thirty. Before then I want you to have seen your patients, collated all the necessary information to present during the rounds. Is that clear?"

Fairweather looked at Carpin in dismay. He leaned over and whispered in Carpin's ear, "Christ, I'll have to get up before I go to bed!"

"Do you have a question, Mr. Fairweather?" demanded Bellows.

"No," answered Fairweather rapidly. He was intimidated by the fact that Bellows knew his name.

"As for the rest of the morning," said Bellows, eyeing his watch again. "First I will take you to the ward and introduce you to the nursing staff, who will be thrilled to meet you all, I'm sure," said Bellows with a wry smile.

"We have experienced their joy already," said Susan, speaking for the first time. Her voice brought Bellows's eyes around and held them. "We didn't expect a brass band for our arrival but at the same time we didn't expect a cold shoulder."

Susan's appearance had already somewhat unnerved Bellows. With the animation that the sound of her voice provided, Bellows's pulse quickened slightly. There was a certain surge within his body which reminded him of watching cheerleaders in high school and wishing that they were naked. Bellows searched for words.

"Miss Wheeler, you'll have to understand that the nurses here are primarily interested in one thing."

Niles winked in agreement to Goldberg, who didn't understand what Niles was implying.

"And that is patient care, damn good patient care. And when new medical students and/or new interns arrive that becomes a rather difficult goal. From actual experience they have all learned that new house staff is probably more deadly than bacteria and virus put together. So don't expect to be greeted as saviors here, least of all from the nurses."

Bellows paused but Susan did not respond. She was thinking about Bellows. At least he was a realist and that was a glimmer of hope in the otherwise poor impression he had made on her.

"At any rate, after showing you the ward, we'll head up to surgery. There's a staff gallbladder at ten-thirty and it will give you all a chance to get into a scrub suit and see the inside of an OR."

"And the handle of a retractor," added Fairweather. For the first time the atmosphere lightened and everyone laughed.

Down in the OR area Dr. David Cowley was absolutely pissed and he spared no one. The circulating nurse had broken into tears before the case was over and had to be replaced. The anesthesiology resident had had to weather one of the worst bombardments of foul words and captious epithets that had ever been hurled over an anesthesia screen. The surgical resident first assisting had a small cut in his right index finger from Cowley's scalpel.

Cowley was one of the more prosperous of the general surgeons at the Memorial with a spacious private office on Beard 10. He had been spawned, trained, and now nurtured by the Memorial. When things went well, he was a most pleasant chap, full of jokes and ribald stories, always eager to offer an opinion, to bet on a game, to laugh. But when things went contrary to his wishes, he was a firebrand of the most vicious nature, a seething cauldron of invective. In short, he was a juvenile in adult clothing.

His only case that day had gone poorly. To start with, the circulating nurse had put out the wrong surgical instruments. She had set up the Mayo stand with the gallbladder instruments used by the residents. Dr. Cowley had responded by picking up the whole tray and dashing it to the floor. Next the patient quivered a little as he made the initial incision. It was only with great self-discipline that Cowley had curbed his inclination to hurl the scalpel at the anesthesiology resident. Then there was X-ray, who failed to show up at exactly the moment he called. Cowley's viciousness had so unnerved the poor technician that the first couple of films were totally black.

Somehow Cowley forgot the real reason the case went poorly. Cowley himself had accidentally pulled off the proximal tie on the artery to the gallbladder, causing the wound to fill up with blood in seconds. It had been a struggle to reisolate the vessel and get a tie around it without disturbing the integrity of the hepatic artery. Even after the bleeding had been controlled, Cowley still was not positive that he had not compromised the blood supply to the liver.

Coming into the deserted doctors' lounge, Cowley was raging. He was mumbling inaudibly as he passed down the row of lockers to his own. With emphasis he flung his scrub hat and mask onto the floor. Then he kicked his locker with jarring force.

"Fucking incompetent assholes. This Goddamned place is going to the dogs."

The fury of his kick followed by an overhead fist which he brought against the door of the locker did several things. First, it raised a cloud of previously undisturbed dust which had settled on top of the locker over some five years. Second, it dislodged a single scrub shoe, which fell, just missing Cowley's head. Third, it jarred open the locker next to Cowley's, causing some of the contents to spill out onto the floor.

Cowley dealt with the shoe first. He threw it as hard as he could against the far wall. Then he kicked open the locker next to his in preparation to replace the objects which had fallen out. One glance into the locker, however, made him pause.

Looking closer, Cowley was astonished to see that the locker contained an enormous collection of medications. Many were open, half-used containers and vials, but there were also many unopened. There were ampules, bottles, and pills in a bewildering assortment. Of the drugs that had fallen out, Cowley noted Demerol, succinylcholine, Innovar, Barocca-C, and curare. Within the locker were many more varieties, including an entire carton of unopened morphine bottles, syringes, plastic tubing, and tape.

Quickly Cowley replaced the medicines that had fallen to the floor. Then he locked the locker once again. In his calendar book he wrote the number 338. Cowley was going to check on that locker and see to whom it was assigned. Despite his anger, he had the presence of mind to realize that such a cache was important and had serious implications for the entire hospital. And with things that bothered him, Cowley had the memory of a sage.

Susan Wheeler could not go into the doctors' lounge to change into a scrub suit because the doctors' lounge was synonymous with the men's lounge. Susan had to go into the nurses' locker, which was synonymous with women's lounge. So creeps society from day to day, thought Susan angrily. To her it was just another blatant example of male chauvinism and it gave her a momentary lift to think that she was up-setting this unfair identification. The locker room was at that moment deserted and Susan located an empty locker with ease and began to change by hanging up her white coat. Nearby the shower entrance she found the scrub suits. They were one-piece pale blue dresses made from plain cotton fabric. They were actually for the scrub nurses. She held it up and then against herself. Looking into the mirror, she felt suddenly rebellious despite the intimidating surroundings.

"Screw the dress," said Susan to the mirror. The scrub dress arched in a tumble into the canvas hamper while Susan retraced her steps into the hall. She paused before the doctors' lounge, and she almost lost her nerve. Impulsively she pushed open the door.

Bellows was at that very instant next to the door that Susan opened. He was reaching into one of the cabinets at the en-trance for a scrub suit. He was clothed in his James Bond-style skivvies (that's what he called them) and black socks. He looked as if he belonged in the beginning of a grade C porno movie. Horror spread across his face as he caught sight of Susan. In a flash, he fled into the safety of the depths of the dressing room. As in the nurses' locker room, one could not see into the dressing room from the door. Spurred by her rebelliousness despite the unexpected encounter, Susan advanced to the cabinet and selected a small scrub top and pants; then she left as quickly as she had entered. She could hear a tangle of excited voices in the interior of the doctors' lounge.

Back in the nurses' locker, she completed changing rapidly. The pale green shirt was too large, as were the pants. Because of her narrow waist she had to cinch up the pants to their absolute maximum before tying the cord. Mentally she began to prepare for the inevitable diatribe from Bellows, the mighty surgeon-to-be, by deciding how she would counter. During their brief introductions on the ward, Susan had been very aware of the condescending attitude Bellows had directed toward the nurses. This attitude was ironical coming so soon after the commendable defense of the nurses he had made to explain their lack of enthusiasm toward new medical students. It was pretty obvious to Susan that Bellows was, among other things, a typical chauvinist. Susan decided that she would challenge that aspect of Bellows's personality. Maybe it would make the surgical rotation at the Memorial a bit more bearable. Of course she had not planned to see Bellows in his underwear in the dressing room, but the image and symbolic aspects made Susan laugh out loud before she passed through the door into the OR area.

"Miss Wheeler, I presume," said Bellows as Susan emerged. Bellows was leaning casually against the wall to the left of the doorway, obviously waiting for Susan to appear. His right elbow was on the wall, with the hand supporting his head. Susan literally jumped at the sound of his voice since she hardly expected him to be waiting there for her.

"I must admit," continued Bellows, "you really caught me with my pants down." A broad smile spread across his face, changing him in Susan's eyes to a rather human individual. "That was one of the funniest things that has happened to me in a long time."

Susan smiled in return but it was a half-smile. She was expecting the tirade to commence immediately.

"After I recovered and realized what you were after,"

continued Bellows, "I started to think that it was a pretty ridiculous response on my part to bolt. If I had had any sense I would have stood there and faced you despite my dress . . . or the lack of it. At any rate, it made me think that I might have been relying on appearances a bit too much this morning. I'm a second-year resident, that's all. You and your friends are my first group of students. What I really want to do is to make this time here as profitable as possible for you all, and in the process, profitable for me as well. Last of all, we should enjoy ourselves."

With a final smile and slight nod of the head, Bellows walked away from the stunned Susan to check which room the staff gallbladder was in. It was Susan's turn to feel a sense of confusion as she looked after him. The resolve her feelings of anger and rebelliousness had evoked had been undermined by Bellows's sudden insight into himself. In fact it made her rebelliousness seem a trifle foolish and out of place. The fact that Susan had stimulated the insight fortuitously made it obvious that she couldn't take credit for it and that she would have to revise some of her impressions about Mark Bellows. She watched Bellows walk all the way over to the main OR desk; he was obviously at home in the alien environment. For the first time Susan was a little impressed. In fact, she thought that he really wasn't that bad looking either.

The others were already prepared to go down to the OR. George Niles showed Susan how to put on the paper booties over her shoes and tuck in the conductive tape. Next she put on the hood and finally the mask. Once everyone was so attired, they passed the main OR desk and pushed through the swinging doors into the "clean" area of the ORs themselves.

Susan had never been in an OR before. She had seen a couple of operations through the gallery windows but such an experience was akin to watching it on TV. The glass partition effectively isolated the drama. One did not feel a part of it. While walking down the long corridor Susan felt a certain excitement mixed with fear of the mortality of people. As they passed OR after OR, Susan could see clusters of figures bent over what she knew were sleeping patients with their fragile insides open to the elements. A hospital gurney approached them with a scrub nurse pulling and an anesthesiologist pushing. As the group came abreast Susan could see that the anesthesiologist was matter-of-factly holding the patient's chin back while the patient retched violently. "I hear there's almost forty inches of packed powder at Waterville Valley," said the anesthesiologist to the scrub nurse. "I'm going Friday right after work," returned the scrub nurse as the pair passed by Susan toward the recovery room. The image of the tortured face of the patient so recently operated on imprinted itself in Susan's susceptible consciousness and she shuddered involuntarily.

The group pulled up in front of room 18.

"Try to keep the chatter to a minimum," said Bellows, looking through the window in the door. "The patient is already asleep. Too bad, I wanted you to see that. Well, no matter. There will be a lot of moving around during the draping procedure, etcetera, so stay back against the right wall. Once they get underway, move around so that you can see something. If you have questions, save them until later, OK?" Bellows looked at each student. He smiled anew when he met Susan's gaze, then pushed open the OR door.

"Ah, Professor Bellows, welcome," boomed a large, gowned, gloved, and sterile figure hovering in the background near some X-rays. "Professor Bellows has brought his brood of students to watch the fastest hands in the East," he said laughing. He held up his arms in an exaggerated Hollywood surgical fashion with the hands up and bent outward as far as they would go. "I hope you have told the impressionable youths that the spectacle they are about to see is a rare treat."

"That hulk," said Bellows to the students while motioning toward the laughing character by the X-rays and loud enough for all in the OR to hear, "is the result of staying in the program too long. That's Stuart Johnston, one of the three senior residents. We only have to put up with him for four more months. He had promised me he'd be civil, but I cannot be sure of that."

"You're just a poor sport, Bellows, because I stole this case from you," said Johnston, still laughing. Then to his two assistants he said without laughing, "Let's get the patient draped, you guys. What are you trying to do, make this your life's work?"

The draping proceeded rapidly. A small piece of tubular metal arched over the top of the patient's head and separated the anesthesiologist from the surgical area. By the time the draping was completed, only a small portion of the patient's right upper abdomen was exposed. Johnston moved to the patient's right side; one of the assistants went over to the left side. The scrub nurse moved over the draped Mayo stand, straining with a full complement of surgical instruments. A profusion of hemostats was lined up in a perfect array along the back of the tray. The scalpel had a new razor-sharp blade snapped into its jaws.

"Knife," said Johnston. The scalpel slapped into his gloved right hand. With his left hand he pulled the abdominal skin away from him to provide countertraction. The medical students all moved forward silently and strained to see with a foreboding curiosity. It was like watching an execution. Their minds tried to prepare themselves for the image that was going to be imminently transmitted to their brains.

Johnston held the scalpel about two inches above the pale skin while he looked over the screen at the anesthesiologist. The anesthesiologist was slowly letting the air out of the blood pressure cuff and watching the gauge. 120/80. He looked up at Johnston and gave an imperceptible nod, tripping the poised guillotine. The scalpel dived deep into the tissues, and then with a smooth soundless slice, slid down the skin at an angle of approximately 45 degrees. The wound fell open and little jets of pulsating arterial blood sprayed the area, then ebbed and died.

Meanwhile curious phenomena occurred in George Niles's brain. The image of the knife plunging into the skin of the patient was displayed instantly in his occipital cortex. Association fibers picked up the message and transported the information to his parietal lobe, where it was associated. The association spread so rapidly and so widely that it activated an area of his hypothalamus, causing widespread dilation of his blood vessels in his muscles. The blood literally drained from his brain to fill all the dilated vessels, causing George Niles to lose consciousness. In a dead faint he fell straight backward. His flaccid neck snapped his head against the vinyl floor with a reasonant thump.

Johnston spun around in response to the sound of George's head smashing against the floor. His surprise quickly metamorphosed into typically labile surgical anger.

"For Christ sake, Bellows, get these kids outa here until

they can stand the sight of a few red cells." Shaking his head, he went back to catching bleeders with his hemostats.

The circulating nurse broke a capsule under George's nose and the acrid smell of the ammonia shocked him back to consciousness. Bellows bent down and felt along his neck and the back of his head. As soon as George was fully conscious, he sat up, somewhat confused about his whereabouts. Realizing what had happened, he felt immediately embarrassed.

Johnston meanwhile wouldn't let the matter rest.

"Holy shit, Bellows, why didn't you tell me these students were absolute greenhorns? I mean, what would have happened if the kid fell into my wound here?"

Bellows didn't say anything. He helped George to his feet by degrees until he was satisfied George was really OK. Then he motioned for the group to leave OR No. 18.

Just before the OR door shut, Johnston could be heard angrily yelling at one of his junior residents, "Are you here to help me or hinder me . . . ?"

**Monday
February 23
11:15 A.M.**

George Niles's pride was hurt more than anything else. He developed a rather sizable lump on the back of his head but there was no laceration. His pupils stayed equal in size and his memory was unimpaired. Consensus had it that he was going to make it. However, the episode dampened the spirits of the whole group. Bellows was nervous that the fainting would reflect on his judgment to bring the students into the OR on the first day. George Niles was concerned lest the incident foreshadowed similar responses every time he tried to watch a surgical case. The others were bothered to a greater or lesser degree simply because within a group, the actions of one individual tend to reflect the whole group's performance. Actually Susan was not concerned with this aspect as were the others. Susan was more distressed about the sudden and unexpected response and change in attitude of Johnston and, to a lesser extent, Bellows. One minute they were jovial and friendly; the next minute they were angry, almost vengeful, simply because of an unexpected turn of events. Susan rekindled her preconceptions regarding the surgical personality. Perhaps such generalizations were appropriate.

After changing back to their street clothes, they all had a cup of coffee in the surgical lounge. It was surprisingly good coffee, thought Susan, trying to overcome the oppressive haze of cigarette smoke which hung like Los Angeles smog from the ceiling to a level about five feet from the floor. Susan was mindless of the people in the lounge until her eyes met the stare of a pasty white-skinned man hovering in the corner near the sink. It was Walters. Susan looked away and then back again, thinking that the man was not really watching her. But he was. His beady eyes burned through the cigarette haze. Walters's omnipresent cigarette hung by some partially dried saliva holding the extreme tip in the corner of his lips. A trail of smoke snaked upward from the ash. For some unknown reason he reminded Susan of the hunchback of Notre Dame, only without a hunchback: a ghoulish figure out of place yet obviously at home in the shadows of the Memorial surgical area. Susan tried to look away but her eyes were involuntarily drawn toward the uncomfortable stare of Walters. Susan was glad when Bellows motioned to leave and they drained their cups. The exit was near to the sink, and as the group left the room, Susan had the feeling she was walking down Walters's line of vision. Walters coughed and the phlegm rattled. "Terrible day, eh, Miss," said Walters as Susan passed.

Susan didn't respond. She was glad to be rid of the staring eyes. It had added to her nascent dislike of the surgical environment of the Memorial.

The group moved en masse into the ICU. As the oversized ICU door closed, the outside world faded and disappeared. A surrealistic alien environment emerged out of the gloom as the students' eyes adjusted to the lower level of illumination.

The usual sounds like voices and footsteps were muted by the sound-absorbing baffling in the ceiling. Mechanical and electronic noises dominated, particularly the rhythmical beep of the cardiac monitors and the to-and-fro hiss of the respirators. The patients were in separate alcoves, in high beds with the side rails pulled up. There was the usual profusion of intravenous bottles and lines hanging above them, connected to impaled blood vessels by sharp needles. Some of the patients were lost in layer upon layer of mummylike bandages. A few of the patients were awake and their darting eyes betrayed their fear and the fine line that divided them from acute insanity.

Susan surveyed the room. Her eyes caught the fluorescent blips racing across the front of the oscilloscope screens. She realized how little information she could garner from the instruments in her present state of ignorance. And the I.V. bottles themselves with their complicated labels signifying the ionic content of the contained fluid. In an instant, Susan and the other students felt the sickening feeling of incompetence; it was as if the entire first two years of medical school had meant nothing.

Feeling a modicum of safety in numbers, the five students moved even closer together and walked in unison to one of the center desks. They were following Bellows like a group of puppies.

"Mark," called one of the ICU nurses. Her name was June Shergood. She had thick luxurious blonde hair and intelligent eyes that looked through rather thick glasses. She definitely was attractive and Susan's keen eye could detect a certain change in Bellows's demeanor. "Wilson has been having a few runs of PVCs, and I told Daniel that we should hang a lidocaine drip." She walked over to the desk. "But good old Daniel couldn't seem to make up his mind, or . . . something." She extended an EKG tracing in front of Bellows. "Just look at these PVCs."

Bellows looked down at the tracing.

"No, not there, you ninny," continued Miss Shergood, "those are his usual PVCs. Here, right here." She pointed for Bellows and then looked up at him expectantly.

"Looks like he needs a lidocaine drip," said Bellows with a smile.

"You bet your ass," returned Shergood. "I mixed it up so

I could give about 2 mg per minute in 500 D5W. Actually it's all hooked up and I'll run over and start it. And when you write the order include the fact that I gave him a bolus of 50 mg when I first saw the runs of PVCs. Also maybe you should say something to Cartwright. I mean, this is about the fourth time he couldn't make up his mind about a simple order. I don't want any codes in here we can avoid."

Miss Shergood bounced over to one of the patients before Bellows could respond to her comments. Deftly and with assurance she sorted out the twisted I.V. lines to determine which line came from which bottle. She started the lidocaine drip, timing the rate of the drops falling into the plastic chamber below the bottle. This rapid exchange between the nurse and Bellows did little to buoy the already nonexistent confidence of the students. The obvious competence of the nurse made them feel even less capable. It also surprised them. The directness and seeming aggressiveness of the nurse was a far cry from their rather traditional concept of the professional nurse-physician relationship under which they all still labored.

Bellows pulled out a large hospital chart from the rack and placed it on the desk. Then he sat down. Susan noticed the name on the chart. *N. Greenly.* The students crowded around Bellows.

"One of the most important aspects of surgical care, any patient care really, is fluid balance," said Bellows, opening the chart, "and this is a good case to prove the point."

The door to the ICU swung open, allowing a bit of light and hospital sounds to spill into the room. With it came Daniel Cartwright, one of the interns on Beard 5. He was a small man, about five seven. His white outfit was rumpled and blood-spattered. He sported a moustache but his beard was not very thick and each hair was individually discernible from its origin to its tip. On the crown of his head he was going bald rather rapidly. Cartwright was a friendly sort and he came up to the group directly.

"Hi, Mark," said Cartwright making a gesture of greeting with his left hand. "We finished early on the gastrectomy so I thought I'd tag along with you if I may."

Bellows introduced Cartwright to the group and then asked him to give a capsule summary on Nancy Greenly.

"Nancy Greenly," began Cartwright in a mechanical fashion, "twenty-three-year-old female, entered the Memorial approximately one week ago for a D&C. Past medical history entirely benign and noncontributory. Routine pre-op workup normal, including negative pregnancy test. During surgery she suffered an anesthetic complication and she has been comatose and unresponsive since that time. EEG two days ago was essentially flat. Current status is stable: weight holding; urine output good; BP, pulse, electrolytes, etcetera, all OK. There was a slight temperature elevation yesterday afternoon but breath sounds are normal. All in all, she seems to be holding her own."

"Holding her own with a good deal of help from us," corrected Bellows.

"Twenty-three?" asked Susan suddenly while glancing around at the alcoves. Her face reflected a tinge of anxiety. The soft light of the ICU hid this from the others. Susan Wheeler was twenty-three years old.

"Twenty-three or twenty-four, that doesn't make much difference," said Bellows as he tried to think of the best way to present the fluid balance problem.

It made a difference to Susan.

"Where is she," asked Susan, not sure if she really wanted to be told.

"In the corner on the left," said Bellows without looking up from the input-output sheet in the chart. "What we need to check is the exact amount of fluid the patient has put out versus the exact amount that has been given. Of course this is static data and we are more interested in the dynamic state. But we can get a pretty good idea. Now let's see, she put out 1650 cc of urine . . ."

Susan was not listening at this point. Her eyes fought to discern the motionless figure in the bed in the corner. From where she was standing, she could make out only a blotch of dark hair, a pale face, and a tube issuing from the area of the mouth. The tube was connected to a large square machine next to the bed that hissed to and fro, breathing for the patient. The patient's body was covered by a white sheet; the arms were uncovered and positioned at forty-five-degree angles from the torso. An I.V. line ran into the left arm. Another I.V. line ran into the right side of her neck. Heightening the somber effect, a small spotlight directed its concentrated beam down from the ceiling above the patient, splashing over the head and upper body. The rest of the corner was lost in shadow. There was no motion, no sign of life save for the rhythmical hiss of the breathing machine. A plastic line curled down from under the patient and was connected to a calibrated urine container.

"We also have to have an accurate daily weight," continued Bellows.

But for Susan his voice drifted in and out of her awareness. "A twenty-three-year-old woman . . ." The thought reverberated in Susan's mind. Without the aid of an extensive clinical experience, Susan was instantly lost in the human element. The age and sex similarity struck too close to home for her to avoid the identification. In a naive way she associated such serious medicine with old people who had had their fling at life.

"How long has she been unresponsive," asked Susan absently, without taking her eyes from the patient in the corner, without even blinking.

Bellows, interrupted by this non sequitur, turned his head up to glance at Susan. He was insensitive to Susan's state of mind. "Eight days," said Bellows, slightly vexed at the interruption of his harangue about fluid balance. "But that has little to do with today's sodium level, Miss Wheeler. Could you kindly keep your mind on the subject at hand."

Bellows shifted his attention to the others. "I'm going to be expecting you people to start writing routine fluid orders by the end of the week. Now where the hell was I?" Bellows returned to his input-output calculations, and everyone except Susan leaned over to catch the expanding figures.

Susan continued to stare at the motionless individual in the corner, racing through a mental checklist of her friends who had had D&Cs, wondering what really divided herself or her friends from the plight of Nancy Greenly. Several minutes passed as she bit her lower lip, as was her custom when in deep thought.

"How'd it happen?" asked Susan, again unexpectedly.

Bellows's head popped up for the second time, but more rapidly, as if he expected some imminent catastrophe. "How'd what happen?" he countered, scanning the room for some telltale activity.

"How'd the patient become comatose?"

Bellows sat up straight, closed his eyes and put his pencil down. As if counting to ten, he paused before speaking.

"Miss Wheeler, you've got to try to give me a hand," said Bellows slowly and condescendingly. "You've got to stay with us. As for the patient, it was just one of those inexplicable twists of the fickle finger of fate. OK? Perfect health . . . routine D&C . . . anesthesia and induction without a ripple. She just never woke up. Some sort of cerebral hypoxia. The squash didn't get the oxygen it needed. OK? Now let's get back to work. We'll be here all day getting these orders written and we've got Grand Rounds at noon."

"Does that kind of complication occur often?" persisted Susan.

"No," said Bellows, "rare as hell, maybe one in a hundred thousand."

"One hundred percent for her, though," added Susan with an edge on the tips of her words.

Bellows looked up at Susan without any idea of what she was driving at. The human element in Nancy Greenly's case had ceased to be a part of his concern. Bellows was intent on keeping the ions at the right level, keeping the urine output up, and keeping the bacteria at bay. He did not want Nancy Greenly to die while she was on his service because if she did, it would reflect on the kind of care he was capable of providing, and Stark would have some choice comments for him. He remembered all too well what Stark had said to Johnston after a similar case had resulted in death while Johnston was on the service.

It wasn't that Bellows didn't care about the human element, it was just that he didn't have time for it. Besides the sheer number of cases he had been and was involved with provided a cushion or a numbness associated with anything done repeatedly. Bellows did not make the association between Susan's and Nancy Greenly's ages, nor did he remember the emotional susceptibility associated with an individual's initial clinical experiences in the hospital environment.

"Now for the hundredth time, let's get back to work," said Bellows, pulling his chair in closer to the desk and running his hand nervously through his hair. He looked at his watch before going back to his calculations. "OK, if we use 1/4 normal saline, let's see how many milliequivalents we'll get in 2500 cc."

Susan was totally detached from the conversation, almost in a fugue. Following some inner curiosity, she moved around the desk and approached Nancy Greenly. She moved slowly, warily, as if she were approaching something dangerous, and absorbing all the details of the scene as they came available. Nancy Greenly's eyes were only half closed and the lower edges of her blue irises were visible. Her face was a marble white, which contrasted sharply with the sable brown of her hair. Her lips were dried and cracked, her mouth held open with a plastic mouthpiece so she wouldn't bite the endotracheal tube. Brownish material had crusted and hardened on her front teeth; it was old blood.

Feeling slightly giddy, Susan looked away for a moment and then back. The harshness of the image of the previously normal young woman made her tremble with undirected emotion. It wasn't sadness per se. It was another kind of inner pain, a sense of mortality, a sense of the meaningless of life which could be so easily disrupted, a sense of hopelessness, and a sense of helplessness. All these thoughts cascaded into the center of Susan's mind, bringing unaccustomed moisture to the palms of her hands.

As if reaching for a delicate piece of porcelain, Susan lifted one of Nancy Greenly's hands. It was surprisingly cold and totally limp. Was she alive or dead? The thought crossed Susan's mind. But there directly above was the cardiac monitor with its reassuring electronic blip tracing excitedly its pattern.

"I shall assume you are a whiz at fluid balance, Miss Wheeler," said Bellows at Susan's side. His voice broke the semitrance Susan had assumed and she replaced carefully Nancy Greenly's hand. To Susan's surprise the whole group had moved over to the bedside.

"This, everybody, is the CVP line, the central venous pressure," said Bellows holding up the plastic tube whose tip snaked into Nancy Greenly's neck. "We just keep that open for now. The I.V. goes in the other side, and that's where we'll hang our 1/4 normal saline with the 25 milliequivalents of potassium to run at 125 cc per hour."

"Now then," continued Bellows after a slight pause, obviously thinking while looking vacantly at Nancy Greenly, "Cartwright, be sure to order electrolytes on her urine today but leave the standing order for daily serum electrolytes. Oh yeah, include magnesium levels too, OK."

Cartwright was madly writing these orders down on the index card he had for Nancy Greenly. Bellows took his reflex hammer and absently tried for deep tendon reflexes on Nancy Greenly's legs. There were none.

"Why didn't you do a tracheostomy?" asked Fairweather.

Bellows looked up at Fairweather and paused. "That's a very good question, Mr. Fairweather." Bellows turned to Cartwright, "Why didn't we do a tracheostomy, Daniel?"

Cartwright looked from the patient to Bellows, then back to the patient. He became visibly flustered and consulted his index card despite the fact that he knew the information was not there.

Bellows looked back at Fairweather. "That's a very good question, Mr. Fairweather. And if I remember correctly I did tell Dr. Cartwright to get the ENT boys over here to do a trach. Isn't that right, Dr. Cartwright?"

"Yeah, that's right," enjoined Cartwright. "I put in the call but they never called back."

"And you never followed up on it," added Bellows with uncamouflaged irritation.

"No, I got involved . . . ," began Cartwright.

"Cut the bullshit, Dr. Cartwright," interrupted Bellows. "Just get the ENT boys up here stat. It doesn't look like this one is going to come to, and for long-term respiratory care we need a trach. You see, Mr. Fairweather, the cuffed endotracheal tube will eventually cause necrosis of the walls of the trachea. It is a good point."

Harvey Goldberg fidgeted, wishing he had asked Fairweather's question.

Susan revived from the depths of her daydream as a result of the verbal exchange between Bellows and Cartwright.

"Does anybody have any idea why this horrible thing has happened to this patient?" asked Susan.

"What horrible thing?" asked Bellows nervously while he mentally checked the I.V., the respirator, and the monitor. "Oh, you mean the fact that she never woke up. Well . . ." Bellows paused. "That reminds me. Cartwright, while you're calling consults, have neurology get their asses up here and do another EEG on this patient. If it is still flat, maybe we can get the kidneys."

"Kidneys?" questioned Susan with horror, trying not to think about what such a statement meant for Nancy Greenly.

"Look," said Bellows putting his hands on the railing with his arms extended. "If her squash is gone, I mean wiped out, then we might as well get the kidneys for someone else, provided of course, we can talk the family into it."

"But she might wake up," protested Susan with color rising in her cheeks, her eyes flashing.

"Some of them wake up," shrugged Bellows, "but most don't when they have a flat EEG. Let's face it; it means the brain is infarcted, dead, and there is no way to bring it back. You can't do a brain transplant although there are some cases where it might be very useful." Bellows looked teasingly at Cartwright, who caught the innuendo and laughed.

"Doesn't anyone know why this patient's brain didn't get the oxygen it needed during surgery?" asked Susan, going back to her previous question in a desperate attempt to avoid even the thought of taking the kidneys out of Nancy Greenly.

"No," said Bellows plainly and looking directly at Susan. "It was a clean case. They've gone over every inch of the anesthesia procedure. It happened to be one of the most compulsive of all the anesthesiology residents and he's sucked the case dry. I mean, he's been merciless on himself. But there's been no explanation. It could have been some sort of stroke, I guess. Maybe she had some condition which made her susceptible to having a stroke. I don't know. In any case, oxygen was apparently kept from the brain long enough so that too many of the brain cells died. It so happens that the cells of the cerebrum are very sensitive to low levels of oxygen. So they die first when the oxygen falls below a critical level and the result is what we have here"—Bellows made a gesture with his hand, palm up, over Nancy Greenly—"a vegetable. The heart beats because it doesn't depend on the brain. But everything else must be done for the patient. We have to breathe her with the respirator there." Bellows motioned toward the hissing machine to the right of Nancy's head. "We have to maintain the critical balance of fluids and electrolytes as we were doing a few moments ago. We have to feed her, regulate the temperature . . ." Bellows paused after he said the word *temperature*. The concept keyed off his memory. "Cartwright, order a portable chest X-ray today. I almost forgot about the temp elevation you mentioned a little while ago." Bellows looked at Susan. "That's how most of these brainstem patients depart from this life, pneumonia . . . their only friend. Sometimes I wonder what the shit I'm doing when I treat the pneumonia. But in medicine we don't ask questions like that. We treat the pneumonia because we have the antibiotics."

At that moment the page system came to life as it had been doing intermittently. This time it paged "Dr. Wheeler, Dr. Susan Wheeler, 938 please." Paul Carpin nudged Susan and informed her about the page. Susan looked up at Bellows quite surprised.

"That was for me?" asked Susan in disbelief. "It said 'Doctor Wheeler.' "

"I gave the nurses on the floor a list of your names to put on the charts in order to divide up the patients among you. You'll be paged for all the blood work and other fascinating scut."

"It's going to be strange getting used to being called Doctor," said Susan looking around for the nearest phone.

"You'd better get used to it because that's the way you'll be paged. It's not meant to flatter you. The idea is to make it easier on the patients. You shouldn't hide the fact that you're students, but don't advertise it either. Some of the patients wouldn't let you touch them if they thought you were med students; they'd yell and scream they were being used as guinea pigs. Anyway go answer the page, Dr. Wheeler, and then catch up with us. After we finish here we'll be up in the conference room on ten."

Susan walked over to the main desk and dialed 938. Bellows watched her cross the room. He couldn't help but notice that under the white coat lurked a sensuous figure. Bellows was being attracted to Susan Wheeler by quantum leaps.

It gave Susan a feeling of unreality to answer a page for "Dr. Wheeler." She felt transparent as if she were an actress playing the role of a doctor. She had on the white coat and the scene was melodramatic and appropriate. Yet on the inside she just didn't feel like the part, and there was the thought that she would be exposed at any moment as a charlatan.

At the other end of the phone line, the nurse was matter-of-fact and to the point.

"We need an I.V. started on a pre-op. The case has been delayed and anesthesia wants some fluid in him."

"When would you like me to start it?" asked Susan twisting the phone cord.

"NOW!" answered the nurse before hanging up.

The other members of Susan's group had moved on to another patient and were again huddled about the desk, straining to see the chart Bellows had pulled from the rack and had in front of him. No one looked up as Susan traversed the half-light of the ICU. She reached the door and her left hand wrapped around the upturned stainless steel handle. Turning her head slowly to the right she chanced another glance at the immobile and lifeless-appearing Nancy Greenly. Once again Susan's mind stumbled through a painful identification. She left the ICU with difficulty but also with a sense of relief.

The sense of relief was short-lived. Hurrying along the crowded corridor, Susan began to prepare herself for the next mini-hurdle. Susan had never started an I.V. before.

She had drawn blood from several patients, including her lab partner, but she never had started an I.V. Intellectually she knew what was required and she knew that she could do it. After all, it only involved punching a razor-sharp needle through some thin skin and impaling a vein without going all the way through the vessel. The difficulties arose from the fact that frequently the vein was only the size of thin spaghetti with a corresponding smaller lumen. In addition, sometimes the vein could not be seen from the surface of the skin and had to be attacked blindly with only the help of the sense of touch.

With these difficulties in mind Susan knew that even something as mundane as starting an I.V. was going to be a challenge of sorts. Her biggest concern was that it was going to be very apparent that she was new at the game, and perhaps the patient might rebel and demand a real doctor. Besides, she was in no frame of mind to have to put up with any exasperated ridicule from any of those bitchy nurses.

When Susan arrived at Beard 5, the scene was unchanged. The bustle of activity was as hectic as ever. Terry Linquivist gave a fleeting look at Susan before disappearing into the treatment room. One of the other nurses, whose cap had a bright orange stripe and whose name tag read "Sarah Sterns," responded to Susan's arrival by handing her the I.V. tray and a bottle of I.V. fluid.

"The name's Berman. He's in 503," said Sarah Sterns. "Don't worry about the rate. I'll be down there in a few minutes to regulate it."

Susan nodded and headed for 503. En route she examined the I.V. tray. There were all sorts of needles: scalp needles, long-dwelling catheters, CVP lines, and traditional disposable needles. There were packets of alcohol sponges, a few lengths of flat rubber tubing to be used as the tourniquets, and a flashlight. Eyeing the flashlight, Susan wondered how many times she would repeat the scene of trudging off in the middle of the night to start an I.V.

Susan passed 507, then 505. As 503 loomed she rummaged in the I.V. tray among the scalp needles until she located a #21 in a bright yellow packet. That was the needle she had seen an I.V. started with in the past. She was tempted to try one of the impressive-looking long-dwells but she decided to keep the experimenting to a minimum, at least on her first I.V.

"Room 503" was stenciled plainly on the door. It stood slightly ajar. Susan didn't know whether she should knock or just walk in. With a self-conscious glance over her shoulder to make sure she was not being watched, she knocked.

"Come in," said a voice from within.

Susan pushed open the door with her foot, clutching the I.V. tray in her right hand and the D5W bottle in her left. Expecting to see an elderly ill individual, Susan moved into the room. It was a typical private room at the Memorial: small, old, the floor tiled with vinyl squares. The window was curtainless and dirty. An old radiator stood in the corner covered with a dozen layers of paint.

Contrary to Susan's expectations, the patient was neither old nor infirm. Propped up in the hospital bed was a youngish man, seemingly in perfect health. Susan quickly estimated that he was about thirty. He was wearing the usual hospital garb with the sheet pulled up to his waist. His hair was dark and very thick, and it was brushed back on both sides of his temples so that it covered the top part of each ear. His face was narrow, intelligent, and tanned despite the winter season. He had a sharp nose with flared nostrils, making him appear as if he were constantly breathing in. He looked athletic and in good physical condition. His muscular arms encircled his updrawn knees. His hands worked at each other nervously as if they were cold. Susan sensed immediately the man's anxiety through a patina of contrived calmness.

"Don't be bashful, come right in. It's like Grand Central here," smiled Berman. The smile wavered. It was apparent that the man welcomed an interruption in the tenseness of waiting to be called for surgery.

Susan entered and allowed herself only a short look at Berman while she returned the smile. She then pushed the door to its original position. She put the tray on the foot of the bed and hung the I.V. bottle from the stand at the head of the bed. She consciously avoided Berman's eyes while she wondered why in God's name did Berman have to be so young, healthy, and obviously in charge of all his faculties. Susan certainly would have preferred an unconscious centenarian.

51

"Not another needle!" said Berman with partially feigned overconcern.

"I'm afraid so," said Susan opening a package of I.V. tubing, which she inserted into the bottle of D5W on the stand, allowing some of the fluid to run through the tube before securing it with a stopcock. With that accomplished, Susan looked up at Berman, to find that he was staring intently at her.

"Are you a doctor?" asked Berman with a tone of disbelief.

Susan didn't respond immediately. She continued to look directly into Berman's deep brown eyes. In her mind she weighed the possibilities of her response. She wasn't a doctor, that was obvious. What did she want to say? She wanted to say that she was a doctor. But Susan was a realist and she wondered if she would ever be able to say she was a doctor and believe it herself.

"No," said Susan with finality while returning her gaze to the #21 scalp needle. The reality disappointed her and she thought that it would add to Berman's anxiety. "I'm just a medical student," she added.

Berman's hands stopped their nervous activity. "There's no need to be defensive about that," he said with sincerity. "You just don't look like a doctor or a doctor-to-be."

Berman's innocent comment struck a tender chord in Susan's mind. Her embryonic professionalism made her rather paranoid and she immediately misconstrued Berman's comment, which was meant as a backhanded compliment.

"What is your name?" continued Berman, totally unaware of the effect of his previous comment. He shielded his eyes from the glare of the overhead fluorescent lights and motioned for Susan to turn slightly to the left so he could see her name tag on her lapel. "Susan Wheeler . . . Dr. Susan Wheeler. It has a natural sound to it."

Susan quickly realized that Berman was not challenging her as a doctor after all. Still she did not respond. Something about Berman was distantly but comfortably familiar to her but she could not characterize it. Her mind tried but it was too subtly hidden in the immediacy of their encounter. It had something to do with Berman's charming authoritarian manner.

Partially as a method to concentrate her own thoughts and partially to control the conversation, Susan plunged into the I.V. affair. In a businesslike manner she placed the tourniquet about Berman's left wrist and pulled it tight. She tore open the packets containing the scalp needle and the alcohol sponge. Berman's eyes followed these preparations with great interest.

"Gotta admit from the start, I'm not crazy about needles," said Berman, trying to maintain a degree of aplomb. He looked back and forth from his hand to Susan.

Susan sensed Berman's mounting concern and she wondered what he'd say if she told him that it was her first attempt at starting an I.V. She was quite certain that he would simply become unhinged. She felt certain because she realized that if the roles were reversed, that would be how she would react.

The tourniquet combined forces with Berman's ectomorphic body to make the veins on the back of his hand stand out like garden hoses. Susan took a deep breath and held it. Berman did the same. After a swipe with the alcohol pledget, Susan tried to jam the needle into the back of Berman's hand. But the skin advanced, resisting penetration.

"Ahhh," cried Berman gripping the sheet with his free right hand. He was purposely overdoing the theatrics as a self-preservation maneuver. However, its effect was to unnerve Susan, who desisted in her attempt to break the skin.

"If it's any consolation, you feel just like a doctor," said Berman looking at the back of his left hand. The tourniquet was still in place and the hand had an overall bluish discoloration.

"Mr. Berman, you're going to have to be a little more cooperative," said Susan, mustering her forces for a renewed attempt and wishing to spread the responsibility for any failure.

"Cooperate, she says," echoed Berman while rolling his eyes up inside of his head. "I've been as quiet as a sacrificial lamb."

Susan replaced Berman's left hand flat on the bed. With her own left hand she effected countertraction on Berman's skin. With the same amount of effort the needle entered the scanty tissue.

"I give up," pleaded Berman with a tinge of humor.

Susan concentrated on the submerged needle point. At first it tended to push the vein in front of itself. She tried the countertraction trick: same problem. She tried the countertraction combined with a decisive lunge with the needle. She could feel the pop as the needle burst into the vein. Blood flowed back through the needle, filling the attached plastic tubing. Quickly she hooked up the I.V. line, opened the stopcock, and removed the tourniquet. The I.V. flowed smoothly.

Both parties felt definite relief.

Having actually accomplished something, something medical for a patient, Susan felt a tinge of euphoria. It was a small affair, a mere I.V., but nonetheless a definite service. Maybe there was a future for her overall. The euphoria brought a feeling of expansiveness to Susan which included a heightened sense of warmth with a shade of condescension toward Berman in spite of the hospital environment.

"You said before that I don't look like a doctor," said Susan, getting the tape out to secure the I.V. line to the back of Berman's hand. "What does it mean, to look like a doctor?" There was a slight tease to her voice as if she were more interested in hearing Berman speak than in actually listening to what he had to say.

"Maybe it was a silly comment," said Berman, watching every move Susan made while taping the I.V. line. "But I do know a few girls who went into medicine from my graduating class in college. Several of them were OK; all of them were bright; there was no doubt about that, but they were hardly feminine."

"They probably weren't feminine to you because they went into medicine rather than vice versa," said Susan, slowing the I.V. to a steady drip.

"Possible . . . possible . . . ," said Berman thoughtfully. He recognized that Susan's interpretation represented a new perspective. "But I don't think so. Two of them I happen to know quite well. In fact I knew them all the way through college. They really didn't decide on medicine until the last year. They were just as nonfeminine before as after their decision. Whereas you, Dr. Wheeler-to-be, have a distinct aura of femininity that envelops you like a cloud."

Susan, eager to take exception to Berman's comment regarding his friends' femininity, was caught off guard by Berman's reference to her own femininity. On the one hand she was tempted to respond, "Are you for real, buddy?" while on the other hand she thought that Berman might be serious and actually paying her a compliment. Berman himself decided which way Susan's mind would turn.

"If I had to pick what your vocation was," continued Berman, "I'd have to say you were a dancer."

Having stumbled on to Susan's own fantasy concerning her alter ego, Berman opened the door on Susan's personality. To her, appearing like a dancer was definitely a compliment, and therefore she was more than willing to accept Berman's comment about her femininity as a compliment as well.

"Thank you, Mr. Berman," said Susan with sincerity.

"Please call me Sean," said Berman.

"Thank you, Sean," repeated Susan. She stopped her activity of gathering up the debris from the I.V. paraphernalia and looked out the dirty window. She didn't notice the dirt, the brick, the dark clouds, nor the lifeless trees. She looked back at Berman. "You know, I wouldn't be able to tell you how much I appreciate your compliment. It might sound rather strange to you, but to be quite honest I haven't felt feminine over the last year or so. To hear someone like yourself say so is enormously reassuring. It's not that I have dwelt on it, but just the same I have begun to think of myself as . . ." Susan paused, thinking of the right word. "Neutral, or neuter. Yes that's the right word, neuter. It has happened slowly, in degrees, and I guess I'm really only aware of it by comparison when I get together with some of my former college classmates, especially my former roommate."

Susan suddenly stopped in the middle of her thought and straightened up. She was slightly embarrassed and surprised at her own unexpected candor. "What am I talking about? Sometimes I can't believe myself." She smiled and then laughed at herself. "I can't even act like a doctor, much less look like one. I'm sure that the last thing you want to hear about is my professional adjustment difficulties!"

Berman looked up at Susan with a broad smile. He was obviously enjoying the interlude.

"The patient is the one who is supposed to do the talking," continued Susan, "not the doctor. Why don't you tell me what you do so that I have to shut up?"

"I'm an architect," said Berman. "One of the million or so that haunt the Cambridge scene. But that is another story. I'd much prefer to get back to you. You cannot guess how reassuring it is to me to hear you talk like a human being in this place." Berman's eyes swept around the room. "I don't mind having a little operation, but this waiting around is driving me up the wall. And everybody is so Goddamn matter-of-fact." He looked back at Susan. "Tell me what you were going to say about your former roommate; I'd like to hear."

"Are you putting me on?" asked Susan with narrowed eyes.

"Honest."

"Well it's not all that important. It's just that she was smart. She went to law school and has maintained herself as a woman yet has satisfied her urge and capacity to compete and contribute intellectually."

"I have no idea how you have been doing intellectually but there is no doubt about you being a woman. You couldn't be any less than the absolute antithesis of neuter."

At first Susan was tempted to get into an argument with Berman over the fact that he equated being a woman with outward appearance. She felt that was only a part, a small part. But she caught herself and refrained. After all, Berman was on his way to surgery and didn't need a debate.

"I can't help the way I feel," said Susan, "and 'neuter' is the best description. Initially I thought that medicine would be good for a number of reasons, including the fact that it would provide the social insurance I needed; I didn't want to think or worry about any social pressure to get married. Well," sighed Susan, "it provided social insurance all right, and a good deal more. Actually, I have begun to feel excommunicated from normal society."

"In that vein I would love to be of assistance," said Berman, pleased with his pun. "Provided, of course, you consider architects normal society. There are some who don't, I can assure you. Anyway . . ." Berman scratched the back of his head while he put his words in order. "I hardly feel capable of carrying on a reasonable conversation in this humiliating nightgown, in this depersonalized milieu, and I would like very much to continue this conversation. I'm sure you get accosted continuously and I hate to add to your burden, but perhaps we could get together for some coffee or a drink or something after I get this Goddamn knee taken care of." Berman held up his right knee. "Screwed the thing up years ago playing football. It's been my Achilles heel ever since, so to speak."

"Is that what you're scheduled for today?" asked Susan while she thought about how to respond to Berman's offer. She knew that it was hardly professional by any stretch of the imagination. At the same time she was attracted to Berman.

"That's right, a minuscule-ectomy, or something like that," said Berman.

A knock at the door, followed by the rapid entry of Sarah Sterns before Susan could even respond, made Susan jump, and nervously she began to fuss with the stopcock on the I.V. Almost at the same time Susan realized how childish this action was, and it made her angry that the system could affect her to such a degree.

"Not another needle!" voiced Berman, dejected.

"Another needle. It's your pre-op. Roll over, my friend," said Miss Sterns. She crowded Susan in order to put her tray on the night table.

Berman glanced at Susan in a self-conscious way before rolling over on his right side. Miss Sterns bared Berman's left buttock and grabbed a handful of flesh. The needle flashed into the muscle. It was over almost before it began.

"Don't worry about the I.V. rate," said Miss Sterns on her way to the door. "I'll adjust it shortly." She was gone.

"Well, I must be going," said Susan quickly.

"Is it a date?" asked Berman, trying not to lean on his left buttock.

"Sean, I don't know. I'm not sure how I feel about it; I mean professionally and all that."

"Professionally?" Berman was genuinely surprised. "You must be being brainwashed."

"Maybe I am," said Susan. She looked at her watch, the door, and back at Berman. "All right," said Susan finally, "we'll get together. Meanwhile you have to get back to normal. I'll live with being unprofessional but I don't want to be accused of taking advantage of a cripple. I'll stop in here before you go home. Do you have any idea how long you are going to be in the hospital?"

"My doctor said three days."

"I'll stop back before you go," said Susan already on her way to the door.

At the door she had to give way to an orderly arriving with a gurney to transport Berman to the OR, to room No. 8, for his meniscectomy. Susan glanced back at Berman before turning down the corridor. She gave him the thumbs-up sign, which he returned with a smile. As she moved down toward the nurses' station, Susan pondered over her mixed emotions. There was the warmth of meeting someone with whom she felt a rather immediate chemical attraction; at the same time there was the nagging reality of the unprofessionalism of it all. Susan couldn't help but acknowledge that for her to be a doctor was going to be very difficult in every respect.

Monday
February 23
12:10 P.M.

Like a slalom skier Susan wove her way down the hospital corridor crowded with lunch carts filled with an assortment of colorless food. The reasonably pleasant aromas emanating from the evenly stacked trays reminded her that she hadn't eaten that day: two pieces of toast on the run hardly constituted a meal.

The arrival of the lunch carts added to the appearance of utter chaos at the nurses' station on Beard 5. It seemed to Susan that it was a wonder indeed that the right patient got the right drug, therapy, or meal. To Susan's pleasant surprise, Sarah Sterns had a smile and a quick thank-you for Susan before pointing to the resting place for the I.V. tray. No one else even acknowledged Susan's presence and she left. It took her about three seconds to decide to use the stairs rather than wait for the crowded elevator. After all, it was only three floors down to the ICU.

The stairs were made of metal with an embossed surface like beaten silver. The color had been orange but now had become something approaching a dirty tan except in the center of each step, which was worn shiny by multitudinous footsteps. The walls of the stairwell were made of cinder block, painted dark gray. But the paint was old and peeling. Some previous plumbing catastrophe or accident had provided a series of longitudinal stains that descended from above along the wall to the right. The stains reappeared each time. Susan rounded the platform and started down another flight. The only light in the stairwell came from a bare bulb at each floor landing. On the fourth floor the bulb had blown, and because of the relative darkness Susan had to proceed with caution, advancing her foot to find the first stair on the next flight down to three. The distances between the floors seemed remarkably long to Susan.

By leaning out over the metal banister Susan could see down into the subbasement and up to where the spiraling stairs became lost in collapsing perspective. Susan felt slightly ill at ease in the stairwell. The decaying darkness of the walls seemed to move in on her, awakening some atavistic fear. Perhaps it reminded her of a recurrent dream she used to have as a child. Although she had not had the dream for a long time, she remembered it well. It did not concern a stairwell but the overall effect was similar. The dream involved moving through a tunnel of twisted shapes which would progressively impede her progress. She never made it to the end of the tunnel in her dream despite the fact that the goal seemed very important.

In spite of the mildly disquieting atmosphere in the stairwell, Susan descended slowly, step by step. Her deliberate footsteps rang out with a dull metallic echo. She was alone. There were no people and it gave her a few uninterrupted moments to think. For a short period of time the immediacy of the hospital receded from Susan's consciousness.

The encounter with Berman became more complicated in her mind. The lack of professionalism was diluted because, in reality, Berman was not Susan's patient. She had been called simply to provide a peripheral service. The fact that Berman was a patient was important only in facilitating their chance meeting. But Susan wasn't sure if she were just rationalizing. Rounding the landing on the third floor, she paused at the head of the next flight.

She had reacted to Berman as a woman. For a constellation of inexplicable reasons, Berman had appealed to her in a basic, natural, even chemical way. To an extent that was encouraging and reassuring. There was no doubt in Susan's mind that she had begun to think of herself in a sexless sort of way over the first two years of medical school. She had used the word *neuter* in talking with Berman but only because she had been forced on the spur of the moment to find a term for it. Obviously she was female; she felt female and her monthly menstrual flow emphasized its reality. But was she a woman?

Susan started down the next flight of stairs. For the first time events had forced her to intellectualize a tendency which had been developing for several years. She wondered if Carpin had been called instead of her and if Berman had been some equally attractive female, would Carpin have responded as a male? Susan stopped again, considering this hypothetical situation.

From her experience she decided that there was a very good possibility that Carpin would have performed in an equivalent fashion.

Susan recommenced descending the stairs, very slowly now. But if it were true that a male would respond in a way similar to hers, why was it so different for her? Why did she dwell on it?

It was more than the debatable question of medical ethics. Berman had made Susan feel like a woman. All at once it came to Susan. The biggest difference between herself and Carpin was that Susan had an extra obstacle. She knew that both of them wanted to become doctors; to act like doctors, think like doctors, to be taken for doctors. But for Susan there was an additional step. Susan wanted also to become a woman; to feel like a woman, to be taken for and respected as a woman. When she had entered medicine, she knew it was a male-dominated career choice. That had been one of the challenges. Susan had never imagined that medicine would make it difficult for her to achieve fulfillment in a social sense. Academically she could compete; she was reasonably sure of that. The next step was going to be harder, an uncharted course. And Carpin? Well, for him the social part was easy. He was a male in a recognized male role. Being in medicine only supported his image of himself as a man. Carpin only had to worry about convincing himself he was a doctor; Susan had to convince herself that she was a doctor and a woman.

Arriving on the second floor, Susan was greeted by a sign

which stated in bold letters: "Operating Room Area: Unauthorized Entry Forbidden." But the sign wasn't necessary. To Susan's momentary consternation, the door was locked! Her overly active imagination suddenly had all the doors from the stairwell locked, and she thought of herself caught within a vertical prison. It was a fleeting thought, totally irrational. "Wheeler, you're too much," she said aloud for her own benefit and encouragement. She quickly descended to the first floor. The door opened easily and Susan joined the surging mob on the main floor.

She took the elevator and returned to the ICU entrance. It took a bit of fortitude to begin to open the door. Once she started, it took strength. The ICU door was massive and very heavy.

Susan stepped once again into the nether world of the ICU interior. One of the nurses looked up from the desk but then went back to an EKG tracing in front of her. As Susan scanned the room, she was again struck by the purely mechanical appearance, the lack of human voices, even the lack of movement save for the fluorescent blips tracing their incessant patterns. And there was Nancy Greenly, as immobile as a statue, a casualty of medicine, a victim of technology. Susan wondered about her life, her loves. Everything was gone, all because of a simple menstrual irregularity, a routine D&C.

Susan forced her eyes away from Nancy Greenly and ascertained that her group had since departed from the ICU, presumably for Grand Rounds. At the same instant Susan acknowledged to herself her acute discomfort about being in the ICU. The psychological and technical complexity of the room caused any residual euphoria from the I.V. episode to vanish. Her imagination forced her to ponder the situation if something suddenly went wrong with one of the patients while she was standing there. What if someone expected her to make some life-death decision to go along with her white coat and her impotent stethoscope in her pocket?

Controlling the urge to succumb to a minor panic, Susan tugged at the inertia of the door and escaped into the corridor. Retracing her steps to the elevator, Susan mused about the difference between fact and fancy, between reality and mythology, between what it really was like being a medical student and what people thought it was like.

Remembering Bellows's comment about Grand Rounds on

10, Susan pushed the tenth-floor button and allowed herself to be compressed toward the rear of the elevator. It was a miserable trip. The car was a potpourri of human beings with every conceivable affliction, and it stopped at every floor. The air was heavy and hot, particularly since one rude passenger was smoking despite the sign plainly forbidding it. The occupants did not look at each other; they stared blankly at the light progressing from number to number, as did Susan, wishing the doors would open and close more quickly.

Impetuously she pushed her way to the front of the elevator at the ninth floor. At 10, she broke from the crowded cubicle with relief.

The atmosphere changed immediately. The tenth floor was carpeted and the walls shone with an even luster of newly applied semigloss paint. Gilded frames set off portraits of former Memorial greats in their sartorial academic splendor. Chippendale tables topped with a variety of lamps were interspersed between comfortable chairs along the length of the corridor. Neat piles of *New Yorker* magazines were arranged at rational intervals.

A large sign opposite the elevator directed Susan to the conference room. As she walked down the corridor she could see into the offices. These were the private offices for some of the more established doctors at the Memorial. A few patients were scattered along the corridor, reading and waiting. They all looked up as Susan passed. Their faces were uniformly expressionless.

At the end of the corridor Susan passed the office of the Chief of Surgery, Dr. H. Stark. The door was ajar, and inside Susan caught a glimpse of two secretaries typing furiously. Just beyond Stark's office and on the other side of the corridor was a second stairwell. At the very end of the corridor, over two swinging mahogany doors an illuminated sign proclaimed: "Conference in Progress."

Susan entered the conference room, letting the doors close quietly behind her. It took a few moments for her eyes to adjust to the darkness, since the room lights were out. The focal point of light at the end of the room was the projected image of a Kodachrome of a human lung. Susan could just make out the outline of a man with a pointer describing the details of the photograph.

From the gloom in the foreground Susan began to discern

the rows of seats and their occupants. The room was about thirty feet wide and some fifty feet long. There was a gentle downward slope of the floor to the podium, which was raised by two steps. The projection equipment was professionally hidden from view. The projected beam of light, however, was visible throughout its entire path due to the swirls of cigarette and pipe smoke. Even in the darkness Susan could tell that the conference room was new, well designed, and sumptuously appointed.

The next color slide was a microscopic section, and it provided relatively more light in the room. Susan was able to pick out the back of Niles's head with its prominent lump. He was sitting in an aisle seat. She walked down to the proper row and tapped Niles on the shoulder. Susan could see that they had saved a seat for her. She had to squeeze past Niles and Fairweather before she could sit down. It was next to Bellows.

"Did you do a laparotomy or start an I.V.?" whispered Bellows sarcastically, leaning toward Susan. "You were gone over a half-hour."

"It was an interesting patient," said Susan, bracing for another lecture on punctuality.

"You can think of a better one than that, I hope."

"To tell the truth, it was a dressing change on Robert Redford's circumcision." Susan pretended to be absorbed in the projected slide for a few moments. Then she looked over at Bellows, who snickered and shook his head.

"You're too much, I . . ."

Bellows was interrupted by becoming aware that the man on the podium was directing a question at him. All he heard was ". . . you can enlighten us on that point, Dr. Bellows, can you not?"

"I'm sorry, Dr. Stark, but I did not hear the question," said Bellows, mildly flustered.

"Has she shown any signs of pneumonia?" repeated Stark. A large X-ray of a chest with the right side clouded silhouetted Stark's thin figure on the podium. His features could not be seen.

A fellow resident sitting directly behind Bellows, leaned forward and whispered for Bellows's benefit, "He's talking about Greenly, you asshole."

"Well," coughed Bellows, rising to his feet. "She did have a low-grade temperature elevation yesterday. However, her chest is still clear to auscultation. A chest film two days ago was normal, but we have one pending for today. There has been some bacteria in her urine and we believe that cystitis rather than pneumonitis is the cause of the temperature elevation."

"Is that the pronoun you intended to use, Dr. Bellows?" demanded Dr. Stark, as he walked over to the lectern, placing his hands on each side. Susan struggled to see the man; this was the infamous and famous Chief of Surgery. But his face was still lost in shadow.

"Pronoun, sir?" intoned Bellows rather meekly and with obvious confusion.

"Pronoun. Yes, pronoun. You do know what a pronoun is, don't you, Dr. Bellows?"

There was a bit of scattered laughter.

"Yes, I think I do."

"That's better," said Stark.

"What's better?" persisted Bellows. As soon as he said it he wished that he hadn't. More laughter.

"Your pronoun choice is better, Dr. Bellows. I'm getting rather tired of hearing *we* or some indeterminate third person singular. Part of your training as surgeons involves being able to deal with information, assimilate it, and then make a decision. When I ask a question of one of you residents, I want *your* opinion, not the group's. It doesn't mean that other people don't contribute to the decision process but once you have made the decision, I want to hear *I*, not *we* or *one*."

Stark walked a few steps from the lectern and leaned on the pointer. "Now then, back to the care of the comatose patient. I want to stress again that you must be fully vigilant with these patients, gentlemen. Although it can be frustrating because of the intense chronic care that is required and, perhaps, because of the grim ultimate prognosis, the rewards can be fabulous. The teaching aspect alone is priceless. Homeostasis is indeed extremely difficult to maintain over protracted periods of time when the brain . . ."

A red light on the side wall suddenly sprang to life, blinking frantically. All eyes in the conference room turned toward it. Silently a message flashed onto a TV screen below the red light: "Cardiac Arrest Intensive Care Unit Beard 2."

"Shit," muttered Bellows as he jumped up. Cartwright and Reid followed at his heels, and the three pushed their way to the aisle. Susan and the other four med students hesitated for a moment, looking at each other for encouragement. Then they followed en masse.

"As I was saying, homeostasis is difficult to maintain when the brain is damaged beyond repair. Next slide, please," said Stark consulting his notes on the lectern, hardly paying heed to the group storming from the room.

Monday
February 23
12:16 P.M.

There was no doubt that Sean Berman was very nervous about being in the hospital, facing imminent surgery. He knew very little about medicine, and although he wished that he were better informed, he had not bothered to inquire intelligently about his problem and its treatment. He was frightened about medicine and disease. In fact he tended to equate the two rather than think of them as antagonists. Hence the thought of undergoing surgery offended his sensibility; there was no way for him to deal rationally with the idea that someone was going to cut his skin with a knife. The thought made his stomach sink and sweat appear on his forehead. So he tried not to think about it. In psychiatric terms this was called *denial*. He had been reasonably successful until he had come to the hospital the afternoon before his scheduled surgery.

"The name is Berman. Sean Berman." Berman remembered the admission sequence all too well. What should have been a smooth affair got hopelessly caught in the bureaucratic tangle of the hospital.

"Berman? Are you sure you're to come to the Memorial

today?" questioned the well-meaning, overly made-up receptionist, who wore black nail polish.

"Yes, I'm sure," returned Berman, marveling at the black nail polish. It made him realize that hospitals were monopolies of sorts. In a competitive business someone would have the sense to keep the receptionist from wearing black nail polish.

"Well, I'm sorry but I don't have a file for you. You'll have to take a seat while I handle these other patients. Then I'll call Admitting and I'll be with you shortly."

So commenced the first of several snafus which characterized Sean Berman's admission. He sat down and waited. The big hand of the clock worked its way through an entire revolution before he was admitted.

"May I have your X-ray request, please?" asked a young and extremely thin X-ray technician. Berman had waited over forty minutes in X-ray before being called.

"I don't have an X-ray request," said Berman, glancing through the papers he'd been given.

"You must have one. All admissions have one."

"But I don't."

"You must."

"I tell you I don't."

Despite the obvious frustration, the ridiculous admission sequence had had one positive effect. It had totally occupied Berman's consciousness, and he did not dwell upon his impending surgery. But once in his room, hearing the random moans through partially closed hospital doors, Sean Berman was forced to confront his imminent experience. Even more difficult to dismiss were the people with bandages or even tubes that issued forth mysteriously from areas of the human body without natural orifices. Once in the hospital environment, *denial* was no longer an effective means of psychological defense.

Berman then tried another tactic; he switched to what the psychiatrists call *reaction formation*. He let himself think about his upcoming operation to the point where he seemingly made light of the idea.

"I'm one of the dieticians and I'd like to discuss your meal selection," said an overweight woman with a clipboard who entered Berman's room after a sharp knock. "You are here to have surgery, I presume."

"Surgery?" Berman smiled. "Yeah, I have it about once a year. It's a hobby."

The dietician, the lab technician, anyone who would listen, became a victim of Berman's offhand comment about his scheduled operation.

To an extent this method of defense was successful, at least until the actual morning of the operation. Berman had been awakened at six-thirty by the sound of some jangling cart in the corridor. Try as he might, he had been unable to fall back to sleep. Reading had been impossible. The time had dragged horribly, slowly yet inexorably toward 11, when his surgery was scheduled. His stomach had growled from its emptiness.

At 11:05 the door to his room burst open. Berman's pulse fluttered. It was one of the harried nurses.

"Mr. Berman, there's going to be a delay."

"A delay? How long?" Berman forced himself to be civil. The agony of anticipation was taking its toll.

"Can't say. Thirty minutes, an hour." The nurse shrugged.

"But why? I'm starved." Berman really wasn't hungry; he was too nervous.

"The OR's backed up. I'll be back later to give you your pre-op meds. Just relax." The nurse departed. Berman's mouth was open, ready for another question, a hundred questions. Relax? Fat chance. In fact, until Susan's appearance, Sean Berman had spent the entire morning in an uninterrupted cold sweat, dreading the passage of each moment, yet at the same time wishing time would hurry by. Several times he had felt a tinge of embarrassment at the depth of his anxiety, and he wondered if his feelings were relative to the seriousness of the anticipated surgery. If that were the case, he felt he could never undergo a truly serious operation. Berman was worried about feeling pain, worried that his leg might not be ninety-eight percent better, as his doctor had promised, worried about the cast he would have to wear on his leg for several weeks after the operation. He wasn't worried about the anesthesia. If anything, he worried that they might not put him to sleep. He did not want local anesthesia; he wanted to be out cold.

Berman did not worry about possible complications, nor did he worry about his mortality. He was too young and healthy for that. If he had, he would have thought twice about having the operation. It had always been one of Berman's faults, to miss the forest for the trees. Once he had designed an architecturally award-winning building only to have it turned down by the local city council just because it did not fit into the surroundings. Fortunately Berman was unaware of the stricken Nancy Greenly in the ICU.

For Berman, Susan Wheeler had been a star on a cloudy night. In his overly sensitized and anxiety-ridden state, she had seemed like an apparition coming to help him pass the time, to ease his mind. But she had done more. For the first few moments of the morning Berman had been able to think of something besides his knee and the knife. He had given every ounce of concentration to Susan's comments and all too brief self-revelation. Whether it was Susan's attractiveness or her obvious wit or just Berman's own emotional vulnerability, he had been charmed and delighted and felt immeasurably more comfortable on his ride in the elevator down to the operating room. He also considered that the shot Ms. Sterns had given him might have contributed, because he began to get a little light-headed and images began to be slightly discontinuous.

"Guess you see a lot of people on their way to surgery," said Berman to the orderly, as the elevator approached floor two. Berman was on his back, his hands beneath his head.

"Yup," said the orderly, uninterested, cleaning under his nails.

"Have you ever had surgery here?" asked Berman, enjoying a sensation of calmness and detachment spreading through his limbs.

"Nope. I'd never have an operation here," said the orderly, looking up at the floor indicator as the car eased to a stop on two.

"Why not?" asked Berman.

"I've seen too much, I guess," said the orderly, pushing Berman into the hall.

By the time his gurney was parked in the patient holding area, Berman was happily inebriated. The shot he had received on orders from the anesthesiologist, a Dr. Norman Goodman, was 1 cc of Innovar, a relatively new combination of extremely potent agents. Berman tried to talk to the woman next to him in the patient holding area, but his tongue seemed to have become unresponsive, and he laughed at his own ineffectual efforts. He tried to grab a nurse who walked by, but he missed, and he laughed. Time ceased to be a concern and Berman's brain no longer recorded what happened.

Down in the OR things were progressing well. Penny O'Rilley was already scrubbed and gowned and had brought in the steaming tray of instruments to put out on the Mayo stand. Mary Abruzzi, the circulating nurse, had located one of the pneumatic tourniquets and had carried it into the room.

"One more to go, Dr. Goodman," said Mary, activating the foot pedal to raise the operating table to gurney height.

"How right you are," said Dr. Goodman cheerfully. He let I.V. fluid run through the tube onto the floor to remove the bubbles. "This should be a rapid case. Dr. Spallek is one of the fastest surgeons I know and the patient is a healthy young man. I bet we're out of here by one."

Dr. Norman Goodman had been on the staff at the Memorial for eight years and held a joint appointment at the medical school. He had a lab on the fourth floor of the Hilman Building with a large population of monkeys. His interests involved developing newer concepts of anesthesia by selectively controlling various brain areas. He felt that eventually drugs were going to be specific enough so that just the reticular formation itself would be altered, thereby reducing the amount of drugs necessary to control anesthesia. In fact, only a few weeks earlier he and his laboratory assistant, Dr. Clark Nelson, had stumbled onto a butyrophenone derivative which had slowed the electrical activity only in the reticular formation of a monkey. With great discipline he had kept himself from becoming overly encouraged at such an early time, especially when the results had been from a single animal. But then the results had become reproducible. So far he had tested eight monkeys and all had responded the same.

Dr. Norman Goodman would have preferred to give up all activities and devote twenty-four hours a day to his new discovery. He was eager to advance to more sophisticated experiments with his drug, especially a trial on a human. Dr. Nelson, if anything, was even more eager and optimistic. It had been with difficulty that Dr. Goodman had talked Dr. Nelson out of trying a small subpharmacological dose on himself.

But Dr. Goodman knew that true science rested on a foundation of painstaking methodology. One had to proceed slowly, objectively. Premature trials, claims, or disclosure could be disastrous for all concerned. Accordingly Dr. Goodman had to rein in his excitement and maintain his normal schedule and commitments unless he was willing to divulge his discovery; and that he was unwilling to do as yet. So on Monday morning he had to "pass gas," as they called it in the vernacular . . . devote time to clinical anesthesia.

"Damn," said Dr. Goodman straightening up. "Mary, I forgot to bring down an endotracheal tube. Would you run back to the anesthesia room and bring me a number eight."

"Coming up," said Mary Abruzzi, disappearing through the OR door. Dr. Goodman sorted out the gas line connectors and plugged into the nitrous oxide and oxygen sources on the wall.

Sean Berman was Dr. Goodman's fourth and final case for February 23, 1976. Already that day he had smoothly anesthetized three patients. A two-hundred-and-sixty-seven-pound flatulent female with gallstones had been the only potential problem. Dr. Goodman had feared that the enormous bulk of fatty tissue would have absorbed such large quantities of the anesthetic agent that termination of the anesthesia would have been very difficult. But that had not proved to be the case. Despite the fact that the case had been prolonged the patient had awakened very quickly and extubation had been carried out almost immediately after the final skin suture had been tied.

The other two cases that morning had been very routine: a vein stripping and a hemorrhoid. The final case for Dr. Goodman, Berman, was to be a meniscectomy of the right knee and Dr. Goodman expected to be in his lab by 1:15 at the latest. Every Monday morning Dr. Goodman thanked his lucky stars that he had had enough foresight to have continued his research proclivities. He found clinical anesthesia a bore; it was too easy, too routine, and frightfully dull.

The only way he kept his sanity those Monday mornings, he'd tell his neighbor, was to vary his technique to provide food for his brain, to force him to think rather than just sit there and daydream. If there were no contraindications, he liked balanced anesthesia the best, meaning he did not have to give the patient some gargantuan dose of any one agent, but rather he balanced the needs by a number of different agents. Neurolept anesthesia was his favorite because in certain respects it was a crude precursor to the types of anesthetic agents he was looking for.

Mary Abruzzi returned with the endotracheal tube.

"Mary, you're a doll," said Dr. Goodman, checking off his preparations. "I think we're ready. How about bringing the patient down?"

"My pleasure. I'm not going to get lunch until we finish this case." Mary Abruzzi left for the second time.

Since Berman did not offer any contraindications, Goodman decided to use neuroleptanesthesia. He knew Spallek didn't care. Most orthopedic surgeons didn't care. "Just get them down enough so I can put on the Goddamn tourniquet, that's all I care about" was the usual orthopedic response to the query about which anesthetic agent they might prefer.

Neurolept anesthesia was a balanced technique. The patient was given a potent neurolept, or tranquilizing agent, and a potent analgesic, or painkiller. Both agents provided easily arousable sleep as a side effect. Dr. Goodman liked droperidol and fentanyl best of the agents cleared for use. After they were given, the patient was put to sleep with Pentothal and maintained asleep on nitrous oxide. Curare was used to paralyze the skeletal muscles for entubation and surgical relaxation. During the case aliquots of the neurolept and analgesic agents were used as needed to maintain the proper depth of anesthesia. The patient had to be watched very closely through all this, and Dr. Goodman liked that. For him the time passed more quickly when he was busy.

The OR door was opened by one of the orderlies helping to guide Berman's gurney into room No. 8. Mary Abruzzi was pushing.

"Here's your baby, Dr. Goodman. He's sound asleep," said Mary Abruzzi.

They put down the arm rails.

"OK, Mr. Berman. Time to move over onto the table." Mary Abruzzi gently shook Berman's shoulder. He opened his eyelids about halfway. "You have to help us, Mr. Berman."

With some difficulty they got Berman over onto the table. Smacking his lips, turning on his side, and drawing up the sheet around his neck, Berman gave the impression that he thought he was home in his own bed.

"OK, Rip Van Winkle, on your back." Mary Abruzzi

coaxed Berman onto his back and secured his right arm to his side. Berman slept, apparently unaware of the activity about him. The cuff of the pneumatic tourniquet was placed about his right thigh and tested. The heel of his right foot was placed in a sling and hung from a stainless steel rod at the foot of the operating table, lifting the entire right leg. Ted Colbert, the assisting resident, began the prep by scrubbing the right knee with pHisoHex.

Dr. Goodman went right to work. The time was 12:20. Blood pressure was 110/75; pulse was seventy-two and regular. He started an I.V. with deftness which belied the difficulties of handling a large-bore intravenous catheter. The whole process from skin puncture to tape took less than sixty seconds.

Mary Abruzzi attached the cardiac monitor leads, and the room echoed with the high-pitched but low-amplitude beeps.

With the anesthesia machine rigged and ready, Dr. Goodman attached a syringe to the I.V. line.

"OK, Mr. Berman, I want you to relax now," kidded Dr. Goodman, smiling at Mary Abruzzi.

"If he relaxes any more, he's going to pour off the table," laughed Mary.

Dr. Goodman injected intravenously a 6 cc bolus of Innovar, the same droperidol and fentanyl combination that had been used as the pre-op medication. Then he tested the lid reflex and noted that Berman had already achieved a deep level of sleep. Consequently Dr. Goodman decided that the Pentothal was not needed. Instead he began the nitrous oxide/oxygen mixture by holding the black rubber mask over Berman's face. Blood pressure was 105/75; pulse was sixty-two and regular. Dr. Goodman injected 0.40 mg of d-tubocurarine, the drug which represents a debt modern society owes to the Amazon peoples. There were a few muscle twitches in Berman's body, then relaxation followed; breathing stopped. The entubation was rapid and Dr. Goodman inflated Berman's lungs with the ventilating bag while he listened to each side of the chest with his stethoscope. Both sides aerated evenly and fully.

Once the pneumatic tourniquet was cajoled into functioning, Dr. Spallek breezed into the room, and the case went rapidly. Dr. Spallek was into the joint in one dramatic slice.

"*Voilà,*" he said, holding the scalpel in the air and tilting his head to admire his handiwork. "And now for the Michelangelo touch."

Penny O'Rilley's eyes rolled up inside of her head in response to Dr. Spallek's theatrics. She handed him the meniscus knife with a trace of a smile on her lips.

"Anoint my blade," said Dr. Spallek holding the knife out for the resident to squirt irrigation fluid over its tip.

The knife was then inserted into the joint and for a few moments Dr. Spallek rooted around blindly, his face upturned toward the ceiling. He was cutting by feel alone. There was a faint grinding sound, then a snap.

"OK," said Dr. Spallek tightening his teeth, "here comes the culprit."

Out came the damaged cartilage. "Now I want everyone to see this. See this little tear on the inside edge. That's what's been causing this chap's problems."

Dr. Colbert looked from the specimen to Penny O'Rilley. They both nodded approval while both secretly wondered if the little tear hadn't been caused by the blind cutting with the meniscus knife.

Dr. Spallek stepped back from the table, pleased with himself. He snapped off his gloves. "Dr. Colbert, why don't you close up. 4 - 0 chromic, 5 - 0 plain, then 6 - 0 silk for the skin. I'll be in the lounge." Then he was gone.

Dr. Colbert dabbed ineffectually at the wound for a few moments.

"How much longer do you estimate?" questioned Dr. Goodman over the ether screen.

Dr. Colbert looked up. "Fifteen or twenty minutes, I guess." He palmed a pair of toothed forceps and took the first suture from Penny O'Rilley. He took a bite with the suture and Berman moved. At the same time Dr. Goodman felt a tenseness in the ventilating bag when he tried to breathe Berman. He sensed that Berman was trying to breathe on his own. Concurrently the blood pressure rose to 110/80.

"He must be a little light," said Dr. Colbert, trying to sort out the layers of tissue in the wound.

"I'll give him a bit more of this love potion," said Dr. Goodman. He injected another full cc of Innovar, since the syringe with the Innovar was still connected to the I.V. line. Later he admitted that this could have been a mistake. He should have used only the analgesic, fentanyl. The blood pressure responded rapidly and fell as Berman's anesthesia deepened again. The blood pressure leveled off at 90/60. The pulse increased to 80 per minute, then fell to a comfortable 72 per minute.

"He's OK now," said Dr. Goodman.

"Good. OK, Penny, feed me those chromic sutures and I'll get this joint closed," said Colbert.

The resident made fine headway, closing the joint capsule and then the subcutaneous tissues. There was no conversation. Mary Abruzzi sat down in the corner and turned on a small transistor radio. Very faint rock music trickled through the room. Dr. Goodman started the final notations on the anesthesia record.

"Skin sutures," said Dr. Colbert, straightening up from his crouch over the knee.

There was the familiar slapping sound as the needle holder was thrust into his open hand. Mary Abruzzi changed her worn-out gum for a new stick by lifting the lower part of her mask.

At first it was only one premature ventricular contraction followed by a compensatory pause. Dr. Goodman's eyes looked up at the monitor. The resident asked for more suture. Dr. Goodman increased the oxygen flow to wash out the nitrous oxide. Then there were two more abnormal ectopic heartbeats and the heart rate increased to about 90 per minute. The change in the audible rhythm caught the attention of the scrub nurse, who looked at Dr. Goodman. Satisfied that he was aware, she went back to supplying the resident with skin sutures, slapping a loaded needle holder in his hand every time he reached up.

Dr. Goodman stopped the oxygen, thinking that maybe the myocardium or heart muscle was particularly sensitive to the high oxygen levels that were obviously in the blood. Later he admitted that this might have been a mistake as well. He began to use compressed air for aerating Berman's lungs. Berman was still not breathing on his own.

In quick succession there were several back-to-back runs of the strange premature-type heartbeats, which made Dr. Goodman's own heart jump in his chest from fright. He knew all too well that such runs of premature ventricular contractions often were the immediate harbinger of cardiac arrest. Dr. Goodman's hands visibly trembled as he inflated the blood pressure cuff. Blood pressure was 80/55; it had fallen for no apparent reason. Dr. Goodman looked up at the monitor as the premature beats began to increase in frequency. The beeping sound became faster and faster, screaming its urgent information into Dr. Goodman's brain. His eyes swept over the anesthesia machine, the carbon dioxide canister. His mind raced for an answer. He could feel his bowels loosen and he had to clamp down voluntarily with the muscles of his anus. Terror spread through him. Something was wrong. The premature beats were increasing to the point that normal beats were being crowded out as the electronic blip on the monitor began to trace a senseless pattern.

"What the hell's going on?" yelled Dr. Colbert, looking up from his suturing job.

Dr. Goodman didn't answer. His trembling hands searched for a syringe. "Lidocaine," he yelled to the circulating nurse. He tried to pull the plastic cap from the end of the needle but it would not come off. "Christ," he yelled and flung the syringe against the wall in utter frustration. He tore the cellophane cover from another syringe and managed to get the cap off the needle. Mary Abruzzi tried to hold the lidocaine bottle for him but his trembling hands made it impossible. He snatched the bottle from her and thrust in the needle.

"Holy shit, this guy's going to arrest," said Dr. Colbert in disbelief. He was staring at the monitor. The needle holder was still in his right hand; a pair of fine-toothed forceps were in his left hand.

Dr. Goodman filled the syringe with the lidocaine, dropping the bottle in the process so that it shattered on the tile floor. Struggling with his trembling he tried to insert the needle into the I.V. line and succeeded only in jabbing his own index finger, bringing a drop of blood. Glen Campbell whined in the background from the transistor.

Before Dr. Goodman could get the lidocaine into the I.V. line, the monitor abruptly returned to its steady, pre-crisis rhythm. In utter disbelief Dr. Goodman looked at the electronic blip moving through its familiar and normal pattern. Then he grasped the ventilating bag and inflated Berman's lungs. Blood pressure read 100/60 and the pulse slowed evenly to about seventy per minute. Perspiration coalesced on Dr. Goodman's forehead and dripped off the bridge of his nose onto the anesthesia record. His own heart rate was over one hundred per minute. Dr. Goodman decided that clinical anesthesia was not always dull.

"What in God's name was all that about?" asked Dr. Colbert.

"I haven't the slightest idea," said Dr. Goodman. "But finish up. I want to wake this guy up."

"Maybe it's something wrong with the monitor," said Mary Abruzzi, trying to be optimistic.

The resident finished the skin sutures. For a few minutes Dr. Goodman had them hold off deflating the tourniquet. When they did, the heart rate increased slightly but then returned to normal.

The resident started to cast Berman's leg. Dr. Goodman continued to aerate the patient while he kept one eye on the monitor. The rate stayed normal. Dr. Goodman tried to record the events on the anesthesia record in between compressions of the ventilating bag. When the cast was completed, Dr. Goodman waited to see if Berman would breathe on his own. There was no breathing effort at all, and Dr. Goodman took over again. He looked at the clock. It was 12:45. He wondered if he should give an antagonist for the fentanyl to try to curtail the respiratory depressant effect it was apparently causing. At the same time he wanted to keep the medication that he gave to Berman to a minimum. His own clammy skin reminded him vividly that Berman was no routine case.

Dr. Goodman wondered if Berman was getting light despite the fact that he was not breathing. He decided to test the lid reflex to find out. There was no response. Instead of stroking the lid, Dr. Goodman lifted the lid and he noted something very strange. Usually the fentanyl, like other strong narcotics, produced very small pupils. Berman's pupils were enormous. The black area almost filled the clear cornea. Dr. Goodman reached for a penlight and directed the beam into Berman's eye. A ruby red reflex flashed back but the pupil did not budge.

In total disbelief, Dr. Goodman did it again, then again. He did it once more before his own eyes looked up at nothing. Dr. Goodman said two words out loud . . . "Good God!"

For Susan Wheeler and the other four medical students, the charge down the hall to the elevator fitted perfectly their preconceptions of the excitement of clinical medicine. There was something horribly dramatic about the headlong rush. Startled patients sitting there casually leafing through old *New Yorker* magazines while waiting to see their doctors reacted to the stampeding group by drawing their legs and feet more closely to their chairs. They stared at the running figures who clutched at pens, penlights, stethoscopes, and other paraphernalia to keep them from flying from their pockets.

As the group came abreast of, then passed, each patient, the patient's head swung around to watch the group recede down the corridor. Each assumed that a group of doctors had been called on an emergency, and it was reassuring for the patients to see how earnestly the doctors responded; the Memorial was a great hospital.

At the elevator there was momentary confusion and delay. Bellows repeatedly pushed the "down" button as if manhandling the plastic object would bring the elevator more quickly. The floor indicator above each elevator door suggested that the elevators were taking their own sweet time, slowly rising from floor to floor, obviously discharging and taking on passengers in the usual slow motion. For such emergencies there was a phone next to the elevators. Bellows snatched it off its cradle and dialed the operator. But the operator didn't answer. It usually took the operators at the Memorial about five minutes to answer a house phone.

"Fucking elevators," said Bellows striking the button for the tenth time. His eyes darted from the exit sign over the stairwell back to the floor indicator above the elevator. "The stairs," said Bellows with decision.

In rapid succession the group entered the stairwell and began the long twisting plunge from the tenth floor to the second floor. The journey seemed interminable. Taking two or three steps at a time, constantly turning to the left, the group began to spread out a bit. They passed the sixth floor, then the fifth. At the fourth floor the whole group slowed to a cautious walk in the dark because of the missing light bulb. Then down again at the previous pace.

Fairweather began to slow and Susan passed him on the inside.

"I don't know what the hell we are running for," panted Fairweather as Susan passed.

Susan managed to brush her hair from her face, hooking it behind her right ear. "As long as Bellows *et al.* are in the lead, I don't mind running. I want to see what goes on but I don't want to be the first one on the scene."

Fairweather assumed a comfortable walk and was quickly left behind. Susan was nearing the third floor landing when she heard Bellows pound on the locked door on two. He yelled at the top of his lungs for someone to open the door, and his voice carried up the stairwell, reverberating strangely, taking on a warbling quality. As Susan rounded the final landing, the door on two was opened. Niles kept the door open for her and she entered the hall. The constant turning to the left in the stairwell made Susan feel a bit dizzy, but she did not stop. Following the others, she ran directly into the ICU.

In sharp contrast to the former dimness of the room, it was now brightly illuminated with stark fluorescent light that provided a shimmering aura to objects within the room. The white vinyl floor added to this effect. In the corner the three ICU nurses were engaged in giving closed chest massage to Nancy Greenly. Bellows, Cartwright, Reid, and the medical students crowded around the bed.

"Hold up," said Bellows watching the cardiac monitor. The nurse giving the closed chest massage straightened up from her efforts. She was kneeling on the edge of the bed on the right side of Nancy Greenly. The monitor pattern was wildly erratic.

"She's been fibrillating for four minutes," said Shergood watching the monitor. "We started the massage within ten seconds."

Bellows moved rapidly over to the right of Nancy Greenly and while watching the monitor, he thumped the patient's sternum with his fist. Susan winced at the dull sound of the blow. The monitor's pattern did not alter. Bellows began closed chest massage.

"Cartwright, feel for a pulse in the groin," said Bellows without taking his eyes from the monitor. "Charge the defibrillator to 400 joules." The last command was directed to anyone. One of the ICU nurses carried it out.

Susan and the other students backed up against the wall, acutely aware that they were mere observers, and although they wanted to, they could not help in the frantic activity occurring before them.

"You've got a good pulse going," said Cartwright with his hand pressed in Nancy Greenly's groin.

"Was there any warning for this or did it drop out of the blue?" said Bellows with some difficulty between compressions of the chest. He nodded his head toward the monitor.

"Very little warning," answered Shergood. "She began to have a suggestion of increased excitability of her heart by having a few premature ventricular beats and a suggestion of a mild atrioventricular conduction defect which we picked up on the recorder." Shergood held up a strip of EKG paper for Bellows to see. "Then she had a sudden run of extra systoles, and wham . . . fibrillation."

"What has she got so far?" asked Bellows.

"Nothing," said Shergood.

"OK," said Bellows. "Push an amp of bicarbonate and draw up 10 cc of a 1:1000 epinephrine in a syringe with a cardiac needle."

One of the ICU nurses injected the bicarbonate; another prepared the epinephrine.

"Somebody draw blood for stat electrolytes and calcium," said Bellows, letting Reid take over the massage. Bellows felt the femoral pulse under Cartwright's hand and was satisfied.

"From what Billings said at the complication conference

on this case, the same thing is happening here that happened in the OR to cause all her troubles in the first place," said Bellows thoughtfully. He took the 10 cc syringe with the epinephrine from the nurse, holding it up to let the last traces of air escape.

"Not quite," said Reid between compressions. "She never fibrillated in the OR."

"She didn't fibrillate but she did have premature ventricular contractions. Obviously she had an excitable heart then as now. All right, hold up!" Bellows moved along Nancy Greenly's left side, brandishing the syringe with the cardiac needle. Reid straightened up from his resuscitative efforts so that Bellows could feel along Nancy Greenly's sternum for the landmark called the angle of Louis. Using that as a guide, he located the fourth interspace between the ribs.

The needle on Bellows's syringe was three and a half inches long and a sparkle of reflected light danced off its stainless steel shaft. Decisively Bellows pushed it into the girl's chest, all the way to the hilt. When the plunger was pulled back, dark red blood swirled up into the clear epinephrine solution.

"Right on," said Bellows as he rapidly injected the epinephrine directly into the heart.

Susan's skin crawled with the vivid thought of the long needle tearing its way down into Nancy Greenly's chest and spearing the quivering mass of cardiac muscle. Susan could almost feel the coldness of the needle in her own heart.

"Go to it," said Bellows to Reid as he stepped back from the bed. Reid immediately recommenced his cardiac massage. Cartwright nodded, indicating that there was a strong femoral pulse. "Stark is going to be pissed when he hears about this," continued Bellows, eyeing the monitor, "especially right after his lecture on vigilance in these cases. Shit, I really don't deserve this kind of headache. If she croaks, my ass is grass."

Susan had trouble comprehending that Bellows had actually said what he did. Once again she was faced with the fact that Bellows and probably the entire crew were not thinking of Nancy Greenly as a person. The patient seemed more like the part of a complicated game, like the relationship between the football and the teams at play. The football was important only as an object to advance the position and advantage of one of the teams. Nancy Greenly had become a technical challenge, a game to be played. The final, ultimate result had become less important than the day-to-day plays and moves and ripostes.

Susan felt a strong surge of ambivalence toward clinical medicine. Her nascent female sensitivities seemed to be a handicap within the mechanistic and tactically oriented atmosphere. She silently longed for the old familiar lecture hall and its abstractions. Reality was too bitter, too cold, too detached.

And yet there was something fascinating and academically satisfying seeing the application of the basic scientific knowledge she had acquired. From physiology experiments with animal hearts, she comprehended the disorganization that the fibrillating heart within Nancy Greenly represented. If only the whole mass could be depolarized to stop all electrical activity, then the intrinsic rhythm could possibly begin again.

Susan strained to watch as Bellows placed the defibrillating paddles on Nancy Greenly's exposed chest. One of the paddles was held directly over the sternum, the other was placed against the left lateral chest, slightly distorting the left breast with its pale nipple.

"Everyone away from the bed!" ordered Bellows. His right thumb made contact and a powerful electric charge spread through Nancy Greenly's chest, arcing from one paddle to the other. Her body jerked upward; her arms flopped across her chest with her hands twisting inward. The electronic blip disappeared from the screen, then it returned. It traced a relatively normal pattern.

"She's got a good pulse," said Cartwright.

Reid held up on the external massage. The rate held steady for several minutes. Then a premature ventricular contraction appeared. The rate was again steady for several minutes followed by three premature ventricular contractions in a row.

"V tach," said Shergood confidently. "The heart is still very easily excitable. There has to be something very basic wrong here."

"If you know what it is, don't keep it from us," said Bellows. "Meanwhile let's have some lidocaine, 50 cc."

One of the nurses drew up the lidocaine and handed it to Bellows. Bellows injected it into the I.V. line. Susan moved so that she could see the monitor screen more clearly.

Despite the lidocaine, the rhythm rapidly deteriorated to

senseless fibrillation once more. Bellows swore, Reid started massage, and the nurse recharged the defibrillator.

"What the hell is going on here?" queried Bellows, motioning for another amp of bicarbonate to be given. He didn't expect an answer; he was posing a purely rhetorical question.

Another dose of epinephrine given I.V., followed by a second defibrillation attempt, returned the rate to a semblance of normal. But premature contractions returned, despite additional lidocaine.

"This has to be the same problem that they had in the OR," said Bellows, watching the premature contractions increase in frequency until the rhythm dissolved into fibrillation. "You're up again, Reid ole boy. Let's go, team."

By 1:15 Nancy Greenly had been defibrillated twenty-one times. After each shock a relatively normal rhythm would return only to disintegrate into fibrillation after a short duration. At 1:16 the ICU phone rang. It was answered by the ward clerk, who took the information. It was the lab calling with the stat electrolyte values. Everything was normal except the potassium level. It was very low, only 2.8 milliequivalents per liter.

The ward clerk handed the results to one of the nurses, who showed them to Bellows.

"My God! 2.8. How in Christ's name did that happen? At least we have an answer. OK, let's get some potassium in her. Put 80 milliequivalents into that I.V. bottle and speed it up to 200 cc per hour."

Nancy Greenly responded to this command by immediately lapsing back into fibrillation for the twenty-second time. Reid started compression while Bellows readied the paddles. The potassium was added to the I.V.

Susan was totally absorbed by the whole resuscitation procedure. In fact, her concentration had been so great that she had almost missed hearing her name crackle out of the page system speaker near the main desk. The page system had been intermittently active throughout the entire cardiac arrest procedure by calling out the names of physicians followed by an extension number. But the sound had blended and merged with the general background noise, and Susan had been oblivious to it. At least until her own name floated out into the room along with the extension 381.

Somewhat reluctantly Susan left her place by the wall and used the phone at the main desk to answer her page.

381 turned out to be the extension of the recovery room and Susan was quite surprised to be paged from there. She gave her name as Susan Wheeler, not Dr. Susan Wheeler, and said that she had been paged. The clerk told her to hold the line. He returned immediately.

"There's an arterial blood gas to be drawn on a patient up here."

"Blood gas?"

"Right. Oxygen, carbon dioxide, and acid levels. And we need it stat."

"How did you get my name?" asked Susan, twisting the cord on the phone. She hoped it was by some sort of mistake that she had been called.

"I just do as I'm told. Your name is on the chart. Remember it's stat." The line went dead. The clerk had hung up before Susan could respond again. Actually she had little else to say. She replaced the receiver and walked back to Nancy Greenly's bedside. Bellows was repositioning the paddles again. The shock swept through the patient's body, the arms ineffectually flopping across the chest. It seemed both dramatic and pitiful at the same time. The monitor showed a normal rhythm.

"She's got a good pulse," said Cartwright at the groin.

"I think she's holding her sinus rhythm better now that some of the potassium has gotten into her system," said Bellows, his eyes glued to the monitor screen.

"Dr. Bellows," said Susan during the lull in the action. "I got a call to draw an arterial blood gas on a patient in the recovery room."

"Enjoy yourself," said Bellows, distracted. He turned to Shergood. "Where in heaven's name are those medical residents? God, when you need them they lie low. But just try to take someone to surgery and they hang around like a group of vultures, canceling your case because of a borderline serum porcelain."

Cartwright and Reid forced a laugh for political reasons.

"You don't understand, Dr. Bellows," continued Susan. "I've never drawn an arterial blood gas. I've never seen one drawn."

Bellows turned from the monitor to Susan. "Jesus Christ,

as if I don't have enough to worry about. It's just like getting venous blood only you get it out of an artery. What the hell did you learn during the first two years of medical school?"

Susan felt a defensive surge; her face reddened.

"Don't answer that," added Bellows quickly. "Cartwright, head over with Susan and . . ."

"I've got that thyroidectomy you put me on with Dr. Jacobs in five minutes," interrupted Cartwright, looking at his watch.

"Shit," said Bellows. "OK, Dr. Wheeler, I'll head over with you and show you how to do an arterial stick but not until things are reasonably quiet here. Things are looking a little better; I've got to admit that." Bellows turned to Reid. "Send up another blood sample for a repeat potassium. Let's see how we are doing. Maybe we are out of the woods."

While she was waiting, Susan thought about Bellows's last comment. He had used the pronoun *we* rather than saying that Nancy Greenly was out of the woods. It fit the pattern and she pondered about depersonalization. It also reminded her of Stark. He didn't seem to care for Bellows's pronouns either.

**Monday
February 23
1:35 P.M.**

"Some days are like this," said Bellows, holding the door open for Susan as they left the ICU. "Lunch can be considered a luxury. Even a nice . . ." Bellows paused as they walked down the corridor. They were both eyeing the floor. Bellows was searching for a word. Then he changed his incompleted sentence. "On occasion it is even hard to find time to relieve oneself."

"You meant to say 'a nice shit,' didn't you?"

Bellows glanced at Susan. She looked up at him with a slight smile. "You don't have to act differently on my account," said Susan.

Bellows continued to study her face, which she carefully kept as neutral as possible. They walked in silence past the holding area for surgery.

"As I mentioned before, an arterial stick is just about the same as a venous stick," said Bellows, changing the subject. He sensed the unnerving effect Susan had on him and he sought to regain the upper hand. "You isolate the artery, either the brachial, radial, or femoral, it really doesn't matter which, with your middle and index fingers, like this . . ." Bellows held up his left hand and extended his middle and index fingers and pretended to palpate an artery in the air. "Once you have the artery between the fingers, you can feel the pulse. Then simply guide the needle in by feel. The best method is to let arterial pressure fill the syringe. In that way you can avoid air bubbles, which tend to distort the values."

Bellows backed into the recovery room door, still gesturing the technique of the arterial stick. "Two important points: you have to use a heparinized syringe to keep the blood from clotting, and you have to keep pressure over the site for five minutes after the stick. The patient can get a frightful hematoma from an arterial stick if the pressure part is forgotten."

To Susan the recovery room seemed superficially similar to the ICU except that it was brighter, noisier, and more crowded. There were about fifteen to twenty spaces designated for beds. Each space had a complement of equipment built into the wall, including monitors, gas lines, and suction lines. Most of the spaces were occupied by high beds with the side rails pulled up. In each bed was a patient with fresh bandages over some part of his body. Bottles of intravenous fluid were clustered on the tops of poles, like some hideous fruit on leafless trees.

New patients were arriving, others leaving, causing mini-traffic jams of moving beds. Conversation flowed freely from those who worked there and felt at home in the environment. There was even some occasional laughter. But there were also some groans, and a baby was wailing an unheeded lament in a crib by the nurses' station. Some of the beds had groups of doctors and nurses busily engaged in adjusting the hundreds of lines, valves, and tubes. Some of the doctors were dressed in wrinkled scrub suits, stained with all sorts of secretions, although blood was the most prevalent. Others wore long white coats starched painfully stiff. It was a busy place, a crossroad filled with patients, charts, motion, and talk.

Bellows was anxious to dispense with the task ahead and approached the main desk, which was strategically placed in the center of the large room. In response to his inquiry he was handed a tray with a heparinized syringe and directed to one of the recovery room beds to the left, opposite the door through which they had entered.

"Why don't I go ahead and do this one, and you do the next one," said Bellows. Susan nodded in agreement as they approached the bed. They could not see the patient because of the people standing in the way. There were several nurses on the left, two doctors in scrub suits at the foot, and a tall black doctor in a long white coat on the right. As Bellows and Susan drew near, it was obvious that the latter individual had been talking although at that moment he was adjusting the pressure setting on the respirator. Susan sensed the emotional climate instantly. Both of the doctors in scrub suits were obviously intensely concerned. The smaller individual, Dr. Goodman, was visibly shaking. The other, Dr. Spallek, had his mouth angrily set with clenched teeth, audibly breathing through his nostrils as if he were about to attack the next person in his path.

"There's got to be some sort of an explanation," snarled the infuriated Spallek. He took hold of his face mask still tied around his neck and yanked it free, snapping the cord. He flung it to the floor. "That doesn't seem too much to ask," he hissed before abruptly turning away and leaving. He collided with Bellows, who miraculously managed to juggle the small tray he was carrying without dropping any of its contents. There were no words of apology from Dr. Spallek. He crossed the recovery room and blasted open the doors to the hall.

Bellows went directly to the left of the bed and put down the tray. Susan advanced warily, watching the expressions of the remaining people. The black doctor straightened up and his dark eyes followed the exit of the irate Dr. Spallek. Susan was immediately taken by the imposing image of the man

His tag gave his name: Dr. Robert Harris. He was tall, well over six feet, his dark hair textured into a restrained Afro. His blemishless tawny skin shone, and his face reflected a curious combination of culture and restrained violence. His movements were calm, almost to the point of deliberate slowness. As his eyes returned from watching Spallek's exit they passed over Susan's face before returning to the respirator at the side of the bed. If he had noticed Susan, he gave no hint whatsoever.

"What did you use for the pre-op, Norman?" asked Harris, pronouncing each word carefully. He had a cultured Texas accent—if that were possible.

"Innovar," said Goodman. The pitch of his voice was abnormally high and cracking under the strain.

Susan moved up to the foot of the bed where Spallek had been standing. She studied the crumpled man next to her, Dr. Goodman. He looked pale and his hair was matted with perspiration to his forehead. He had a prominent nose, which Susan saw in perfect profile. His deep-set eyes were riveted to the patient. He did not blink.

Susan looked down at the patient, her eyes wandering to the wrist which Bellows was prepping for the arterial stick. With an exaggerated double-take, her eyes shot back to the face of the patient as recognition occurred. It was Berman!

In contrast to the tanned visage Susan recalled from their meeting in room 503 only ninety minutes ago, Berman's face was a dusky gray color. The skin was pulled taut over his cheekbones. An endotracheal tube protruded from the left side of his mouth and some dried secretion was crusted along his lower lip. His eyes were closed but not completely. His right leg was in a huge plaster cast.

"Is he all right?" blurted Susan looking from Harris to Goodman. "What happened?" Susan spoke from emotion, without thinking; she sensed something was wrong and she reacted impulsively. Bellows was surprised at her sudden questions and looked up from his work, holding the syringe in his right hand. Harris straightened up slowly and turned toward Susan. Goodman's eyes did not stray.

"Everything is absolutely perfect," said Harris with a pronunciation suggesting an Oxford sojourn some time in his past. "Blood pressure, pulse, temperature all perfectly normal. However, he has apparently enjoyed his anesthetic slumber so much that he has decided not to wake up."

"Not another one," said Bellows, switching his attention to Harris and concerned that he was going to be saddled with another problem like Greenly. "What does the EEG look like?"

"You'll be the first to know," said Harris with a trace of sarcasm. "It's been ordered."

Comprehension for Susan was delayed by emotion, for hope was momentarily stronger than reason. But eventually it flooded over her.

"EEG?" asked Susan apprehensively. "You mean he's like the patient down in the ICU?" Her eyes darted back and forth between Berman and Harris, then to Bellows.

"Which patient is that?" asked Harris, picking up the anesthesia record.

"The D&C mishap," said Bellows. "You remember, about eight days ago, the twenty-three-year-old girl."

"Well I hope not," said Harris, "but it's beginning to look that way."

"What was the anesthesia?" asked Bellows lifting Berman's right eyelid and glancing down into the widely dilated pupil.

"Neurolept anesthesia with nitrous," said Harris. "The girl's was halothane. If the problem is the same clinically, it wasn't the anesthetic agent." Harris looked up from the anesthesia record toward Goodman. "Why did you give this extra cc of Innovar toward the end of the case, Norman?"

Dr. Goodman did not respond immediately. Dr. Harris called his name again.

"The patient seemed to be getting too light," said Goodman, suddenly breaking his trance.

"But why Innovar so late in the case? Wouldn't fentanyl alone have been more prudent?"

"Probably. I should have used the fentanyl alone. The Innovar was just handy and I knew that I'd only use an additional cc."

"Can't something be done?" asked Susan with a hint of desperation. Images of Nancy Greenly streamed back with bits and pieces of the recent conversation with Berman. She could distinctly remember his vitality, which was in sharp contrast to the waxy, lifeless-appearing figure before her.

"It's been done, whatever it was," said Harris with finality, returning the anesthesia record to Goodman. "All we can do now is watch and see what kind of cerebral function returns, if any. The pupils are widely dilated and they do not react to light. That is not a good sign, to say the least. It probably means that there was extensive brain death."

Susan experienced a sickening feeling rise up within herself. She shuddered and the feeling passed but she felt lightheaded. Above all, she felt helplessly desperate.

"This is too much," said Susan suddenly and with obvious emotion. Her voice quivered. "A normal healthy man with a minor peripheral problem ends up like a . . . like a vegetable. My God, this can't go on. Two young people within just a couple of weeks. I mean, it's an unacceptable risk. Why doesn't the Chief of Anesthesia close the department? Something's got to be wrong. It's absurd to allow . . ."

Robert Harris's eyes began to narrow as Susan began her tirade. Then he interrupted her with an obvious edge to his voice. Bellows's mouth had dropped open in total dismay.

"I happen to be the Chief of Anesthesia, young lady. And who, may I ask, are you?"

Susan started to speak, but Bellows cut in nervously. "This is Susan Wheeler, Dr. Harris, a third-year medical student who is rotating on surgery, and, ah . . . we just wanted to get this blood drawn here, then we'll be off." Bellows recommenced his prep on Berman's right wrist, stroking rapidly with the Betadine sponge.

"Miss Wheeler," continued Harris in a condescending tone, "your emotionalism is out of place and frankly will not serve constructive purposes. What one needs in these cases is to establish a causal factor. I've just mentioned to Dr. Bellows that the anesthetic agent was different in these two cases. The anesthetic care was unimpeachable save for a few minor debatable points. In short, both these cases were obviously unavoidable idiosyncratic reactions to the combination of anesthesia and surgery. One needs to try to determine from these people if there is a way in order to forecast this kind of disastrous sequelae. To condemn anesthesia across the board and deprive the populace of needed surgery would be far worse than to accept a certain minimal risk involved in anesthesia. What . . ."

"Two cases in eight days is hardly a minimal risk," interrupted Susan contentiously.

Bellows tried to catch Susan's eye to get her to break off

with Harris, but Susan was staring directly at Harris, converting her emotionalism to defiance.

"How many such cases have there been in the last year?" asked Susan.

Harris's eyes scanned Susan's face for several seconds before he responded. "I suddenly find this conversation somewhat akin to being cross-examined, and in that sense intolerable and unnecessary." Without waiting for a response, Harris walked past Susan toward the recovery room door.

Susan turned to face him. Bellows reached for her right arm to try and shut her up. Susan fended him off. She called after Harris, "Without wishing to sound impertinent, it does seem to me that some questions need to be asked by someone, and something done."

Harris stopped abruptly about ten feet from Susan and turned very slowly. Bellows shut his eyes tightly, as if he expected to receive a blow to the head.

"And I suppose that someone should be a medical student! For your information, in case you are planning to be our Socratic gadfly, there have been six cases prior to this present problem in the last few years. Now if I may have your permission, I will get back to work."

Harris turned again and started for the door.

"I suppose *your* emotionalism serves constructive purposes," called Susan. Bellows supported himself by leaning onto the bed. Harris stopped for the second time, but he did not turn around. Then he continued, and he too blasted open the door to the hall.

Bellows put his left hand up to his forehead. "Holy fuck, Susan, what are you trying to do, commit medical suicide?" Bellows reached out and turned Susan around to face him. "That was Robert Harris, Chief of Anesthesia. Christ!"

Bellows commenced the prep for the third time, rapidly, nervously. "You know, just being here with you when you act like that makes me look bad. Shit, Susan, why did you want to get him pissed?" Bellows palpated the radial artery and then jammed the needle of the heparinized syringe into the skin on the thumb side of Berman's wrist. "I'm going to have to say something to Stark before he hears about it through the grapevine. Susan, I mean, what's the point of getting him mad? You obviously don't have any idea what hospital politics are like."

Susan watched Bellows performing the arterial stick. She consciously avoided looking at Berman's sickly face. The syringe began to fill with blood spontaneously. The blood was a very bright crimson.

"He got mad because he wanted to get mad. I don't think I was impertinent until that last question, and he deserved that."

Bellows didn't answer.

"Anyway I really didn't want to make him angry . . . well, maybe I did in a way." Susan thought for a few moments. "You see, I talked with this patient only an hour or so ago. He was the patient I had to leave the ICU for. It's just so unbelievable; he was a functioning, normal human being. And . . . I . . . we had a conversation and I felt like I knew something about him. I even took a liking to him in a way. That's what makes me mad or sad or both. And Harris, his attitude made it worse."

Bellows didn't respond immediately. He searched in the tray for a syringe cap. "Don't tell me anymore," he said at length. "I don't want to hear about it. Here, hold the syringe for me." Bellows gave Susan the syringe while he prepared the ice bed. "Susan, I'm afraid you're going to be poison for me around here. You have no idea how miserable someone like Harris can make it. Here, put pressure on the puncture site."

"Mark?" said Susan pressing on Berman's wrist but looking at Bellows directly. "You don't mind if I call you Mark, do you?"

Bellows took the syringe and placed it into the ice bath. "I'm not sure, to be perfectly honest."

"Well, anyway, Mark, you have to admit that six, and maybe seven, cases, if Berman proves to be like Greenly, represents a lot of cases of brain death, or vegetables, as you call them."

"But a lot of surgery goes on here, Susan. It's often more than a hundred cases a day, some twenty-five thousand per year. That drops the six cases below some two hundredths of one percent in incidence. That's still within the surgical anesthesia risk."

"That may be true, but these six cases represent only one type of possible complication, not surgical-anesthesia risk in general. Mark, it's got to be too high. In fact, down in the

ICU this morning you said that the particular complication Nancy Greenly represented occurred only about one in a hundred thousand. Now you're trying to tell me that six in twenty-five thousand is OK. Bullshit. It's too high whether you or Harris or anybody in the hospital accept it. I mean would *you* want to have some minor surgery tomorrow with that kind of risk? You know this whole thing really bothers me, the more I think about it."

"Well then, don't think about it. Come on, we've got to get moving."

"Wait a minute. You know what I'm going to do?"

"I can't guess and I'm not sure I want to know."

"I'm going to look into this particular problem. Six cases. That should be enough for some reasonable conclusions. I do have a third-year paper to do and I think I owe that much to Sean here."

"Oh for Christ sake, Susan, let's not be melodramatic."

"I'm not being melodramatic. I think I'm responding to a challenge. Sean challenged me earlier with my image of myself as a doctor. I failed. I wasn't detached or professional. You might even say I acted like a schoolgirl. Now I'm challenged again. But this time intellectually with a problem, a serious problem. Maybe I can respond to this challenge in a more commendable fashion. Maybe these cases represent a new symptom complex or disease process. Maybe they represent a new complication of anesthesia because of some peculiar susceptibility these people had from some previous insult which they suffered in the past."

"All the more power to you," said Bellows getting the remains from the arterial stick together. "Frankly though, it sounds like a hell of a hard way to work out some emotional or psychological adjustment problem of your own. Besides, I think you'll be wasting your time. I told you before that Dr. Billing, the anesthesiology resident on Greenly's case, went over it with a fine-toothed comb. And believe me, he's bright. He said that there was absolutely no explanation for what happened."

"Your support is appreciated," said Susan. "I'll start with your patient in the ICU."

"Just a minute, Susan dear. I want to make one point crystal clear." Bellows held up his index and middle finger like Nixon's victory sign. "With Harris on the rag, I don't want to be involved, no how. Understood? If you're crazy enough to want to get involved, it's your bag from A to Z."

"Mark, you sound like an invertebrate."

"I just happen to be aware of hospital realities and I want to be a surgeon."

Susan looked Mark directly in the eye. "That, Mark, in a nutshell, is probably your tragic flaw."

**Monday
February 23
1:53 P.M.**

The cafeteria at the Memorial could have been in any one of a thousand hospitals. The walls were a drab yellow that tended toward mustard. The ceiling was constructed of a low-grade acoustical tile. The steam table was a long L-shaped affair with brown, stained trays stacked at the beginning.

The excellence of the Memorial's clinical services did not extend into the food service. The first food seen by an unlucky customer coming into the cafeteria was the salad, the lettuce invariably as crisp as wet Kleenex. To heighten the disagreeable effect, the salads were stacked one on top of the other.

The steam table itself presented the hot selections, which posed a baffling mystery. So many things tasted alike that they were indistinguishable. Only carrots and corn stood aside. The carrots had their own disagreeable taste; the corn had absolutely no taste at all.

By quarter to two in the afternoon, the cafeteria was almost empty. The few people who were sitting around were mostly kitchen employees, resting after the mad lunchtime rush. As bad as the food was, the cafeteria was still heavily patronized because it enjoyed a monopoly. Few people in the hospital complex took more than thirty minutes for lunch, and there simply was not enough time to go elsewhere.

Susan took a salad but after one look at the limp lettuce, she replaced it. Bellows went directly to the sandwich area and took one.

"There's not much they can do to a tuna sandwich," he called back to Susan.

Susan eyed the hot entrees and moved on. Following Bellows's lead, she selected a tuna sandwich.

The woman who was supposed to be at the cash register was nowhere to be seen.

"Come on," motioned Bellows, "we ain't got much time."

Feeling a bit like a shoplifter by not paying, Susan followed Bellows to a table and sat down. The sandwich was repellent. Somehow too much water had gotten into the tunafish and the tasteless white bread was soggy. But it was food and Susan was famished.

"We've got a lecture at two," garbled Bellows through a huge bite of sandwich. "So eat hearty."

"Mark?"

"Yeah?" said Bellows as he gulped half his milk in one swig. It was apparent that Bellows was a speed eater of Olympic caliber.

"Mark, you wouldn't be hurt if I cut your first surgery lecture, would you?" Susan had a twinkle in her eye.

Bellows stopped the second half of his tuna sandwich midway to his mouth and regarded Susan. He had an idea that she was flirting with him, but he dismissed it.

"Hurt? No, why do you ask?" Bellows had a helpless feeling that he was being manipulated.

"Well I just don't think I could sit through a lecture at this moment in time," said Susan, opening her milk carton. "I'm a little spaced from this affair with Berman. . . . *Affair* is not the right word. Anyway I'm really uptight; I couldn't handle a lecture. If I do something active I'll be much better off. I was thinking that I'd go to the library and look up something about anesthesia complications. It will give me a chance to start my 'little' investigation as well as sort out this morning in my mind."

"Would you like to talk about it?" asked Bellows.

"No, I'll be OK, really." Susan was surprised and touched by his sudden warmth.

"The lecture isn't critical. It's an introductory kind of thing by one of the emeritus professors. Afterwards I planned for you students to come on the ward to meet your patients."

"Mark?"

"What?"

"Thanks."

Susan stood up, smiled at Bellows, and left.

Bellows put the second half of his tuna sandwich into his mouth and chewed it on the right side, then he moved it over to the left cheek. He wasn't even sure what Susan had thanked him for. He watched her cross the cafeteria and deposit her tray in the rack. She rescued her unfinished milk and sandwich before leaving. At the door she turned and waved. Bellows waved in return but by the time he got his hand up, she had already disappeared.

Bellows looked around self-consciously, wondering if anyone had noticed him with his hand in the air. Replacing his hand on the table, he thought about Susan. He had to admit that she attracted him in a refreshing, basic way, reminding him of the way he felt early in his social career: an excitement, an unsettling impatience. His imagination conjured up sudden romantic pursuits with Susan as the object. But as soon as he did so, he reprimanded himself for being juvenile.

Bellows polished off his milk with another gigantic gulp while carrying his tray to the dirty-dish cart. En route he wondered if he dared to ask Susan out. There were two problems. One was the residency and Stark. Bellows had no idea how the chief would react to one of his residents dating a student assigned to him. Bellows was not sure if such a worry was rational or not. He did know that Stark tended to favor married residents. The idea was that the married ones would be more dependable, which, as far as Bellows was concerned, was pure bunk. But there was little hope of keeping a relationship between himself and one of the students a secret. Stark would find out and it could be bad. The second problem was Susan herself. She was sharp; there was no question about that. But could she be warm? Bellows had no idea. Maybe she was just too busy, or too intellectualized, or too ambitious. The last thing that Bellows wanted to do was to squander his limited free time on some cold, castrating bitch.

And what about himself? Could Bellows handle a sharp girl who was in his own field even if she were warm and lovable? He had dated a few nurses, but that was different because nurses were allied with but distinct from doctors. Bellows had never dated another doctor or even doctor-to-be. Somehow the idea was a bit disturbing.

Leaving the cafeteria, Susan enjoyed a greater sense of direction than she had felt all day. Although she had no idea how she was actually going to investigate the problem of prolonged coma after anesthesia, she felt that it represented an intellectual challenge which could be met by applying scientific methods and reasoning. For the first time all day she had a feeling that the first two years of medical school had meant something. Her sources were to be the literature in the library and the charts of the patients, particularly Greenly's and Berman's.

Near to the cafeteria was the hospital gift shop. It was a pleasant place, populated and run by an assortment of gracefully aging suburbanite women dressed in cute pink smocks. The windows of the shop faced the main hospital corridor and were mullioned, giving the shop an appearance of a cottage smack dab in the middle of the busy hospital. Susan entered the gift shop and quickly found what she was after: a small black looseleaf notebook. She slipped the purchase into her pocket of her white coat and left for the ICU. Her jumping-off point would be the case of Nancy Greenly.

The ICU was back to its pre-arrest hush. The harsh illumination had been dampened to the level Susan recalled from her first visit. The instant the heavy door closed behind her, Susan tasted the same anxiety she had noted before, the same feeling of incompetence. Again she wanted to leave before something happened and she was asked the simplest of questions to which she would undoubtedly have to answer a demoralizing "I don't know." But she did not bolt. Now she at least had something to do which gave her a modicum of confidence. She wanted the chart of Nancy Greenly.

Looking to the left, Susan noticed that no one was standing by Nancy Greenly's bed. The potassium level had apparently been rectified and the heart was beating normally once again.

The crisis over, Nancy Greenly was forgotten and allowed to return to her own infinity. Willing machines resumed the vigil over her vegetablelike functions.

Drawn by an irresistible curiosity, Susan walked over to Nancy Greenly's side. She had to struggle to keep her emotions in check and to keep the identification transference to a minimum. Looking down at Nancy Greenly, it was difficult for Susan to comprehend that she was looking at a brainless shell rather than a sleeping human being. She wanted to reach out and gently shake Nancy's shoulder so that she would awaken so that they could talk.

Instead, Susan reached out and picked up Nancy's wrist. Susan noted the delicate pallor of the hand as it drooped, lifelessly. Nancy was totally paralyzed, completely limp. Susan began to think about paralysis from destruction of the brain. The reflex circuits from the periphery would still be intact, at least to some degree.

Susan grasped Nancy's hand as if she were shaking it and slowly flexed and extended the wrist. There was no resistance. Then Susan flexed the wrist forcefully to its limit, the fingers almost touching the forearm. Unmistakenly Susan felt resistance, only for an instant but nonetheless definite. Susan tried it with the other wrist; it was the same. So Nancy Greenly was not totally flaccid. Susan felt a certain sense of academic pleasure; the irrational joy of the positive finding.

Susan found a percussion hammer for tendon reflexes. It was made of hard red rubber with a stainless steel handle. She had had one used on herself and had tried one on fellow students in physical diagnosis classes, but never used one on a patient. Clumsily Susan tried to elicit a reflex by tapping Nancy Greenly's right wrist. Nothing. But Susan was not exactly sure where to tap. Instead she pulled up the sheet on the right side and tapped under the knee. Nothing. She flexed the knee with her left hand and tapped again. Still nothing. From neuroanatomy class Susan remembered that the reflex she was searching for came from a sudden stretch of the tendon. So she stretched Nancy Greenly's knee more, then tapped. The thigh muscle contracted almost imperceptibly. Susan tried it again, eliciting a reflex that was no more than a slight tightening of the flaccid muscle. Susan tried it on the left leg, with the same result. Nancy Greenly had weak but definite reflexes, and they were symmetrical.

Susan tried to think of other parts of the neurological examination. She remembered level-of-consciousness testing. In Nancy Greenly's case the only test would be reaction to pain stimulus. Yet when she pinched Nancy Greenly's Achilles tendon, there was no response no matter how hard she squeezed. Without any specific reason other than wondering if the pain sensation would be more potent the closer to the brain, Susan pinched Nancy Greenly's thigh and then recoiled in horror. Susan thought that Nancy Greenly was getting up because her body stiffened, arms straightening from her sides and rotating inward in a painful contraction. There was a side-to-side chewing motion with her jaw almost as if she were awakening. But it passed and Nancy Greenly reverted to her limpness equally suddenly. Eyes widening, Susan had moved back, pressing herself against the wall. She had no idea what she had done or how she had managed to do it. But she knew she was toying in the area well beyond her present abilities and knowledge. Nancy Greenly had had a seizure of some kind, and Susan was immensely thankful that it had passed so quickly.

Guiltily, Susan glanced around the room to see if anyone was watching. She was relieved to note that no one was. She was also relieved that the cardiac monitor above Nancy Greenly continued its steady and normal pace. There were no premature contractions.

Susan had the uncomfortable feeling that she was doing something wrong, that she was trespassing, and that any moment she would be deservedly reprimanded, perhaps by Nancy Greenly's arresting once again. Susan quickly decided that she would withhold further patient examination until after some serious reading.

With great effort at appearing nonchalant, Susan made her way over to the central desk. The charts were kept in a circular stainless steel file built into the counter top. With her left hand she began to turn the chart rack slowly. It squeaked painfully. Susan turned it more slowly. The squeak persisted.

"Can I help you?" asked June Shergood from behind Susan, causing her to start and to withdraw her hand as if she were a child caught at the cookie jar.

"I'd just like the chart," said Susan, expecting some sour words from the nurse.

"What chart?" Shergood's voice was pleasant.

"Nancy Greenly's. I'm going to try to get an idea about her case so that I can participate in her care."

June Shergood rummaged among the charts, coming up with Nancy Greenly's. "You might find it easier to concentrate in there," said Shergood with a smile, pointing toward a door.

Susan thanked her, welcoming the opportunity to withdraw. The door that Shergood had indicated opened into a tiny room ringed about with glass-faced, locked medicine cabinets. A counter top ran around three sides of the room, providing desk space. On the right was a sink, and in the left corner was the omnipresent coffeepot.

Susan sat down with the chart. Although Nancy Greenly had not been in the hospital for even two weeks, her chart was voluminous. That was usual for a case placed in the ICU. The elaborate, constant care generated reams of paper.

Susan took out the remains of her tuna sandwich and milk and poured herself a cup of coffee. Then she took out her notebook and removed a number of blank pages. She started to work. Unaccustomed to using a patient chart, she spent a few minutes figuring out its organization. The order sheets were first, followed by the graphs of the patient's vital signs. Next was the history and physical examination dictated on the day of admission. The rest of the chart included the progress notes, the operative and anesthesia notes, the nurses' notes, and the innumerable laboratory values, X-ray reports, and records of sundry tests and procedures.

Since she did not know what she was looking for, Susan decided to make copious notes. At this early stage there was no way of determining what was going to be the important information. She started with Nancy Greenly's name, age, sex, and race. Next she included the meager medical history attesting to the fact that Nancy Greenly had been a healthy individual. There were bits and pieces of family history, including reference to a grandmother who had had a stroke. The only illness of note in Nancy's past was a case of mononucleosis at age 18, with an apparently uneventful recovery. The reviews of Nancy's systems, including her cardiovascular and respiratory systems, were normal. Susan wrote down the laboratory values from her routine pre-op screen: the blood and urine were both normal. She also wrote down the results of the pregnancy test, negative; various blood clotting studies, blood type, tissue type, chest X-ray, and EKG. There was also the chemistry profile, which included a wide battery of tests. Nancy Greenly's reports were well within normal limits.

Susan ate the last of the tuna sandwich and washed it down with a slug of milk. Turning the pages of the operative section and locating the anesthesia record, she noted the pre-op medication: Demerol and Phenergan given at 6:45 A.M. by one of the nurses on Beard 5. The endotracheal tube was a number 8. Pentothal 2 grams given I.V. at 7:24 A.M. Halothane, nitrous oxide, and oxygen started at 7:25. The halothane concentration was initially 2 percent through the Fluotec Temperature Compensated Vaporizer. Within several minutes it was reduced to 1 percent. The nitrous oxide and oxygen flow rates were 3 liters and 2 liters per minute respectively. For muscle relaxation a 2 cc dose of 0.2 percent succinylcholine was given at 7:26 and a second dose at 7:40.

Susan noted that the blood pressure fell at 7:48 after maintaining a plateau of 105/75. The halothane percentage was reduced to 1/2 percent at that point, while the nitrous oxide and oxygen flow was changed to 2 and 3 liters. The blood pressure drifted back up to 100/60. Susan made a rough copy of the information which was graphed in the anesthesia record.

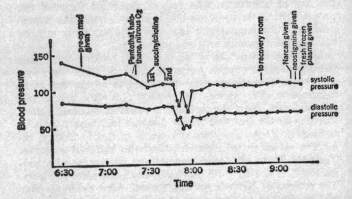

But from that point on the anesthesia record became hard to decipher. As far as Susan could tell, the blood pressure and the pulse stayed about 100/60 and seventy per minute respectively. Although the heart rate stayed stable, there was some sort of variation in the rhythm, but Dr. Billing had not described it.

From the record Susan could see that Nancy Greenly had been moved from the OR into the recovery room at 8:51. A Block Ade square-wave nerve stimulator had been used to test the function of Nancy's peripheral nerves. It had been originally suspected that she had been unable to metabolize the additional dose of succinylcholine. But the nerve function had been detected in both ulnar nerves, meaning that the problem was most likely central, in the brain.

Over the following hour Nancy Greenly had been given Narcan 4 mg to rule out an idiosyncratic hypersusceptibility to her pre-op narcotic. There had been no response. At 9:15 she had been given neostigmine 2.5 mg to see if the block on her nerves and hence her paralysis was due to a curarelike competitive block despite the result of the nerve stimulator test. Nancy Greenly had also been given two units of fresh frozen plasma with documented cholinesterase activity to try to eliminate any succinylcholine that might have still remained. Both these measures resulted in some mild twitching of a few muscles but no real response.

The anesthesia record ended with the terse statement in Dr. Billing's handwriting: "Delayed return of consciousness post anesthesia; cause unknown."

Susan next turned to the operative report dictated by Dr. Major.

DATE: February 14, 1976
PRE OP DIAGNOSIS: Dysfunctional uterine bleeding
POST OP DIAGNOSIS: Same
SURGEON: Dr. Major
ANESTHESIA: General endotracheal using halothane
ESTIMATED BLOOD LOSS: 500 cc
COMPLICATIONS: Prolonged return to consciousness after the termination of anesthesia
PROCEDURE: After appropriate pre-op medication (Demerol and Phenergan) the patient was brought to the operating room and attached to the cardiac monitor. She was smoothly inducted under general anesthesia utilizing an endotracheal tube. The perineum was

prepped and draped in the usual fashion. A bimanual examination was carried out revealing normal ovaries, adnexa and an antero-flexed uterus. A #4 Pederson speculum was inserted into the vagina and secured. Blood clots were sucked from the vaginal vault. The cervix was inspected and appeared normal. The uterus was sounded to 5 cm with a Simpson sound. Cervical dilation was carried out with ease and minimal trauma. Cervical dilators #1 through #4 were passed with ease. A #3 Sime curette was passed and the endo-metrium was curetted. A specimen was sent to the laboratory. Bleeding was minimal at the termination of the procedure. The speculum was removed. At that point it became apparent that the patient was making a slow recovery from anesthesia.

Susan rested her weary right hand by letting it dangle by her side. She had a habit of writing by holding a pencil or pen so tightly that blood flow was restricted. The blood tingled as it returned to her fingertips. Before going back to work, she took several sips of her coffee.

The pathology report described the endometrial scrapings as proliferative in character. The diagnosis was then listed as anovulatory uterine bleeding with a proliferative endo-metrium. No clue there.

Next Susan turned to the most interesting page: the initial neurology consult, signed by a Dr. Carol Harvey. Without knowing the meaning of most of what she wrote, Susan copied the consult note as well as she could. The handwriting was atrocious.

HISTORY: The patient is a twenty-three-year-old, white female admitted to the hospital with a problem of (illegible phrase). Past medical history of self and family negative for significant neurological disorders. Patient's pre-op workup (illegible phrase). Surgery itself uneventful and immediate result diagnostic and most likely curative of the presenting complaint. How-ever, during surgery some minor problems with the blood pressure were noted, and after surgery there was noted a prolonged unconsciousness and apparent paralysis. Overdose of succinylcholine and/or halothane ruled out. (Entire sentence totally illegible.)

EXAMINATION: Patient in deep coma unresponsive to spoken word, light touch or deep pain. Patient appears to be paralyzed although trace deep tendon reflexes elicited from both biceps and quadriceps symmetrically. Muscle tone decreased but not totally flaccid. Pendulousness increased. No tremor.

Cranial nerves: (illegible phrase) . . . pupils dilated and unresponsive. Absent corneal reflex.

Square-Wave Nerve Stimulator: Persistent although decreased function of the peripheral nerves.

Cerebral Spinal Fluid (CSF): Atraumatic puncture, clear fluid, opening pressure 125 mm of water.

EEG: Flat wave in all leads.

IMPRESSION: (illegible sentence). (illegible phrase) . . . with no localizing signs . . . (illegible phrase) . . . coma due to diffuse cerebral edema is the primary diagnosis. The possibility of a cerebral vascular accident or stroke cannot be ruled out without cerebral angiography. An idiosyncratic response to any of the agents used for anesthesia remains a possibility although I believe . . . (illegible phrase). Pneumoencephalography and/or a CAT scan may be of help but I believe it would be of academic interest only and would not provide any additional information for diagnosis in this difficult case. The EEG with its suppression of all organized and otherwise activity certainly suggests extensive brain death or damage. This same picture has been seen with tranquilizer/alcohol combinations but it is extremely rare. There are only three cases in the literature. Whatever the cause, this patient has suffered an acute insult to the brain. There is no chance that this patient represents any degenerative neurological syndrome.

Thank you very much for letting me see this very interesting patient.

DR. CAROL HARVEY, resident, neurology

Susan cursed the handwriting as she surveyed the many blanks on her own notebook sheet. She took another sip of coffee and turned the page in the chart. On the next page was another note from Dr. Harvey.

February 15, 1975. Follow up by Neurology
Patient status = unchanged. Repeat EEG = no electrical activity. CSF laboratory values were all within normal limits.

IMPRESSION: I have discussed this case with my attending and with other neurology residents who agree on the diagnosis of acute brain insult leading to brain death. It is also the general consensus that cerebral edema from acute hypoxia was the immediate cause of the problem. The cause of the hypoxia was probably some sort of cerebral vascular accident perhaps due to a transient blood clot, platelet clot, fibrin clot, or other embolus related to the endometrial scraping. Some sort of acute idiopathic polyneuritis or vasculitis may have played a part. Two papers of interest are: "Acute Idiopathic Polyneuritis; a Report of Three Cases," *Australian Journal of Neurology*, volume 13, Sept. 1973, pp 98-101.
"Prolonged Coma and Brain Death Following Ingestion of Sleeping Pills by Eighteen Year Old Female," *New England Journal of Neurology*, volume 73, July 1974, pp 301-302.
Cerebral angiography, pneumoencephalography, and a CAT scan can be done, but it is the combined opinion that the results would be normal.
Thank you very much

DR. CAROL HARVEY

Susan let her aching hand rest for a few moments after copying the lengthy neurology notes. She moved on in the chart, passing the nurses' notes until she reached the laboratory results. There were numerous X-ray reports, including a normal series of skull X-rays. Next came the extensive chemistry and hematology reports, which Susan laboriously copied into her notebook pages. Since all the results were essentially normal, Susan concentrated on finding out if there were any changes between the pre-op values and the post-op values. There was only one value that fell into this category;

after the operation Nancy Greenly had exhibited a higher serum sugar as if she had developed a diabetic tendency. The serial EKGs were not very revealing, although they did show some nonspecific S and ST wave changes following the D&C. However, there was no pre-op EKG to compare.

Finishing, Susan closed the cover of the chart and leaned back, stretching her hands up toward the ceiling. At the very limit of her stretch, she grunted and exhaled. She leaned forward and glanced over the eight pages of minute handwriting which she had just completed. She felt no further in her investigation but she did not expect to. Much of what she had copied she really did not understand.

Susan believed in the scientific method and she believed in the power of books and knowledge. For her there was no substitute for information. Although she did not know very much about clinical medicine, she had the positive feeling that by combining method with information she could solve the problem at hand—why had Nancy Greenly lapsed into coma. First she had to gather as much observational data as possible; that was the purpose of the charts. Next she had to understand the data; for that she must turn to the literature. Analysis leading to synthesis: pure Cartesian magic. Susan was optimistic at this stage. And it did not faze her that she did not understand much of the material she had taken from Nancy Greenly's chart. She felt confident that within the maze of information were critical points which could lead to the solution. But to see it Susan needed more information, a lot more.

The hospital medical library was on the second floor of the Harding building. After multiple false starts Susan was directed to a flight of stairs which led up to the personnel office, and past it, to the library itself.

It was called the Nancy Darling Memorial Library, and as Susan entered she passed a small daguerreotype of a matronly woman dressed in black. A copper plaque on the frame was engraved: *In fond memory of Nancy Darling*. Susan thought the name Nancy Darling, with its amorous connotations, hardly fitted the prim scowling figure. But it was New England one hundred percent.

With the reassuring warmth of the books about her, Susan felt instantly at home in the library, in sharp contrast to her feelings in the ICU and the hospital in general. She put down her notebook and got her bearings. The center of the room, with its two-storied ceiling, had large oak tables with black academic colonial-style chairs. The end of the room was dominated by a large window that reached up to the ceiling, giving out onto the small inner courtyard of the hospital, which contained a patch of anemic grass, a single leafless tree, and a tennis court. The net on the tennis court sagged sadly from midwinter disuse.

Bookshelves flanked both sides of the tables and were oriented at right angles to the long axis of the room. There was a cast-iron circular staircase which led up to the balcony. On that level the shelves to the right contained books, while bound periodicals were in stacks to the left. Against the wall opposite the window stood the dark mahogany card catalogue.

Consulting the card catalogue, Susan searched out the books on anesthesiology. Once in the proper area, she went from book to book. She knew next to nothing about anesthesiology and needed a good introductory text. Specifically she was interested in anesthetic complications. She picked out five books, the most promising of which was titled *Anesthetic Complications: Recognition and Management*.

As she was carrying the books over to the table where she had placed her notebook, her name came over the page system, gently subdued, distinctly followed by the number 482.

Susan let the books slide from her hands onto the table. She turned and eyed the phone. Then she turned back to the table and looked down at the books and her notebook. With her hands resting on the back of one of the chairs, Susan vacillated. She felt torn between her strongly reinforced compulsion to do as she was told and her newly discovered challenge, the problem of prolonged coma after anesthesia. It was not an easy choice. Following the accepted pathways had served her well in the past. She owed her current position to that. And that position was particularly important for Susan because of her sex. All of the females in medicine tended to follow a rather conservative road simply because they were a minority and hence had the feeling that they were constantly on trial.

But then Susan thought about Nancy Greenly in the ICU and Sean Berman in the recovery room. She didn't think about them as patients but rather as people. She thought about their personal tragedies. Then she knew what she had to do. Medicine had already forced her to make many compromises. This time she was going to do what she thought was right, at least for a couple of intensive days.

"Screw 482," she said half out loud, smiling at the rhyme. She sat down deliberately and cracked the book on anesthetic complications. The more she thought about Greenly and Berman, the more convinced she was that she was doing the right thing.

Monday
February 23
2:45 P.M.

Bellows impatiently tapped the top of the extension telephone No. 482, expecting it to ring any second. He was going to answer it before the first ring was completed. In the background the droning voice of the aging professor emeritus, Dr. Allen Druery, could be heard, extolling the virtues of Halstead. The four students appeared lost within the emptiness of the surgical conference room. Bellows had originally thought that the atmosphere of the conference room would add a positive note to the lectures he had planned for the students. But now he wasn't so sure. The room was too big, too cold for four students, and the lecturer looked a bit ludicrous standing at the podium and facing tier after tier of empty seats.

From where Bellows was sitting, he could see only the backs of the four students. Goldberg was busy taking notes in a furious fashion, getting every word. Dr. Druery's lecture was mildly interesting but certainly not worth notetaking. Bellows knew the syndrome, though. He'd seen it in action a thousand times and even suffered from it to an extent himself. As soon as the lights would dim, and someone would start speaking, many medical students would respond in a Pavlovian fashion by taking notes, madly trying to get every word down onto paper without any thought as to the content. The medical student responded in this utterly unintellectual way because, more often than not, he was asked to regurgitate whatever trivia he had been fed.

Bellows was sorry he had not told Susan that he indeed would be hurt if she missed the lecture. In such a small group, her absence was painfully apparent above and beyond the fact that she was so visually distinctive. Bellows was nervous that Stark would decide to pop in and welcome the group. Of course he'd wonder where the fifth student was, and what could Bellows say? He thought about saying that she was scrubbing on a case. But so early in the game, that was unlikely.

The worry about Stark had finally caused Bellows to page Susan so that he could retract his previous silent acquiescence to her cutting the lecture. It was a bad precedent to establish. So he thought he would just inform her that she was sincerely missed and should get herself up to the tenth-floor conference room on the double. Bellows specifically decided to use the word *sincerely* because in the context it was used, it had several implications.

Bellows had made up his mind to ask Susan out on a date. There were several unanswerable questions and aspects involved in such a move, yet the payoff was worth the risk. Susan was bright and spirited, and Bellows was almost positive she had a dynamite figure. Whether she could be feminine and warm according to Bellows's interpretations of those qualities remained to be seen. The trouble was that Bellows had some pretty outdated notions about femininity. For him surgery and his schedule came first; thus an important aspect of Bellows's definition of femininity concerned availability. He expected his female friends to respect his schedule as much as he did and to rearrange their schedules to accord with it. An interesting aspect of Susan's situation, it occurred to Bellows, was that for the next month or so, they would have similar schedules. That was encouraging. And if all else failed, Bellows reasoned that at least Susan would be a damn interesting screw.

But the phone remained silent under Bellows's expectant hand. Impatiently he redialed the page operator and told her to repeat the page for Dr. Susan Wheeler for 482. Replacing the receiver, he again waited for the ring as the minutes slid by. Bellows began to think that maybe things would not go so smoothly with Susan. Perhaps she wouldn't even go out with him. She could already be tight with someone else. Under his breath he cursed females in general, and he told himself that he should be sensible and leave well enough alone. At the same time he knew that Susan was triggering off his keen sense of competition. He also visualized that curve of Susan's low back as it spread out over her ass. He decided to page once more.

Gerald Kelley was as Irish as one could be and still live in Boston and not Dublin. His hair was reddish blond and thick and curly despite the fact that he was fifty-four years old. His face had a ruddy hue, almost as if he wore theatrical makeup, especially over the crests of his cheekbones.

Kelley's most notable feature and by far the dominant aspect of his profile was his enormous paunch. Every night three bottles of stout contributed to its awe-inspiring dimensions. For the last few years it had been pointed out that when Kelley was vertical, his belt buckle was horizontal.

Gerald Kelley had worked for the Memorial since he was fifteen years old. He had started out in the maintenance department, the boiler room to be exact, and now he was in charge. From his long experience and mechanical aptitude he knew the power plant of the hospital inside and out. In fact, he knew almost all the mechanical aspects of the building by heart. It was for this reason that he was in charge and also why he was paid $13,700 a year. The hospital administration knew he was indispensable, and they would have paid more if Gerald Kelley had made an issue of it. The fact was, each party was satisfied.

Gerald Kelley sat at his desk in the machinery spaces of the basement, thumbing through work orders. He had a day crew of eight men, and he tried to distribute the work according to need and capability. Any work on the power plant itself, though, Kelley did himself. The work orders in front of him were all routine, including the drain in the nurses' station on the fourteenth floor. That plugged up on schedule, once per week. Placing the work orders in the sequence he felt they should be done, Kelley began to match them up with his crew.

Although the general din in the machinery spaces was at a relatively high level, especially for people unaccustomed to the area, Kelley's ears were sensitive to the character of the mixed sounds. Thus when the clank of metal on metal reached his ears from the direction of the main electrical panel, he turned his head. Most people would not have heard the sound amid all the other mechanical noises. However, it did not repeat itself and Kelley returned to his administrative job at hand. He did not like the paperwork attached to his position; he would have preferred to fix the sink on the fourteenth floor himself. Yet he also understood that organization was a necessity if he were to keep things running. There was no way he could attend to every repair himself.

The clank recurred, louder than before. Kelley turned again and surveyed the area near the electrical panel, behind the main boilers. He returned to his papers but found himself staring ahead, trying to understand what could have caused the kind of sound he had heard. It had a sharp, brief metallic resonance foreign to the indigenous sounds of the area. Finally curiosity got the best of him and he wandered over to the main boiler. To get near to the electrical panel situated next to the main chase, which contained all the piping rising up in the building, he had to go around the boiler in either direction. He chose to go right, which gave him an opportunity to check the gauges on the boiler. This was an unnecessary maneuver because the system had been fully automated with backup safety devices and automatic cutoff switches. But it was an instinctive move for Kelley, having originated in the days when the boiler had to be watched minute by minute. So as he rounded the boiler his eyes were on the system, his mind appreciating its marvelous compactness compared to the system when he had started at the Memorial. When he looked ahead toward the electrical panel, he froze in his tracks, his right arm lifted involuntarily in self-defense.

"God, you scared the life out of me," said Kelley, catching his breath and allowing his arm to come back to his side.

"I could say the same," said a slim man dressed in a khaki uniform. The shirt was open at the neck, and the man wore a white crew neck t-shirt which reminded Kelley of navy chiefs during his wartime duty. The man's left breast pocket bulged with pens, small screwdrivers, and a ruler. Above the pocket was embroidered "Liquid Oxygen, Inc."

"I had no idea anyone else was in here," said Kelley.

"Same with me," said the man in khaki.

The two men looked at each other for a moment. The man in khaki was carrying a small green cylinder of compressed gas. A flow meter was attached to the cylinder head. "Oxygen" was stenciled plainly on the side.

"My name is Darell," said the man in khaki. "John Darell. Sorry to have scared you. I've been checking the oxygen lines out to the central storage tank. Everything seems fine. In fact, I'm on my way out. Could you tell me the shortest route?"

"Sure. Through those swinging doors, up the stairway to the main hall. Then you have a choice. Nashua Street is to the right, Causeway Street to the left."

"Thanks a million," said Darell, heading for the door.

Kelley watched him leave, and then looked around in disbelief. He couldn't figure how Darell had managed to get where he had been without being noticed. Kelley had no idea he could get so absorbed in his Goddamn paperwork.

Kelley walked back to his desk and returned to work. After a few minutes he thought of something else that bothered him. There were no oxygen lines in the boiler room. Kelley made a mental note to ask Peter Barker, assistant administrator, about oxygen line checks. The trouble was that Kelley had a poor memory for everything except mechanical details.

With the cloud cover Boston had enjoyed little daylight that day, and by 3:30 dusk settled over the city. It took a bit of imagination to comprehend that above the clouds shone the same six-thousand-degree fiery star which in summer turned the macadam on Boylston Street molten. The temperature had responded to the surrendering sun by precipitously falling to nineteen degrees. Another flurry of minute crystalline bodies wafted over the city. The outside lights along the hospital walkways had been on for almost a half-hour.

From within the illuminated library, it already appeared pitch black outside. The two-story window at the end of the room responded to the dropping temperature by starting an active convection current of cold air across its face. The weighted colder air fell to the floor at the foot of the window and then swept the length of the room under the tables toward the hissing radiators in the back. It was the cold current which first began to nudge Susan from the depths of her intense concentration.

As with so many academic subjects, Susan began to perceive that the more she read about coma, the less she felt she knew. To her surprise, it was an enormous subject, spanning many disciplines of medical specialization. And perhaps the most frustrating of all was Susan's realization that it was not known what determined consciousness, other than saying that the individual was not unconscious. The definition of one consisted of being the opposite of the other. Such a tautologous circle was a travesty of logic until Susan accepted the fact that medical science had not advanced enough to define consciousness precisely. In fact, being fully conscious and being totally unconscious (coma) seemed to represent opposite ends of a continuous spectrum which included partway states like confusion and stupor. Hence the inexact, unscientific terms were more an admission of ignorance than poorly conceived definitions.

Despite the semantics Susan was well aware of the stark difference between normal consciousness and coma. She had observed both states that very day in a patient . . . Berman. And despite the lack of precision in definition, there was no lack of information regarding coma. Under the heading of "acute coma," Susan began to fill page after page in her notebook with her characteristically small handwriting.

Her particular interest was in causation. Since science had not decided on what particular aspect of brain function had to be disrupted, Susan had to be content with precipitating factors. Being interested in acute coma, or coma of sudden onset, also helped to narrow the field but still was impressive and growing. Susan looked back over the list of causes that she had noted so far:

Trauma = concussion, contusion, or any type of stroke
Hypoxia = low oxygen:
        (1) mechanical
            — strangulation
            — blocked airway
            — insufficient ventilation
        (2) lung abnormality
            — alveolar block
        (3) vascular block
            — blood cannot get to brain
        (4) cellular block of oxygen use
High Carbon Dioxide
Hyper (hypo) Glycemia = high (low) blood sugar
Acidosis = high acid in the blood
Uremia = kidney failure with high uric acid in the blood
Hyper (hypo) Kalemia = high (low) potassium
Hyper (hypo) Natremia = high (low) sodium
Hepatic Failure = increase of toxins which would normally be detoxified by the liver

Addison's Disease = severe endocrine or glandular ab-
                    normality
Chemicals or Drugs . . .

Susan took an extra couple of pages for the chemicals and
drugs associated with acute coma and listed them alpha-
betically, each with a separate line to make it possible to add
information as she got it:

Alcohol	Insulin
Amphetamines	Iodine
Anesthetics	Mercurial diuretics
Anticonvulsants	Metaldehyde
Antihistamines	Methyl bromide
Aromatic hydrocarbons	Methyl chloride
Arsenic	Naphazoline
Barbiturates	Naphthaline
Bromides	Opium derivatives
Cannabis	Pentachlorophenol
Carbon disulfide	Phenol
Carbon monoxide	Salicylates
Carbon tetrachloride	Sulfanilamide
Chloral hydrate	Sulfides
Cyanide	Tetrahydrozaline
Glutethimide	Vitamin D
Herbicides	Hypnotic agents
Hydrocarbons	

Susan knew that the list was not complete but nonetheless
it gave her something to go on, something to keep in mind
during her subsequent investigations, and it could be en-
larged at any time.

Turning next to the general internal medicine textbooks,
Susan opened the ponderous *Principles of Internal Medicine*
and read the appropriate sections dealing with coma. The
articles in Cecil and Loeb were about the same. Both books
provided a rather good overview, although no new concepts
were added. Several references were cited which Susan duly
copied down in an ever-expanding list of necessary reading.

It felt good to get up and stretch. Susan allowed a deep
comforting yawn. She wiggled her toes to try to encourage
the blood to go there. The cold draft along the floor had

made her stir sooner than she might have otherwise. But once up she turned to the *Index Medicus,* the exhaustive listing of all articles published in all the medical journals.

Starting with the most recent volumes and working backward, Susan searched for and extracted every article concerning acute coma and every article under the heading "Anesthetic complications: delayed return to consciousness." By the time she had worked herself back to 1972, Susan had a list of thirty-seven prospective papers worth reading.

One title especially caught Susan's attention: "Acute Coma at the Boston City Hospital: A Retrospective Statistical Study of Causes," *Journal of the American Association of Emergency Room Physicians,* volume 21, August 1974, pp. 401-3. She found the bound volume containing the article and was soon immersed in it, taking notes as she read.

Bellows had to call her by name before she looked up at him. He had come into the library, located her, and had taken the seat directly across from her. But she did not look up from her reading. Bellows had tried clearing his throat with absolutely no effect. It was as if Susan were in a trance.

"Dr. Susan Wheeler, I believe," said Bellows, leaning over the table, his shadow falling across the journal in front of her.

Susan finally responded and looked up. "Dr. Bellows, I presume." Susan smiled.

"Dr. Bellows is right. God, what a relief. I thought for a moment you were in a coma." Bellows shook his head up and down, as if he were agreeing with himself.

Neither one of them spoke for a few moments. Bellows had prepared a short speech during which he was going to correct any impression he might have given Susan that she was free to cut lectures. He had decided to tell her in plain language that she had to get her ass in gear. But once confronting her, sense of purpose failed, leaving him as directionless as a sailboat becalmed. Susan remained silent because her intuition had informed her that Bellows had something to say. The silence soon became mildly awkward.

Susan broke it.

"Mark, I've been doing a bit of interesting reading here. Look at these figures."

She stood up and leaned across the table, holding out the journal so that Bellows could see the page. As she did so, her blouse fell away from her chest. Bellows found himself staring down at her splendid breasts, barely contained by a sheer flimsy bra, their skin of a smoothness Bellows imagined to be like velvet. He tried to concentrate on the page Susan was showing him, but his peripheral vision continued to record the insistent image of Susan's lovely torso. Self-consciously Bellows scanned the library, certain that his preoccupation would be transparent to anyone in the room.

Susan was oblivious to the mental havoc she was inadvertently causing.

"This chart here shows the order of incidence of the various types of acute fatal coma appearing at the emergency room at the Boston City Hospital," said Susan, running her fingers along the lines. "One of the most amazing facts is that only fifty percent of the cases are ever diagnosed. I find that amazing; wouldn't you agree? That means that fifty percent of the cases are never diagnosed. They just come in to the ER in coma and die. Just like that."

"Yeah, it's amazing," said Bellows, putting his left hand up to his temple to try to keep from seeing what he was seeing.

"And look here, Mark, at the causes of the cases which they do diagnose: sixty percent are due to alcohol, thirteen percent due to trauma, ten percent to strokes, three percent to drugs or poisons, and the rest divided up among epilepsy, diabetes, meningitis, and pneumonia. Now obviously . . . ," said Susan, sitting back down and relieving the stress on Bellows's hypothalmus.

Bellows glanced around once more to make sure that no one had noticed the episode.

". . . we can dismiss alcohol and trauma as far as causing acute coma in the OR is concerned. So . . . that leaves us with strokes, then drugs or poisons, and the others in decreasing probability as possible culprits."

"Wait a second, Susan," said Bellows pulling himself together. He put his elbows on the table with his forearms up in the air, his hands drooped but engaged. His head was down at first, then he picked it up and looked at Susan. "That's all very interesting. A little farfetched, but interesting."

"Farfetched?"

"Yeah. You cannot possibly extrapolate data from the ER to the OR. But anyway, I didn't come in here looking for you to argue about that. I came in here because you haven't been answering your pages. I know, because it was me who was paging you. Look, I'm going to have trouble if you don't show up for conferences. You're going to make trouble for yourself, and the fact of the matter is that, while you're on my service, your trouble is my trouble. I can only make excuses for you for so long. I mean, you can be drawing blood or scrubbing just so often. Stark will be asking questions before you know it. He's phenomenal. He knows everything that's going on around here. Besides, you'll get the reputation of being a phantom among your own section students. Susan, I'm afraid you're going to have to restrict your research proclivities to after-hours."

"Are you finished?" asked Susan, rising to the defense.

"I'm finished."

"Well, answer me this one question. Has Berman or Greenly awakened yet?"

"Of course not . . ."

"Then frankly, I believe that my current activities eclipse the importance of a few boring surgical conferences."

"Oh my aching back! Susan, be reasonable. You're not going to save the world during your first week on surgery. I'm going out on a limb for you as it is."

"I appreciate it, Mark. Really I do. But listen. My few hours here in the library have already provided some very interesting information. The complication of prolonged coma after anesthesia is about one hundred times more prevalent here at Memorial than the incidence given for the rest of the country over the past year. Mark, I think I'm onto something. When I started, it was more of an emotional thing which I thought I could work out in a day or two here in the library. But one hundred times! God, I could be on the track of something big, like a new disease, or a lethal combination of normally safe drugs. What if this is some sort of viral encephalitis, or even the result of a previous infection which makes the brain somehow more susceptible to certain drugs or mild lack of oxygen?"

Susan had been part of the medical world for only two years, and yet she was already cognizant of the potential benefits which would accrue to someone who discovered a new disease or syndrome. She thought this one might become known as the Wheeler syndrome, and Susan's success within the medical community would be guaranteed. More often than not, the discoverer of the new disease became far more famous than the discoverer of the cure for the same disease. Eponyms abound in medicine like the tetralogy of Fallot, Cogan's disease, the Tolpin syndrome, or Depperman's degeneration. Whereas names like the Salk vaccine are an anomaly. Penicillin is called penicillin, not Fleming's agent.

"We could call it the Free Wheeler Syndrome," said Susan, allowing herself to laugh at her own enthusiasm.

"Christ," said Bellows, cradling his head in his hands. "What an imagination. But that's OK. Naiveté has a certain license. But, Susan, you are in a real world situation with certain specific responsibilities. You are still a medical student, low man—or woman—on the totem pole. You'd better get your tail in gear and honor your surgery rotation obligations or, believe me, your ass will be grass. I'll give you one more day for this project, provided you show up for rounds in the morning. After that you work on it in your free time. Now, if I need you I'll page Dr. Wheels instead of Wheeler, so answer it, understand?"

"Understood," said Susan looking squarely at Bellows. "I'll do that, if you do something for me."

"What's that?"

"Pull out these articles and have them Xeroxed. I'll pay you later." Susan tossed her list of references to Bellows, jumped up from the table and breezed out of the room before Bellows could respond. He found himself looking at a list of thirty-seven journal articles. Since he knew the library like the bones of his hand, he located the volumes with ease, marking each article with a piece of paper. He took the first group over to the desk and told the girl to copy the indicated articles and put it on his library charge. Bellows knew that he had been manipulated again, but he didn't mind. It had taken only ten minutes. He would get them back with interest.

And he had been right; she had a dynamite figure.

As she had been telling Bellows that the incidence of coma
following anesthesia at the Memorial was one hundred times
the national incidence, Susan had realized that she was basing
her calculations on the six cases Harris had mentioned in his
outburst. Susan had to check that figure. If it was actually
higher, she would have more ammunition to base her commitment to the project. Besides, she needed the names of the
coma victims so that she could obtain their charts. What she
needed more than anything else, she recognized, was hard
data.

Susan knew that she had to get access to the central computer. Harris would be unwilling to supply the names of the
patients. Susan was certain of that. Bellows might have been
able to get them if he were sufficiently motivated. But that
was a big if. Susan felt that the best route was for her to try
to get the information herself. So she was thankful she had
taken the introductory course in PL 1 computer program-
ming as a junior in college. Already it had paid off in surprising ways, and her need for the information at hand was just
another example.

The computer center in the hospital was located in the
Hardy wing, occupying the entire top floor. Many people
joked about the symbolic aspects of the computer being
above everything else in the hospital, and it had added a
new meaning to the phrase "with a little help from above."

As the elevator door slid open on the foyer of the eigh-
teenth floor, Susan knew she was going to have to improvise

if she were to be successful. Beyond the foyer Susan could see through glass partitions into the main computer reception area. The place had the appearance of a bank. The only difference was that the medium of exchange here was information, not currency.

Susan entered the reception room and walked directly to a counter top that ran the length of the room along the right wall. There were about eight other people in the room, most of them sitting in comfortable-looking blue corduroy chairs. A few were at the counter top bent over computer request forms. All looked up as Susan traversed the room, but they quickly returned to their own affairs. Without the slightest hint of uncertainty Susan took one of the computer request forms. Ostensibly concentrating on the form, Susan had her real attention on the room.

In the back of the room, about twelve feet from Susan, was a large white Formica desk. Above it hung a sign: "Information." It was so appropriate that it brought a smile to Susan's face. The man at the desk sat motionlessly, a slight proud smile on his face. He was about sixty, pudgy but neat. Behind him, visible through another glass partition, were the gleaming input-output terminals of the computer itself. While Susan was pretending to be absorbed in the form in front of her, the man at the desk accepted several computer request forms. Each time he went over the form, converting the request to computer language and writing it on the lower portion of the form. He also checked the authorization by calling the department involved, unless he knew the requesting individual personally. Finally he placed the form—or several stapled together—in the "in" box on the corner of the desk. The requesting individual was told when to expect the information, depending on the priority assigned to the request.

Having assessed the procedure, Susan gave full attention to the form before her. It was certainly simple enough. She filled in the date in the indicated box. She left blank the box for the authorizing department, and she also omitted the name of the requesting party or organization. Susan also left blank the box reserved for method of payment for computer time. She concentrated on the information desired. Susan was not sure how she should word the request for several reasons. One was the concern that the hospital might be uptight about leaking information on cases of coma resulting from anesthesia. Perhaps they might have programmed a subroutine into the computer so that any requests for information would be automatically canceled, or at least alert the computer that the information had been requested. Another point that occurred to Susan was that a disease or disease process might have several modes or degrees of expression. Prolonged coma after an anesthetic might be one of them, maybe the most severe. Susan wanted to obtain a wide range of information and in that way be able to select what she thought was significant.

But requesting all cases of coma for the past year might yield a printout that was too extensive. Since coma was a symptom and not a disease itself, Susan could end with a list of every heart attack, stroke, and cancer victim who had succumbed to those diseases over the last year. Susan decided to call only for cases of coma occurring in people who had no known chronic or debilitating disease. Then she realized that she was already making assumptions. If she were on the track of a new disease, there was no reason why it couldn't affect people who had other diseases. In fact, if it were infectious in nature, other disease processes would encourage its expression by lowering defenses.

Susan changed her request to all cases of coma occurring to inpatients (in hospital) which were unrelated to the patient's known disease processes. Susan next asked for a correlate between her sample and those having surgery during their stay at the Memorial prior to their coma, with a time correlation between surgery and the onset of the coma. With a certain amount of difficulty Susan translated her request into computer language. She had not used it for almost a year, and it took a few moments to get it right. This portion of the request was below two red lines and the admonishment "Do not write below this line."

Susan then waited for the next request to be turned in to the man at the desk. Luckily she did not have to wait long. About four minutes after she finished writing, the elevator arrived. Through the glass she saw a man squeeze past the elevator door before it had fully opened and approach the reception desk at a lope. About forty, slight of build, with flaxen hair parted from a deeply recessed hairline, the man waved a handful of the computer request forms nervously.

"George," said the man pulling up in front of the reception desk, "you gotta help me."

"Ah, my old friend Henry Schwartz," said the man behind the desk. "We're always ready to help the accounting department. After all, that's where our checks come from. What can I do for you?"

Susan carefully penciled in "Henry Schwartz" onto her own form in the box for the requesting party. In the area for authorizing department, Susan wrote "Accounting."

"I need a couple of things, but most of all I need a list of all the Blue Cross-Blue Shield subscribers who have had surgery in the last year," said Schwartz in a rapid-fire fashion. "If you asked why I need it, you'd crack up, I swear you would. But I need it and fast. The day shift was supposed to have had it ready for me."

"We can run it in an hour or so. I'll have it for you by seven," said George, stapling Schwartz's requests together and tossing them into the box.

"George, you're a lifesaver," said Schwartz, running his hand through his hair over and over again. He then headed toward the elevator. "I'll be back at seven sharp."

Susan watched Schwartz press the "down" button and then walk back and forth in the elevator foyer. It looked as if he was talking to himself. He hit the "down" button several more times. After the elevator picked him up, Susan watched the floor indicator above the elevator. It stopped at six, then three, then one. Susan would have to look up which floor the accounting department was located on.

Susan took another blank request form and, carefully placing it over her own, she headed for the desk.

"Excuse me," said Susan, marshaling a smile she hoped would be convincing. George looked up at her, over the tops of his black-rimmed glasses, which perched midway down his nose. "I'm a medical student," continued Susan, making her voice as sweet as possible, "and I'm very interested in the computer here at the hospital." She held up the request forms, the blank one hiding the one she had filled out.

"You are, are you?" said George, sitting back with a smile broadening on his own face.

"I am," repeated Susan shaking her head in the affirmative. "I think that the potential of the computer in medicine is very great, and since it is obviously not a part of our formal orientation here, I thought I'd just come up and sort of get acquainted."

George looked at Susan, then over his shoulder through the glass partition at the gleaming IBM hardware. When he turned back to Susan his pride was effervescing.

"It's a marvelous set up, Miss . . ."

"Susan Wheeler."

"It is a fantastic machine, Miss Wheeler," said George, leaning forward in his seat and lowering his voice and emphasizing his words, suggesting that he was telling Susan a tremendous secret. "The hospital couldn't do without it."

"In order to get an idea how it is used, I've been studying the request form here." Susan held the request forms so that George would see only the blank one, but he had turned again to look into the terminal room.

"I was interested to see a completed form," continued Susan reaching over and taking the top group of stapled forms from the "in" box. "I was curious about how the requests were fed into the computer. Is it all right if I look at one of these?" She placed the forms Schwartz had delivered over her own.

"Sure," said George turning back to Susan. He stood up and leaned over toward Susan, placing his left hand on the desk. With his other hand he pointed to the space where the request was written in normal English.

"Here the requesting party indicates what it is they want. Then down here . . ." George's finger moved down below the red lines ". . . we have the area where the request is translated into a language that the computer will understand."

Susan slipped her blank form from under the pile of Schwartz's forms, as if comparing them and she put it down on the desk beside them—leaving her own filled-out form beneath Schwartz's.

"So if someone wants several different kinds of information, they have to fill out separate forms?" asked Susan.

"Exactly, and if . . ."

Susan turned Schwartz's first request form back from the rest of them rapidly, pulling it free of the staple in the upper left corner.

"Oh, I'm terribly sorry," said Susan putting the top sheet back in position. "Look what I've done. Let me staple it for you."

"No matter," said George, fumbling for the staple machine himself. "One staple will fix it." George pressed the staple machine as Susan held the completed forms, together with her own request on the underside.

"Let me put these back before I destroy them completely," said Susan contritely, replacing the forms in the "in" box.

"No harm done," reassured George.

"Now once the request is in, what happens to it?" asked Susan looking into the terminal room and taking George's attention from the "in" box.

"Well, I take them inside to the key puncher, who prepares the cards for the card reader. Then . . ."

Susan was not listening; she was thinking of how best to terminate her visit. About five minutes later she was down at the directory for the hospital, looking up Henry Schwartz of the accounting department.

With a spare hour and a half, Susan left the Memorial for her dorm. Her stomach growled in opposition to her forgetfulness of basic needs. The tuna sandwich, as bad as it was, had long since disappeared into her metabolic mill, and Susan looked forward to dinner.

Monday
February 23
6:55 P.M.

It was a little before seven when Susan alighted from the MBTA at the North Station stop. Crossing the footbridge spanning the street, Susan was exposed to the rush of wind whipping up from the partially frozen harbor water. She bent against its force, clutching her sheepskin ski hat with her left hand and the lapels of her peajacket with her right hand.

She tried to keep the cold from her neck by snuggling her chin as far as possible into the recesses of her collar.

When she rounded the edge of the building, the wind increased. An empty beer can tumbled past her into the street. The familiar rush hour sea of red taillights and wisps of exhaust fumes stretched as far as Susan could see. The windows on the cars were frosted, and they reflected the images about them with a silver sheen, giving the impression of the often white, unseeing pupils of the blind.

Susan began to run at a slow jog with an exaggerated to and fro roll of her body since her arms were pressed against herself. The main entrance to the hospital yawned in front of her, and with relief she pushed through the revolving door.

Susan stuffed her hat into the right sleeve of her coat and left it in the coatroom behind the main information desk. Then she used the hospital telephone directory and rang up the computer center.

"Hello, this is the accounting department," said Susan slightly out of breath and struggling to make her voice sound normal. "Has Mr. Schwartz picked up his material yet?"

The answer was affirmative; he had collected it about five minutes earlier. The timing seemed perfect as far as Susan was concerned, and she left for the Hardy building elevator and the third floor accounting offices.

The evening accounting crew was a mere skeleton compared to the day shift. When Susan entered the room only three people were visible at the far end. Two men and one woman looked up in unison as Susan entered.

"Excuse me," called Susan, approaching the group. "Can you tell me where I can find Mr. Schwartz?"

"Schwartz? Sure. He's in the office in the corner," said one of the men, pointing down the opposite side of the room.

Susan's eyes followed his finger. "Thanks," she said, reversing her direction.

Henry Schwartz was in the middle of the computer printout he had requested. The office was small but extraordinarily neat. The books in the bookcase were arranged so that their heights descended in an orderly fashion. The depth of the book backs in the shelves was one inch, no more, no less.

"Mr. Schwartz?" asked Susan smiling and walking up to his desk.

"Yes?" said Schwartz without removing his index finger from his place in the printout.

"It seems that my printout got mixed up with yours, or at least that was the combined opinion upstairs. I was wondering if you had noticed any material you had not requested?"

"No, but I haven't looked through it all yet. What was it you're missing?"

"It's some information on coma we need for a section presentation. Do you mind if I see if it's included with your material?"

"Not at all," said Schwartz, lifting sections of the printout to find the break points.

"If it's there, it would be the last section," offered Susan. "They said it was run right after yours."

Schwartz lifted the bulk of the material from the desk. Remaining was the information Susan needed. Attached to the top was her request form.

"That's it," said Susan.

"But the form indicates I requested it," questioned Schwartz glancing at the request form.

"No wonder they got it mixed up with your material," said Susan, reaching for the material. "But I assure you, you wouldn't be interested in this stuff. And it's certainly not your fault, by any means."

"I'd better say something to George . . . ," said Schwartz replacing his own printout in front of him.

"No need," said Susan, exiting. "We already discussed it at length. Thanks a million."

"You're welcome," said Schwartz, but Susan had already left.

"Susan, you are too much, really too much," said Bellows between spoonfuls of custard he had taken from the tray of a patient who was too nauseated to eat. "You skip the lecture, afternoon rounds, and avoid your patients, and now you're hanging around here until eight P.M. The only consistency about your performance so far is constant variation." Bellows laughed as he scraped the bottom of the custard cup.

Susan and Bellows were sitting in the lounge on Beard 5 where the hospital day had begun for Susan. She was sitting in the same seat she had occupied that morning. Spilling over onto the floor was the IBM printout sheet she had obtained. She was running down the list of names and marking appropriate ones with a yellow felt-tip pen.

Bellows took a drink from his coffee.

"Well, that proves it," said Susan, putting the cap on the pen.

"Proves what?" asked Bellows.

"Proves that there haven't been six cases of unexplained coma, excluding Berman, here at the Memorial this last year."

"Hurray," cheered Bellows, toasting with his coffee mug. "Now I can stop worrying about anesthesia and have my hemorrhoids fixed."

"I would recommend that you stick to your suppositories," said Susan, counting the names she'd marked. "There haven't been six because there've been eleven. And if Berman continues on his present course, then there will have been twelve."

"Are you sure?" Bellows's tone changed abruptly and he showed interest in the IBM printout sheet for the first time.

"That's all that came out on this printout," said Susan. "I wouldn't be surprised if there were a few more if I had been able to call up the information straight away."

"You really think so? God, eleven cases!" Bellows leaned over toward Susan, his tongue working at the empty spoon. "How'd you manage to get this IBM printout?"

"Henry Schwartz was nice enough to help me," said Susan nonchalantly.

"Who the hell is Henry Schwartz?" asked Bellows.

"Damned if I know."

"Spare me," said Bellows covering his eyes with his hand, "I'm too tired for mental games."

"Is that a chronic ailment or an acute affliction?"

"Cut the crap. How'd you get this data? Something like this has to be cleared through the department."

"I went upstairs this afternoon, filled out one of those M804 forms, gave it to the nice man at the desk, and then went back tonight and picked it up."

"I'm sorry I asked," said Bellows getting up and waving his spoon to suggest he would let the issue ride. "But eleven cases. Did they all happen during surgery?"

"No," said Susan, going back to the printout. "Harris was on the level when he said six. The other five were from inpatients on the medical service. Their diagnosis was idiosyncratic reaction. Doesn't that strike you as pretty odd?"

"No."

"Oh, come on," said Susan impatiently. "The word idiosyncratic sounds great but it really means that they had no idea what the diagnosis was."

"That might be true, but Susan, dear, this happens to be a major hospital, not a country club. It serves as a referral base for the whole New England area. Do you know how many deaths we have here on an average in a single day?"

"Deaths have causes . . . these cases of coma do not . . . at least not as yet."

"Well, deaths don't always have apparent causes. That's the purpose of autopsy."

"There, you hit the nail on the head," said Susan. "When someone dies, then you do an autopsy and you find out what was the cause of death so that you can possibly add to your fund of knowledge. Well, in the coma cases you can't do an autopsy because the patients are somewhere hovering between life and death. That makes it even more important that you do another kind of 'opsy,' a live-opsy, if you will. You study all the clues you have available, short of dismembering the victim. The diagnosis is just as important, maybe even more important than the autopsy diagnosis. If we could find out what was wrong with these people, maybe we could bring them out of their comas. Or better still, avoid the coma in the first place."

"Even the autopsy," said Bellows, "doesn't always provide the answers. There are plenty of deaths where the exact cause is never determined whether they do an autopsy or not. I happen to know that two patients threw in the towel today, and I doubt very much if a diagnosis will be made."

"Why do you think that the diagnosis won't be made?" asked Susan.

"Because both patients expired from respiratory arrest. They apparently just stopped breathing, very calmly with no warning. They were just discovered dead. And in respiratory arrest you don't always find anything to hang the blame on."

Bellows had captured Susan's interest. She was staring at him without moving, without blinking.

"Are you OK?" asked Bellows, waving his hand in front of her face. Still Susan did not move until she looked down at the IBM printout.

"What the hell do you have, psychomotor epilepsy or something?" asked Bellows.

Susan looked up at him. "Epilepsy? No, of course not. You said these cases today died of respiratory arrest?"

"Apparently. I mean they stopped breathing. They just gave up."

"What were they in the hospital for?"

"I'm not positive. I think one of them was in for some problem with his leg. Maybe he had phlebitis and they might find a pulmonary embolus or something. The other one was in for Bell's palsy."

"Were they both on I.V.s?"

"I don't remember but I wouldn't be surprised if they had been. Why do you ask?"

Susan bit her lower lip, thinking about what Bellows had just told her.

"Mark, do you know something? These deaths you mentioned could be related to the coma victims." Susan patted the printout with the back of her hand. "You might have hit on something. What were the names? Can you remember?"

"For Christ's sake, Susan, you've got this thing on the brain. You're working overtime and you're starting to have delusions." Bellows switched to an artificially concerned tone. "Don't be concerned, though; it happens to the best of us after we've stayed up for two or three nights in a row."

"Mark, I'm serious."

"I know you're serious, that's what worries me. Why don't you give yourself a break and forget about it for a day or so? Then you can pick it up and be more objective. I tell you what. I've got tomorrow night off and with a little luck I can get out of here by seven. How about some dinner? You've only been here a day but you have to get away from the hospital as much as I do."

Bellows hadn't planned on asking Susan out quite so soon and in such a fashion. But he was pleased because it had come so apparently spontaneously and consequently it would be easy to deal with a refusal if it occurred. It sounded more like an offer to get together than an actual date.

"Dinner's fine, can't pass up an offer for a dinner even with an invertebrate. But really, Mark, what were the names of the two deaths today?"

"Crawford and Ferrer. They were patients on Beard 6."

Susan pursed her lips as she wrote the names down in her notebook. "I'll have to look into those in the morning. In fact . . ." Susan looked at her watch ". . . maybe tonight. If they were going to do an autopsy on these cases, when would it be?"

"Probably tonight or first thing in the morning," shrugged Bellows.

"Well then I better check tonight."

Susan refolded her printout.

"Thanks, Mark, old boy; you've been a help again."

"Again?"

"Yeah. Thanks for those articles you Xeroxed for me. You'll make a good secretary someday."

"Up yours."

"Tut, tut. See you tomorrow night. How about the Ritz? I haven't eaten there for several weeks," teased Susan, heading for the door.

"Not so fast, Susan. I'll see you at rounds in the morning at six-thirty. Remember our deal. I'll cover for you another day if you come to rounds."

"Mark, you've been such a dear, really. Let's not louse it up so soon." Susan smiled and pulled some of her hair across her face with coquettish exaggeration. "I'll be up till all hours reading all this material you got for me. I need one more full day. We'll discuss it further tomorrow night."

Then she was gone. Again Bellows felt encouraged about Susan as he sipped his coffee. Then he got up. He had plenty of work to do.

**Monday
February 23
8:32 P.M.**

The pathology lab was in the basement of the main building. Susan descended the stairs and emerged in the middle of a basement corridor which disappeared into utter darkness to the right and twisted out of view to the left. Stark bare light bulbs glowed from the ceiling at intervals of twenty to thirty feet. The light from each bulb met the light from the next in an uneasy penumbra, causing a strange interplay of shadows from the tangle of pipes along the ceiling. In a vain attempt to provide color to the dim subterranean world, angled stripes of bright orange paint had been painted on the walls.

Directly opposite Susan, partially hidden from view, was an arrow pointing to the left, with the word *Pathology* stenciled above it. Susan turned down the corridor, her shoes making hollow noises on the concrete floor, competing with the hiss of the steam pipes. The atmosphere was oppressive; the location within the bowels of the hospital was sinisterly appropriate. She was not heading for the pathology lab with any favorable anticipation. As far as Susan was concerned pathology represented the black side of medicine, the specialty that seemed to derive its nourishment from medical failure, death. Arguments about the benefits of biopsies which the pathologists analyzed or the obvious beneficial spinoffs for the living from the autopsies the pathologists performed were all lost on Susan. She had only seen one autopsy done during her course in pathology, and that had been one too many. Life had never seemed quite so fragile nor had death seemed quite so final as when Susan had watched the two overweight pathologists disembowel the body of a recently deceased patient.

The memory of that event slowed Susan's steps but it did not halt them. She was determined. But she had seemingly been walking for a hundred yards as the corridor twisted first in one direction then in another. She cast a nervous glance over her shoulder, wondering if she could have missed the door to the lab. With increased misgivings she continued. At several places, the light bulbs were not functioning and Susan's shadow would appear in front of her and lengthen. Then as she moved into the sphere of influence of the next functioning light her shadow would pale and disappear.

Finally she faced two swinging doors. The upper portion of each contained opaque windows.

"Unauthorized Entry Forbidden" was lettered boldly across the cracked, frosted glass on each door. Stenciled in peeling gold paint below the window on the right door was "Pathology Laboratory." Susan hesitated at the door, building up her confidence, wondering what sort of scene to prepare herself for. Cracking the door, she got a glimpse of the interior. A long black stone table dominated the room, running most of its length. Cluttered about on the table were microscopes, slides, slide boxes, chemicals, books, and an array of other equipment. Susan pushed open the door and stepped into the lab. The acrid smell of formaldehyde hung over the room.

The entire wall on the right had shelving from floor to ceiling. With hardly a square inch remaining, the shelves were full of varying sized bottles and jars. Looking more closely, Susan realized that the amorphous colorless mass in the large jar closest to her was an entire human head cut neatly in half, sagitally. Just behind the halved tongue in the wall of the throat was a granular mass. The label on the glass simply said, "Pharyngeal carcinoma, #304-A6 1932." Susan shuddered and tried to keep herself from glancing at other equally gruesome specimens.

At the far end of the room was another set of swinging doors identical to those from the corridor. From the room beyond, Susan could hear a mixture of voices and metallic sounds. She walked toward the doors as silently as possible, feeling herself an intruder in an alien and potentially hostile environment.

Susan tried to peer through the crack between the doors. Although her visual field was limited she knew immediately that she was looking into the autopsy room. Slowly she began to open the left door.

A loud ringing noise echoed around the room causing Susan to spin around, letting the autopsy room door snap shut behind her. At first she thought that she had tripped some alarm system and she felt the urge to bolt for the door into the corridor. But before she could move, a pathology resident appeared out of another side door.

"Well, hello there," said the resident to Susan as he walked over to the sink and picked up a distilled water irrigator. He smiled at Susan as he squirted water over a tray of slides he was staining. The color went from deep violet to clear. "Welcome to the path lab. You a med student?"

"Yes." Susan forced a smile.

"We don't see many med students this time of day . . . or night. Is there anything special we can do for you?"

"No, not really. I'm just looking around. I'm quite new here," said Susan putting her hands in the pockets of her white coat, her pulse racing.

"Make yourself at home. There's coffee in the office here if you're interested."

"No thanks," said Susan walking back along the desk, aimlessly touching some of the slide boxes.

The resident added another amber stain to the tray of slides and reset the timer.

"Actually, maybe you could help me," said Susan fingering a few slides on the table. "Several patients from Beard 6 expired today. I wondered if they've been . . . um . . ." Susan tried to think of the right word.

"What were the names?" asked the resident wiping his hands. "There's a post going on right now."

"Ferrer and Crawford."

The resident walked over to a clipboard hanging from a nail on the wall.

"Hmmm . . . Crawford. That rings a bell. I think that was a medical examiner's case. Here's Ferrer . . . that's a medical examiner's case. And I was right, Crawford is too. They're both medical examiner's cases, but hold on."

The resident walked quietly over to the doors into the autopsy room and banged one open with the palm of his

133

hand. With his right hand holding the edge of the remaining closed door he leaned into the room beyond, his head just out of Susan's view.

"Hey, Hamburger, what's the name of the case you're doing?"

There was a pause and a voice but Susan could not hear it.

"Crawford! I thought that was an examiner's case." There was another pause.

The resident came back into the room as the timer went off again. The ringing noise made Susan jump once more. The resident squirted more distilled water onto the slides.

"The medical examiner released both cases to the department, as usual. Lazy son of a bitch. Anyway they're doing Crawford right now."

"Thanks," said Susan. "All right if I go in and take a look?"

"By all means, our pleasure," said the resident, shrugging his shoulders.

Susan paused momentarily at the doors, but she knew the resident was watching her, so she pushed open one of the doors and entered the room.

The room was probably forty feet square, old and dingy. Its walls were surfaced in white tile, which was ancient, cracked, and missing in places. The floor was a type of gray terrazzo. In the center of the room there were marble tables built with slanted tops. A stream of water constantly ran down each table toward a drain at the foot, which emitted a constant sucking noise. Over each table hung a hooded light, a scale, and a microphone. Susan found herself standing on a level three to four steps above the level of the main floor. Immediately to her right were several wooden benches on progressively lower tiers. These benches were a remnant from older days when groups would assemble to observe autopsies.

Only one of the hooded lights was on, that over the table nearest to Susan. It cast its relatively narrow beam down onto the naked corpse on the table immediately below. On each side of the table stood a pathology resident wearing an oilcloth apron and rubber gloves. The focal point of light caused the rest of the room to slide into graded burnt umber shadow like a sinister Rembrandt painting. The table in the center of the room was in shadow but it was possible for Susan to see that it also held a naked corpse, a manila tag tied around its right big toe. A large Y-shaped sutured incision crossed the thorax and abdomen. The third table was barely visible in the darkness, but it appeared to be empty.

Susan's entrance stopped all progress in the room. Both residents were staring at her with their heads tilted down to avoid the glare of the overhead light. One of the residents with a large moustache and sideburns, was in the process of suturing the Y-shaped incision on the male corpse under the light. The other resident, taller by almost a foot, was standing before a basin containing the disemboweled organs.

Having sized up Susan, the taller resident went back to work. He reached into the tangle of organs with his left hand, grasping the liver. His right hand gripped a large, razor-sharp butcher knife. A few strokes freed the liver from the other organs. The liver made a sloshing sound as it oozed into the scale. The resident stepped on a foot pedal on the floor, speaking into the microphone. "The liver appears reddish brown with a lightly mottled surface, period. The gross weight is . . . a . . . two point four kilograms, period." He then reached into the pan and lifted the liver out, dropping it back into the basin.

Susan descended several steps toward the group. The smell was slightly fishy; the air seemed greasy and heavy, like an uncleaned bus depot restroom.

"The liver consistency is more firm than usual but definitely pliant, period." The knife flashed in the light and the liver surface separated. "The cut surface demonstrates an enhanced lobar pattern, period." The knife sliced across the liver in four or five more places, then finally cut a piece out of the center. "The cut specimen demonstrates the usual friable character, period."

Susan moved up to the foot of the table. The sucking drain was directly in front of her. The taller resident on the left reached into the basin for another organ but he stopped when the moustached resident spoke.

"Well, hello . . ."

"Greetings," said Susan; "sorry to bother you."

"No bother. Join the party, except we've almost finished."

"Thanks, but I'm happy to just watch. Is this Crawford or Ferrer?"

"This is Ferrer," said the resident. Then he pointed at the other body. "That's Crawford."

"I was wondering if you've determined a cause of death."

"No," said the taller resident. "But we haven't opened the lungs on this case yet. Crawford was clean grossly. Maybe the microscopic sections will shed some light."

"Do you expect something in the lungs?" asked Susan.

"Well, from the history of apparent respiratory arrest, we were considering pulmonary embolism. But I don't think we're going to find anything, though. Maybe there'll be something in the brain sections."

"Why don't you think you'll find anything?"

"Well, because I've posted a few cases like this before, and I've never found anything. And the history is exactly the same. Relatively young, somebody comes by and they're not breathing. There's a resuscitation attempt but without luck. Then we get them, or at least after the medical examiner turns them over to us."

"About how many such cases would you estimate?"

"Over what time span?"

"Whatever . . . a year, two years."

"Maybe six or seven over the last two years. I'm guessing."

"And you don't have any ideas about the cause of death?"

"Nope."

"None?" asked Susan, a bit surprised.

"Well, I think it's something with the brain. Something turns off their breathing. Maybe a stroke, but I did brain sections like you wouldn't believe on two similar cases."

"And?"

"Nothing. Clean as a whistle."

Susan began to feel a bit queasy. The atmosphere, the smell, the images, the noises all joined forces to make her feel light-headed and she shuddered with a mild wave of nausea. She swallowed.

"Are the hospital charts for Ferrer and Crawford down here?"

"Sure, they're in the coffee room through the lab."

"I'd like to look at them for a few minutes. If you find anything significant, would you give me a yell? I'd be interested in seeing it."

The taller resident lifted the heart and placed it on the scale. "These your patients?"

"Not exactly," said Susan, starting toward the exit, "but they might be."

The taller resident looked quizzically over at the other as Susan left. His companion was watching Susan exit, trying to figure out a smooth way of getting her name and number.

The coffee room could have been anywhere in the hospital. The coffee machine was an ancient device, the paint on one side burned and the wire frayed to the point of being a real hazard. The countertop desk along both side walls was spread with charts, paper, books, coffee cups, and a welter of ballpoint pens.

"That was quick," said the resident who had been staining the slides. He was sitting at one of the desks, with a half-filled cup of coffee and a half-eaten doughnut. He was busy signing a large stack of typed pathology reports.

"Autopsies are apparently too much for me," admitted Susan.

"You get used to it, like everything else," said the resident, stuffing more doughnut into his mouth.

"Possibly. Where would I look for the charts of the patients they are posting?"

The resident washed down the doughnut with coffee, swallowing with some effort.

"In that shelf marked 'Post.' When you finish with them, put them over there in the shelf marked 'Medical Records' because we're finished with them."

Turning to the rear wall, Susan faced a series of cubic shelves. One of the shelves was marked "Post." On it she found Ferrer's and Crawford's charts. Clearing one of the desks of debris, Susan sat down and took out her notebook. At the top of an empty page she wrote, "Crawford," on the top of another page she wrote, "Ferrer." Methodically she began to extract the charts as she had done with Nancy Greenly's.

**Tuesday
February 24
8:05 A.M.**

Susan had found it unbelievably difficult to emerge from the warmth and comfort of her bed when the radio alarm went off the following morning. The fact that it was a Linda Ronstadt selection was a big help in that it caused some degree of pleasant association in Susan's mind and instead of turning the radio off, she lay there and let the sounds and rhythm course through her. By the time the song was over Susan was fully awake, her mind beginning to race over the events of the previous day. The night before, at least until three A.M., had been passed in deep concentration with the large pile of journal articles, the books on anesthesiology, her own internal medicine book, and her clinical neurology text. She had amassed an enormous amount of notes, and her bibliography had increased to some one hundred articles that she planned to drag from the library stacks. The project had become more complex, more demanding, yet at the same time more fascinating, more absorbing. As a consequence Susan had become even more determined, and she realized that she was going to have to accomplish a great deal that day.

Shower, dressing, and breakfast were dispatched with commendable speed. During breakfast, she reread some of her notes, realizing that she would have to reread the last few articles she had read the night before.

The walk to the MBTA stop on Huntington Avenue proved to Susan that the weather had not changed and she cursed the fact that Boston had to be situated so far north. With luck she found a seat on the aging street car and was able to unfold a portion of her IBM printout. She wanted to check once more the number of cases which it suggested.

"Good to see you, Susan. Don't tell me you're going to go to lecture today?"

Susan looked up into the grinning face of George Niles, who was holding on to the bar above her head.

"I'd never miss lecture, George; you know that."

"Looks like you missed rounds. It's after nine."

"I could say the same to you." Susan's tone hovered between being friendly and combative.

"I was told in no uncertain terms that I had to be seen in Student Health to rule out a comminuted compound skull fracture from yesterday's gala event in the OR."

"You are OK, aren't you?" asked Susan with genuine sincerity and concern.

"Yeah, I'm fine. It's just hard to patch up my injured ego. That was the only thing that broke. But the clinic doc said that the ego had to heal itself."

Susan allowed herself to laugh. Niles joined. The car stopped at Northeastern University.

"Missing half of your first day at Surgery at the Memorial, then skipping rounds the next day, that's commendable, Miss Wheeler." George assumed a serious expression. "In no time at all you'll be able to run for medical student Phantom of the Year. If you keep it up you'll be able to challenge the record set by Phil Greer during second-year Pathology."

Susan didn't answer. She went back to her IBM sheets.

"What are you working on, anyway?" asked Niles, twisting himself in an attempt to view the printout right side up.

Susan looked up at Niles. "I'm working on my Nobel Prize acceptance speech. I'd tell you about it but you might miss lecture."

The car plunged down into the tunnel, beginning its transit under the city. Conversation became impossible. Susan resumed her check of the IBM printout sheet. She wanted to be damn sure of the numbers.

With its private offices Beard 8 resembled Beard 10. Susan walked down the corridor, stopping at room 810. The door had crisp black lettering across its aged but polished mahogany surface: "Department of Medicine, Professor J. P. Nelson, M.D., Ph.D."

Nelson was Chief of Medicine, Stark's counterpart, but associated with internal medicine and its subspecialties. Nelson was also a powerful figure in the medical center but not quite as influential as Stark, nor was he as dynamic, and as a fund raiser, he couldn't even compare. Nevertheless, it took a bit of fortitude on Susan's part to get up the nerve to approach this Olympian figure. With some hesitation she pushed open the mahogany door and faced a secretary with wire-rimmed glasses and a comfortable smile.

"My name is Susan Wheeler and I called a few minutes ago to see Dr. Nelson."

"Yes of course. You're one of our medical students?"

"That's right," said Susan, unsure of what "our" meant in that context.

"You're lucky, Miss Wheeler, to catch Dr. Nelson in. Plus I believe he remembers you from a class or something. Anyway, he'll be with you shortly."

Susan thanked her and retreated to one of the stiff black waiting-room chairs. She pulled out her notebook to scan more of her notes, but instead found herself viewing the room, the secretary, and the lifestyle it meant for Dr. Nelson. As far as the value system in medical school was concerned, such a position represented the final triumph of years of effort and even luck. It was just the kind of luck Susan felt could be behind her present quest. All someone needed was one lucky break and the doors would open.

The reverie was cut short by the door to the inner office being opened. Two doctors in long white coats came from within, continuing their conversation at the door. Susan could get bits and pieces and it seemed to be about an enormous amount of drugs that had been located in a locker in the surgical lounge. The younger of the two men was quite agitated and spoke in a whisper whose sound level was approximately equal to normal speech. The other gentleman had the portly bearing of a mature physician, replete with soft, knowing eyes, luxuriant graying hair, and a consoling smile. Susan knew it had to be Dr. Nelson. He seemed to be trying to console the other with reassuring words and a lingering pat on the shoulder. Once the other doctor had left, Dr. Nelson turned to Susan and beckoned for her to follow him.

Nelson's office was a tumble of reprinted journal articles, scattered books, and stacks of letters. It appeared as if a tornado had swept through the room several years previously with no subsequent effort at reconstruction. The furniture consisted of a large desk and an old cracked leather chair that squeaked as Dr. Nelson lowered his weight into it. There were two other smaller leather chairs facing the desk. Susan was motioned to take one of them as Dr. Nelson took one of his briars and opened a tobacco canister on the desk. Before filling the pipe he hit it on the palm of his left hand a few times. The few ashes that appeared were carelessly scattered on the floor.

"Ah yes, Miss Wheeler," began Dr. Nelson, scanning a note card on his desk. "I remember you well from physical diagnosis class. You were from Wellesley."

"Radcliffe."

"Radcliffe, of course." Dr. Nelson corrected his note card. "What can we do for you?"

"I'm not sure how to start. But I've become very interested in the problem of prolonged coma, and I have begun to look into it."

Dr. Nelson leaned back, the chair squeaking in agony. He placed the tips of his fingers together.

"That's fine, but coma is a big subject, and, more important, it is a symptom rather than a disease in itself. It is the cause of the coma that is important. What is the cause of the coma you have become interested in?"

"I don't know. In short, that's why I'm interested in it. I'm interested in the kind of coma that just seems to happen and no cause is found."

"Are you concerned with emergency room patients or in-hospital patients?" asked Dr. Nelson, whose voice changed slightly.

"Inpatients."

"Are you referring to the few cases that have occurred during surgery?"

"If you call seven few."

"Seven," said Dr. Nelson taking several long pulls from his pipe, "I believe is a rather high estimate."

"It's not an estimate. Six previous cases occurred during surgery. Presently there is another case upstairs, operated on yesterday, that appears to fit into the same category. In addition, there have been at least five cases on the medical floor occurring in patients admitted for some seemingly unrelated complaint."

"How did you get this information, Miss Wheeler?" asked Dr. Nelson with an altogether different tone of voice. The previous warmth was gone. His eyes regarded Susan without blinking. Susan was unaware of this change in apparent mood.

"I got the information from this computer printout right here." Susan leaned forward with the printout and handed it across the desk to Dr. Nelson. "The cases I've mentioned have been indicated with yellow ink. You'll see that there is no mistake. Besides, this represents only coma cases for the last year. I don't know what the incidence was before then, and I think it would be essential to get a year-by-year printout. In that way one could have a better idea if this problem is static or on a dynamic upswing. And perhaps even more important, or at least equally important, I have a feeling that a number of sudden deaths here at the Memorial could be ascribed to the same unknown category. I believe the computer could help on that as well. Anyway, it is for these reasons that I wanted to speak with you. I was wondering if you would support me on this endeavor. What I need is full clearance to use the computer and the opportunity to get the hospital charts on these patients. I came to you because I have an intuitive feeling that it represents some sort of unknown medical problem."

With her case presented, Susan allowed herself to sit back into the chair. She felt she had put the matter fairly and completely; if Dr. Nelson was going to be interested, he certainly had enough to go on to make up his mind.

Dr. Nelson did not speak right away. Instead he continued to regard Susan; then he studied the printout, taking short, quick puffs on his pipe.

"This is all very interesting information, young lady. Of course I have been aware of the problem. However, there are other implications in these statistics and I can assure you that this apparent high incidence is occurring because . . . well, frankly . . . we have been lucky over the last five or six years that we haven't had any such cases. Statistics have a way of catching up with you, though . . . and indeed that seems to be the case at present. As to your request, I'm afraid I'm not in a position to grant it. You undoubtedly understand one of the major impediments to our establishing our central computer information bank was the creation of adequate safeguards concerning the confidentiality of most of the information stored. It is impossible for me to give blanket authorization. In fact, this type of endeavor is really . . . what should I say . . . hmm . . . beyond . . . or above that which a medical student of your level is equipped to deal with. I think it would be in everyone's best interest, yours included, if you would limit your research interests to more scientific projects. I'm certain I could find room for you in our liver lab, if you were interested."

Susan was so accustomed to academic encouragement that she was totally caught off guard by Dr. Nelson's negative response to her investigation. Not only was he not interested, but he was obviously trying to talk Susan out of the project as well.

Susan hesitated, then stood up.

"Thank you very much for the offer. But I've just gotten so involved with this study that I think I'll follow it up for a while."

"Suit yourself, Miss Wheeler. But I'm sorry; I cannot help you."

"Thank you for your time," said Susan, reaching out for her computer printout.

"I'm afraid this information cannot be made available for you any longer," said Dr. Nelson interposing his hand between Susan's and the IBM sheet.

Susan kept her hand extended for a second of indecision. Once again Dr. Nelson had caught her off guard with an unexpected response. It seemed absurd that he would actually have the gall to confiscate material she already had.

Susan did not say another word and she avoided looking at Dr. Nelson. She got her things together and left. Dr. Nelson instantly picked up the telephone and placed a call.

In Dr. Harris's office there was an entire bookcase full of the latest books on anesthesiology, some still in prepublication bound galleys, sent for his endorsement. For Susan this was a boon, and her eyes scanned the titles for any books specifically on complications. She located one, and she wrote down the title and publisher. Next she looked for any general texts which she had not seen in the library. And her eyes registered another find: *Coma: Pathophysiological Basis of Clinical States.* Excitedly she withdrew the volume and thumbed through it, noticing the chapter headings. She wished she had had the book at the onset of her reading.

The door to the office opened and Susan looked up to face Dr. Robert Harris for the second time. Instantly she felt a certain sense of intimidation or scorn as Dr. Harris regarded her without the slightest sign of recognition or friendliness. It had not been Susan's idea to wait for him in his office; it had been the direct order of the secretary who had arranged the meeting for Susan. Now Susan felt an uneasiness, as if she were an interloper in Dr. Harris's private sanctum. The fact that she was holding one of his books made it that much worse.

"Be sure to put the volume back where you found it," said Harris as he turned to close the door, his speech slow and deliberate as if addressed to a child. He removed his long white coat and hung it on the hook on the back of the door. Without another word he retreated behind his desk to open a large ledger and make several notations. He acted as if Susan were not even there.

Susan closed the textbook and replaced it on the shelf. Then she returned to the director's chair in which she had started her wait for Dr. Harris thirty minutes before.

The only window was directly behind Harris, and its light, combining with the overhead fluorescent light, gave a strange shimmering quality to Harris's appearance. Susan had to squint against the glare coming directly at her.

The smooth tawny color of Harris's arms was a perfect setting for the gold digital watch on his left wrist. His forearms were massive, tapering to surprisingly narrow shafts. Despite the time of year and the temperature, Dr. Harris was dressed in a short-sleeved blue shirt. Several minutes went by before he finished with the ledger. After closing the cover he pressed a buzzer for his secretary to come in and take it. Only then did he turn and acknowledge Susan's existence.

"Miss Wheeler, I am certainly surprised to see you in my office." Dr. Harris slowly leaned back in his chair. He seemed to have some difficulty looking directly at Susan. Because of the background lighting Susan could not see the details of his face. His tone was cold. There was a silence.

"I would like to apologize," began Susan, "for my apparent impertinence yesterday in the recovery room. As you probably are aware, this is my first clinical rotation, and I'm unaccustomed to the hospital environment, particularly to the recovery room. On top of that there had been a strange coincidence. About two hours prior to our meeting I had spent some time with the very patient you were attending. I had started his I.V. prior to surgery."

Susan paused, hoping for some sign of acknowledgment from the faceless figure in front of her. There was none. There was no movement whatsoever. Susan continued.

"The fact of the matter was that my conversation with the patient had not remained on an entirely professional level; in fact, we had tentatively agreed to meet sometime on a social basis."

Susan paused again but silence continued from Dr. Harris.

"I'm offering this information more as an explanation than an excuse for my reaction in the recovery room. Needless to say, when I was confronted with the reality of the patient's condition, I became quite upset."

"So you reverted to the vestiges of your sex," said Harris condescendingly.

"Excuse me?" Susan had heard his comment, but by reflex she questioned whether she had heard him correctly.

"I said, so you reverted to the vestiges of your sex."

Susan felt a flush spread across her cheeks. "I'm not sure how to take that."

"Take it at face value."

There was an awkward pause. Susan fidgeted, then spoke. "If that is your opinion of being a woman, then I plead guilty; emotionalism under such circumstances is understandable from any human being. I admit the fact that I was not the archetypical professional at the first meeting with the patient, but I think that if the roles had been reversed, I being the patient and the patient being the doctor, it probably would have come out the same. I hardly think that susceptibility to human responses is a frailty reserved for female medical students, especially when I have to put up with the patronizing attitudes of my male counterparts with the female nurses. But I did not come here to discuss such matters. I came here to apologize for impertinence to you and that is all. I'm not apologizing for being a woman."

Susan paused again, expecting some sort of reply. None was forthcoming. Susan felt a definite feeling of irritation spread through her.

"If my being a woman bothers you, then that's your problem," said Susan with emphasis.

"You're being impertinent again, my dear," said Harris.

Susan stood up. Gazing down, she looked at Harris's face, his narrowed eyes, his full cheeks and broad chin. Light played through the edge of his hair, making it appear like silver filigree.

"I can see this is getting us nowhere. I'm sorry I came. Goodbye, Dr. Harris."

Susan turned and opened the door to the corridor.

"Why did you come?" said Harris after her.

With her hand on the door, Susan looked out into the corridor and considered Harris's question. Obviously debating with herself whether to leave or not, she finally turned and faced the Chief of Anesthesiology again.

"I thought I'd apologize so that we could let bygones be bygones. I had the irrational hope that you might be willing to lend me some assistance."

"In what regard?" said Harris, his voice relaxing its aloofness by a degree.

Susan hesitated again, debating, then let the door shut. She walked up to the chair she had been sitting in but she did not sit down. She eyed Harris and thought that she had nothing to lose and should say what she had originally come to say despite his coldness.

"Since you said that there have been six cases of prolonged coma following anesthesia during the last year, I decided to look into the problem as a potential subject for my third-year paper. Well, I found out that you were absolutely correct. There have been six cases following anesthesia during the last year. But there also have been five cases of sudden unexplained coma occurring in patients on the medical floors during the past year. Yesterday there were two deaths for apparent respiratory arrest. These patients gave no history to suggest that such an event might take place. They were in the hospital for essentially peripheral problems; one had a minor foot operation followed by phlebitis, the other had Bell's palsy. Both were essentially well individuals, except one of them had glaucoma. There was no explanation for their respiratory arrest and I have a feeling that they are possibly related to the other coma cases. In other words, I think I have twelve cases representing gradations of the same problem. And if Berman turns out to be in the same boat as the others, then there are thirteen people suffering from some unexplained phenomenon. Perhaps worst of all, the incidence seems to be on the upswing, especially for the cases occurring during anesthesia. The interval between cases seems to be getting shorter and shorter. Anyway, I have decided to try to look into the problem. In order for me to continue my investigation I need some help from someone like yourself. I need authorization to search the data bank and see how many cases the computer could find if it's asked directly. Also I need the charts of the previous victims."

Harris leaned forward and slowly placed his arms on his desk.

"So the Medical Department has had some trouble too," he murmured. "Jerry Nelson didn't mention that."

Looking up at Susan, he spoke louder.

"Miss Wheeler, you are dabbling in troubled waters. It's refreshing to hear someone, fresh from the basic science years of medical school, interested in clinical research. But this is not the proper subject for you. There are many reasons for my saying this. First of all, the problem of coma is far more complex than might be apparent to you. It is a wastepaper-basket term, a mere description. And for someone to immediately assume all cases of coma are related simply because the causative agent is not precisely known is intellectually absurd. Miss Wheeler, I advise you to stick to something more specific, less speculative, for your so-called third year paper. As far as helping you is concerned, I must admit I do not have the time. And let me admit something else that might be rather apparent to you. I don't try to hide it. I'm not keen on women in medicine."

Harris pointed his finger at Susan and aimed it across, almost as if it were a gun.

"They treat it like a game, something to do for now . . . something chic . . . later, who knows. It's a fad. And on top of that, they are invariably, impossibly emotional and . . ."

"Dr. Harris, cut the bullshit," interrupted Susan, lifting up the back of the chair and letting it fall a few inches. She was furious. "I didn't come here to listen to this type of nonsense. In fact it's people like you who keep medicine in the old rut, unable to respond to the challenge of relevancy and change."

Harris pounded the top of the desk with his open hand causing a few papers and pencils to flee for safety. Almost in one step he came from behind his desk with a speed that caught Susan off guard. His movement brought his face only inches from Susan's. She froze before the unexpected fury she had unleashed.

"Miss Wheeler, you do not know your place here," hissed Harris, holding himself in check with great difficulty. "You are not to be the Messiah who is going to miraculously deliver us from a problem which has already been under the scrutiny of the best minds in this hospital. In fact, I see you as a very destructive influence and I can promise you this: you'll be out of this hospital in twenty-four hours. Now get out of my office."

Susan backed up, afraid to expose her unguarded back

to this man who seemed about to explode with hatred. She opened the door and ran down the corridor, feeling the tears well up from her mixture of fear and anger.

Behind her, Harris kicked the door shut and snatched the phone off the hook. He told his secretary to get him the director of the hospital without delay.

Tuesday
February 24
11:00 A.M.

Susan slowed to a deliberate walk, avoiding the questioning expressions of the people using the corridor. Her emotions, she was afraid, could be read from her face like an open book. Usually when she cried or was about to cry, her cheeks and eyelids turned bright crimson. Although she knew she wasn't going to cry now, the proper neural connections had been made. If someone she knew stopped her and said something innocuous, like "What's the matter, Susan?" she probably would have cried. So Susan wanted to be alone for a few moments. As it was, she was more angry and frustrated than anything else as the fear generated by her encounter with Harris evaporated. Fear seemed so out of place in the context of a meeting with a professional superior that she wondered if she was becoming delusional. Had she really crossed Harris to the extent that he had had to keep himself in check to avoid some sort of physical encounter? Was he just about to strike her, as she had feared, when he came bounding out from behind his desk? The idea seemed ludicrous and it was difficult for her to believe that the situation had been so precipitous. She knew that she could never make someone else believe what she had felt. It reminded her of the situation with Captain Queeg in *The Caine Mutiny*.

The stairwell was the only haven she could think of, and she pushed through the metal door. It closed behind her rapidly, cutting off the raw fluorescent lights and the voices. The single bare incandescent bulb above her had a warmer glow and the stairway offered a soothing silence.

Susan was still clutching her notebook and a ballpoint pen. Gritting her teeth, and swearing loudly enough to hear an echo, she threw the notebook and the pen down the course of stairs to the landing below. The notebook bounced on the edge of a stair, then fell flat, cover down, onto the floor. It skidded across the landing and struck the wall, coming to a rest unhurt and open. The pen flipped over the edge of the stairs and a few telltale sounds suggested that it had descended to the bowels of the hospital.

Uninviting as it was, Susan sat down on the top stair, her feet on the very next step, bringing her knees up at acute angles. Her elbows rested on the tops of her knees. She closed her eyes tightly. So much of her experience in medicine with relationships had been reemphasized in the short time she had been at the Memorial. Professional superiors, instructors to professors, reacted to her in a manner that unpredictably varied from warm acceptance to overt hostility. Usually the hostility was more passive-aggressive than Harris's had been; Nelson's reaction was more typical. Nelson had been friendly at first, then later had slipped into an obstructive stance. Susan felt an old familiar feeling, a feeling which had developed ever since she had chosen medicine as a career: it was a paradoxical loneliness. Although constantly surrounded by people who reacted to her, she felt apart. The day and a half at the Memorial had not been an auspicious beginning for her clinical years. Even more than during her first days at medical school, she felt that she was entering a male club; she was an outsider forced to adapt, to compromise.

Susan opened her eyes and looked down at her notebook sprawled on the landing below. Throwing the book had given some vent to her frustrations, and she felt a degree more relaxed. Control was returning. At the same time the childish aspect of the gesture surprised her. It was not like her to do such a thing. Perhaps Nelson and Harris were, in the final analysis, right. Perhaps being a medical student so early in training, she was not the right person to investigate such a serious clinical problem. And perhaps her emotionalism was a built-in handicap. Would a male have responded in the same way to Harris's reaction? Was she more emotional than her male counterparts? Susan thought about Bellows and his cool detached manner, how he could concentrate on the sodium ions while confronting a tragedy. Susan had found fault with his behavior the day before, but now, daydreaming in the stairwell, she was no longer so sure. She wondered if she could achieve that type of detachment if it were necessary.

A door opening somewhere far above brought Susan to her feet. There were some hushed and hurried footsteps on the metal stairs, then the sound of another door, then silence returned. The crude cement walls of the stairwell combined with the curious longitudinal rust-colored stains enhanced Susan's sense of isolation. In slow motion she descended to where her notebook lay. By chance it had opened to the page copied from Nancy Greenly's chart. Reaching for the book, Susan read her own handwriting. "Age 23, Caucasian, previous medical history negative except for mononucleosis at age 18." Quickly Susan's mind conjured up the image of Nancy Greenly, her ghostly pallor, lying in the ICU. "Age twenty-three," Susan said aloud. In a rush she reexperienced the intensity of her feelings of transference. Susan felt a rekindling of her commitment to investigating the coma problem to the limit of her abilities despite Harris, despite Nelson. Without questioning why, she felt a strong urge to find Bellows. Within a single day her feeling toward Bellows had taken a one-hundred-and-eighty-degree turn.

"Susan, for Christ's sake, haven't you had enough yet?" With his elbows on the table, Bellows placed his palms against his face so that his fingers could lightly massage his closed eyes. His hands rotated, bringing his fingers below his ears. With his face cradled in his hands, he looked at Susan sitting across from him in the hospital coffee shop. The place had a relatively clean appearance with indeterminate modern furnishings. It was primarily meant for visitors to the hospital, although the staff frequented it on occasion. The prices were higher than the cafeteria's but the quality was equivalently better. At eleven-thirty it was crowded but Susan had found a table in the corner and had paged Bellows. She was pleased when he agreed to see her immediately.

"Susan," continued Bellows after a pause, "you've got to give up this self-destructive crusade. I mean it's absolutely sure suicide. Susan, there's one thing about medicine, you've got to flow with the river or you'll drown. I've learned that. God, whatever could have possessed you to go to Harris, especially after that little episode yesterday?"

Susan sipped her coffee in silence, keeping her eyes on Bellows. She wanted him to talk because it sounded good; he seemed to care. But also she wanted him to get involved, if that were at all possible. Bellows shook his head as he took a drink of his coffee.

"Harris is powerful, but he's not omnipotent around here," added Bellows. "Stark can reverse anything Harris does if he has reason to do so. Stark has raised most of the money for construction around here, millions. So people listen to what he says. So why not give him a reason; why not pretend to be a normal medical student for a few days? Christ, I need it myself. Guess who was on rounds this morning to welcome you medical students? Stark. And the first thing he wanted to know was why there were only three students out of five. Well I told him that, foolishly enough, I had taken you all in to see a case on the first day, and one of you had fainted and smashed his head on the floor. You can guess how that went over. And then I couldn't think of anything appropriate to say about you. So I said you were doing a literature search on coma following anesthesia. I decided that since I couldn't think of a good lie I might as well tell the truth. Well he immediately assumed that it had been my idea to put you on the project. I cannot repeat what he said to me in response. It should be enough for me to say that I need you to behave like a normal medical student. I've covered for you to the extent that I'm already overdrawn."

Susan felt an urge to touch Bellows, kind of a reassuring people-to-people hug. But she didn't; instead she played with her coffee spoon with her head down. Then she looked at Bellows.

"I'm really sorry if I've caused you some difficulties, Mark, really I am. Needless to say, it was unintentional. I'm the first to admit this thing has gotten out of hand so rapidly that it's uncanny. I started because of an emotional crisis of sorts.

Nancy Greenly is the same age as I, and I've had some occasional irregularities with my periods, probably just like Nancy Greenly. I cannot help but feel some . . . some kinship with her. And then Berman . . . what a Goddamned coincidence. By the way, did Berman have an EEG?"

"Yeah, it was completely flat. The brain is gone."

Susan searched Bellows's face for some response, some sign of emotion. Bellows lifted the coffee cup to his lips and took a sip.

"The brain is gone?"

"Gone."

Susan bit her lower lip and looked down into her coffee cup. A small amount of oil opalesced on the surface in colorful swirls. Somehow she had expected the news, but it still cut into her and she fought with her mind, suppressing emotion as best she could.

"Are you OK?" asked Bellows, reaching across and gently lifting her chin with his hands.

"Don't say anything for a second," said Susan, not daring to look at him. The last thing she wanted to do was cry and if Bellows persisted, it would happen. Bellows cooperated and returned to his coffee while keeping his eyes on Susan.

After a few moments Susan looked up; her eyelids were slightly reddened.

"Anyway," continued Susan, avoiding eye contact with Bellows, "I started with an emotional sort of commitment, but that quickly mixed with intellectual commitment. I really thought I had stumbled onto something . . . a new disease or a new complication of anesthesia or a new syndrome . . . something, I don't know what. But then there was another change. The problem loomed bigger than I had imagined initially. They've had coma cases on the medical floors as well as in surgery. On top of that, there were those deaths you told me about. I know you think it's crazy, but I think they are related, and the pathologist intimated they have had a number of such cases. My intuition tells me there is something else in all this, something . . . I don't know how to explain it . . . call it supernatural or call it sinister . . ."

"Ah, now paranoia," said Bellows, nodding his head in mock understanding.

"I can't help it, Mark. There was something very strange

about the reaction of Nelson and Harris. You have to admit that Harris's reaction was totally inappropriate."

Bellows tapped his forehead in succession with the heel of his hand. "Susan, you've been staying up watching old horror movies. Admit it, Susan . . . admit it or I'll think you're having a psychotic break. This is absurd. What do you suspect, some sort of sinister inversion layer spreading evil forces, or is it a crazed killer who hates people with minor ailments? Susan, if you hypothesize so extravagantly and with such creativity, then come up with some ideas of motive. I mean, a demented killer was OK for Hollywood and George C. Scott in *Hospital* just to create an artificial mystery . . . but it's a little too farfetched for reality. I admit Harris's performance sounds a bit weird, there's no doubt about that. But at the same time I think I could come up with some reasonable explanation for his unreasonable behavior."

"Try."

"OK, I'm sure Harris is already completely uptight about this problem of coma. After all, it's his department which essentially has to shoulder the responsibility. And here comes a young medical student to drive in the painful spikes a little more. I think it's understandable for an individual to overreact under that kind of stress."

"Harris did a little more than overreact. This nut came from behind his desk with the intent of knocking me around the room."

"Maybe you turned him on."

"What?"

"On top of everything else maybe he was reacting to you sexually."

"Come on, Mark."

"I'm serious."

"Mark, this guy's a doctor, a professor, a chief of a department."

"That does not rule out sexuality."

"Now you're the one being absurd."

"A lot of doctors spend so much time with the nuts and bolts of their profession that they fail to ever really adequately resolve the usual social crises of life. Socially speaking, doctors are not very accomplished, to say the least."

"Are you speaking for yourself?"

"Possibly. Susan, you have to realize you are a very seductive girl."

"Fuck you."

Bellows looked at Susan, stunned. Then he glanced around to see if anyone was listening to their conversation. He had not forgotten they were in the coffee shop. He took a sip of coffee and then regarded Susan for several minutes. She returned his stare.

"Why did you say that?" said Bellows with a lowered voice.

"Because you deserved it. I get a little tired of that kind of stereotyping. When you say I'm seductive you imply to me that I am actively trying to seduce. Believe me, I am not. If medicine has done anything to me, it certainly has cut into my image of myself as conventionally female."

"All right, maybe it was a bad word. I didn't mean to imply it was your fault. You're an attractive girl . . ."

"Well there's a helluva difference between saying someone's attractive and saying someone's seductive."

"OK, I meant attractive. Sexually attractive. And there are people who may find that hard to deal with. Anyway, Susan, I didn't mean to get into an argument. Besides, I've got to go. I've got a case in fifteen minutes. If you want, we can talk about it tonight over dinner. That is, if you still want to have dinner?" Bellows started to get up, taking his tray.

"Sure, dinner's fine."

"Meanwhile, couldn't you try to be normal for a little while?"

"Well, I have one more stone to turn over."

"What's that?"

"Stark. If he doesn't help me, I'll have to give up. Without some support I'm doomed to failure, unless of course you want to get the computer information for me."

Bellows let his tray drop back onto the table. "Susan, don't ask me to do anything like that, because I can't. As for Stark, Susan, you're crazy. He'll eat you alive. Harris is a jewel in comparison to Stark."

"That's a risk I have to take. It's probably safer than undergoing minor surgery here at the Memorial."

"That's not fair."

"Fair? What a choice word. Why don't you ask Berman if he thinks it's fair?"

"I can't."

"You can't?" Susan paused, waiting for Bellows to explain himself. Susan did not want to think of the worst but it came to her automatically. Bellows started toward the tray rack without explaining himself.

"He's still alive, isn't he?" asked Susan with a tingle of desperation in her voice. She got up and walked behind Bellows.

"If you call that heart beating being alive, he's alive."

"Is he in the recovery room?"

"No."

"The ICU?"

"No."

"OK, I give up, where is he?"

Bellows and Susan put their trays into the rack and walked from the coffee shop. They were immediately engulfed by the mob in the hall and forced to quicken their steps.

"He was transferred to the Jefferson Institute in South Boston."

"What the hell is the Jefferson Institute?"

"It's an intensive care facility built as part of the area's Health Maintenance Organization design. Supposedly it's been designed to curtail costs by applying economics of scale in relation to intensive care. It's privately run but the government financed construction. The concept and plans came out of the Harvard-MIT health practices report."

"I've never even heard about it. Have you visited it?"

"No, but I'd like to. I saw it from the outside once. It's very modern . . . massive and rectilinear. The thing that caught my eye was that there were no windows on the first floor. God only knows why that caught my eye." Bellows shook his head.

Susan smiled.

"There's a tour organized for the medical community," continued Bellows, "to visit the place on the second Tuesday of each month. Those that have gone have been really impressed. Apparently the program is a big success. All chronic-care ICU patients who are comatose or nearly so can be admitted. The idea is to keep the ICU beds in the acute-care hospitals available for acute cases. I think it's a good idea."

"But Berman just became comatose. Why would they transfer him so quickly?"

"The time factor is less important than stability. Obviously he's going to be a long-term-care problem and I guess he was very stable, not like our friend Greenly. God, she's been a pain in the ass. Just about every complication known, she's had it."

Susan thought about emotional detachment. It was difficult for her to understand how Bellows could be so out of touch emotionally with the problem Nancy Greenly represented.

"If she were stable," continued Bellows, "even threatened stability, I'd transfer her to the Jefferson in a flash. Her case demands an inordinate amount of time with thin rewards. Actually, I have nothing to gain by her. If I keep her alive until the services switch, then at least I've suffered no professional harm. It's like all those Presidents keeping Vietnam alive. They couldn't win, but they didn't want to lose either. They had nothing to gain but a lot to lose."

They reached the main elevators and Bellows made sure one of the silently waiting crowd had pushed the "up" button.

"Where was I?" Bellows scratched his head, obviously preoccupied.

"You were talking about Berman and the ICU."

"Oh, yeah. Well, I guess he was stable." Bellows looked at his watch, then eyed the closed doors with hatred. "Goddamn elevators.

"Susan, I'm not one to give advice usually, but I can't help myself. See Stark if you must, but remember I've gone out on a limb for you, so act accordingly. Then after you see Stark, give this crusade up. You'll ruin your career before you begin."

"Are you worried about my career or your own?"

"Both, I guess," said Bellows standing aside for the disembarking elevator passengers.

"At least you're honest."

Bellows squeezed into the elevator and waved to Susan, saying something about seven-thirty. Susan presumed he meant their dinner date. At that moment her watch said eleven forty-five.

Bellows looked up at the floor indicator above the door. He
had to cock his head way back, as he was almost directly
under it. He knew that he had to hustle in order to be on
time for his case, a hemorrhoid operation on a sixty-two-
year-old man. It wasn't his idea of a fascinating case but he
loved to operate. Once he got going and felt the strange
sense of responsibility which the knife afforded, he didn't
really care where he was working, stomach or hand, mouth
or asshole.

Bellows thought about seeing Susan that night, and he felt
a sense of pleasurable anticipation. Everything would be fresh
and unspoiled. Their conversation could range over any one
of a thousand topics. And physically? Bellows had no idea
what to expect. In fact he wondered how he would be able
to bridge the colleaguelike rapport they had already established. Within himself he sensed a very positive physical
reaction toward Susan but it began to trouble him. In a lot
of ways, sex meant aggression to Bellows, and he didn't feel
any aggression toward Susan, not yet.

A smile crept over his face as he imagined himself kissing
Susan impulsively. It made him remember those awkward
adolescent moments in his early youth when he would continue some banal conversation with his pimpled date right
up to her doorstep. Then without warning he would kiss the
girl, hard and sloppy. Then he'd step back to see what happened, hoping for acceptance but fearing rejection. It had
never ceased to amaze him when he found acceptance, be-

cause in many ways he didn't know why he was kissing the girl in the first place.

The concept of seeing Susan socially reminded Bellows of those early years of dating because he felt an inner urge for physical contact yet did not expect it. Susan was obviously palpable and luscious, yet she was going to be a doctor, as he was. Hence she would have little appreciation for the trump card Bellows always felt in a social situation—most everyone was impressed when he said he was a doctor, a surgeon! It didn't matter that Bellows himself knew that being a doctor did not assure any special attributes, contrary to popular mythology. In fact, if he used many of the attending surgeons at the Memorial as examples, the effect of admitting such an association should have been a handicap. But what really bothered Bellows was the knowledge that a penis would hold little fascination for Susan; in all probability she had dissected one.

Bellows did not reduce his own sexual urges and fantasies to anatomical and physiological realities, but what about Susan? She looked so normal with her smile, her soft skin, the hint of her breast gently rising with her breathing. But she had studied the parasympathetic reflexes, and the endocrine alterations that make sex possible, even enjoyable. Maybe she had studied too much, too much of the wrong thing. Maybe even if the occasion was auspicious, Bellows would find his penis limp, impotent. The thought made Bellows doubtful about seeing Susan. After all, once away from the hospital, Bellows wanted to escape, and mindless sex was a superb method. With Susan, if it happened at all, it wasn't going to be mindless. It couldn't be. Finally there was the sticky question about the wisdom of dating a student currently under his supervision on the surgery rotation. Bellows was undoubtedly going to be called upon to evaluate Susan's performance as a student. Dating her represented a ridiculous conflict of interest.

The elevator door opened on the OR floor and Bellows quickly crossed to the main OR desk. The clerk was preparing the OR schedule of the following day.

"What room is my case in? It's a Mr. Barron, a hemorrhoid."

The clerk looked up to see who it was, then down at the current schedule.

"You're Dr. Bellows?"

"None other."

"Well, you have been taken off that case."

"Taken off? By whom?" Bellows was perplexed.

"By Dr. Chandler, and he left word for you to meet him in his office when you appeared."

To be taken off one of his own cases was very strange for Bellows. Certainly it was within George Chandler's prerogative since he was the chief resident. But it was highly irregular. Occasionally Bellows had been removed from a scrub on which he was to assist, usually to help on some other case, and usually for purely logistic reasons. But to be removed from one of his own cases where the patient had been assigned to Beard 5 was a totally new experience.

Bellows thanked the OR clerk without bothering to hide his surprise and irritation. He turned and headed for George Chandler's office.

The chief resident's office was a windowless cubicle on 2. From this tiny area came the tactical edicts that ran the surgical department from day to day. Chandler was in charge of all the schedules for all the residents, including the on-call and weekend duty assignments. Chandler was also in charge of the operating room schedule, assigning the staff and clinic cases as well as the assists for the attending surgeons who asked for them.

Bellows knocked on the closed door, entering after hearing a muffled "Come in." George Chandler was sitting at his desk, which nearly filled the tiny room. The desk faced the door, and Chandler had to squeeze past to gain access to the seat. Behind him was a file cabinet. In front of the desk was a single wooden chair. The room was bare; only a bulletin board adorned the walls. Blank but neat, the room was somewhat like Chandler himself.

The chief resident had successfully risen up the competitive pyramidal power structure of the lower world of students and residents. Now he was the liaison between the upper world, the full-fledged surgeons certified by specialty boards, and the lower world. As such he was a member of neither class. This fact was the source of his power as well as his weakness and isolation. The years of competition had taken their inexorable toll. Chandler was still young by most standards: thirty-three years old. He was not tall: about five eight. His hair was half-heartedly combed in some sort of modern Caesar look. His face had a gentle pudginess that belied his easily aroused temper. In many ways Chandler represented the young boy who has been bullied too much.

Bellows took the wooden chair opposite Chandler. At first no words were spoken. Chandler regarded a pencil he had in his fingers. His elbows were resting on the arms of his chair. He had rocked back from what he had been working on when Bellows knocked.

"Sorry about taking you off your case, Mark," said Chandler without looking up.

"I can manage without another hemorrhoid," said Bellows, maintaining a neutral tone.

There was another pause. Chandler tipped his chair forward to the level position and looked directly at Bellows. Bellows thought that he'd be a perfect individual to play Napoleon in a play.

"Mark, I'm going to assume you're serious about surgery, surgery here at the Memorial, to be exact."

"I think that's a fair assumption."

"Your record has been reasonable. In fact I've heard your name on several occasions in relation to possibly being considered for the chief residency. That leads me to one of the reasons I wanted to talk with you. Harris gave me a call not too long ago and he was completely strung out. I wasn't even sure what he was talking about for a few minutes. Apparently one of your students has been nosing around about these coma cases, and it's got Harris bullshit. Now, I have no idea what's going on, but he thinks that you might be behind getting the student interested and helping him."

"It's a her."

"Him, her, I don't give a damn."

"Well, it might be significant. She happens to be a very well put-together specimen. As for my role in the matter, it's a big fat zero! If anything, I have constantly tried to talk her out of the whole affair."

"I'm not about to argue with you, Mark. All I wanted to do is warn you of the situation. I'd hate to have you gamble your chances on the chief residency because of some student's activities."

Mark looked at Chandler and wondered what Chandler

would say if he told Chandler that he was going to see Susan that night on a social basis.

"I have no idea if Harris has said anything to Stark about all this, Mark, and I can assure you that I won't unless it gets to the point where I have to cover my own tracks. But let me emphasize that Harris was livid, so you'd better tone your student down and tell him . . ."

"Her!"

"OK, tell her to find something else to get interested in. After all there must be ten people who are working on the problem already. In fact most of Harris's department has been doing nothing else since the present run of anesthetic coma catastrophes."

"I'll try to tell her again, but it's not as easy as it may sound. This girl has a mind of her own, with a rather fertile imagination." Bellows wondered why he chose that way to describe Susan's imagination. "She's gotten into this thing because the first two patients she came in contact with are victims of the problem."

"Anyway, let's just say you have been warned. What she does is going to reflect on you, especially if you aid her in any way at all. But that was only one of the reasons I wanted to talk with you. There is another problem, more serious, to be sure. Tell me, Mark, what is your locker number up in the OR?"

"Eight."

"What about number 338?"

"That was my temporary locker. I used it for about one week before number eight became available."

"Why didn't you stay with 338?"

"I guess it actually belonged to someone else, and I got to use it until I could get one of my own."

"Do you know the combination of 338?"

"Maybe, if I thought long enough. Why do you ask?"

"Because of a strange finding by Dr. Cowley. He claims that 338 opened by magic when he was changing his clothes and the whole Goddamn thing was filled with drugs. We checked it out and he was right. Every kind of drug that you could imagine and a few more, including narcotics. The locker list I have has you down for 338, not eight."

"Who's down for eight?"

"Dr. Eastman."

"He hasn't done a case in years."

"Exactly. Tell me, Mark, who gave you number eight? Walters?"

"Yup. Walters first told me to use 338, and then he gave me number eight."

"OK, don't say anything to anybody about this, least of all to Walters. Finding a hoard of drugs like this is a pretty serious business, considering all the rigmarole you have to go through to get a narcotic in the first place. Because of my locker list, you will probably be contacted by the hospital administration. For obvious reasons they are not excited about letting this information out, especially with the recertification deal coming up. So keep it under your hat. And for God's sake, get your student interested in something else besides anesthesia complications."

Bellows emerged from Chandler's cubicle with a strange feeling. He wasn't surprised about hearing that he was being associated with Susan's activities. He was already afraid of that. But the news about the drugs found in a locker to which he was assigned, that was a different story. His mind conjured up an image of Walters oozing around the OR area. He questioned why anyone would hoard drugs like that. Then there was the suggestion of association. Susan had used the words *supernatural* and *sinister*. Bellows wondered exactly what kind of drugs were stored in locker 338. He also wondered if he should tell Susan about the discovery.

Tuesday
February 24
2:30 P.M.

Susan allowed her eyes to wander around the Chief of Surgery's office. It was spacious and exquisitely decorated. Large

163

windows occupying most of two walls afforded a splendid view of Charlestown in one direction and a corner of Boston and the North End in the other. The Mystic River bridge was partially concealed by gray snow clouds. The wind had shifted from the sea and was now blowing in from the northwest with arctic air.

Stark's teak desk, with its white marble top, was situated cater-corner in the northwest section of the office. The wall behind and to the right of the desk was mirrored from floor to ceiling. The fourth wall contained the door from the reception room and carefully constructed, recessed bookshelves. A section of the shelves was hinged; partly ajar, it revealed gleaming glasses, bottles, and a small refrigerator.

In the southeast corner, where the huge expanse of windows met the bookshelves, there was a low, glass-topped table surrounded by molded fiberglass chairs. Their leather cushions were made of bright colors ranging through the oranges and greens.

Stark himself was seated behind his massive desk. His image was recreated a hundred times in the mirror to the right thanks to the reflection from the tinted window glass to his left. The Chief of Surgery had his feet propped up on the corner of his desk so that daylight fell over his shoulder onto the paper he was reading.

He was impeccably dressed in a beige suit tailored to fit close to his lean body, accented by an orange silk scarf in his left breast pocket. His graying hair was moderately long and brushed back from his high forehead, just covering the tops of his ears. His face was aristocratic, with sharp features and a thin nose. He wore executive half-glasses framed in delicate reddish tortoiseshell. His green eyes rapidly scanned back and forth across the sheet of paper in his hand.

Susan would have been greatly intimidated by a combination of the impressive surroundings and Stark's awe-inspiring reputation as a surgical genius had it not been for his initial smile and his seemingly incongruous posture. The fact that he had his feet up on the corner of the desk made Susan feel more comfortable, as if Stark really didn't take his power position within the hospital too seriously. Susan correctly surmised that his skill as a surgeon and his ability as a medical administrator-businessman made it possible for

Stark to ignore conventional executive posturing. Stark finished reading the paper and looked up at Susan sitting in front of him.

"That, young lady, is very interesting. Obviously I am totally aware of the surgical cases, but I had no idea a similar problem was occurring on the medical floors. Whether they are indeed related is uncertain but I must give you credit for coming up with the idea that they may be related. And these two recent respiratory arrests and deaths; associating them is . . . well, both far-out and brilliant at the same time. It gives food for thought. You have related them because you feel that depression of respiration is the common ground for all the cases. My first reaction to that—now, this is just my first reaction—is that it does not explain the anesthesia cases because in that circumstance, the respiratory pattern is being artificially maintained. You suggest some previous encephalitis or brain infection making people more susceptible to complications during anesthesia . . . let me see."

Stark swung his feet from his desk and turned toward the window. Unconsciously he took his reading glasses from his nose and lightly chewed one of the earpieces. His eyes narrowed in concentration.

"Parkinsonism has now been related to previous unsuspected viral insult, so I suppose your theory is possible. But how could it be proved?"

Stark rotated around, facing Susan.

"And you must be assured that we investigated the anesthesia complication cases ad nauseam. Everything—and I mean everything—was studied with a fine-tooth comb by a host of people, anesthesiologists, epidemiologists, internists, surgeons . . . everybody we could think of. Except, of course, a medical student."

Stark smiled warmly and Susan found herself responding to the man's renowned charisma.

"I believe," said Susan, her confidence rallying, "the study should start with the central computer bank. The computer information I obtained was only for the past year and called up by an indirect method. I have no idea what data would emerge if the computer was asked directly for all cases over, say, the last five years of respiratory depression, coma, and unexplained death.

"Then with a complete list of the potentially related cases,

165

the charts would have to be painstakingly reviewed to try to elicit any common denominators. The families of the involved patients would have to be interviewed to obtain the best possible record of previous viral illness and patterns of illnesses. The other task would be to obtain serum from all existing cases for antibody screens."

Susan watched Stark's face, intently preparing herself for an untoward response like that she had experienced with Nelson and then more dramatically with Harris. In contrast, Stark maintained an even expression, obviously in thought over Susan's suggestions. It was apparent that he had an open, innovative mind. Finally he spoke.

"Shotgun-style antibody screening is not very productive; it is time-consuming and it is horribly expensive."

"Counter-immunoelectrophoresis techniques have relieved some of these disadvantages," offered Susan, encouraged by Stark's response.

"Perhaps, but it still would represent an enormous outlay of capital with a very low probability of positive results. I'd have to have some specific evidence before I could justify that type of resource commitment. But maybe you should suggest this to Dr. Nelson, down in Medicine. Immunology is his special field."

"I don't think Dr. Nelson would be interested," said Susan.

"Why is that?"

"I haven't the faintest idea. To tell the truth, I already spoke with Dr. Nelson. So I already know he's not interested. And he wasn't the only one. I mentioned my ideas to another department head and I thought I was going to get swatted like some naughty child that needed chastising. Trying to incorporate that episode into the whole picture, I get a feeling that something else could be operating here."

"And what is that?" asked Stark, glancing over the figures Susan had provided.

"Well, I don't know what word to use . . . foul play . . . or something sinister."

Susan stopped talking quite suddenly, expecting either laughter or anger. But Stark merely rotated in his chair, looking out over the city again.

"Foul play. You do have an imagination, Dr. Wheeler, no doubt about that."

Stark turned back toward the room, rising up and walking around his desk.

"Foul play," he repeated. "I must admit I'd never even considered that." Stark had been briefed only that morning about Cowley's discovery of the drugs in locker 338; that information had disturbed him. He leaned against his desk and looked down at Susan.

"If you think about foul play, motive becomes of paramount importance. And there just isn't any motive for such a series of heartbreaking episodes. They are too dissimilar. And coma? You'd have to implicate some very clever psychopath operating on a premise that's beyond rationality. But the biggest problem with the idea of foul play is that it would be impossible in the OR. There are too many people involved who are watching the patient too closely.

"Certainly investigative activities should be carried out with an open mind, but I don't think foul play is possible in this instance. But, I must admit, I had not thought of it."

"Actually," said Susan, "I hadn't planned on suggesting foul play to you, but I'm glad that I did so that I can forget it. But back to the problem itself. If antibody screening is too expensive, the chart review and interviews would be comparatively cheap. I could take that on myself, except I'd need a little help from you."

"What kind of help?"

"First of all, I'd need to have authorization to use the computer. That's number one. Secondly, I'd need authorization to get the charts. Thirdly, I may have run into a problem downstairs."

"What kind of a problem?"

"Dr. Harris. He's the one who blew his cool. I think he intends to have my surgical rotation here at the Memorial cut short. It seems that he is not fond of women in medicine, and perhaps I have served to underline that prejudice."

"Dr. Harris can be difficult to get along with. He's an emotional type. But at the same time he's probably the best mind in anesthesiology in the country. So don't damn him until you see his other side. I believe he has specific personal reasons for his attitude toward women in medicine. It's not admirable, perhaps, but it is potentially understandable. Anyway, I'll see what I can do for you. At the same time I must tell you that you have picked a very touchy subject to become involved in. You have undoubtedly considered the malpractice implication, the potential bad publicity for the hospital and even the Boston medical community. Tread lightly, young lady, if you choose to tread at all. You'll make no friends on the course you are embarking on, and it's my opinion you should drop the whole affair. If you choose to go on, I'll try to help you, although I can guarantee nothing. If you do turn up any information, I will be happy to offer an opinion. Obviously the more information you have, the easier it will be for me to get you what you need."

Stark moved toward the door from his office, opening it.

"Give me a call later this afternoon and I'll let you know if I've had any luck with your requests."

"Thank you for your time, Dr. Stark." Susan hesitated in the doorway, looking at Stark. "It is reassuring that you have not lived up to your reputation of being a man-, or should I say, woman-eater."

"Perhaps you will agree with the others when you find time to come on teaching rounds," said Stark, with a laugh.

Susan said goodbye and left. Stark returned to his desk and spoke into his intercom, talking to his secretary.

"Call Dr. Chandler and see if he has talked with Dr. Bellows yet. Tell him that I want to get to the bottom of those drugs in the locker room as soon as possible."

Stark turned and looked out over the complex of buildings that made up the Memorial. His life was so closely linked to the hospital that at certain points they merged. As Bellows had told Susan, Stark had personally raised an enormous amount of the money it had taken to revitalize the hospital and build its seven new buildings. It was partly due to his fund-raising abilities that he was Chief of Surgery at the Memorial.

The more he thought about the drugs in 338 and their possible implications, the angrier he got. It was just another glaring example of how people in general could not be trusted to think in terms of the long-run effects.

"Christ," he said out loud, his eyes mesmerized by the swirling snow clouds. Fools could undermine all his efforts at insuring the Memorial's position as the number one hospital in the country. Years of work could go down the drain. It underscored his belief that he had to attend to everything if he wanted it done right.

The gloom of the winter Boston night had long since invaded the city when Susan alighted from the Harvard line train at the open-air Charles Street MBTA station. The wind, still blowing in from the Arctic, whistled in the river end of the station and traversed the length of the platform in short turbulent gusts. Susan bent over as she headed toward the stairs. The train lunged and slid out of the station, passing her on her right, its wheels screeching as it turned into the tunnel.

Susan used the pedestrian overpass to cross the intersection of Charles Street and Cambridge Street. Underneath, the traffic had dissipated to a minor dribble of cars, but the noxious odor of exhaust gases still fouled the night air. Susan descended to Charles Street. In front of the all-night drugstore there was the usual collection of wayward individuals, either drunk or stoned. Several of them reached toward Susan, asking for spare change. She responded by quickening her step. Then she collided with a seedy, bearded fellow who had deliberately stepped into her way.

"*Real Paper* or *Phoenix*, beautiful?" asked the bearded fellow with seborrheic eyelids. He held several newspapers in his right hand.

Susan recoiled, then pressed on, ignoring the lurid jibes and laughter of the night people. She passed down Charles Street and presently the surroundings changed. A few antique shop windows beckoned for her to dally, but the cold night wind urged her on. At Mount Vernon Street she turned up to the left and began to ascend Beacon Hill. From the numbers on the doors she knew she had a way to go. She passed Louisburg Square. The orange glow from the mullioned windows cast warm rays in the cold night. The houses gave a sense of peace and security behind their solid brick facades.

Bellows's apartment was in a building on the left, about a hundred yards beyond Louisburg Square. The buildings along here sat back behind small lawns and towering elms. Susan pushed open a squeaking metal gate and went up the stone steps to the heavy paneled door. In the foyer she blew on her blue fingers while walking in place to encourage circulation in her feet. She always had cold feet and hands from November to March. While she blew and stamped she scanned the names next to the buzzer. Bellows was number five. She pushed the button hard, and was rewarded with a raucous buzz.

In a minor panic she reached for the doorknob, scraping her knuckle on the metallic guard on the door frame as the door swung open. A small amount of blood oozed from her knuckle, and she lifted her hand to her mouth. In front of her was a staircase twisting up to the left. A shining brass chandelier hovered above, and a gilded frame mirror served to make the hall seem more spacious. By reflex she checked her hair in the mirror, pressing it down at her temples. As she climbed she noticed attractively framed Brueghel prints on every landing.

Exaggerating her exhaustion, she reached the top flight and paused, gripping the banister. Down the stairwell she could see to the tiled floor of the foyer, five storeys below. Bellows opened his door before Susan knocked.

"There's an oxygen bottle in here if you need it, Grandma," he said, smiling.

"God, the air is thin up here. Maybe I should sit here on the steps and recuperate for a few moments."

"A glass of Bordeaux will fix you up perfectly. Give me your hand."

Susan allowed Mark to help her into his apartment. Then she took off her coat, her eyes wandering around the room. Mark disappeared into the kitchen, returning with two glasses of ruby red wine.

Susan threw her coat over a straight-back chair near the

door and pulled off her high boots. Distracted, she took the wine and sipped it. Her attention had been captured by the room she found herself in.

"Pretty tastefully decorated for a surgeon," said Susan, walking into the center of the room.

It was about twenty by forty feet. At each end was a large old-fashioned fireplace, and in each glowed a cheerful fire. The beamed cathedral ceiling was very high, perhaps twenty feet at the peak, slanting down toward both fireplaces. The far wall was an enormous complex of geometric shapes, some housing bookshelves, others with objets d'art and a large stereo, TV, and tape system. The near wall was of exposed brick and covered with paintings, lithographs, and medieval sheet music, attractively framed. An antique Howard clock ticked unobtrusively over the fireplace to the right, a ship model adorned the mantelpiece to the left. Through the windows, on either side of both fireplaces, a myriad of crooked chimneys was silhouetted against the night sky.

The furnishings were of a minimum; Bellows had relied on a collection of thick scatter rugs, dominated by a blue and cream Bukhara in the center of the room. On it was a low onyx coffee table, surrounded by a large number of sizable pillows covered in shocking shades of corduroy.

"This is beautiful," said Susan twisting around in the center of the room and then collapsing on an armful of cushions. "I never expected anything like this."

"What did you expect?" Mark sat down on the other side of the low table.

"An apartment. You know, tables, chairs, couch, the usual."

They both laughed, aware that they really did not know each other very well. Conversation remained on a frivolous level as they enjoyed the wine. Susan hopefully pointed her stocking feet toward the fire, to warm her toes.

"More wine, Susan?"

"For sure. It tastes wonderful."

Mark disappeared into the kitchen for the bottle. He poured each of them another glass.

"No one would ever believe the day I've had today, incredible," said Susan, holding the glass of wine between her eye and the fire and appreciating its deep luscious red glow.

"If you haven't abandoned your suicidal crusade, I believe anything. Did you go and see Stark?"

"You bet your ass, and contrary to your fears, he was very reasonable . . . more than I can say about Harris or even Nelson, for that matter."

"Be careful, that's all I can say. Stark is like an emotional chameleon. I usually get along with him extremely well. Yet today, out of the blue, I found out he's furious at me because of some nut putting half-used medicine in a locker that I had used for a while. He doesn't come to me and ask me about it the way a normal human being would. Instead he sics poor old Chandler, the chief resident, onto me, and Chandler cancels a case of mine to ask me about it. Then later he calls me out of rounds to tell me Stark wants me to get to the bottom of it. You'd think I had nothing to do."

"What's this about drugs in a locker?" Susan remembered the doctor talking to Nelson.

"I'm not sure I have the whole story. Something about one of the surgeons coming across a whole bunch of drugs in an OR locker which old friggin' Walters still had assigned to me. Apparently there were narcotics, curare, antibiotics—a whole pharmacy."

"And they don't know who put them there or why?"

"I guess not. It's my idea that somebody's been saving the stuff to ship off to Biafra or Bangladesh. There's always a couple of people around with some cause like that. But why they've been storing them in a locker in the lounge is beyond me."

"Curare is a nerve blocker, isn't it, Mark?"

"Yup, a competitive nerve blocker. A great drug. Oh, in case you haven't guessed, we're dining here tonight. I got some steaks, and the hibachi is all set on the fire escape outside the kitchen window."

"Couldn't be better, Mark. I'm exhausted. But I'm also hungry."

"I'll put the steaks on." Mark walked into the kitchen with his wineglass.

"Does curare depress respiration?" asked Susan.

"Nope. It just paralyzes all the muscles. The person wants to breathe but can't. They suffocate."

Susan stared into the fireplace, resting the edge of her glass against her lower lip. The dancing flames hypnotized her and she thought about curare, about Greenly, about Berman. The fire crackled suddenly and angrily spat a red-hot coal against the screen. A piece of the coal ricocheted off the screen, landing in the rug to the side of the fireplace. Susan jumped up, flicked it off the rug and pushed it harmlessly onto the slate hearth. She then walked over to the kitchen door, watching Mark season the steaks.

"Stark actually was interested in what I had found out and has already tried to help. I had asked him to help me get the charts of the patients on my list. When I called back later this afternoon, he said he had tried to get them for me but had been told that they were all signed out to one of the professors of neurology, a Dr. Donald McLeary. Do you know him?"

"No, but that doesn't mean anything. I don't know very many of the nonsurgical types."

"To my way of thinking, it makes McLeary look rather suspicious."

"Oh oh, here we go again, imagination plus! Dr. Donald McLeary mysteriously destroys the cerebrum of six patients . . ."

"Twelve . . ."

"OK, twelve, and then he signs all their charts out to eliminate any chance of suspicion. I can just picture all this in the headlines of the Boston *Globe*."

Mark laughed as he put the steaks on the hibachi through the open window, then drew it down against the cold.

"Go ahead and laugh, but at the same time come up with an explanation for McLeary. Everyone else so far has expressed surprise at the idea of relating all these cases together. Everyone except this Dr. McLeary. He has all the charts. I just think it's worth looking into. Maybe he's been investigating this thing for some time and he's far ahead of me. That would be nice to believe and if so, maybe I could help him."

Mark didn't answer. He was wondering exactly how he was going to try to talk Susan out of the whole business. He was also concentrating on the salad dressing, his culinary specialty. When he reopened the kitchen window, the cold wind brought in the sizzling aroma of the cooking steaks. Susan leaned against the door frame, watching him. She thought about how marvelous it would be to have a wife, to be able to come home and have a wife keeping the house in order, the meals on the table. At the same time it seemed ridiculously unfair that she could never have a wife. It was a mental game that Susan played with herself, always to the same impasse, at which time she would simply deny the whole problem or at least postpone it until some indeterminate future date.

"I called the Jefferson Institute today."

"What'd they have to say?" Mark handed Susan some plates, silver and napkins, and pointed toward the onyx table.

"You were right about it being difficult to visit," said Susan, carrying the material to the table. "I asked if I could come out and visit the facility because I wanted to see one of the patients. They laughed. They told me that only the very immediate family can visit and only on prearranged, brief visits. They said that the mass methods of taking care of the patients is generally unacceptable, emotionally, to the families, so they have to make special arrangements for them to visit. They did tell me about the monthly tour you mentioned. My being a medical student counted about the same as a wooden nickel, so far as making them alter their routine. Actually the place sounds interesting, especially since, as you say, the concept has been successful in keeping chronic cases from taking up acute-care beds in the local hospitals."

Susan finished setting the table, then returned to staring into the fire. "I'd really like to visit, though, mostly to see Berman once more. I have a feeling that if I saw him again that I'd probably be able to ease up on this . . . crusade, as you call it. Even I realize I've got to get back to a semblance of normality."

Mark straightened up from his activities in the kitchen at this last sentence, entertaining a ray of hope. He turned the steaks over again and closed the window.

"Why don't you just show up there? I mean, it must be like any other hospital when it comes right down to it. It's probably as chaotic as the Memorial. If you acted like you belong, probably nobody would even question you. You could even wear a nurse's uniform. If anybody came into the Memorial dressed like a doctor or a nurse, they could go anywhere they chose."

Susan looked back at Mark, who was standing in the kitchen door.

"That's not a bad idea . . . not bad. But there's a catch."

"What's that?"

"Simply that I wouldn't know where the hell I was going even if I were able to walk into the building. It's hard to look like you belong when you're totally lost."

"That's not an insurmountable obstacle. All you'd have to do is visit the building department in City Hall and get a copy of the building plans or floor plans. There are plans on file of all public buildings. You'd have yourself a map."

Mark returned to the kitchen to get the steaks and the salad.

"Mark, that's ingenious."

"Practical, not ingenious." He brought the food into the room and served up the steaks and a generous helping of salad. There were also asparagus with hollandaise sauce and another whole bottle of red Bordeaux.

Each thought the meal perfect. The wine tended to smooth any potential rough edges, and the conversation flowed freely as each learned bits and pieces of the other's background to fill in the gaps of the personality mosaics each was constructing of the other. Susan from Maryland, Mark from California. There was little intellectual common ground, for Mark's education had been severely skewed in the direction of Descartes and Newton, while Susan's tended toward Voltaire and Chaucer. But skiing emerged as a love of both, as well as the beach, and the outdoors in general. And they both liked Hemingway. There was an awkward silence after Susan asked about Joyce. Bellows had not read Joyce.

With the dishes cleared, they settled on a random grouping of pillows before the fireplace at the far end of the room. Bellows put on some additional oak logs, turning the smoldering embers into a crackling blaze. Grand Marnier and Fred's Home Made vanilla ice cream made them quiet for some moments, both enjoying the peaceful and contented silence.

"Susan, getting to know you just a little better, and liking every minute of it, makes me even more motivated to urge you to forget this coma problem," said Mark, after a while. "You've got an enormous amount of learning to do, and believe me, there's no place better than the Memorial. In all likelihood this coma problem will be around for some time, plenty of time for you to begin again when you have a real background in clinical medicine. I'm not trying to suggest you cannot contribute; maybe you can. But the chances of making a contribution are small, just like in any research project, no matter how well conceived. And you have to consider the effect your activities will undoubtedly have, in fact already have had, on your superiors. It's a poor gamble, Susan; the odds are stacked against you."

Susan sipped her Grand Marnier. The viscous, smooth fluid slid down her throat, and sent warm sensations down her legs. She took in a deep breath and felt a certain levitation.

"Being a female medical student must be hard enough," continued Bellows, "without adding a further handicap."

Susan raised her head and looked at Bellows. He was staring into the fire. "Exactly what do you mean by that statement?" asked Susan with a sudden slight edge to her voice. Bellows was suddenly brushing against sensitive areas.

"Just what I said." Bellows did not look up from the fire. The dancing flames had captured his attention. "I just think it must be particularly difficult being a female medical student. I never really thought too much about it until you forced me to come up with an alternative explanation for Harris's behavior. Now, the more I think about it, the more I think I am right because . . . well, to be truthful, I can't say I reacted to you as a medical student first. As soon as I saw you, I reacted to you as a woman, and maybe in kind of an immature way. I mean I found you immediately attractive—not seductive." Bellows added the last comment quickly and turned to make sure Susan appreciated his reference to their previous conversation in the coffee shop.

Susan smiled. The defensive attitude, which Bellows's initial statement had rekindled, had melted.

"That was why I reacted so foolishly when you walked into the dressing room yesterday and caught me in my shorts. If I had thought of you asexually, I wouldn't have budged. But it was pretty apparent that was not the case. Anyway, I think most of your professors and instructors are going to react to you first as female and only second as a student of medicine."

Bellows looked back into the fire; he almost had the attitude of a contrite sinner who has confessed. Susan felt a resurgence of the warmth she had begun to feel toward him. She felt again the urge to give him one of her people hugs, as she thought of them. In truth Susan was a physical person, although she did not show it often, especially since entering medicine. Even before applying to medical school, Susan had decided that the physical aspects of her personality had to be suppressed if she was going to make it in medicine. Now instead of reaching for Mark, she sipped her Grand Marnier.

"Susan, you are very apparent in any group and if you don't show up at my lecture, I'm going to have to account for you."

"The luxury of anonymity," said Susan, "has not been something I could enjoy ever since I started medical school. I understand what you are saying, Mark. At the same time I feel I need just one more day. One more." Susan held up one finger and tilted her head in a coquettish fashion. Then she laughed.

"You know, Mark, it is reassuring to hear you say that you think being a female medical student is difficult, because it is. Some of the girls in my class deny it, but they're fooling themselves. They're using one of the oldest and easiest defense mechanisms; get around a problem by saying it's not there. But it is. I remember reading a quote by Sir William Osler. He said there were three classes of human beings: men, women, and women physicians. I laughed when I read that the first time. Now I don't laugh anymore.

"Despite the feminist movement there still lingers the conventional image of wide-eyed feminine naiveté and all that bullshit. As soon as you enter a field which demands a bit of competitive and aggressive action, the men all label you as a castrating bitch. If you sit back and try to use passive, compliant behavior, you find yourself being told that you can't respond to the competitive atmosphere. So you're forced to try to find your own compromise somewhere in the middle, which is difficult because all the while you feel like you're on trial, not as an individual but as a representative of women in general."

There was silence for a few moments, each digesting what had been said.

"The thing that bothers me the most," added Susan, "is that the problem gets worse, not better, the farther into medicine one goes. I cannot imagine how these women with families do it. They have to apologize for leaving work early and then they have to apologize for getting home late, no matter what time it is. I mean, the man can work late, no problem, in fact it makes him seem that much more dedicated. But a woman physician: her role is so diffuse. Society and its conventional female mores make it very difficult.

"How did you get me on this platform?" asked Susan suddenly, realizing the vehemence with which she had been speaking.

"You were just agreeing to my statement that being a female medical student was difficult. So how about agreeing to the last part, about not taking on any more handicaps?"

"Shit, Mark, don't push me right at this moment. Obviously you can see that once I got involved in this thing, I probably need to resolve it somehow. Maybe it's related to my feeling like I'm on trial for women. God, I'd like to show that Harris where to get off. Maybe if I can see Berman again, I'll be able to give up without any loss of intellectual face or . . . what should I say, self-image or self-confidence. But let's talk about something else. Would you mind if I were to give you a hug?"

"Me, mind?" Bellows sat up quickly but slightly flustered. "Not at all."

Susan leaned over and gave him a squeeze with a force that surprised him. Instinctively his arms went around her and he felt her narrow back. Somewhat self-consciously he patted it, as if he were comforting her. She pulled back.

"I hope you're not waiting for me to burp."

For several moments they studied each other in the firelight. Then tentatively their lips sought each other, gently at first, then with obvious emotion, finally with abandon.

The alarm jangled in the darkness, making the air in the room vibrate with its piercing sound. Susan sat bolt upright from a dead sleep. At first she wondered why her eyes wouldn't open; then she realized that they were open. It was just that they could not pierce the utter blackness in the room. For several seconds she had no idea where she was. Her only thought was to try to find the alarm clock and deaden its awful nerve-shattering noise.

As suddenly as it had started, it stopped with a metallic click. At the same time Susan became conscious that she was not alone. The memory of the previous evening swept over her, and she remembered that she was still at Mark's apartment. She lay back, bringing up the covers to cover her nakedness.

"What in God's name was that noise for?" said Susan to the blackness.

"It's an alarm. I suppose you've never heard one before," said a voice from beside her.

"An alarm. Mark, it's the middle of the night."

"Like hell it is; it's five-thirty and time to get rolling."

Mark threw back the covers and put his feet onto the floor. He turned on the lamp next to the bed and rubbed his eyes.

"Mark, you've got to be out of your squash. Five-thirty, Christ." The voice was muffled; Susan had her head underneath the pillow.

"I've got to see my patients, grab a bit to eat, and be

179

ready for rounds at six-thirty. Surgery starts at seven-thirty sharp." Mark stood up and stretched. Disregarding his nakedness and the coldness, he started for the bathroom.

"You surgical masochists defy imagination. Why don't you start at nine or some other reasonable time? Why seven-thirty?"

"It's always been seven-thirty," said Bellows, pausing in the doorway.

"That's a great reason. It's seven-thirty because it's always been seven-thirty—God, it's that type of reasoning that's so typical in medicine. Five-thirty in the morning. Shit, Mark, why didn't you tell me about this when you invited me to stay last night? I would have gone back to the dorm."

Bellows walked back to the bedside, looking down at the mound of covers indicating Susan's body. The pillow was still over her head.

"If you'd take your surgical rotation a bit more seriously, I wouldn't have to tell you what is the normal modus operandi. Time to get up, beauty queen."

Bellows grabbed the edge of the blankets and, with a forceful jerk, pulled all the covers from the bed, leaving Susan bared to the elements, except for her head, still concealed by the pillow.

"Some hospitality," said Susan, jumping up. She grabbed a blanket and twisted herself into an instant cocoon, then collapsed back onto the bed.

"Ah, but today is the first day of your new leaf. You're going to be a normal medical student."

A tug of war ensued with Susan's wrapping.

"I need one more full day, just one. Come on, Mark, one more. You can understand that it's important for me. If I don't get the charts today, which I think I won't, then it's all over. Besides, if I can see Berman, I'll probably give up. Then you'll have your normal medical student. But I need one more day."

Bellows let go of the blankets. Susan fell back, one breast exposed in a fetching Amazonian way.

"All right, one more day. But if Stark is on rounds today, he'll know that you are phantomizing. I wouldn't be able to come up with any cover story. I hope you realize that."

"Let's just play it by ear, almighty surgeon. I'm sure you'll think of something."

"Susan, I'll just have to say that I had told you to be on rounds."

"OK, have it your way. But I'm spending one more whole day on this thing. I've got some investment into it already."

Susan snuggled into the warm bed. She barely heard the shower start in the bathroom. She thought she'd wait until Bellows finished before getting up.

When Susan awoke the second time, it was already quite light. Sudden gusts of wind blew rain against the window panes with a sound like rice hitting glass. With a contrariness typical of Boston weather, the wind had shifted during the night from northwest to due east. Thanks to the Gulf Stream, the temperature had risen into the high thirties, so precipitation was in the liquid rather than solid phase. The commuters were relieved, the skiers disgusted.

It was hard for Susan to believe the clock next to the bed, because it said almost nine. Bellows had showered, dressed, and exited without having reawakened her. Susan was amazed, for she was a relatively light sleeper. Just to be sure, she checked the bathroom and the living room for any sign that Bellows might still be there. She was alone.

Susan found a clean towel, then showered vigorously, remembering the previous night's passion with a pleasant sense of warmth. Bellows had turned out to be a far more sensitive and innately generous lover than Susan had surmised. She was genuinely pleased, although she had some serious reservations about the relationship going very far. Bellows's commitment to surgery seemed somehow too encompassing, as if everything else in his life would necessarily be relegated to a secondary position like a hobby.

In the refrigerator, Susan found some cheese and an orange. She helped herself to Grapenuts and toast while thumbing through the Yellow Pages. Checking to be sure that she had everything, she left Bellows's apartment, locking the door securely behind her. It was going to be a busy day.

The rain had let up significantly by the time Susan hit the street. The weather did not appear to be clearing, but now it would be more pleasant to walk about. Susan turned left up Mt. Vernon toward the State House. She crossed the Boston Common at its northern tip and entered the downtown shopping area.

Of all the young girls who had come to the Boston Uniform Company retail store seeking a nurse's uniform, the salesman found Susan the easiest and fastest customer. She seemed totally uninterested in the bewildering permutations of the plain white dress. She asked for size ten and told the salesman that any size ten would do.

"We have this style here which you might like," he said, bringing out one uniform.

Susan took the dress and held it against herself as she looked into the mirror.

"The changing rooms are in the back if you'd like to try it."

"I'll take it."

The salesman was stunned if gratified at the speed of the sale.

The rain started again half-heartedly as Susan walked up Washington Street toward Government Center. As she reached the middle of the bricked mall in front of the ultrageometric City Hall, the wind brought in another moisture-laden cloud over the city. As the rain came down in earnest Susan ran for cover.

The girl at the information booth told Susan that the building department was on the eighth floor. It was easy to find. Once there, though, things were different. Susan waited for twenty-five minutes at the main counter only to be told that she was at the wrong place. This happened twice before she was directed to the rear of the vast room. There was another wait of a quarter of an hour despite the fact she was the only customer. Behind the counter were five desks, of which three were occupied. Two men and one woman. The two men looked surprisingly alike, with large red noses, plastic black-rimmed glasses, and tasteless ties. They were engaged in a heated argument about the Patriots. The woman had a ratted hairdo recalling the early sixties and shocking red lipstick that used the natural lip borders only as suggestions. She was engrossed with a pocket mirror, examining her face from every possible angle.

The smaller of the two men eventually eyed Susan and realized that she was not going to disappear despite the fact that she was being ignored. He rambled over, uninterested. When he reached the counter he took his cigarette from his mouth. A few of the ashes from the tip dusted down the front of his tie. He crushed the butt repeatedly in a cheap and already overflowing metal ashtray.

"What can I do for you?" said the bureaucrat, looking at Susan for a moment. He turned before she could answer.

"Hey, Harry, that reminds me. What are you going to do about the GRI 5 request? Remember, it was filed as urgent and it's been in your box for two months." Looking back at Susan, "What is it, honey? Let me guess. You want to file a complaint about your landlord. Well, this isn't the right place."

He looked back at his colleague. "Harry, if you're going for coffee, pick me up a regular and a Danish. I'll pay you later." His red eyes turned to Susan. "Now then . . ."

"I'd like to look at some plans; the floor plans for the Jefferson Institute. It's a relatively new hospital in South Boston."

"Plans. What do you want plans for? How old are you, fifteen?"

"I'm a medical student and I'm interested in hospital design and construction."

"Kids today! With your looks you don't have to be interested in anything." He laughed obnoxiously.

Susan closed her eyes, resisting the retort the comment deserved.

The state employee started toward a stack of oversized books on the counter. "What ward is it in?" he asked with obvious ennui.

"I haven't the slightest idea."

"All right then," said the man, making an about-face. "First we'll have to find out which ward it is in."

A smaller book on the counter supplied the needed information.

"Ward 17."

With calculated slowness, he returned to the large books on the counter. From his side pocket he withdrew a crumpled pack of cigarettes. He put one cigarette in his mouth, leaving it unlit. After picking several wrong volumes, he found the Ward 17 volume. The other books were pushed aside. Turning back the cover, he slobbered over his index finger. He flipped the pages forcefully, running his finger across his tobacco-stained tongue every four or five pages. Having found the reference, he copied the figures onto a piece of scrap paper. Motioning for Susan to follow, he started toward a large bank of filing cabinets.

"Harry!" called the bureaucrat, continuing his conversation with his colleague en route to the filing cabinets, the unlit cigarette bobbing up and down in his mouth. "Before you go downstairs, call up Grosser and find out if Lester is coming in today. Somebody's goin' to have to file that stuff on his desk if he's not; that's been there longer than your GRI 5 request."

It was a simple affair to find the correct drawer and extract a large packet of plans. "Here you are, Goldilocks; there's a Xerox machine over in that room beyond the counter, if you want. It takes nickels." He pointed with his unlit cigarette.

"Maybe you could show me which of these are floor plans." Susan had withdrawn the contents from the jacket.

"You're interested in hospital construction and you don't know what floor plans look like? My God. Here, these are the floor plans . . . basement, first floor, and second floor." He lit his cigarette with a pocket lighter.

"How do you decipher these abbreviations?"

"For Christ's sake, right here in the lower corner. It says 'OR,' means operating room. 'W (main)'; that means main ward. And 'Comp. R.' stands for computer room and so forth." The man showed signs of incipient irritation.

"And the Xerox machine?"

"Over there. There's a change machine on the wall. When you finish with the plans, just put them in the metal bin on the counter."

Susan carefully Xeroxed the floor plans and labeled the rooms on the copy with a felt-tipped pen. Then she headed for the Memorial.

Susan entered the Memorial through the main entrance. It was just after ten in the morning. Yet the inevitable daily crowds were already there. Every conceivable seat was occupied. There were people of all ages, waiting, forever waiting. These were not people seeking attention in either the clinic or the emergency room. They were people waiting for a relative to be admitted or discharged, or perhaps they were patients who had been seen and treated and were now waiting to be picked up and taken home. There was little conversation and no smiles. These were all distinct and separate islands, united only by their healthy awe of the hospital and its shrouded mysteries.

The dense crowd impeded Susan's progress, forcing her to push her way through to the directory. The plastic letters spelled out "Neurology Department, Beard 11." Susan made her way to the Beard elevators and waited with the crowd. The person next to her turned and Susan recoiled in ill-concealed horror. The man's—or was it a woman's—eyes were surrounded by dark areas of hemorrhage. The nose was swollen and distorted, with nasal packs partially extruding from the nostrils. Several wires came from within the nose and were taped to either cheek. The visage was that of a monster. Susan tried to keep her eyes on the elevator indicator, unprepared for the visual surprises of the hospital.

Dr. Donald McLeary was one of the younger members of the fulltime neurology staff and, because of the ever-mounting pressure of space, had not been given an office on eleven. Susan had to take the stairs up to twelve before she found the door with "Dr. Donald M. McLeary" stenciled on it in black letters. She opened the door and squeezed into a tiny outer office; the door could not be opened all the way because of a filing cabinet. The desk, of average size, appeared huge in the room. An aging secretary looked up. She had extraordinarily thick makeup, including rouge and false eyelashes. Her totally bleached hair was glued into short, tight curls. She wore a tight pink pants-suit outfit that strained over unnatural bulges.

"Excuse me, is Dr. McLeary in?"

"He's in, but he is very busy." The secretary was annoyed at the intrusion. "Have you an appointment?"

"No. No, I haven't, but I only want to ask him a quick question. I'm a medical student rotating here at the Memorial."

"I'll check with the doctor."

The secretary stood up, eyeing Susan from head to foot. Even more irritated at Susan's lissome figure, she entered the inner office to Susan's right. Susan looked around the outer office for any signs of the hospital charts she wanted.

Almost immediately, the woman returned, sat down at

her desk, put a piece of stationery into the typewriter and typed several lines. Only then did she look up.

"You may go in; he says he has a moment for you."

The secretary resumed her typing before Susan could respond. Whispering some choice epithets under her breath, Susan opened the door and entered the inner office.

Reminiscent of Dr. Nelson's office, McLeary's office was equally messy, with journals and papers in innumerable haphazard stacks. Several of the stacks had tipped over at some previous time and had never been reerected. Dr. McLeary was a thin, intense-looking man with a deep crease that ran down through the middle of each cheek. His sharply angular nose and chin were separated by a small mouth that twitched as he eyed Susan over his glasses and through his bushy eyebrows.

"Susan Wheeler, I presume," said Dr. McLeary, with no friendliness in his voice.

"Yes." Susan was surprised that he knew her name. She could not decide if that were propitious or not.

"And you have come concerning these ten charts I have here." McLeary half-turned in his chair, waving toward a large group of hospital charts in his bookcase.

"Ten? Is that all you have?"

"Isn't ten enough?" asked McLeary somewhat sarcastically.

"Fine. I just thought that maybe you'd have more. Are those the charts of the coma victims?"

"Possibly. What do you have in mind if they are?"

"I'm not sure. Dr. Stark told me you had the charts, and I thought I'd come by and ask if I could perhaps look at them or help you extract them."

"Young lady, I'm a neurologist with considerable training. My expertise is neurology, and I am evaluating the extensive neurological evaluations that were done on these patients by our resident staff. I really don't need any help."

"I'm not insinuating that you need help, Dr. McLeary, least of all in a professional capacity. I admit that I know next to nothing about neurology. But these patients all have suffered a tragedy akin to death and there is something very strange about the whole affair. I think these cases have to be viewed in terms of some kind of association rather than as random events."

"And of course you are going to be the one to do that."

"Well, somebody has to do it."

McLeary paused and Susan had the uncomfortable feeling that the conversation was rapidly deteriorating.

"Well, let me tell you this," continued McLeary with a forceful quality to his voice. "This kind of a problem is far broader than your current capabilities. Not only that, but your efforts so far are already responsible for a disproportionate amount of trouble in this hospital. Rather than a help you are fast becoming a definite handicap. What I want you to do now is sit down." McLeary pointed to one of the chairs in front of his desk.

"I beg your pardon?" Susan had heard but the tone was confusing. McLeary wasn't asking; he was ordering.

"I said, sit down!" The anger in his voice now was unmistakable.

Susan sat down in the only chair without a complement of journal articles.

McLeary picked up the phone and dialed. He looked directly at Susan with unblinking, beady eyes. His mouth twitched as he waited for a connection.

"Director's office, please. . . . I'd like to speak to Philip Oren."

There was a longer pause. McLeary's expression did not change.

"Mr. Oren, Dr. McLeary here. You were quite right. She is sitting here in front of me. . . . The charts? Of course not, you must be joking . . . All right . . . fine."

McLeary hung up the phone, still looking directly at Susan. Susan could not detect even an iota of human warmth. She thought that he deserved the secretary he had. After an awkward silence Susan started to get up.

"I have a feeling that I should not . . ."

"Sit down!" shouted McLeary even more loudly than before.

Susan sat down quickly, surprised at the sudden outburst.

"What is going on here? I came in here to see if you could use some help in looking into the coma problem, not to be shouted at."

"I really have nothing more to say to you, young lady. You have overstepped your boundaries here at the Memorial. I was told that you would probably come snooping for these charts. I was also told you obtained unauthorized information from the computer. And on top of that, you managed to alienate Dr. Harris. Anyway, Mr. Oren will be here in a moment and you can talk with him. This is his problem, not mine."

"Who is Mr. Oren?"

"The director of the hospital, my young friend. He is the administrator, and personnel problems are in his bailiwick."

"I'm not personnel. I'm a medical student."

"True enough. And that actually puts you on somewhat of a lower plane. You are a guest here . . . a guest of the hospital . . . and as such, your conduct should be suitable to the hospitality extended to you. Instead you have chosen to be disruptive and to ignore rules and regulations. You medical students of today somehow have gotten your sense of position in the scheme of things reversed. The hospital does not exist for your benefit. The hospital does not owe you an education."

"This is a teaching hospital and is associated with the medical school. Teaching is supposed to be one of the major functions of this hospital."

"Teaching, of course, but that certainly doesn't mean just medical students. It means the whole medical community."

"Exactly. Supposedly it is a symbiotic atmosphere for everyone's benefit: student and professor alike. The hospital doesn't exist for the benefit of the medical student nor for the benefit of the professor. In fact, it's supposed to be primarily for the patient."

"Well, it is indeed easy to understand Harris's reaction to you, Miss Wheeler. As he said, you lack respect for people as well as institutions. But it is a reflection of youth in general today. They believe their very existence alone entitles them to all the luxuries of society, education being one of them."

"Education is more than a luxury; it is a responsibility that society owes to itself."

"Society undoubtedly has a responsibility to itself but not to individual students, not to youth just because they are youth. Education is a luxury in that it is expensive beyond belief and the major burden, particularly in medicine, falls on the public at large, the workingman. The students themselves pay a small amount of the money needed. Not only does it cost an enormous amount of money to have you here,

Miss Wheeler, but your being here means that you are economically unproductive. Hence the cost to society automatically doubles. And besides, your being a woman means that your future per-hour productivity . . ."

"Oh save me," said Susan sarcastically, standing up. "I've heard about as much bullshit as I can stand."

"Stay put, young lady," shouted McLeary, furious. He too stood up.

Susan tried to look behind the face of the man trembling with anger in front of her. She thought about Bellows's suggestion relative to sexuality explaining Harris's behavior. She was hard put to believe that was a factor in McLeary's performance. Once again she was facing very irregular behavior, to say the least. The man was breathing rapidly, his chest heaving. She had apparently and unknowingly challenged the man. But how? In what capacity? She had no idea. Susan debated whether she should just walk out. A mixture of curiosity and respect for the apparent irrationality of McLeary's actions made her stay. She sat down, watching McLeary, who now couldn't decide what to do. He too sat down and began nervously playing with an ashtray. Susan sat motionless. She wouldn't have been surprised if the man cried.

She heard the outer office door opening. Voices drifted into the inner office. Then the inner office door opened. Without being announced or knocking, an energetic individual entered. He appeared like a businessman, in a smartly tailored blue suit. Reminding Susan of Stark's attire, a silk handkerchief peeked out of his left breast pocket. His hair was carefully combed and frozen with a ruler-straight part on the left side. There was a definite aura of authority about the man; he exuded an air of assurance at handling a wide spectrum of problems.

"Thank you for your call, Donald," said Oren.

Then he faced Susan condescendingly.

"So this is the infamous Susan Wheeler. Miss Wheeler, you have been causing a great commotion in this hospital. Are you aware of that?"

"No, I haven't been aware of that."

Oren leaned back on McLeary's desk, folding his arms in a professional fashion.

"Out of curiosity, Miss Wheeler, let me ask you a rather

simple question. What do you think is the major goal of this institution?"

"Caring for the sick."

"Good. At least we agree in general. But I must add a crucial phrase to your answer. We are caring for the sick of this community. That might sound redundant to you because obviously we are not caring for the sick of Westchester County, New York. Yet this is an extremely important distinction because it underlines our responsibility to the people right here in Boston. As a direct corollary, anything that could interrupt or otherwise disturb this relationship to the community would, in effect, negate our primary mission. Now this may sound very . . . what should I say . . . irrelevant to you. But quite the contrary. I have been receiving complaints about you over the last few days which have grown from being irritated to intolerable. Apparently you are bent on specifically disrupting our carefully maintained relationship with the community."

Susan felt color rising in her cheeks. Oren's condescending manner began to irritate her.

"I suppose bringing to the forefront of everyone's awareness that the chances of becoming a vegetable, of losing one's brain, is very high, intolerably high, by being a patient here would ruin the reputation of the hospital."

"Exactly."

"Well, it seems to me that the reputation of the hospital is nothing compared to the irreparable damage suffered by these people. I have become more and more convinced that the reputation of the hospital deserves to be ruined if that's what it takes to solve the problem."

"Now, Miss Wheeler, you can't be serious. Where would all the people turn . . . all the people who are in daily need of the facilities in this hospital? Come . . . come. And by glibly drawing attention to an unfortunate but nevertheless unavoidable complication . . ."

"How do you know it's unavoidable?" interrupted Susan.

"I can only believe what the chiefs of the respective departments assure me. I am not a doctor nor a scientist, Miss Wheeler, nor do I pretend to be. I am an administrator. And when I am faced with a medical student who is here to learn surgery, but instead spends her time calling attention to a problem which is already under investigation by qualified people such as Dr. McLeary here—a problem whose indiscreet disclosure has the potential to cause irreparable harm to the community, I am forced to react quickly and decisively. Obviously the warnings and exhortations you have already received to assume your normal duties have gone unheeded. But this is not a debate. I'm not here to argue with you. On the contrary, with all due respect, I thought it best to give you an explanation for my decision about your surgery rotation. Now, if you'll excuse me, I will phone your dean of students."

Oren picked up McLeary's telephone and dialed.

"Dr. Chapman's office, please. . . . Dr. Chapman, please. Phil Oren calling. . . . Jim, Phil Oren here. How's the family? Everyone in our house is just fine. . . . I suppose I told you that Ted's been accepted at the University of Pennsylvania. . . . I hope so. . . . The reason I called is about one of your third-year students rotating on surgery, a Susan Wheeler. . . . That's right. . . . Sure, I'll hold."

Oren looked at Susan. "You are a third-year student, Miss Wheeler?"

Susan nodded. Her nascent anger had melted into dejection.

Oren looked back at McLeary, who suddenly stood up, apparently bored. "I'm sorry, Don, for this intrusion," said Oren. "I suppose we should have gone to my office. I'll be finished . . ." Oren redirected his attention into the telephone. "Yes, I'm here, Jim . . . well that's nice to know she's been a good student. But nonetheless she has exhausted her welcome here at the Memorial. She is supposed to be on surgery but has decided never to attend rounds, conferences, or surgery. Instead, she has been irritating the staff, particularly our Chief of Anesthesia, and exacting unauthorized information from our computer storage facility by some devious means. We obviously have enough trouble around here without her kind of help. . . . Sure, I'll tell her you want to see her . . . this afternoon at four-thirty. Good enough. I'm sure the V.A. would be happy to have her . . . right (chuckle). Thanks, Jim. Speak to you soon, and let's get together."

Oren hung up the phone and smiled diplomatically at McLeary. Then he turned to Susan.

"Miss Wheeler, your dean, as you have plainly heard, would like to have a word with you this afternoon at four-thirty.

From this moment on, your professional welcome at the Memorial has been terminated. Goodbye."

Susan looked from Oren to McLeary and then back. McLeary's expression was unchanged. Oren sported a self-satisfied smile, as if he had just won a debate. There was an awkward silence. Susan realized that the scene was over, and she got up without a word, picked up the parcel containing the nurse's uniform, and left.

Wednesday
February 25
11:15 A.M.

Finding the hospital intolerably oppressive from an emotional point of view, Susan fled. She pushed her way through the lingering crowds, out into the rainy, raw February day. Once outside and without any particular destination in mind, she just walked, aimlessly, lost in her own thoughts. She turned on New Chardon Street and then on Cambridge Street.

"Assholes," she hissed as she kicked a stray, partially crunched Campbell's soup can. The light rain flattened her hair against her forehead. Small droplets coalesced and dripped from the tip of her nose. She wandered up Joy Street into the back side of Beacon Hill, preoccupied with her stream of consciousness. She saw but her mind did not record the clutter of life, dogs, garbage, and other debris of the decaying urban surroundings.

She could not remember ever feeling quite so rejected and isolated. She felt totally alone, and sudden fears of failure kept reoccurring in her compulsively conditioned brain. Waves of depression alternated with anger as she went over the conversations with McLeary and Oren. She yearned to talk with someone, someone whose counsel she could trust and respect. Stark, Bellows, Chapman; each was a possibility but each had a specific disadvantage. Bellows's objectivity would have to be suspect; Stark's and Chapman's overriding loyalties would be to their respective institutions.

Susan thought of the worst: being dismissed from medical school in disgrace. Not only would it be a personal failure but she felt it would be a failure for all women in medicine. Susan wished there were some woman doctor to whom she could turn, but she did not know any. There were so few on the medical school staff, and none in any positions that made them accessible for counseling.

In the middle of her tormented musing, Susan felt her right foot slide as she put her weight on it. She had to steady herself with her hand on a nearby building to keep from falling. Expecting the worst, she looked down to see that she had stepped in a large steaming pile of dog feces.

"God damn Beacon Hill." Susan cursed Boston and all the literal and figurative shit a city government tolerated. Using the curb to dislodge most of the material, Susan choked on the odor. Still she couldn't help but think about the symbolic aspect of her misfortune. Perhaps she had been stepping into a pile of shit, and as she was forced to do in regard to the actual shit in the city, she should try to ignore the whole affair. Just walk around it. Her responsibility was to become a doctor; that should take precedence over everything. The Bermans and the Greenlys were not her concern.

The rain continued and rivulets ran down her cheeks. She began to walk more carefully, prudently noticing the innumerable piles of dog crap that characterized Beacon Hill as much as the gas lamps or the red brick. She watched where she put her feet and the going was easier. But she could not dismiss her sense of responsibility to the Bermans and the Greenlys so easily. She thought about the age similarity between herself and Nancy Greenly. She thought about her own periods and the several episodes when she had bled more heavily than usual; how it had frightened her and made her feel helpless and out of control. She might have had to have a D&C herself, possibly at the Memorial.

But now she was out of the Memorial, maybe out of medical school. There was little that was up to her at that point, whether she wanted to pursue the problem or not. It was finished. It embarrassed her slightly to think of the frame of mind she had when she started the affair. "A new disease!" Susan laughed at her own vanity and deluded sense of ability.

Susan strolled down Pinckney Street, crossed Charles Street and headed for the river. As aimlessly as on her Beacon Hill wandering, Susan mounted the stairs to the Longfellow Bridge. The graffiti stood out in bold outlines and she lingered, reading some of the nonsensical phrases, the faceless names. In the center of the span she paused, gazing up the Charles River toward Cambridge and Harvard and the B.U. Bridge. The river was a curious pattern of ice patches and open water, like a gigantic piece of abstract art. A flock of seagulls stood motionless on one of the floes of ice.

Susan did not know what it was that drew her attention to the left, the way she had come. She saw a man in a dark overcoat and hat who turned toward the river and stopped when Susan looked in his direction. She returned to her undirected musing and the scene in front of her without giving the man in the dark overcoat a thought. But after five to ten minutes passed, Susan noticed the man had not moved. He was smoking and gazing up the river, seemingly as oblivious to the rain as was Susan. Susan thought that it was a coincidence to have two people standing on a bridge on a rainy day in February brooding over the river when as a rule the bridge was deserted even in nice weather.

Susan crossed the bridge to the Cambridge side and walked up the river bank toward the MIT boat house. She felt a little cold as some moisture worked its way into her collar. The mild discomfort was somewhat therapeutic. But presently she decided that getting back to the dorm and a hot bath were in order.

Abruptly she turned, intending to recross the Longfellow Bridge and take the MBTA home. But she stopped. The same man with the dark coat was about a hundred yards away, still staring out over the expanse of the Charles River. Susan felt an uneasiness that she couldn't characterize. She changed her plans, to avoid passing the man. She would traverse the corner of the MIT campus and take the MBTA at Kendall Station.

As she crossed Memorial Drive, she noticed that the man began to move in her direction. Obviously it was stupid, she assured herself, to concern herself with some stranger. She had difficulty explaining to herself why she would be so apt to have ungrounded paranoia. She decided that she was more upset than she had imagined. Just to be sure, she turned another corner and walked to the end of the block, stopping in front of the Political Science Library. Trying to be natural, she adjusted the string on her parcel.

The man appeared almost immediately but did not turn into the block. Instead, he crossed the street and disappeared from sight. But Susan had not convinced herself that he was not following her. There had been the slightest suggestion that the man had reacted to her delaying tactics. Susan mounted the steps and entered the library. She used the ladies' room and relaxed for a few moments. In the mirror her face reflected a definite uneasiness. She thought about calling someone but dismissed the idea. What could she say that wouldn't sound ridiculous? Besides, she felt better and was willing to forget the episode as a construct of her imagination.

Emerging from the ladies' room, she had regained her composure enough to appreciate the architecture of the library. It was ultra-modern with a sense of serenity and space. There was none of that overbearing stuffiness one associated with old university libraries. The chairs were bright orange canvas. The shelves and the card catalogues were highly polished oak.

Then Susan saw the man again! This time at a very close range. She knew it was he although he did not look up from the magazine he appeared to be reading. He was obviously out of place in the library, dressed in a dark overcoat, white shirt, and white tie. His plastered-down hair had a shiny appearance suggesting multiple layers of Vitalis. His irregular face was pockmarked from adolescent years of acne.

Susan mounted the stairs to the mezzanine, watching the man whenever she could. He did not seem to look up from his reading. From the outside of the building Susan had noted a connection between the library and the building immediately adjacent. She found the overpass and quickly crossed. The adjacent building was a classroom-office building and a number of people were milling through it. Susan felt more comfortable as she descended to the street floor. She left the building and headed rapidly for Kendall Square.

Since the area was unfamiliar to Susan, it took her a few minutes to find the entrance to the MBTA underground. Just before she descended she hesitated, then she looked around. To her amazement and consternation, the man in the dark coat was about a block away, coming toward her. Susan felt a sinking feeling in her abdomen and a quickening pulse. She also felt undecided about what to do.

A slight breeze moving up the stairs and a low threatening rumble helped her make up her mind. A train was coming into the station. A train filled with people.

In a partially controlled panic she descended the stairs and entered the shadowy subterranean world. She fumbled for a quarter at the turnstile. She knew she had several in her pocket, but her mitten made it impossible. She tore off her mitten and pulled out her change. A few coins fell to the concrete and rolled spiraling away. No one got off the train. A few people blankly watched Susan's uncoordinated efforts at the turnstile. The quarter dropped into the slot and Susan tried to push through. With a gasp she realized she had pushed too soon; the arm of the turnstile dug into her stomach rather than giving way. She let up, and the quarter dropped into the release mechanism. On her second attempt the turnstile turned so freely that she stumbled forward, just managing to keep herself from falling. The doors to the train closed as she ran up to them.

"Please!" she shouted but the train began to pull away from the station. Susan ran alongside for a few steps. Then as the end of the train slid by her, Susan caught the image of the conductor looking at her through the glass with a blank face. The train receded rapidly into the inbound tunnel as Susan panted and looked after it.

The station was totally deserted. Even the outbound platform on the other side was empty. The sound of the departing train fell off astoundingly rapidly, to be replaced by the regular sound of dripping water. Kendall Station was not a busy station and had not been renovated. The mosaic walls which had once been fashionable were a study in decay; the place recalled some ancient archeological site. Soot covered everything, and the platform was strewn with paper debris. Stalactite forms hung from the ceiling with droplets of moisture falling from their tips, as if it were a limestone cave of the Yucatán.

Susan leaned out over the tracks as far as she could and peered into the tunnel toward Cambridge, hoping to see another train materialize. Straining her ears, she heard only the dripping water. Then there was the unmistakable sound of unhurried footsteps on the subway stairs. Susan rushed over to the heavily grated change booth. It was empty. A sign said that it was occupied only at rush hour, from 3 to 5 P.M. The footsteps on the stairs grew closer and Susan backed away from the entrance. She turned and ran down the platform toward the Cambridge end of the station. At the extreme end of the platform, she once again looked into the darkness of the tunnel. There was only the steady sound of dripping water. And footsteps.

Looking back toward the entrance, Susan watched the man in the dark coat enter through the turnstile. He stopped, cupping his hands over a match to light a cigarette, casually tossing the used match onto the tracks. Obviously in no hurry, he took several puffs from his cigarette before starting toward Susan. He seemed to savor the fear he was causing. His shoes echoed metallically as he came closer and closer.

Susan wanted to scream or run but she could do neither. It occurred to her that she might be dreaming up the terrifying situation. Perhaps it was just a series of coincidences. But the appearance and the expression of the man approaching her convinced her that this was no dream.

Susan began to panic. She was cornered unless she wanted to enter the tunnel. She discarded that idea despite her panic. The other platform? She looked across the inbound and outbound tracks to the other side. Between the tracks were steel I-beam uprights with room to squeeze through between them. But next to the uprights, running along on either side of them, were the third rails, the power source for the trains with enough voltage and amperage to fry a person instantly.

About ten to twenty feet within the tunnel, the I-beam uprights terminated and the power rails switched to the outsides of the respective tracks. Susan estimated that it would be relatively easy to sprint into the tunnel just far enough to round the end of the row of uprights. That way she could avoid stepping over the third rails.

The man was within fifty feet of Susan, and he flipped his unfinished cigarette onto the tracks. He appeared to take something from his pocket. A gun? No, it wasn't a gun. A knife? Perhaps.

Susan needed no more encouragement. She switched the nurse's uniform parcel to her right hand and squatted down at the edge of the platform, placing her left palm on the edge. Then she vaulted the four feet down onto the tracks, landing on her feet but allowing herself to absorb the shock by bending her legs. In an instant she was up, running into the tunnel.

Panic flooded over her and she stumbled on the wooden ties. She fell sideways toward the third rail. Instinctively she let go of her parcel and grabbed for one of the I-beams, managing to deflect herself enough so that she missed the third rail by inches. As she landed, her left hand hit a small piece of wood, which flipped up and landed against the third rail and the ground. With a blinding flash of electricity and a popping noise the piece of wood was incinerated. The acrid smell of an electrical fire filled the air.

Scrambling to her feet despite a sharp pain in her left ankle, mindlessly clutching at her package, Susan tried to run again on the ties. Just within the mouth of the tunnel, there was a series of switches, creating a maze of tracks and a bewildering pattern of rail and ties underfoot. With no time to figure out the intricacies of the track, Susan stumbled ahead. But her dragging left boot snagged between two rails. She fell again.

Expecting her pursuer to be on her at any second, Susan struggled to one knee. Her left foot was jammed fast between the two rails. She pulled to try to extricate herself, straining forward with effect. All she managed to do was to aggravate the pain in her ankle. Bending down, she clutched at her leg with her hands and pulled in desperation. She didn't allow herself to look back.

Suddenly an agonizing screech filled the air, forcing Susan to let go of her leg and gasp for breath. She thought that something had happened to her but she was still alive. Then it happened again; a noise so loud in the underground cavern that she instinctively covered her ears with her palms. Even so, the noise caused a sharp pain deep within her middle ears. Then she knew what it was. It was the train! It was the shriek of the train whistle.

Susan looked up into the blackness of the tunnel and saw the single penetrating light. She began to feel the thundering vibration of the tons of steel bearing down at her at great speed. Then there was another sound, deeper yet even more penetrating than the whistle. It was the rasp of steel against steel as the wheels of the oncoming train locked in a vain and desperate attempt to stop. But it was useless. The momentum was too great.

Susan had no idea which track her foot was caught in, nor could she tell which track bore the train. The light seemed to be coming directly at her. With a desperate, manic jerk she pulled her foot from her boot and wrenched herself in the direction of the outbound track.

Her outstretched arms and hands cushioned the fall as she sprawled across a rail. By reflex she pulled herself into a ball and covered her head with her arms. The vibration and the rasp came to a crescendo and with a whoosh the train passed some five feet away.

Susan didn't move for a moment. She couldn't believe what had happened. Her pulse was racing and her hands were wet. But she was alive and, except for some bruises, she was all right. Her overcoat was torn and several buttons had popped off. There was a band of grease across it and part of the white lab coat she wore beneath it. Her pens and penlight were gone, scattered in the tunnel. One of the earpieces to her stethoscope was bent at right angles.

She stood up and brushed off the larger pieces of debris and reclaimed her boot. By merely depressing the heel and lifting the toe, she extricated it with ease that belied her earlier difficulties. By the time she had it on, she could see several men running toward her with lights.

When she was helped onto the platform, the whole experience already seemed like a total figment of her imagination, as if she were totally out of control. There was no man in a dark coat. There was just a large crowd of people who excitedly shouted with each other about what had happened and what should happen. Someone found her parcel on the track and brought it to her.

Susan denied injury. She thought about saying something about the man, but then again she was unsure of her own grasp of what had been real and what had been imagined. She had panicked and was still overwrought. She couldn't think and she wanted to go home more than anything else.

She had to spend fifteen minutes assuring the train crew that she had simply slipped off the platform, was now perfectly fine, and definitely didn't need an ambulance. Susan insisted that all she wanted was to get to Park Street to catch the Huntington line. Finally Susan and the others entered the train, the doors closed, and it pulled out of the station.

Susan inspected her clothes in the light. She noticed that the man across from her was staring at her. And the woman next to him was doing the same. In fact as Susan's eyes moved around the car, she realized that everyone was staring at her as if she was some sort of freak. The eyes and the faces were unbearable. She tried to look outside as the train crossed the Longfellow Bridge. Still there was no conversation. Everyone was watching her fixedly.

The train pulled into Charles Street. With great relief Susan jumped off the car and ran down the platform. In front of the Phillips Drugstore she caught a cab. Only then did she begin to calm down. Looking at her hands, she realized she was visibly trembling.

**Wednesday
February 25
1:30 P.M.**

By one-thirty in the afternoon, Bellows had already had a full day by most people's standards. He wasn't physically tired, because he was well accustomed to his schedule. But he was emotionally tired, on edge. The day had begun auspiciously enough when he had awakened with Susan still at his side. He had enjoyed their evening together immensely, although he was doubtful about the potential longevity of their affair. Susan was hardly the type of girl he was accustomed to escape with. She had none of that wide-eyed feminine naiveté which formed the basis of Bellows's idea of women. To his pleasant surprise, and despite his fears, sex had come naturally with Susan, although for him it was without the aggressive overtones he had learned to recognize as normal. Susan, and his own response to her, remained an absorbing enigma.

Getting up and leaving Susan sleeping in his bed had provided a certain comforting feeling for Bellows. It made his role more traditional. Had Susan gotten up and come to the hospital at the same time as he did, it would have diluted his sense of sacrifice. And a sense of sacrifice was important for Bellows since it served as a fertile source of inner satisfaction.

But then the day had deteriorated. To Bellows's horror, Stark had made a surprise appearance on early-morning rounds, and the chief was in a particularly vindictive mood. Stark had started rounds by asking Bellows what he had done to the attractive medical student assigned to him that made it so difficult for her to show up for rounds. Bellows had inwardly shuddered, realizing that Stark's off-color implications were truer than Stark himself realized. For Bellows knew that at that very moment Susan lay sleeping in his bed.

Stark's question had caused some short laughs and a few snide remarks by the others on rounds. Bellows had felt his face tingle with blood flowing through dilated capillaries. At the same time he had felt a sudden defensiveness.

Before Bellows had been given a chance to say anything, Stark had launched into a tirade about attendance and interest, performance, and reward. He had essentially told Bellows that any future absence by Susan would be debited to Bellows's own record. Bellows was to make it his personal goal to see that all the students assigned to him performed exemplarily.

During actual rounds Stark had been as nasty as ever, particularly toward Bellows. In almost every case Bellows had been asked some difficult question and his answers never satisfied the irate chief. Even some of the other residents had realized that Bellows was being raked over the coals and they had tried to interfere by answering questions even when the questions were clearly directed at Bellows.

At the end of rounds, Stark had called Bellows aside to tell him that he was not performing up to his usual level, nor to the department's expectations. Finally Stark had gotten around to what was really bothering him. After a rather lengthy pause, the Chief of Surgery had asked Bellows exactly what role he had played with respect to the drugs found in locker 338.

Bellows had denied any knowledge whatsoever of the drugs, except what Chandler had told him. Bellows had told Stark directly that he had used locker 338 for about one week before his permanent locker came available. Stark's only comment to this information had been that he wanted the affair cleaned up in short order.

For Bellows, even being remotely related to such a situation caused him a disproportionate amount of anxiety. His horribly compulsive mentality magnified the whole affair out of proportion. His tendency toward professional paranoia began to feed on itself and, as the morning passed, his anxiety had waxed rather than waned.

Bellows operated on two cases himself that morning, allowing the students to come into the OR. On the first case, Goldberg and Fairweather had scrubbed, more to wet their hands than actually to help. On the second case, Carpin and Niles had scrubbed. Bellows had been particularly careful and encouraging for Niles and it had paid off. There had been no fainting episodes. In fact, Niles had turned out to be the most dextrous of the students and had been allowed to close the skin.

During lunch Bellows found the opportunity to corner Chandler. The chief resident had reiterated what Bellows already knew—namely, that Stark was really uptight about the drugs.

"The whole Goddamned thing is ridiculous," said Bellows. "Has Stark talked with Walters yet to get me off the hook?"

"I haven't even talked with Walters," said Chandler. "I went into the OR area to talk with him but he hasn't shown up today. Nobody has seen him all day."

"Walters?" Bellows was greatly surprised. "He hasn't missed a day here in a quarter of a century."

"What can I tell you? He's not here."

Bellows responded to this information by going up to the personnel office to get Walters's home phone number. It turned out that Walters did not have a telephone. Bellows had to be satisfied with an address: 1833 Stewart Street, Roxbury.

By one-thirty Bellows was very much on edge. Another call to the OR desk confirmed the fact that Walters still had not appeared, and Bellows made a decision. He decided that he would take the time and make the effort to go and visit Walters. It was the only way that he could think of to extricate himself immediately from the drug affair. It wasn't all that difficult a decision, although it was very irregular for Bellows to leave the hospital in the middle of the day. But Bellows had the distressing feeling that over the last forty-eight hours his comfortable and promising position at the Memorial had been put in jeopardy. As he saw it, he had two problems: the first, the drug problem, was simple, because he knew that he was not involved and that all he had to do was to establish that fact; the second problem, Susan and her so-called project, was something else.

Bellows managed to foist his medical students off on Dr. Larry Beard, a grandson of the Beard wing benefactor. Then, with his beeper on his belt, the operators notified, and a fellow resident by the name of Norris willing to cover for an hour, Bellows slipped out of the hospital at one-thirty-seven, and flagged a cab.

"Stewart Street, Roxbury? You sure about that?" The taxi driver's face contorted into a questioning, disdainful expression when Bellows gave his destination.

"Number 1833," added Bellows.

"It's your money!"

With dirty steaming piles of snow pushed aside here and there, the city looked particularly depressing. It was raining almost as hard as it had been when Bellows had walked to work in the morning. Very few people were visible along the route the driver took. The peculiar, uninhabited look of the city recalled the deserted cities of the Mayans. It was as if things had gotten so bad that everyone decided to just close their doors and leave.

As the cab penetrated Roxbury deeper and deeper, the city got worse. Their route took them down through a disintegrating warehouse area, then through decaying slums. The mid-thirties temperature, the relentless rain, and the rotting snow made it that much more depressing. Finally the cab pulled to the right and Bellows leaned forward, catching sight of the street sign for Stewart Street. At the same time the right front wheel descended into a pothole filled with rain water and the bottom of the front part of the cab crashed against the pavement. The driver swore and threw the steering wheel to the right to avoid the same hole with the rear tire. But the rear of the car slammed down and then lurched upward with a shudder. Bellows's head hit the ceiling hard enough to hurt.

"Sorry, but you wanted Stewart Street!"

Rubbing his head, Bellows looked out at the numbers: 1831, and then 1833. After paying the fare, he stepped out and closed the door. The cab raced off, weaving its way between the potholes and turning off as soon as possible. Bellows watched it disappear from sight, wishing that he had told the driver to wait. Then he looked around, thankful that the rain had stopped. There were several gutted hulks of automobiles with everything of even questionable value removed. There were no other cars parked on the grim street, or moving, for that matter. There were no people in sight either. When Bellows looked up at the row house in front of him, he realized it was deserted, most of the windows boarded up. Then he looked at the surrounding houses. All were the same. Most were boarded up; any windows exposed were smashed.

A torn sign nailed to the front door said that the building was condemned and owned by the BHA, the Boston Housing Authority. The date on the sign was 1971. It was another Boston project that had got completely fouled up.

Bellows was perplexed. Walters had no phone, and this seemed a phony address. Remembering Walters's appearance, it didn't seem so surprising. Curiosity made Bellows mount the stairs to read the BHA sign. There was another smaller sign saying "No Trespassing" and that the police had the premises under surveillance.

The door had once been attractive, with a large oval stained glass window. The glass was now broken and several pieces of roughcut lumber were haphazardly nailed across the opening. Bellows tried the door, and to his surprise it opened. One of the straps of the hasp was unattached, with the screws gone despite the fact that the hasp had a large steel padlock.

The door opened in, scratching over the broken glass. Bellows took one look up and down the deserted street, then stepped over the threshold. The door closed quickly behind him, extinguishing most of the meager daylight. Bellows waited until his eyes adjusted to the semidarkness.

The hall in which he found himself was in ruins. The stairs ascended directly in front of him. The banister had been pushed over and broken into pieces, presumably for firewood. The wallpaper was hanging in streamers. A small dirty drift of snow half-covered the debris on the floor and extended toward the rear of the building. Within six or seven feet it dissipated. But directly in front of him, Bellows saw several footprints. Examining them more closely, he could tell that there were at least two different sets. One set was huge, made by feet half again as large as his own. But more interesting was that the tracks did not seem very old.

Bellows heard a car coming down the street and he straightened up. Conscious of trespassing, Bellows moved over to one of the boarded-up windows in what had been the parlor, to see if the car passed. It did.

Then he climbed up the stairs and partially explored the second floor. Several crumbling mattresses were the only contents. The air had a musty, heavy odor. The ceiling in the front room had collapsed, covering the floor with chunks of plaster. Each room had a fireplace, layers of filth, and dusty cobwebs hanging from the ceiling.

Bellows glanced up the stairs to the third floor but decided not to go up. Instead he returned to the first floor and was preparing to leave when he heard a sound. It was a soft thud coming from the back of the house.

Feeling a certain quickening of his pulse, Bellows hesitated. He wanted to leave. There was something about the house that made him feel uneasy. But the sound was repeated and Bellows walked down the hall toward the rear of the building. At the end of the hall he had to turn right into what had been the dining room. The fixture for the gaslight was still in the center of the ceiling. Walking through the dining room, Bellows found himself in the remains of the kitchen. Everything had been removed except a few naked pipes, which protruded from the floor. The rear windows were all boarded up like those in front.

Bellows took a few steps into the room and there was a sudden movement to his left. Bellows froze. His heart leaped into high gear, thumping audibly in his chest. The movement had come from the direction of several large cardboard boxes.

Having recovered from his sudden fright, Bellows gingerly

approached the boxes. With his foot he nudged them. To his horror several large rats scurried from their cover and disappeared into the dining room.

Bellows's nervousness surprised him. He had always thought of himself as being the calm one, not easily shaken. His reaction to the rats had been one of paralyzing fear, and it took him several minutes to recover. He kicked the cardboard boxes to reassure himself that he was in control and was about to return to the dining room when he noticed another footprint in the dust and debris by the boxes. Looking back and forth from his own footprints to the one he had just found, Bellows realized that the strange footprint must be fairly fresh. Just beyond the cardboard boxes was a door, open by a few inches. The footprint pointed in its direction.

Bellows approached the door and opened it slowly. Beyond was darkness and steps leading down into it. The steps presumably led to the cellar but were quickly swallowed in darkness. Bellows reached into the breast pocket of his white coat and pulled out his penlight. Switching it on, he found that its small beam could penetrate only five or six feet down.

Every ounce of rationality told him to leave the building. Instead he started down the cellar stairs, as much to prove to himself that he wasn't afraid as to find out what was there. But he was afraid. His imagination was working swiftly to remind him how easily horror movies affected him. He remembered the scenes in *Psycho* of the descent into the cellar.

As he advanced step by step, the penlight beam advanced until it played on a closed door. Bellows examined it, and then tried the knob. The door swung open easily.

Bellows had expected that there would be some sunken cellar windows to allow some light in but there was only darkness. He peered ahead after the pale shaft from his penlight into what seemed like a rather large room. His penlight was little help beyond six feet. By moving around the room counterclockwise, Bellows found some broken but serviceable furniture, including a bed covered with newspapers and two moth-eaten blankets. A few cockroaches fled Bellows's encroaching penlight.

There was a fireplace with a large stack of wood on the hearth. Within the fireplace were ashes that suggested a recent fire. Bellows reached down and picked up one of the newspapers to check the date. It was February 3, 1976.

Letting the newspaper drop to the floor, Bellows noticed another door, which was standing ajar about six inches. He started for the door but the penlight dimmed sharply, its miniature batteries drained by the continuous use. Bellows switched the light off for a moment to give it a chance to revive. He found himself in a blackness so dense that he literally could not see his hand in front of his face. And as long as he did not move, total silence reigned.

The sensory deprivation resulted in a building apprehension and Bellows switched on the light before he had planned to do so. The beam was significantly stronger and Bellows could make out white tile on the floor just beyond the door in front of him. A bathroom.

Bellows pushed open the door. It moved hard on its hinges as if it were made of lead. The meager and faltering light from the penlight outlined a toilet without a seat immediately opposite the door. Once the door was half open, Bellows leaned his head into the room. The sink was on the wall to the right around the half-opened door. The light moved over the sink, then up onto the wall and over the mirrored medicine cabinet.

Bellows's scream was totally involuntary. It was not loud, but it came from deep within his brain, a primeval response. The penlight dropped from his hand onto the tiled floor and shattered. Instantly Bellows was plunged into darkness. He turned and ran in the direction of the stairs, falling over the furniture. He was in a total panic, and he slammed into the wall instead of finding the stairs. Running his hand along the wall, he reached a corner and realized that he had come too far. He turned and retraced his steps. Only when he was directly facing the stairs could he see any light from above.

He stumbled up the steps and ran back through the house and out into the street. Only then did he stop, his chest heaving from exertion, his right hand bleeding from one of his falls in the darkness. He looked back at the house, allowing his mind to reconstruct the image that he had seen.

He had found Walters. In the mirror in the bathroom, Bellows had glimpsed Walters hanging by a rope around his neck from a hook on the door. Walters was terribly distorted and bloated by stagnant blood. His eyes were wide open and appeared as if they were about to extrude from his head. Bellows had seen some awful things in emergency rooms during his medical training, but never in his whole life had he seen a more gruesome spectacle than the corpse of Walters.

Wednesday
February 25
4:30 P.M.

Susan entered the dean of students' office with some trepidation, but Dr. James Chapman's demeanor quickly put her at ease. He was not angry, as Susan anticipated, just concerned. A small man with dark hair, closely trimmed, he always looked the same, in his three-piece dark suit complete with a gold chain and a Phi Beta Kappa key. Dr. Chapman paused between his sentences and smiled, not out of emotion, but more as a device to put students at ease. It was a distinctive habit and not unpleasant.

Suggesting the essence of the university, the office of the dean of students at the medical school had a more pleasant atmosphere than offices at the Memorial. A brass antique lamp stood on the desk. The chairs were all of the black academic sort, bearing a decal of the medical school's emblem on the back. An oriental rug brightened the floor. The far wall was covered with pictures of previous classes at the medical school.

After some traditional pleasantries, Susan sat down across from Dr. Chapman. The dean removed his executive reading glasses and carefully placed them on his blotter.

"Susan, why didn't you come to me and discuss this affair before it got out of hand? After all, that's what I'm here for. You could have saved a lot of grief not only for yourself but also for the school. I've got to try to keep everyone as happy as possible. Obviously, keeping everybody happy is impossible, but I do a reasonable job of it. Still, I need warning when there's a special problem. I like to hear when things go poorly and when things go well."

Susan nodded her head in agreement as Dr. Chapman spoke. She was still dressed in the same clothes which she had been wearing during the MBTA mishap. There were obvious abrasions on both of her knees. The parcel containing the nurse's uniform was on her lap. It looked worse than she did.

"Dr. Chapman, the whole affair began innocently enough. The first days of the clinics are difficult enough without the series of coincidences I encountered. They sent me fleeing to the library. As much to get my head together as to learn something, I started to look into anesthetic complications. I thought I could get back to the usual routine in a day or so. But then I got involved so quickly. I turned up some information that astounded me and I thought . . . maybe . . . you're going to laugh when I tell you. It almost embarrasses me to think about it."

"Try me."

"I thought maybe I was on the track of a new disease or syndrome or drug reaction at the least."

Dr. Chapman's face lit up with a genuine smile. "A new disease! Now that would have been a coup for someone's first days as a clinical clerk. Well, one way or the other, it's water under the bridge. I trust you feel differently now?"

"You'd better believe it. I do have a self-preservation reflex. Besides I'm starting to get delusional about the whole thing. I think I had some sort of paranoid reaction this afternoon. I was convinced a man was following me to the point that I actually panicked. Look at my knees and my clothes, as if you haven't already noticed. To make a long story short, I tried to cross from the inbound to the outbound platform at Kendall Station of the MBTA. Idiotic!" Susan tapped her head lightly with her index finger for emphasis.

"After that I realized that it behooved me to get back to normal, quickly. Like right away. But I'm still worried that there is something peculiar about these coma incidents at the Memorial, and I would like to continue studying the problem in some capacity. Apparently there are more cases involved than I originally suspected, and maybe that is why Dr. Harris and Dr. McLeary were irritated at my naive interference. One way or another, I'm sorry I've caused trouble for you at the Memorial. It goes without saying that it was not my intent."

"Susan, the Memorial is a big place. It's probably blown over already. The only tangible legacy is that I'm going to have to switch your surgery to the V.A. hospital. I've already made the arrangements, and you are to report tomorrow morning to Dr. Robert Piles's office." Dr. Chapman paused, looking at Susan intently. "Susan, you have a long road ahead of you. There will be plenty of time to discover new diseases or syndromes, if that is what you want. But now, today, this year, your primary goal should be basic medical education. Let Harris and McLeary work on the coma incidents. I want you to get back to work because I expect nothing but good reports about you. You've done very well so far."

Susan emerged from the medical school Administration Building with a mild sense of euphoria. It was as if Dr. Chapman had powers of absolution. The ponderous problem of being ejected from medical school in disgrace had vanished. Obviously the surgery rotation at the V.A. was not as good as that at the Memorial, but in comparison to what could have happened, the transfer was a mild inconvenience indeed.

Although it was only a little after five, the winter night had begun in earnest. The rain had stopped as another cold front pushed the weakening warm front out over the Atlantic. The temperature had plummeted to about eighteen. The sky was speckled with bright stars, at least directly overhead. Toward the horizon the stars disappeared, their light unable to penetrate the noxious urban atmosphere. Susan crossed Longwood Avenue by running between the cars of impatient commuters in the clogging traffic.

In the lobby of the dorm she passed a few acquaintances, who were quick to notice Susan's skinned knees and the greasy stain of the rail across her coat. There were some clever jibes about how tough surgery rotation must be at the Memorial, to judge by Susan, who looked as if she had been in a barroom brawl. Despite the fact that she thought the comments were rather funny, Susan almost stopped to snap back at the wisecracks. Instead she passed through the lobby and crossed the quad. The tennis court in the center had a sad, neglected winter look.

The well-trodden wooden staircase curved gracefully up, and Susan mounted the steps slowly and deliberately, looking forward to the isolation and security her room promised. She intended to take a long bath, sort out the day mentally, and, above all, relax.

As she always did, Susan entered her room and bolted the door behind her without turning on a light. The switch by the door activated the circular fluorescent bulb in the center of the ceiling, and Susan preferred the richer glow of the incandescent lights, either the lamp by the bed or the modern floor lamp by the desk. With the help of the light coming from the parking lot she walked over to the bed to turn on the lamp. Just as her hand reached for the switch she heard a noise. It was not loud but it was nonetheless distinctive enough to make her aware that it was not part of the normal sounds of her room. It was a foreign noise. She switched on the light, listening for the noise to repeat itself, but it did not recur. She decided it must have come from a neighboring room.

She hung up her coat and her white jacket, and unpacked the new nurse's uniform. It had survived the afternoon remarkably well. Then she unbuttoned and removed her blouse, throwing it onto the pile of dirty laundry in the easy chair. Her bra followed. Reaching behind her with her right hand, she began to struggle with the button on her skirt. At the same time she headed for the bathroom to start the bath water.

She opened the bathroom door and flipped on the fluorescent light, preparing to look in the mirror when the light came on. With a screech of plastic hooks along metal, the shower curtain was whipped back; a figure leaped into the room. Almost at the same instant the fluorescent light blinked and then filled the room with its raw light. There was a flash of a knife and a lightning blow to Susan's head. She twisted backward under its impact, crashing into the wall of the bathroom. By sheer reflex her arms straightened and her hands groped to keep herself from falling. It all happened so quickly that she had no time to react. A cry had started in her throat but the blow to the head had dislodged it.

Instantly the left hand of the intruder grabbed Susan by the throat, forcing her up to her full height against the wall, her naked breasts tensing. Despite all her fantasies about what she would do if she were attacked, knees to the balls, fingernails in the eyes, Susan did nothing but breathe as best she could and gaze at her assailant in utter horror. Her eyes flung open to their very limit. The fury of the unexpected attack had been totally overwhelming. The power of the hand that held her by the throat was unmistakable. And she recognized the man. They had met on the subway platform.

"One sound and you're dead, baby," snarled the man, bringing the knife in his right hand up beneath Susan's chin.

Just as suddenly and roughly as he had originally seized Susan's throat, the man released his hold, causing Susan to stumble forward. Her assailant backhanded her brutally, and she pitched to her hands and knees, with her lip split and numerous small capillaries broken over her left cheekbone.

Hooking his foot under Susan's shoulder, the man forced Susan to rise up on her knees. Then with a callous kick he dumped Susan backward against the wall, where she lay with one arm lewdly draped over the toilet. A trickle of blood ran down from the corner of her mouth and dropped onto a pale breast. The image of the man momentarily swam before her. When he came in focus she could see his pockmarked face crack in a fiendish grin. He was obviously relishing the thought of ravishing her. She felt numb and unable to respond.

"Too bad I'm only authorized on this visit to talk to you, or as we say in my business, to make a preliminary contact. The message is simple. There's a lot of people who are very, very unhappy with the way you have been spending your time lately. Unless you get back to your usual activities and stop getting people mad, I'll have to come back to see you again."

The man paused to let his message sink in. Then he continued: "And just to encourage you a little more, this boy will also get to meet me and maybe even have an unexpected, serious, and probably fatal accident."

The man flipped a picture onto Susan's lap. In slow motion she picked it up.

"And I'm sure you don't want your brother, James, down there in Coopers, Maryland, to suffer from your hobbies. And I don't have to tell you that our little meeting here is just between us. If you go to the cops, the punishment is the same."

Without another word, the man slipped from the bathroom. Susan heard the outside door to her room open and then close quietly. The only sound was a slight buzz from the fluorescent light over the mirror. She did not move for several minutes, uncertain whether her attacker had really left. Her arm was still draped over the toilet.

As the terror subsided, confusion and emotion mounted. Tears welled up in her eyes, forming a bulging meniscus. She lifted the picture of her younger brother with his bike, smiling in front of her parents' home. "Christ," said Susan, shaking her head and closing her eyes tightly. As her eyes closed, the tears overflowed from her lids, running down her cheeks in profusion. There was no doubt that the photograph was authentic.

Footsteps in the hall made Susan suddenly alert, and she pushed herself up onto her feet. The footsteps passed her room and receded down the hall. Susan staggered into her bedroom and rebolted the door. Turning, she scanned her room. Everything seemed undisturbed. Then she realized she felt wet. With her hand she felt herself and couldn't believe it. She had urinated in her panic.

The confusion began to metamorphose into analytical thought, and the thought brought the tears rapidly in check. There had been a host of unexplained episodes in the last couple of days, but one thing began to take definite form in Susan's consciousness. She was now more sure than ever that she had stumbled onto something, something big, something strange.

Looking into the mirror, Susan assayed the damage. Her left eyelids were slightly swollen and might turn into a black eye. Her left cheek sported a contused area about the size of a quarter, and her left lower lip was swollen and tender. By pulling her lip out gently and looking into the mirror Susan could see that she had a two- or three-millimeter laceration on the inside surface. It had been crushed against her lower teeth when she had been struck. The small amount of blood in the corner of her mouth came away easily, improving her appearance tremendously.

Susan decided she was not going to overreact to the latest episode. She also decided that despite Chapman's pleas she was not ready to give up completely. She had a competitive spirit and, although it was deeply buried by years of stereotypical conditioning, it was very strong. Susan had never been challenged in an equivalent capacity before. Never had the potential stakes been so high. But she was also aware of two realities: she had to be extraordinarily careful from then on, and she had to work fast.

Susan got into the shower, turning on the water as hard as it would go. She let it crash down on her head while she slowly rotated. She cupped her hands over her breasts to protect them from the needlelike jets of water. The effect was soothing and it gave her time to think. She thought about calling Bellows but decided against it. Their embryonic intimacy would make it difficult for Bellows to react to the information objectively. He'd probably respond in some idiotic male overprotective fashion. What she needed was a mind with the perspective to challenge her deductions. Then she thought about Stark. He had not been overly influenced by her lowly position as a medical student or by her sex. Besides, his astonishing grasp of medical and business matters was immediately apparent. Above all, he was maturely rational and could be counted on to be objective.

Once out of the shower, Susan wrapped her hair in a towel and donned her terrycloth bathrobe.

She sat down by the phone and dialed the Memorial. She asked for Dr. Stark's office.

"I'm sorry, but Dr. Stark is on another line. Can I have him call you back?"

"No, I'll wait. Just say that it is Susan Wheeler calling and that it is important."

"I'll try, but I cannot promise anything. He's talking long distance and may be on the line for some time."

"I'll hold just the same." Susan was well aware that doctors often ignore returning a call.

Stark finally came onto the line.

"Dr. Stark, you said that I could call you if I found out anything interesting in my little investigation."

"Of course, Susan."

"Well I have found out something extraordinary. This whole affair is definitely . . ." She paused.

"Is definitely what, Susan?"

"Well, I'm not sure how to put it. I guess I'm now sure

that there is a criminal aspect. I don't know how or why, but I'm quite certain. In fact, I have a feeling that some large organization is involved . . . like the Mafia or something."

"Sounds like a pretty wild conjecture to me, Susan. What has brought this idea to mind?"

"I've had a pretty funny afternoon with no laughs." Susan looked closely at her abraded knees.

"And?"

"I've been threatened tonight."

"Threatened with what?" Stark's voice changed from interest to concern.

"My life, I guess." Susan looked at the photo of her brother.

"Susan, if that is true, then this becomes a serious affair, to say the very least. But are you sure this isn't some sort of prank by some of your classmates? Medical school pranks can get rather elaborate on occasion."

"I must admit I hadn't thought of that." Susan gingerly felt her lacerated lip with the tip of her tongue. "But I think this was the real thing."

"Conjecture is not what's needed at this point. I will personally advise the hospital executive committee of this. But, Susan, now is definitely the time for you to withdraw from further involvement. I advised you to do that before, but only because I was afraid it might hurt you academically. Now, it's apparently a different game. I think professionals should take over. Have you reported this to the police?"

"No, the threat included my younger brother, and there was a plain warning not to go to the police. That's why I've called you. Besides, if I went to the police, they'd probably dismiss it as a simple attempted rape rather than a specific threat."

"I doubt it very much."

"Most males would."

"But if the threat included your family, you are probably right to be careful with whom you talk. But my gut reaction suggests that you should report the incident to the police."

"I'll give it some thought. Meanwhile, I wondered if you'd heard that I've been kicked out of my surgery rotation at the Memorial. I have to go to the V.A. to do my surgery."

"No, I've not been told about that. When did this happen?"

"This afternoon. Obviously I'd much prefer to stay at the Memorial. I think that I could prove that I am a good student if given the chance. Since you are Chief of Surgery and since you are aware that I have not been merely goofing off, I thought maybe you might be willing to reverse that decision."

"As Chief of Surgery I should have been told about your dismissal. I will get in touch with Dr. Bellows immediately."

"I don't think he knows about it, either, to tell you the truth. It was a Mr. Oren."

"Oren? Well that's interesting. Susan, I cannot promise anything, but I'll look into it. I must tell you that you have not been the most popular student here with Anesthesia and Medicine."

"I'd appreciate anything you can do. One other question. Would it be possible for you to arrange a visit for me to the Jefferson Institute? I'd very much like to visit the patient, Berman. I'm sort of hoping that if I can see him again that maybe I'll be able to forget this whole affair."

"You certainly have a lot of difficult demands, young lady. But I'll call and see what I can do. The Jefferson is not university-controlled. It was built by government funds through HEW, but its operation has been turned over to a private medical management firm. So I have little voice there. But I'll check. Give me a call after nine tomorrow, and I'll let you know."

Susan hung up the phone. Obviously in deep thought, she bit her lower lip, as was her habit. The result was painful. She stared at one of the posters on her walls but with unseeing eyes. Her mind raced over the events of the last few days, searching for possible associations that she had missed.

Impulsively she got up and took out the nurse's uniform she had purchased. Then she began to dry her hair. Fifteen minutes later, she viewed herself in the mirror. The uniform fitted reasonably well.

She picked up the photograph of her brother for the second time. At least she felt reasonably confident that there was no immediate danger for her family. It was winter vacation for public schools and her family was skiing in Aspen for the week.

Susan had no illusions about her situation. She was in danger and had to be resourceful. Whoever it was that had decided to threaten her undoubtedly expected that she would mend her ways and live in fear, at least for a while. Susan felt that she had about forty-eight hours of relative freedom of movement. After that, who knew.

The thing that encouraged her the most was that someone had decided that she was important enough to be threatened. It might mean that she was on the right track; maybe she had already found more answers than she could associate. She could be like the professor who had carefully discovered all the information necessary to break the secret of DNA. But he had not arranged it properly, and it took the ingenuity of Watson and Crick to pull it all together, to see the whole molecule as the wonderful double helix.

Susan carefully leafed through her notebook, reading all that she had written down. She reread her notes about coma and its known causes; she underlined those articles she still planned to read; she underlined the title of the new anesthesiology text she had seen in Harris's office. Then she reread the extensive material on Nancy Greenly and the two respiratory arrest victims. Susan was sure that the answer was there but she couldn't see it. She knew that she needed more data to increase the likelihood of making correlations. The charts. She needed the charts from McLeary.

It was seven-fifteen when she was ready to leave her room. As if she were in some spy movie, she checked out the parking lot from her window, to see if she were under obvious surveillance. She looked over the cars, but saw no one. Susan pulled the curtains closed and locked her door, leaving her lights on. In the corridor, she stood for a moment, then, extrap-

olating from her movie experience, she rolled a small wad of
paper into a ball and carefully inserted it between the door
and the jamb, next to the floor.

In the basement of the dorm there was a tunnel leading
over to the Anatomy and Pathology Building. It carried steam
pipes and power lines, and Susan and her classmates occasionally used it during inclement weather. Susan had no idea
if she would be followed but she wanted to make it difficult,
hopefully impossible. From the anatomy building Susan used
the passageway to the Administration Building, which she
found unlocked. From there she exited by the medical library,
catching a cab on Huntington Avenue. She had the cab do a
U-turn after a quarter of a mile and drive back, passing the
spot where she had hailed it. Nestling down in her coat to keep
from being seen, Susan tried to see if anyone was following
her. She saw no one at all suspicious-looking. Relaxing, she
told the cab to take her to the Memorial Hospital.

Like any professional "hit man," Angelo D'Ambrosio felt
an inner satisfaction at having successfully completed a job.
After communicating the message he had for Susan, he had
walked back to Huntington Avenue and caught a cab near the
corner of Longfellow. The taxi driver was delighted: finally
he'd found an airport run which meant a decent fare and
undoubtedly a good tip. Prior to D'Ambrosio he'd had nothing but old ladies going to the supermarket.

D'Ambrosio settled back in the cab, content with his day's
work. He had no idea why he had been contracted to do what
he had done in Boston that day. But D'Ambrosio rarely knew
why, and in fact he did not want to know why. On the few
occasions when his information and briefing had been more
complete, he had had more trouble. On the current assignment, he had been merely told to fly to Boston in the evening
of the twenty-fourth and stay at the Sheraton Downtown
under the name of George Taranto. The following morning
he was to proceed to 1833 Stewart Street and to the basement
apartment of a man named Walters. He was to have Walters
write a note saying, "The drugs were mine. I cannot face the
consequences." Then he was to dispose of Walters in a fashion
that would suggest suicide. Then he was to isolate a female
medical student by the name of Susan Wheeler and "scare the
shit out of her," telling her that she would be in danger if she

did not return to her usual occupation. The orders had ended with the usual exhortations about being careful. There was a packet of information about Susan Wheeler, including the photo of her brother, some background, and a schedule of her current activities.

Looking at his watch, D'Ambrosio knew that he could easily make the 8:45 American flight back to Chicago. He also knew his thousand dollars would be in the usual twenty-four-hour locker, number 12 near the baggage claim for TWA. Contentedly, D'Ambrosio watched the play of lights flicker past the window. He thought about the ghoulish Walters and tried to imagine the connection he could have with the attractive Wheeler. D'Ambrosio remembered Susan's appearance, and how he had had to fight with himself not to put it to her. He began to imagine a series of sadistic delights that awakened his sleeping penis. D'Ambrosio found himself hoping that he'd be ordered back to make a second contact with Miss Wheeler. If he ever was, he decided he'd screw her in the ass.

When he reached the airline terminal D'Ambrosio entered a phone booth. There remained one small detail in a routine assignment: he had to call his central contact in Chicago and report that the job was done.

The number rang the agreed-upon seven times.

"The Sandler residence," answered a voice on the other end.

"May I speak to Mr. Sandler, please," said D'Ambrosio, bored. He did not quite understand this maneuver and it took a few minutes. He always had to remember the current name. If the wrong name was used he was supposed to hang up and call an alternate number. D'Ambrosio wet his index finger with his tongue and drew circles of saliva on the phone booth glass. Finally the voice returned.

"It's clear."

"Boston's done, no problems," said D'Ambrosio with no inflection in his voice.

"There's an update. Miss Wheeler is to be disposed of as soon as possible. The method is up to you but it must appear to be a rape. You understand, a rape."

D'Ambrosio couldn't believe his ears. It was like a dream come true.

"There'll be an extra charge," said D'Ambrosio matter-of-factly, carefully concealing his anticipation of sexually assaulting Susan.

"There will be an extra five hundred dollars."

"Seven hundred fifty. This won't be so easy." Easy? It was going to be a breeze. D'Ambrosio thought that he should really be paying.

"Six hundred."

"You're on." D'Ambrosio hung up the phone. He was immensely pleased. He checked the night flight schedule. The last departure for Chicago was 11:45 TWA. D'Ambrosio thought he could get his little kicks and still make that one. He descended to the baggage area and caught a cab. He told the driver to take him to the corner of Longwood and Huntington avenues.

By seven-thirty the ebb and flow of humanity slowed to a trickle at the Memorial. Susan entered through the main entrance. In her nurse's uniform no one even gave her a second look. She first went up to the lounge on Beard 5 and left her coat. Then she checked McLeary's office on Beard 12. The door was locked as she expected and the lights were off. She checked all the nearby offices and labs. All were empty.

Susan returned to the main entrance and walked down the corridor toward the emergency room. Unlike the rest of the hospital, as evening fell the ER became more active. There were a few gurneys with their respective patients parked in the corridor. Susan turned left just before the ER and entered the hospital security office.

The office was small and cluttered. The entire far wall was a bank of TV screens, about twenty or twenty-five of them. Displayed on each screen were images of the entryways, corridors, and key areas of the hospital, including the ER area, televised to these monitors from remote control video cameras. Some of the cameras were stationary; others repeatedly panned over an area. Two uniformed guards and one plainclothes security officer occupied the room. The plainclothesman sat behind a tiny desk, seeming even smaller next to his obese hulk. The skin on his neck overlapped his shirt collar. His breath came in audible gasps.

All three men were oblivious to the TV monitors they were paid to watch. Instead, their eyes were fixed on the screen of a small portable TV set. They were engrossed in the furious combat of a televised hockey game.

"Excuse me, but we have a problem," said Susan, addressing

the plainclothes officer. "Dr. McLeary left tonight without returning some charts to 10 West. And we cannot medicate the patients without the charts. Can you people open his office?"

The security man gave Susan a tenth of a second with his eyes, then returned to the power play in progress. He spoke without looking up.

"Sure. Lou, go up with the nurse here and open the office she needs."

"In a minute, in a minute."

All three watched intently. Susan waited. A commercial came on. The guard leaped to his feet.

"OK, let's get this office open. Let me know if I miss anything, you guys."

Susan had to run a few steps to catch up with the great determined strides taken by the guard. En route he began sorting through an immense collection of keys.

"The Bruins are down by two. If they drop this one too, I'm movin' to Philly."

Susan didn't answer. She hurried along with the guard, hoping that no one would recognize her. She felt a slight sense of relief as they entered the office area. It was deserted.

"Goddamn, where's that key?" cursed the guard as he had to try almost every key on his ring before finding one which would open McLeary's door. The delay made Susan rather nervous, and she began to look up and down the corridor, expecting the worst at any moment. As he opened the door, the guard reached in and flicked on the light.

"Just pull the door closed when you leave. It will lock by itself. I've got to get downstairs."

Susan found herself alone in the outer room of McLeary's office. Quickly she entered the inner room and turned on the light. Then switching off the light in the outer room, she closed herself in McLeary's inner office.

To her dismay, the charts were no longer on the shelf where she had seen them in the morning. She began to search the office. The desk was first. No sign of them. As she closed the center drawer, the phone immediately under her arm began to ring. In the silence the noise seemed earsplitting and it startled her. She looked at her watch and wondered if McLeary often got calls in his office at a quarter of eight in the evening. The sound stopped after three rings, and Susan recommenced her search. The charts were of sufficient bulk so that they could not be hidden in many places. As she pulled out the last drawer of the file cabinet she heard the unmistakable sound of footsteps in the hall. They grew louder. Susan froze, not daring to push the drawer back into the file cabinet for fear of the sound.

To her consternation she then heard the footsteps, and a key go into the lock in the outer door. Susan looked around the room in a panic. There were two doors, one to the outer office, another presumably to a closet. Susan glanced at the position of the furniture, then she snapped off the light. As she did so she heard the outer door open, and the light went on in the outer office. Susan moved toward the closet door, feeling the perspiration appear on her forehead. A metallic sound came from the outer office, then another. The closet door openly easily and Susan eased herself in as quietly as possible. With difficulty she closed the closet door. Almost simultaneously the door to the inner office opened and the light went on. Susan expected the closet door to be yanked open at any second. Instead she heard footsteps going toward the desk. Then she heard the desk chair squeak, as someone sat in it. She thought it was McLeary and she wondered what he was doing in his office at this time. What if he discovered her? The thought made her weak. If he opened the door, Susan decided she would try to bolt.

Then the phone was taken off the hook and Susan heard the familiar sound of dialing. But when the person phoning spoke, the voice confused her. It was female. And the caller was speaking in Spanish. From her own meager Spanish Susan was able to make out a part of the conversation. It was about the weather in Boston, then in Florida. All at once Susan realized that a cleaning lady was plopped down in McLeary's office using the hospital phone to make a personal call to Florida. Maybe that explained hospital overhead.

The call lasted almost a half-hour. Then the cleaning lady emptied the wastebasket, turned out the light, and departed. Susan waited for several minutes before opening the closet door. She headed in the direction of the light switch but her shin thumped painfully into the open file cabinet drawer. Susan cursed and realized what a terrible burglar she would make.

With the light on again Susan resumed her search. Out

of curiosity to see where she had been hiding, she checked the closet. On the lowest shelf, stacked among boxes of stationery, she found the charts she wanted. She wondered if McLeary had actually tried to hide them. But she did not dwell on the mystery. She wanted to get out of McLeary's office.

Drawing on her basic resourcefulness, Susan piled the charts into the freshly emptied wastebasket. Then she left the office, unlocking the door. And as she had done in the dorm, she placed a minute wad of paper between the door and the jamb.

Susan carried the charts up to Beard 5 and entered the lounge. She got out her black notebook and poured herself some coffee. Then she took the first chart and began extracting it, as she had done with Nancy Greenly's.

When D'Ambrosio returned to the medical school dorm, he had no particular plan in mind. His usual method of operation was to improvise, after having observed his quarry for a period of time. He already knew quite a bit about Susan Wheeler. He knew that she rarely went out, once back in her room. He was quite sure she would be there now. What he couldn't be sure of was whether Susan had told the authorities about his initial visit. He decided there was a fifty-fifty chance. If she had told them, there was only a ten percent chance that they would take her seriously or at least that had been D'Ambrosio's experience. And even if they did take her seriously, there was probably only a one percent chance that they would put her under guard. The risk factor was well within D'Ambrosio's normal range. He decided that he would return to her room.

From a telephone in the corner drugstore D'Ambrosio rang Susan's room. No answer. He knew that did not mean anything. She could be there but just not answering. D'Ambrosio could handle the lock on the door; he had determined that in the afternoon. But the bolt; she'd probably have the bolt thrown, and that would be noisy. D'Ambrosio knew he'd have to get her out of her room somehow.

He walked back to the dorm and into the parking lot. Her light was on. He then entered the quad as he had done that afternoon, by picking the padlocks on the gate in the archway.

It was a lock with only three tumblers. It was amazing where the university decided to save money.

He mounted the creaking wooden stairs quickly. D'Ambrosio did not look it, but he was in top physical condition. An athlete, a psychopath. Quickly, he moved over to Susan's door and listened. There were no sounds. He knocked. He was confident she would not open the door without speaking. But at this point D'Ambrosio first wanted to find out if she were there. If she answered, he intended to make it sound as if he were going back down the stairs. That usually worked.

But there was no answer.

He tried again. Still no answer.

He picked the lock in seconds. The door opened. The bolt was off. Susan was gone.

D'Ambrosio checked the closet. The wardrobe had not changed. The two suitcases he had seen on his earlier visit were still there. D'Ambrosio was always thorough and it paid off. He knew, with high probability, that Susan had not left town. That meant she would be back. D'Ambrosio decided to wait.

Wednesday
February 25
10:41 P.M.

Bellows was exhausted. It was going on eleven, and he was still at it. In fact he had not made rounds yet on Beard 5. He had to do that before he left for home. At the nurses' station he got the chart rack and wheeled it toward the lounge. A cup of coffee would help him get through the work. Opening the door, he was genuinely surprised to find Susan in the lounge; she was hard at work.

"Excuse me. I must be in the wrong hospital." Bellows pretended to go back out through the door. Then he looked back at Susan.

"Susan, what in hell's name are you doing here? I was told in no uncertain terms that you had become persona non grata." Without meaning to, Bellows's voice reflected some irritation. It had been a terrible day—with the low spot being his discovery of Walters.

"Who, me? You must be mistaken, sah. I'm Miss Scarlett, the new nurse on 10 West," said Susan, feigning a higher voice with a southern accent.

"Christ, Susan, cut the bullshit."

"You started it."

"What are you doing here?"

"Polishing my shoes, what does it look like I'm doing?"

"OK, OK. Let's start again." Bellows came into the room and sat on the counter top. "Susan, this whole scene has become very serious. It's not that I'm not happy to see you, because I am. I had a fabulous time last night. God, it seems like a week ago. But if you'd been around when the shit hit the fan this afternoon, you'd understand why I'd be a little on edge. Among other things I was told that if I continued to cover and aid you in your, quote, 'idiotic mission,' I'd be out looking for a new residency."

"Ah, poor boy! May have to leave Mama's warm womb."

Bellows looked away for a moment, trying to maintain his composure. "I can sense this conversation is going nowhere. Susan, you cannot understand that I have more to lose in this affair than you do."

"Like hell you do!" Susan's face lit up with sudden anger. "You're so Goddamned self-centered and worried about your residency appointment that you couldn't see a conspiracy if it involved your . . . your mother."

"Jesus Christ! The thanks I get for helping you. What the hell does my mother have to do with all this?"

"Nothing. Absolutely nothing. I just couldn't think of anything else which would come close to your residency in your warped value system. So I took a chance on your mother."

"You're making no sense, Susan."

"No sense, he says. Look, Mark, you're so worried about your career that you're blind. Do I look different to you?"

"Different?"

"Yeah, different. Where's that old clinical expertise, that keen sense of observation that you're supposed to have absorbed during your medical training? What do you think this is here under my eye?" Susan pointed to the bruise on her cheek. "And what do you think this is?" Susan garbled the last few words as she held out her lower lip, exposing the laceration.

"It looks like trauma. . . ." Bellows extended his hand to examine Susan's lip more closely. Susan fended him off.

"Keep your cotton-pickin' mitts off. And you say that you have more to lose in this whole thing. Well, let me tell you something. I was attacked and threatened this afternoon by a man who scared the shit out of me. This man knew about me and what I've been doing these last few days. He even knew about my family. He even included my family in the threat. And you say that you have more to lose!"

"You mean somebody actually hit you?" Bellows was incredulous.

"Oh come on, Mark. Can't you say something intelligent? Do you think these are self-inflicted wounds to make people feel sorry for me? I've stumbled into something big, that I can tell you. And I have a scary feeling that it's some large organization. I just don't know how or why or who."

Bellows looked at Susan for several minutes, his mind racing over her story, which seemed incredible, and his own experience that afternoon.

"I don't have any literal wounds to show, but I had one hell of an afternoon as well. Remember those drugs I told you about? The ones that were found in a locker in the OR doctor's lounge? They were found in a locker assigned to me, as I told you. Like it or not, I was immediately implicated. So I decided that I had to settle the whole thing once and for all by getting Walters to explain why I was still assigned to that locker when he had given me another.

"But Walters didn't come in today. First time in I-don't-know-how-many years. So I decided to visit him." Bellows sighed and poured himself some coffee, remembering the grisly details. "The poor bastard committed suicide over this thing, and I had to be the guy who found him."

"Suicide?"

"Yeah. Apparently he'd learned that the drugs had been

226

found, and he decided to take what he considered the easy way out."

"Are you sure it was suicide?"

"I'm not sure of anything. I didn't even see the note. I called the police and have gotten the details from Stark. But don't suggest it wasn't suicide. God, I couldn't handle that. I'd probably be considered a suspect. What on earth could make you suggest such a thing?" Bellows was intense.

"No reason. It just seems another strange coincidence to have happened at this time. Those drugs that were found may be important somehow."

"I was afraid that your imagination would suggest that they were important. That was one of the reasons why I hesitated to tell you about the drugs in the first place. But look, all this is somewhat peripheral to the present problem, namely your presence here at the Memorial at this rather sensitive time. I mean, Susan, you are not supposed to be here. It's as simple as that." Bellows paused and picked up one of the charts Susan had been extracting. "What the hell are you doing anyway?"

"I finally got some of the charts of the coma patients. Not all of them, but some of them."

"God, you really are amazing. After getting yourself kicked out of the hospital, you still manage to have the balls, so to speak, to come back here and find a way to get these charts. I don't imagine that they leave them lying around for anybody to look at who happens along. How did you manage to get them?"

Bellows looked expectantly at Susan, sipping his coffee and waiting for a response. Susan only smiled.

"Oh no!" said Bellows putting his hand to his forehead. "The nurse's uniform."

"Yup, worked like a charm. Great idea, I must admit."

"Wait a minute. I don't want any credit for it, believe me! What did you do? Get security to open McLeary's or whoever-it-was's office?"

"You're getting more and more clever, Mark."

"You do realize that you're now breaking the law."

Susan nodded in agreement, looking down at the pile of paper filled with her tiny writing.

Bellows's eyes followed hers.

"Well, have they shed any light on this . . . this crusade of yours?"

"Not much, I'm afraid. At least not yet, or at least I've not been clever enough to spot it. I wish I had all the charts. So far the ages have all been relatively young, twenty-five to forty-two. Otherwise they seem to be of random sex, racial background, social background. I can't find any relationship in their previous medical histories. Their vital signs and progress up until the onset of coma were uncomplicated in all cases. Their personal physicians were all different. Of the surgical cases, only two had the same anesthesiologist. The anesthetic agents were varied, as expected. There were some overlaps in the preoperative medications. A number of the cases had Demerol and Phenergan, but others had totally different agents. Innovar was used on two cases. But all that's not surprising.

"It does seem, as far as I can tell without going up in the OR, that most if not all the surgical cases occurred in room eight. That does seem a little strange, but then again that's the room used most often for the shorter operations. And this problem is most often associated with the shorter operations. So that's probably to be expected as well. Laboratory values are all generally normal. Oh, by the way, all cases seemed to have been blood-typed and tissue-typed. Is that normal procedure?"

"They blood-type most surgical patients, especially if they anticipate much blood loss during the operation. Tissue-typing is not usual, although the lab may be doing it as part of a check on new equipment or new tissue-typing sera. See if there is an accounting number on one of the lab reports on the typing."

Susan flipped back through the pages of the chart in front of her until she located the tissue-type report.

"No, there's no accounting number."

"Well, that explains that, then. The lab is doing it at their expense. That's not abnormal."

"The medical patients were all on I.V.s for one reason or another."

"So are ninety percent of the people in the hospital."

"I know."

"Sounds like you got a lot of nothing."

"I'd have to agree at this point." Susan paused, sucking

on her lower lip. "Mark, before the endotracheal tube is placed in a patient during anesthesia, the anesthesiologist paralyzes the patient with succinylcholine. Isn't that right?"

"Succinylcholine or curare, but usually succinyl."

"And when a patient is given a pharmacological dose of succinylcholine, he can't breathe."

"That's true."

"Couldn't an overdose of succinylcholine be the way these patients are rendered hypoxic? If they can't breathe, then oxygen doesn't get to the brain."

"Susan, the anesthesiologist gives succinylcholine and then monitors the patient like a hawk; he even breathes for the patient. If there is too much succinylcholine, it just means the anesthesiologist has to breathe the patient for a longer time until the patient metabolizes the drug. The paralyzing effect is completely reversible. Besides, if something like that were being done maliciously, all the anethesiologists in the hospital would have to be involved, and that's hardly likely. And maybe even more important is the fact that under the combined eye of the anesthesiologist and the surgeon, who can actually see how red the blood is and how well it is oxygenated, it would be absolutely impossible to alter the patient's physiologic state without one or both knowing it. When blood is oxygenated, it is bright red. When oxygen gets low, the blood becomes dark brownish-bluish-maroon. The anesthesiologist meanwhile is breathing the patient, constantly checking the pulse and blood pressure, and watching the cardiac monitor. Susan, you are hypothesizing some sort of foul play, and you don't have a why or a who or a how. You're not even sure you have a victim."

"I'm sure I have a victim, Mark. It might not be a new disease but it's something. One more question. Where do the anesthetic gases come from that the anesthesiologists use?"

"It varies. Halothane comes in cans like ether. It's a liquid and it's vaporized as needed in the OR. Nitrous, oxygen, and air come from central sources and are piped into the OR's. There are standby cylinders of oxygen and nitrous oxide in the OR for emergency use. . . . Look, Susan, I've got a little more work to do, then I'm free. How about coming over to the apartment for a drink?"

"Not tonight, Mark. I want to get a good night's sleep and I've got a few more things to do. But thanks. Also, I've got to get these charts back to their hiding place. After that I intend to look around in OR room number eight."

"Susan, I personally think you should get your ass out of this hospital before you really get yourself in hot water."

"You're entitled to your opinion, doctor. It's just that this patient doesn't feel like following orders."

"I think you're carrying all of this too far."

"You do, do you? Well, I might not have a who, but I've got a number of suspects. . . ."

"Sure you do. . . ." Bellows fidgeted. "Are you going to make me guess or are you going to tell me?"

"Harris, Nelson, McLeary, and Oren."

"You're out of your squash!"

"They all act as guilty as hell and want me out of here."

"Don't confuse defensive behavior with guilt, Susan. After all, complications are hard to live with in medicine, no matter from what cause."

Wednesday
February 25
11:25 P.M.

Susan felt a definite sense of relief when she had returned the charts to their hiding place in McLeary's closet. At the same time, she was very disappointed. Having finally inspected them was an anticlimax of sorts. She had placed a great deal of emphasis on the importance of the charts, but after she had finished studying them, she felt no further in her mission. She had a lot more data but no correlates, no intercepts. The cases still seemed to be random and unassociated.

The elevator slowed and stopped, the door quivered, then opened. Susan stepped out into the OR area. There was still a case going on in room No. 20, a ruptured abdominal aneurysm that had been admitted through the emergency room. The operation had been in progress for over eight hours; that didn't look so good. Otherwise the OR area was in its nightly repose. There were a few people busy cleaning the floor and restocking the supply room with freshly laundered linen. A girl in a scrub dress was behind the main desk, trying to fit the last few cases into the following day's master schedule.

The nurse's uniform ruse was still working well for Susan and the few people in the hall did not seem to notice her passing. She went directly to the nurses' locker rooms and changed into a scrub dress, hanging the nurse's uniform in an open locker.

Reentering the main hall, Susan eyed the swinging doors into the area of the operating rooms. A large sign on the right door said "Operating Rooms: Unauthorized Entry Forbidden." The main desk was just to the side of these doors. The nurse sitting behind the desk was still hard at work. Susan had no idea if she would be challenged if she tried to enter.

In order to survey the scene in its totality, Susan walked the length of the hall several times, half-hoping the girl at the main desk would take a break and leave. But she didn't budge, nor even look up. Susan tried to think of some appropriate explanation in case the girl questioned her. But she couldn't think of any. It was almost midnight and she knew she'd have to have some reasonably convincing story to explain her presence.

Finally, with no cover story in mind except for some weak comment about wanting to check on progress in room No. 20, or being sent up from the lab to do random cultures for contamination, Susan made her move. Pretending not to notice the girl at the desk, she headed for the doors. As she passed, the girl did not look up. A few more steps. When Susan reached the doors, she straight-armed the one on the right. It opened and Susan was about to enter.

"Hey, just a minute."

Susan froze, waiting for the inevitable. She turned to face the girl.

"You forgot your conductive boots."

Susan looked down at her shoes. As it dawned on her what the nurse was concerned about, Susan felt relieved.

"Damn, you'd think this was my second time in the OR."

The nurse's attention went back to the master schedule. "I forget the bastards now and then myself."

Susan walked over to a stainless steel cabinet against the wall. The conductive booties—designed to prevent static electricity, so hazardous where inflammable gas was flowing—were kept in a large cardbox box on the lower shelf. Susan put them on the way Carpin had shown her on the first visit to the OR two days before, tucking the black tapes inside her shoes. When she opened the swinging door the second time, the nurse at the desk didn't even look up. The Memorial was large enough so that new faces were to be expected.

The operating rooms at the Memorial were grouped in a large U-shape with supply, holding area, and anesthesia offices in the center. The entrance to the OR area was at the bottom of the U and the recovery room was on the left arm of the U, closest to the elevators. Susan found that room No. 8 was on the right arm of the U, on the outside.

No. 20, where the operation continued, was in the opposite direction, and Susan found herself quite alone approaching room No. 8. Pausing at the door, she looked through the glass. It looked exactly like room No. 18, where Niles had passed out. The walls were tile, the floor a speckled vinyl. Although the lights were out, Susan could see the large kettledrum operating lights above, and the operating table immediately below. She opened the door and turned on the lights.

Without any specific objective in mind, Susan roamed around the room, noticing the larger objects. Then in a more systematic fashion she began to examine details. She found the gas line terminals, noticing that oxygen had a green male connector. The nitrous connector was blue and structurally different so that no mistake could be made. A third male connector was not labeled or colored. Susan assumed it was the compressed air line. A larger female connector was labeled "suction"; above it was a gauge with a large adjusting dial.

In the back of the room were a number of stainless steel cabinets filled with various supplies. There was a desk of sorts for the circulating nurse. The right wall had an X-ray screen. The rear wall, next to the door, had a large institutional clock. The large red second hand swept around smoothly. Another door led into an adjoining supply room, shared with OR No. 10, which contained the sterilizers and other paraphernalia.

Susan spent almost an hour going over room No. 8, as well as No. 10 for comparison. She found nothing abnormal or even mildly curious about room No. 8. It was an OR room like so many thousands. No. 10 appeared no different.

Without challenge, Susan retraced her steps to the nurses' locker room and changed back into her nurse's uniform. She threw her scrubdress into a hamper and started for the door. But she paused then, looking up at the ceiling. It was a drop ceiling, made with large blocks of acoustical tile.

The wastebasket provided an intermediate step. Susan moved from the wastebasket to the sink to the top of the lockers. The ceiling was about three feet above the top of the lockers. Crouching on all fours, she tried the first ceiling block. It would not lift up because of some piping immediately above it. She tried another. Same problem. The third tile, however, lifted easily, and Susan slid it to one side. She then stood up on top of the locker, projecting half of herself into the ceiling space. Contrary to her estimate, the ceiling space was generous in its size. There was almost five feet of vertical space from the dropped acoustical ceiling to the cement of the floor slabs above. A myriad of pipes and ducts ran through this space, carrying the hospital's vital supplies and wastes. The light was very poor, with only pencil-like beams seeping up from below in scattered locations between ceiling tiles.

The dropped ceiling was composed of the cardboard tile, held in place by thin metal strips, which were in turn hung from the cement slab above. Neither the tiles nor the metal strips were strong enough to carry any weight. In order to enter the ceiling space, Susan had to pull herself up onto the pipes, which she found either ice cold or very hot. Once up in the ceiling space, she replaced the ceiling tile she had moved. It fell back into place, cutting off the direct source of light.

Susan waited until her eyes made the adjustment from the fluorescent world below to the semidarkness above. Eventually outlines took forms and Susan could move ahead along the pipes. She noticed a row of studs which continued through the ceiling space to connect with the concrete above. She guessed that they marked the wall of the corridor.

Progress was slow; it was difficult to move on the pipes, treading on one, keeping hold of another or, here and there, a stud for support. She did not want to make any noise, especially when she guessed she was over the area of the main desk. Once over the OR area itself, the going became definitely easier. The ceilings over the OR and the recovery room were fixed and made of prestressed concrete. Susan could move at will provided she avoided tripping on the piping and provided she bent over considerably, for the space here was only about three feet high.

Susan found a concrete wall which she guessed housed the elevator shafts. Then she discovered that the corridor of the OR area had a dropped ceiling. Beyond the OR corridor, over what was probably part of central supply, Susan could see that the maze of pipes and ducts running through the ceiling space converged in what seemed a tangled vortex. Susan guessed that was the location of the central chase which housed all the piping and ducts coursing vertically in the building.

Susan was interested primarily in locating room No. 8. But that was not easy. There were no specific demarcations from one OR to the next. The pipes seemed to spread out and dive through the concrete to the operating rooms below in utter anarchy. The corridor ceiling led to a solution. By carefully picking up the edges of the ceiling blocks over the corridor, Susan was able to orient herself and locate the ceiling area of rooms No. 8 and No. 10. Susan satisfied herself that the number and configuration of the pipes to and from the two rooms were identical.

The gas lines corresponding to the painted intake connectors she had seen down below in the ORs had the same color codes in the ceiling space. Over room No. 8, Susan found the oxygen line with a splash of green paint. Susan traced the oxygen line from room No. 8. It coursed back to the edge of the corridor then bent at a right angle to run parallel to it, alongside similar oxygen lines coming from other ORs. As Susan passed additional OR rooms, more lines joined the oxygen line she was trailing. In order to be sure she was still following the pipe from No. 8, Susan kept her finger on it all the way to the edge of the central chase. Then her finger hit something. In the dim light she had to bend over to see what it was. She saw a stainless steel female connector. Just over the edge of the chase carrying the pipes up from the hospital depths was a high-pressure T-valve on the oxygen line leading to room No. 8.

Susan stared at the valve. She looked at the other gas lines coming up the chase. There were no similar valves on any of the other lines. With her finger she examined the valve. It was obvious that the oxygen could be tapped from the line at that point. But equally as possible was that something, another gas, could be bled into the oxygen line at the same point.

Keeping to the fixed ceilings of the ORs, Susan worked her way back to the area of the main desk. Then she began the difficult part of crossing the large expanse of non-fixed ceiling. Wishing she had dropped some bread crumbs in the forest of pipes, Susan was forced to reconnoiter. She lifted a corner of a ceiling tile, but it was over the hall. She lifted another tile only to find herself over the doctors' lounge. The third tile was over the nurses' locker, but too far from the lockers she needed to step on. The fourth tile was perfect, and Susan descended with little difficulty.

Thursday
February 26
1:00 A.M.

Like any major city, Boston never completely goes to sleep. But unlike many a major city, Boston becomes almost silent. As Susan settled back in the taxi speeding along Storrow Drive, only two or three cars passed, all going in the opposite direction. She was very tired, and she craved sleep. It had been an unbelievable day.

The laceration of her lip and the bruise on her cheek had grown more painful. Gingerly she touched her cheek to see if the swelling had increased. It had not. She looked out over the Esplanade and the frozen Charles River to her right. The lights of Cambridge were sparse and uninviting. The taxi banked sharply left off Storrow Drive onto Park Drive, requiring Susan to steady herself with her arm.

She tried to assess her progress. It wasn't encouraging. To keep within a reasonable limit of safety, she thought she had another thirty-six hours or so to press her search. But she was stymied. As the cab crossed the Fenway, Susan admitted to herself that she had run out of ideas on how to proceed. She felt she could not chance the Memorial by day with Nelson, Harris, McLeary, and Oren all lined up against her. She doubted the nurse's uniform would work on a direct confrontation.

But she wanted more data from the computer. She needed the other charts, too. Was there a way to do it? Would Bellows help? Susan doubted it. She now knew that he was truly anxious about his position. He really is an invertebrate, she thought.

And what about Walters's suicide? How could those drugs be tied in?

Susan paid her fare and got out of the taxi. Walking up to the door, she decided that in the morning she would try to find out as much as possible about Walters. He had to be related. But how?

Susan stood by the front door with her hand on the knob, expecting to be buzzed in by the watchman at the front desk. But he wasn't sitting there. Susan cursed as she rummaged in her coat for her keys. It was uncanny how the man at the desk seemed to disappear whenever you needed him.

The four flights up to her floor seemed longer than usual to Susan. She paused on several occasions, because of a combination of physical fatigue and mental effort.

Susan tried to remember if Bellows had said succinylcholine was among the drugs found in the locker in the doctors' dressing room. She distinctly remembered his saying curare but she could not remember succinylcholine. She got to the top of the stairs still very much lost in thought. It took another minute to find the correct key. As she had done countless times, she inserted the key in the lock. It took a bit of effort.

Despite her deep thought and exhaustion, Susan remembered about the wad of paper. Leaving the key in the door she bent down to look.

The paper was not there. The door had been opened.

Susan backed away from the door, half-expecting it to open suddenly. She remembered the horrid face of her assailant. If he was within the room, he was undoubtedly poised, expecting her to enter as usual. She thought of the knife he had not used the last time. She knew that she had very little time. The only factor in her favor was that if he were in the room, he would not know Susan suspected his presence. At least for a few moments.

If she called the authorities and the man was found, she'd be safe for some hours perhaps. But she recalled the threat about telling the police, the photograph of her brother. Did that suggest a burglar or a rapist? Not likely. Susan understood that the man who attacked her before was both professional and serious, deadly serious. She should run, perhaps even leave town. Or should she call the police anyway, as Stark had suggested? She was no professional; that was painfully apparent.

Why would they be after her already? She felt confident she had not been followed. Maybe the wad of paper had fallen out by itself. Susan advanced toward the door again.

"What the hell's the matter with this lock?" she said aloud, shaking the keys, playing for time. She remembered that the watchman was not at his desk downstairs. Should she go down and knock on someone else's door, saying that hers was stuck? Susan backed away again and moved over to the stairs. She thought that was the best idea under the circumstances. She knew Martha Fine on three well enough to knock at this hour. She didn't know what she should tell her. It was probably best for Martha if she told her nothing. All she'd say was that she couldn't get into her own room and she needed to sleep on Martha's floor.

Susan stepped slowly onto the wooden stairs. They creaked mercilessly under her weight. The sound was unmistakable and Susan knew it. If someone was poised behind her door he would have heard it. Susan ran down the stairs headlong. As she got to the third floor she heard the latch on her door snap open. She went on down, not bothering to stop. What if Martha wasn't there, or wouldn't answer? Susan knew that she could not let the man get hold of her again. The dorm seemed asleep, although it was only a little after one.

Susan heard her door fly open and hit the wall of the hall. She heard some steps and imagined that someone had run to the banister. Susan dared not to look up. Her mind was made up. She'd leave the dorm. It would be easy to lose whoever was following her within the medical school complex. Susan felt she could run relatively quickly and she knew every inch of the area. She was at the ground floor when she heard her pursuer start down the stairs above.

At the bottom of the stairs Susan turned sharply to the left and ran through a small archway. Quickly she opened the door to the quad outside, but she did not exit. Instead, she let the hydraulic hinge begin to close the door. She turned and passed through the door into the adjacent wing of the dorm, shutting that door after her. She could hear feet running on the landing of the second floor.

Avoiding the noise her shoes would make if she ran normally, Susan moved down the ground-floor hall of the adjacent dorm, keeping her legs relatively stiff. She moved quickly but silently, passing the Student Health Office. At the end of the hall she opened the stairwell door quietly and allowed it to close behind her without a noise. She found herself on a stairway to the basement level and wasted no time in descending.

D'Ambrosio was tricked by the slowly closing door to the quad but not for long. D'Ambrosio was no novice at pursuit and he knew just how much time Susan was ahead of him. As he ran into the quad, he knew immediately that he had been duped. He would have been, except there were no other doors close enough for her to have got back into the building.

D'Ambrosio darted back through the door he had just opened. There were only two alternate routes. He chose the nearest door and ran forward down the hall.

Susan entered the tunnel connecting the dorm with the medical school. She was sure she must be in the clear. The tunnel proceeded straight for twenty-five or thirty yards, then twisted out of sight to the left. Susan moved ahead as quickly as she could: the tunnel was fairly well lit by bulbs in open wire cages.

At the end of the tunnel she reached for the handle on the fire door and opened it. A breeze of air hit her as she went through. A sinking feeling passed over her as she realized that could mean only one thing. The door behind her had to be open at the same time! Then she heard the unmistakable heavy footsteps of a man running in the tunnel.

"My God," she whispered in a panic. Perhaps she had misjudged. She had left a dorm full of people, even if asleep, for the labyrinthine spaces of a dark, deserted building.

Susan rushed up the stairs ahead, feeling a sense of helplessness as she remembered the strength of D'Ambrosio. Quickly she tried to think of the layout of the building she was now in. It was the Anatomy-Pathology Building, which had four floors. There were two large lecture amphitheaters on the first floor as well as several ancillary rooms. The second floor had the anatomy hall with a number of smaller labs. The third and fourth floors were mostly offices, and Susan was not familiar with them.

She opened the door onto the first floor. Unlike the tunnel, the building was totally dark except for light from the street-lamps filtering through infrequent windows. The floor was made of marble and it echoed with her footsteps. The hall followed a circular pattern as it skirted the pit of one of the amphitheaters.

With no particular plan in mind, Susan rushed up to one of the wide but low doors leading into the first amphitheater. It was the door through which patients were wheeled for demonstrations. As Susan closed the door she heard running footsteps on the marble hall behind her. She moved away from the low door into the center of the amphitheater. The banks of seats rose in regular tiers until they were lost in darkness. She mounted the steps leading up one aisle from the pit.

The footsteps got louder and Susan hurried upward, afraid to look back. The footsteps passed and became less audible. Then they stopped altogether. Susan moved higher and higher. Behind her the pit of the amphitheater became more and more difficult to distinguish. Susan reached the upper tier of seats and moved laterally along it. She heard the footsteps on the marble again. She had a few moments to think. She knew there was no way she could cope with this man directly; she had to lose him or hide long enough so that he would give up and leave. She thought about the tunnel to the Administration Building. But she wasn't one hundred percent sure that it would be open. Occasionally it had been locked when she tried to take that route home from the library in the evening.

She froze as she heard the door open into the pit of the amphitheater. The shadowy figure of a man entered. She could barely see him. But she was dressed in the white nurse's uniform and she feared that she was more easily visible. She slowly crouched down behind a row of seats, but the backs of the chairs only rose eight to twelve inches above the level she was on. The man stopped and did not move. Susan guessed that he was trying to scan the room. She carefully lay down on the floor. She could see between the backs of two of the seats. The man walked over to the podium and seemed to be searching. Of course. He was searching for the lights! Susan felt panic again take control. Ahead of her, about twenty feet away, was a door to the hall on the second floor. Susan prayed that the door would be open and not locked. If it were locked she would have to try to make it to the door on the opposite side of the amphitheater. That would take about as long as it would take D'Ambrosio to get from the pit up to her level. If the door ahead of her was locked, she was lost.

There was a snap of a light switch and the lamp on the podium went on. Suddenly and eerily D'Ambrosio's horrid pockmarked face was illuminated from below, casting grotesque shadows and making his eye sockets appear like burnt holes in a ghoulish mask. His hands groped along the side of the podium, and the sound of a second switch reverberated in Susan's ears. A strong ray of light sprang from the darkened ceiling, illuminating the pit in a brilliant beam. Now Susan could see D'Ambrosio clearly.

She crawled forward as rapidly as she could toward the door. Another light switch snapped and a bank of lights lit up the blackboard behind D'Ambrosio. At that point D'Ambrosio noted the switches for the room lights to the left of the blackboard. As he walked over to the switches, Susan got up and broke for the door. She turned the knob as the lights went on in the room. Locked!

Susan stared down into the pit. D'Ambrosio saw her and a smile of anticipation came to his thin, scarred lips. Then he ran for the stairs, taking them in twos and threes.

Susan shook the door in despair. Then she noted that it was bolted from within. She threw the bolt and the door opened. She flung herself through it and slammed the door behind her. She could hear D'Ambrosio's deep breaths as he neared the top row of seats.

Directly across from the second-floor amphitheater door was a CO_2 fire extinguisher. Susan ripped it from the wall and turned it upside down. She spun around, hearing the metallic click of D'Ambrosio's shoes coming closer and closer, and got set just as the knob turned and the door swung open.

At that instant, Susan depressed the button on the fire extinguisher. The sudden phase change and expansion of the gas caused an explosive noise that shrieked and echoed in the silence of the empty building as the spray of dry ice caught D'Ambrosio full in the face. He reeled backward and tripped over the upper row of seats, his big body teetering, then crashing sideways onto the second and third rows. A seat back dug deeply into his side, snapping his left eleventh rib. His arms flew out to protect himself, grabbing at the seat backs as his feet continued over his head. He fell lengthwise facedown into the fourth row, stunned.

Susan herself was amazed at the effect and stepped into the amphitheater, watching D'Ambrosio's fall. She stood there for an instant, thinking that D'Ambrosio must be unconscious. But the man drew his knees up and pulled himself into a kneeling position. He looked up at Susan and managed a smile despite the intense pain of his broken rib.

"I like 'em . . . when they fight back," he grunted between clenched teeth.

Susan picked up the fire extinguisher and threw it as hard as she could at the kneeling figure. D'Ambrosio tried to move, but the heavy metal cylinder struck his left shoulder, knocking him down again, and forcing the upper part of his body to fall over the backs of the seats of the next row down. The fire extinguisher bounced down four or five more rows with a terrific clatter, coming to rest in the eighth row.

Slamming the door to the amphitheater shut on her pursuer, Susan stood panting. My God, was he superhuman? She had to find a way to detain him. She knew that she had been unbelievably lucky in injuring him, but plainly he was not out of the picture. Susan thought of the large deep-freeze in the anatomy room.

The hall was dark except for the window at the far end, which provided a paltry amount of pale light. The entrance to the anatomy room was at the very end of the hall near to the window. Susan ran for the door. As she reached it, she heard the door from the amphitheater open.

D'Ambrosio was hurt but not badly. It was painful to cough or take a deep breath, but it was bearable. His left shoulder was bruised but functioning. More than anything else, he was mad. The fact that this screwy chick had managed to get the best of him even for a few moments pissed him off. Now he'd kill her first and fuck her later. He had his Beretta in his right hand, its silver silencer screwed in place. As he stepped from the amphitheater, he just caught sight of Susan entering the anatomy hall. He fired without really aiming and the bullet missed Susan several inches, slamming into the edge of the door frame and throwing splinters of wood into the air.

The sound of the gun was like that of a rug beater. Susan had no idea what it was until the noise and effect of the slug entering the woodwork made it clear to her that it was a gun, a gun with a silencer.

"All right, you bitch, the game's over," shouted D'Ambrosio, coming down the hall at a walk. He knew he had her cornered and that it would hurt to run.

Inside the anatomy hall, Susan paused for a moment, trying to recall the layout in the faint light. Then she bolted the door behind her. The first-year class at that time of the year was in the middle of their anatomy course. The dissecting tables in the room were covered with green plastic sheets. In the dim light they appeared light gray. Susan ran between the shrouded tables to the freezer door at the far end of the room. There was a large stainless pin through the latch. She pulled the pin free and let it hang by its chain, releasing the latch. With some effort Susan opened the heavy insulated door and squeezed through. She pulled the door shut behind her and heard the heavy click. She groped for a light beside the door and switched it on.

The freezer was at least ten feet wide and thirty feet deep. Susan remembered all too clearly the first day she had seen it. The diener loved to show it to the students, one at a time, and he particularly liked female students for some unknown but undoubtedly perverse reason. He had charge of the cadavers stored here for dissection. After embalming, they were hung up with tongs hooked into the external ear canals. The tongs were connected to roller bearings on tracks in the ceiling, to facilitate movement. The bodies were stiff, naked, misshapen; most were the color of pale marble. The females were mixed with the males, the Catholics with the Jews, the whites with the blacks in the equality of death. The faces were frozen into a wide variety of distorted grimaces. Most of the eyes were closed but here and there was an open one, blankly staring into infinity. The first time Susan had seen these four rows of frozen cadavers hanging up like unwanted clothes in a closet of ice, she had felt sick. She had vowed never to return. And until that night she had avoided the "fridge," as it was affectionately called by the diener. But now it was different.

The anatomy hall had been dark. The inside of the freezer was lit by a single hundred-watt bulb from the rear of the compartment, casting horrid shadows on the ceiling and floor. Susan tried not to look directly at the grotesque bodies. She shivered from the cold and frantically tried to think. There were only a few moments. Her pulse was racing. She knew that D'Ambrosio would be coming into the freezer within minutes. She had to have a plan but she didn't have much time.

Smiling, D'Ambrosio stepped back and kicked the locked door of the anatomy hall, but it held firm. He kicked out a pane of frosted glass, pulled out a few of the splintered pieces, and reached in, opening the door. He looked around the room, not comprehending what it was.

As a precaution against his prey bolting, he closed the door and moved a nearby table in front of it. The room was large, some sixty feet by one hundred feet, with five rows of seven shrouded tables each. D'Ambrosio went up to the nearest table and whipped off the plastic drape.

D'Ambrosio gasped, not even feeling the pain from his broken rib. He was staring at a cadaver. The head was dissected free of skin, the teeth and the eyes were bared. The hair had been undermined and folded back like a pelt. The front of the chest was gone, as was the front of the abdomen.

The organs, which had been removed, were piled back into the opened body haphazardly.

D'Ambrosio walked back to the door and thought about turning on the lights. Then he decided against it because of the large windows and the fear of alerting the security police. Not that he didn't feel confident about handling a couple of inexperienced guards, but he wanted to get Susan without any interference.

Systematically D'Ambrosio removed all the shrouds from all the cadavers in the room. He tried not to look at the dissected bodies. He just wanted to make sure that Susan was not among them.

D'Ambrosio looked around the room. On the right side of the hall several skeletons hung on chains, turning slowly in the air stirred by the opening and closing of the door. Behind the skeletons was a huge cabinet containing numerous specimen jars. At the end of the room were three desks and two doors. One of the doors looked like a freezer door, the other a closet. The closet was empty. Then D'Ambrosio noted the stainless steel pin hanging from the latch on the freezer door. The light smile returned, and he transferred the gun to his left hand. He opened the freezer door and again fell back in horror. The hanging bodies appeared like an army of ghouls.

D'Ambrosio was shaken by the appearance of the bodies and his eyes darted from one to another. Reluctantly he stepped over the threshold of the freezer, feeling the sudden chill.

"I know you're in here, cunt. Why not come out so we can have another talk?" D'Ambrosio's voice trailed off. The close quarters in the freezer and the appearance of the stiffs made him nervous, more nervous than he ever remembered being.

He looked down between the first two rows of frozen corpses. Warily he took two steps to the right and looked down the middle row. He could see the bare light bulb in the rear of the compartment. Glancing back at the door, he took several more steps to the right so he could look down the last corridor.

Susan's fingers were losing their grip around the overhead track in the back of the second row of corpses. She did not know D'Ambrosio's position, not until he called the second time.

"Come on, sweetheart. Don't make me search this place."

Susan was sure that D'Ambrosio was at the head of the last row. She knew it was now or never. With all the force she could muster, she pushed with her legs against the back of the wizened female cadaver in front of her. By holding onto the track above, Susan had lifted her legs up and coiled them against the old woman's back. Her own back was pressed against the rock-hard chest of the last cadaver in the row, a two-hundred-pound black male.

Almost imperceptibly at first, the entire second row of frozen corpses began to move forward. Once the initial inertia was overcome, Susan was able to lunge with her feet, imparting a terrific thrust. Like a row of dominoes the entire group of bodies slid forward on their ball bearings.

D'Ambrosio's ears picked up the sound of the movement. He held himself still for a fraction of a second, trying to locate the weird sound. With the swiftness of a cat, he whirled and retreated toward the door. Not fast enough. As he stepped past the third row, he saw the movement. Instinctively he raised his gun and fired. But his attacker was already dead.

Coming at D'Ambrosio with surprising speed was a ghostly white male whose lips were frozen in a horrid half-smile. Two hundred pounds of frozen human meat slammed into the hit man, sending him crashing into the side of the freezer. In rapid succession the other corpses tumbled after the first, several falling from their hooks, creating a huddle of corpses, a tangle of frozen extremities.

Susan let go of the track, dropping to the floor. Then she ran for the open door. D'Ambrosio was trying to pull the bodies off himself. But he was in pain and had little leverage. The reek of embalming fluid was choking him. As Susan passed he tried to grab her. He struggled to free his gun and aim but it caught in the gnarled hand of a corpse.

"Fuck!" shouted D'Ambrosio as he used all of his might against oppressive weight of dead flesh.

But Susan was through the door.

D'Ambrosio was upright now. Pushing the toppled bodies right and left, he flung himself at the closing door. But outside it Susan was pushing with all her might, and the momentum of the insulated door carried it home. The latch clicked. Susan fumbled with the stainless steel pin. Inside, D'Ambrosio was grabbing for the latch release. Susan beat him by a fraction of a second as the pin dropped home.

Susan backed up, her heart pounding. She heard a muffled cry. Then there was a thud. D'Ambrosio was shooting into the door. But it was twelve inches thick. There were several more ineffectual thuds.

Susan turned and ran. She finally understood the reality of the danger she had been in. Trembling uncontrollably, she fought back tears. She had to find help, real help.

Thursday
February 26
2:11 A.M.

Beacon Hill was definitely asleep. As the cab turned off Charles Street onto Mount Vernon and drove up into the residential area, there were no people, no cars, not even any dogs. The lights in the windows were few; only the gas lamps suggested that the area was populated, not deserted. Susan paid the cab driver, then looked up and down the street to see if anyone was following her.

After escaping from D'Ambrosio in the freezer, Susan was terrified and decided not to return to her room. She had no idea if D'Ambrosio was working alone or with an accomplice, but she was in no mood to find out. She had run out of the Anatomy Building, crossed in front of the Administration Building and had reached Huntington Avenue by passing the School of Public Health. At that hour it had taken fifteen minutes to find a cab.

Bellows. Susan thought that he was the only person she could turn to at two A.M. who would understand her present plight. But she was worried about being followed, and she did not want to involve Bellows in any danger. So as she entered the foyer of Bellows's building she determined to wait five minutes before ringing his apartment, to be certain she had not been followed.

The foyer was not heated and Susan ran in place for a few minutes to keep warm. Becoming rational again after the experience with D'Ambrosio, she tried to understand why D'Ambrosio had returned so quickly. As far as she knew, no one had followed her when she went back to the Memorial to get the charts and explore the ORs. No one even knew that she was there.

She stopped running and looked out at Mount Vernon Street through the glass door. Bellows! He had seen her in the lounge. He was the only one who knew that she had not given up her search. She had shown him the charts. She started running in place again, cursing her own paranoia. Then she stopped as she remembered about Bellows being involved with the drugs that were found in the locker room, about Bellows being the one who found Walters, after Walters had committed suicide.

Susan turned her head and looked through the glass of the locked inner door. The stairway rose upward, its steps covered with a red runner. Could Bellows be involved? The possibility penetrated Susan's overworked brain and fatigued body. She was beginning to suspect everyone. She shook her head and laughed; the paranoia was too obvious. Yet it started her thinking, and the thoughts troubled her.

Her watch said two-seventeen. Bellows was going to be in for a surprise, having a caller at such an hour. At least Susan thought he'd be surprised. What if he were surprised only because he expected her to be quite occupied elsewhere —that he knew all about D'Ambrosio. Susan decided impulsively that was nonsense. She pushed the buzzer with determination. She had to push it again and hold it before Bellows responded.

Susan started up the stairs. She was midway up the second flight when Bellows appeared above in his bathrobe.

"I might have known. Susan, it's after two A.M."

"You asked me if I wanted a drink. I've changed my mind. I want one."

"But that was at eleven." Bellows disappeared into his apartment, leaving the door ajar.

Susan reached Bellows's floor and entered his apartment. He was nowhere to be seen. She closed the door and locked it, throwing both bolts. She found Bellows already back in bed, the covers up under his chin, his eyes closed.

"Some hospitality," said Susan sitting on the edge of the bed. She looked at Bellows. God, she was glad to see him. She wanted to throw herself onto him, feel his arms around her. She wanted to tell him about D'Ambrosio, about the freezer. She wanted to scream; she wanted to cry. But instead she did nothing. She sat there just looking at Bellows, her mind vacillating.

Bellows didn't budge, not at first. Finally the right eye opened, then the left. Then he sat up. "Damn, I can't sleep with you sitting here."

"How about that drink, then? I need it!" Susan forced herself to be calm, analytical. But it was hard. Her pulse was still over one hundred fifty per minute.

Bellows eyed Susan. "You're really too much!" He got up and put his robe back on. "OK, what will you have?"

"Bourbon, if you have it. Bourbon and soda, light on the soda." Susan looked forward to the fiery fluid. Her hands were still visibly trembling. She followed Bellows into the kitchen.

"I had to come over, Mark. I was attacked again." Susan's voice reflected her forced calmness. She watched Bellows's reaction to the information. He stopped with his hands in the freezer, taking out an ice tray.

"Are you serious?"

"I've never been more serious."

"Same person?"

"Same person."

Bellows went back to the ice tray, chipping at it with a fork. Finally it came away. Susan felt that he was surprised at the news but not overly surprised, and not terribly concerned. Susan felt uneasy.

She tried another tack.

"I found something else out when I visited the OR. Something very interesting." She waited for a response.

Bellows poured the bourbon, then opened a bottle of soda and poured it over the ice. The ice snapped in the glass. "OK, I believe you. Are you going to tell me or not?" Bellows handed Susan her drink. She took a slug.

"I traced the oxygen line from room No. 8 up in the ceiling space. Just before it turns down the main chase there is a valve in it."

Bellows took a sip from his drink, motioning for them to return to the living room. The clock over the fireplace chimed. It was two-thirty.

"Gas lines have valves," said Bellows at length.

"The others didn't have them."

"You mean a type of valve which would allow gas to be introduced into the line?"

"I think so. I don't know much about valves and the like."

"Did you trace the others to each room to be sure?"

"No, but room eight was the only line with a valve at the main chase."

"Simply having a valve doesn't surprise me. Maybe they all have one someplace in their lines. I wouldn't use that valve to draw my conclusions, at least not until I had traced all the lines."

"It's too much of a coincidence, Mark. All these cases apparently happened in room No. 8, and room No. 8 has an oxygen line that has a valve in it at a funny place, rather well concealed."

"Susan, look. You're forgetting that some twenty-five percent of your supposed victims weren't even near the OR, much less room No. 8. Now, even under the best of circumstances, I find your crusade ridiculous and threatening. And when I'm exhausted, I find it numbing. Can't we talk about something soothing, like socialized medicine?"

"Mark, I'm sure about this." Susan could sense the exasperation in Bellows's voice.

"I'm sure you're sure, but I'm also sure I'm unsure."

"Mark, the man who attacked me this afternoon warned me, and then he returned tonight, and I don't think he wanted to talk. I think he wanted to kill me. In fact, he tried to kill me. He shot at me!"

Bellows rubbed his eyes, then the sides of his head. "Susan, I don't know what to even think about that, much less have something intelligent to say. Why don't you go to the police if you're so sure?"

Susan did not hear Bellows's last comment; her mind was racing ahead. She started to speak out loud. "It has to be from lack of oxygen. If they were given too much succinylcholine or curare, just enough so that the people would have a hypoxic episode . . ." Susan trailed off, thinking. "That could be why respiratory arrest occurred. The one they autopsied, Crawford." Susan took out her notebook. Bellows took another drink. "Here it is, Crawford. He had severe glaucoma in one eye and was on phospholine iodide. That's an anticholinesterase and that means that his ability to break down the succinylcholine would have been impaired and a sublethal dose could be lethal."

"Susan, I've already told you that succinylcholine would not work in the OR, not with the surgeon and the anesthesiologist right there. Besides you cannot give succinylcholine by gas . . . at least, I've never heard of it. Maybe you could, but anyway, they'd just keep respiring the patient until it was gone; there wouldn't be any hypoxia."

Susan took another slow sip from the bourbon.

"What you're saying is that the hypoxia in the OR has to occur without the color of the blood changing so the surgeon stays nice and happy. How could that be done? . . . You'd have to block the use of oxygen by the brain somehow . . . maybe at the cellular level . . . or block the release of oxygen to the brain cells. It seems to me there is a drug that can block oxygen utilization, but I can't think of it offhand. If the valve on the oxygen line were significant, it would have to be a drug that comes in a gas form. But there's another way to do it. You could use a drug that blocks the uptake of oxygen on the hemoglobin and yet still keeps the color. . . . Mark, I've got it!" Susan sat bolt upright, her eyes wide open, her mouth forming a half-smile.

"Sure you do, Susan; sure you do," soothed Mark sarcastically.

"Carbon monoxide! Carefully bled-in carbon monoxide, by way of the T-valve, titrated to cause just the right amount of hypoxia. The blood color would stay the same. In fact it would get even brighter red, cherry red. Even a very small amount would cause the oxygen to be displaced from the hemoglobin. The brain is starved of oxygen and—coma. In the OR everything has seemed absolutely normal. Then the patient's brain dies; there is not a trace of the cause."

There was a silence as the two people looked at each other. Susan expectantly, Bellows with tired resignation.

"You want me to say something? OK, it's possible. Ridiculous but possible. I mean it's theoretically possible for the OR cases to be caused by carbon monoxide. It's an awful idea, maybe it's even ingenious, but at any rate, it's possible. The trouble is there are still twenty-five percent of the coma victims who didn't even get close to the OR."

"They're the easy ones to explain. That was never hard. It was the OR cases that were hard. It was also hard for me to break away from the idea in the diagnosis of disease in medicine that one should search for single causes. But in this case we're not dealing with a disease. The cases on the medical floors were given sublethal doses of succinylcholine. Something like that happened in a V.A. hospital in the Midwest, and even in New Jersey."

"Susan, you can hypothesize until you're blue in the face," said Bellows with a tinge of anger growing out of frustration. "What you're suggesting is some fantastic organized plan—a criminal plan—with the sole purpose of making people comatose. Well, let me tell you this: you haven't given an ounce of effort to the biggest question: the question of why. Why, Susan? Why? I mean, you're spinning your mental wheels at ninety miles per hour, taking all sorts of risks with your career, and mine, I might add, to come up with a potentially plausible although fantastic explanation for what is a series of unconnected, unfortunate incidences. But at the same time, you've conveniently forgotten to ask why. Susan, there would have to be motive, for Christ's sake. It's ridiculous. I'm sorry, but it is ridiculous. And besides, I've got to go to sleep. Some of us work, you know. . . . And there isn't one bit of solid evidence. A valve on the oxygen line! God, Susan, that's pretty weak. I mean you've got to come to your senses. I can't take any more of this. Really. I'm finished. I'm a surgical resident, not a part-time Sherlock Holmes."

Bellows got up and finished his bourbon in one long drink.

Susan watched him intently, her paranoia awakening once again. Bellows was no longer on her side. Why indeed? The criminal aspect of the matter was horribly apparent to her at that point.

"What makes you so sure," continued Bellows, "that all this has anything to do with Nancy Greenly or Berman? Susan, I think you're jumping to conclusions. There's an easier explanation for this character who seems so interested in getting hold of you."

"I'm waiting." Susan was angry now.

"The guy was probably looking for some action and you . ."

"Screw you, Bellows!" Susan went livid.

"Now she gets mad. God damn it, Susan, you take this whole affair as some sort of complicated game. I don't want to argue with you."

"Every time I tell you about some aggressive behavior from Harris to this fucker who tried to kill me, all you can come up with is some Goddamn sexist explanation."

"Sex exists, my child. You'd better learn to face that."

"I think it's more your problem. You male doctors never do seem to grow up. I guess it's too much fun being an adolescent." Susan got up and put her coat back on.

"Where are you going at this hour?" said Bellows with an authoritarian air.

"I have a feeling I'm safer on the street than here in this apartment."

"You're not going out now," said Bellows with determination.

"Ah, now the male chauvinist is displaying his true colors. The great protector! Bull crap. The egoist says I'm not going. Just watch."

Susan left quickly, slamming the door.

Indecision kept Bellows immobile and silent as he watched the door. He was silent because he knew that she was right in a lot of ways. He was immobile because he really wanted to be rid of the whole mess. "Carbon monoxide, holy shit." He walked back into his bedroom and got into bed once more. Looking at the clock, he realized morning was going to arrive very, very quickly.

D'Ambrosio began to panic. He had never liked confined spaces and the walls of the freezer began to move in on him. He began to breathe faster, gulping for air, and then he thought he might be going to suffocate. And the cold. The deathly cold wormed its way through his heavy Chicago overcoat, and despite constant motion, his feet and hands had gone numb.

But by far the most disturbing aspect of the whole miserable affair was the bodies and the acrid odor of formaldehyde. D'Ambrosio had seen a lot of grisly scenes in his life and had been through some gruesome experiences, but nothing could compare with being in the freezer with the stiffs. At first he had tried not to look at them, but involuntarily and out of mounting fear, his eyes had been drawn to the faces. After some time it had begun to look as if they were all smiling. Then they were laughing and even moving when he didn't watch them carefully. He emptied the clip in his pistol by blasting away at one particularly sneering corpse whom he imagined he recognized.

Finally D'Ambrosio retreated to the corner so he could keep the whole group in view. Slowly he sank into a sitting position. He couldn't feel his knees any longer.

**Thursday
February 26
10:41 A.M.**

The path dipped down to the left, through a thicket of gnarled oak trees standing in a bed of twisted briars. The branches of the trees arched over the pathway, enclosing it like a tunnel and precluding a view for more than a few feet. Susan was running and she dared not look behind her. Safety was ahead; she could make it. But the pathway narrowed and the branches clutched at her, hindering her. The briars caught in her clothing. She desperately tried to force her way through. She could see some lights ahead. Safety. But the harder she pulled, the more entangled she got, as if she were in a giant spider web. With her hands, she tried to free her feet. But then her arms became hopelessly entangled. There were only minutes left. She had to get free. Then she heard a car horn and one arm came free. The horn repeated itself and she opened her arms. She was in room 731 at the Boston Motor Lodge.

Susan sat up in the bed, looking around the room. It had been a dream, a recurrent dream which she hadn't had in years. With wakefulness came relief, and she sank back, pulling the covers up around herself. The auto horn which had awakened her sounded for the third time. There were some muffled shouts, then silence.

Susan looked around the room. Tasteless American. Two large beds with a neutral flower-print spread. The rug was a heavy shag, a shade of spring green. The near wall was papered with a repeating floral design in green. The far wall was a pale yellow. There was a picture over the bed, a tawdry reproduction, portraying an idyllic barnyard scene with a few ducks and sheep. The furniture too was cheap, but there was an impressive, twenty-eight-inch color TV set—the indispensable solace of motel life. Aesthetics had low priority at the Boston Motor Lodge.

But the place was safe. After leaving Bellows's apartment in the wee hours of the morning, Susan had wanted only to find someplace where she could sleep in peace. She had noticed the gaudy motel sign from Cambridge Street on a number of occasions. The sign was awful, certainly not something to beckon the weary. Nonetheless, the room had provided the haven she needed. She had checked in as Laurie Simpson and had waited in the lobby for a good quarter of an hour before going up to the room. When the man at the desk looked at her strangely, she gave him an extra five dollars and told him to call her if anybody inquired about her. She said she was worried about a jealous lover. The desk clerk had winked at her, grateful both for the five dollars and the confidence she extended to him. Susan knew that he accepted the story without question; it was part of the male vanity.

Having taken these precautions, and after moving the desk in front of the door, Susan had allowed herself to fall asleep. She had not slept soundly, as her terminal dream demonstrated, but she felt reasonably refreshed.

She remembered the strong words with Bellows the night before and debated about calling him. She regretted the exchange, feeling that it had been totally unnecessary. She also remembered her feelings of paranoia and felt embarrassed.

Yet she remembered her hyper state of mind and felt that her reactions were understandable. She was surprised that Bellows had not been more tolerant. But of course he wanted to be a surgeon, and she had to recognize that his career aspirations made it difficult if not impossible for him to view the situation with an open mind. Still, she regretted the split, if for no other reason than the fact that Bellows had played an effective devil's advocate to her ideas. After all, he was correct that Susan had no idea of motive, and if some large organization was involved, then there must be one.

Maybe the coma victims were the targets of some gangland vendetta? Susan dismissed the idea instantly, remembering Berman and even Nancy Greenly. No, that couldn't be. Maybe extortion was involved; perhaps the families hadn't paid off and—wham! But that seemed unlikely. It would be too hard to keep the coma business secret. It would be easier to kill people outright, outside the hospital. There had to be some reason for these comas happening in the hospital. There must be some pattern for each victim, some common denominator.

As Susan mused, she lifted the phone onto the bed. She dialed the medical school and asked for the dean's office.

"Is this Dr. Chapman's secretary? . . . This is Susan Wheeler . . . that's right, the infamous Susan Wheeler. Look, I'd like to leave a message for Dr. Chapman. There's no need to bother him. I was supposed to start a surgery rotation at the V.A. today, but I've spent a terrible night and I've got some abdominal cramps that won't quit. I'll be better by tomorrow morning, I'm sure, and I'll call if I'm not. Would you please see that Dr. Chapman is informed of this, and the Department of Surgery at the V.A.? Thanks."

Susan replaced the receiver. The time was quarter to ten. She dialed the Memorial and asked for Dr. Stark's office.

"This is Miss Susan Wheeler calling. I'd like to speak to Dr. Stark."

"Oh, yes, Miss Wheeler. Dr. Stark expected your call at nine. He'll be with you shortly. He was worried when you didn't call."

Susan waited, twisting the cord to the phone between her thumb and index finger.

"Susan?" Dr. Stark's voice was concerned. "I'm very glad to hear from you. After what you described happening to you yesterday afternoon, I became concerned when you didn't call. Are you all right?"

Susan hesitated, wondering if she should use the same cover with Stark as she used for Chapman. Stark might have dealings with Chapman. She decided she'd best be consistent.

"I have some abdominal cramps which have kept me in bed. Otherwise I'm fine."

"The rest will do you good. As for your requests: I have some good news and some bad news. What do you want first?"

"I'll take the bad."

"I've talked with Oren, then Harris, and finally Nelson about getting you reinstated here at the Memorial, but I'm afraid they are adamant. Obviously they don't run the Surgery Department, but we do depend on cooperation around here and, to be truthful, I was not overly insistent. If they had wavered, I would have been more forceful. But they didn't. You certainly stirred the fire, young lady!"

"I see. . . ." Susan was not surprised.

"Besides, if you came back here, I think it would be hard for you to overcome your reputation. It would follow you. It's best to let things cool off."

"I suppose. . . ."

"The V.A. program is a popular affiliated program and you'll get to do more surgery there than you would here."

"That may be true, but as for teaching, it's far inferior to the Memorial."

"But on your other request about the Jefferson Institute, I had some luck. I managed to speak to the director, and I told him about your special interest in intensive care. I also told him you were particularly interested in visiting his hospital. Well, he has obligingly agreed to allow you to come, if you come after the busiest part of the day, sometime after five. But there are some conditions. You must go alone, since only you will be permitted inside."

"Of course."

"And since I have really extended myself and have gone off channels, so to speak, I would prefer that you don't mention your visit to anyone. I must admit, Susan, that I really had to make an effort to get you invited. I'm telling you this not because I want you to feel indebted or anything, but rather as partial atonement for my not getting you reinstated here at the Memorial. The director of the institute told me categorically that he would not allow any others to visit with you. They do allow group visits when they have time to supervise them. It's a rather special place, as I believe you'll see. It would be somewhat embarrassing if you wanted to bring someone else. So you must go alone. You can understand that, I presume."

"Of course."

"Well, then, let me know what you think of the facility. I haven't been there myself yet."

"Thank you very much, Dr. Stark. Oh, there's one other thing. . . ." Susan considered telling Stark about the second experience with D'Ambrosio. She decided against it, because he had wanted Susan to go to the police yesterday; now he'd be insistent. Susan did not want the police, not yet. If it were some large organization behind the whole affair, it was naive to think they didn't have a contingency plan to allow for police probes.

"I'm not sure," continued Susan, "if it's significant, but I found a valve on the oxygen line into room No. 8 in the OR. It's near to the main chase."

"Near the what?"

"The main chase where all the piping in the hospital courses from floor to floor."

"Susan, you're pretty remarkable. How did you find out about that?"

"I went up into the ceiling space and traced the gas lines to the ORs."

"Ceiling space!" Stark's voice rose in irritation. "Susan, that's carrying this affair a bit too far. I cannot condone your climbing around in the ceiling spaces over the operating rooms."

Susan waited for the ax to fall as it had with McLeary or Harris. Instead there was a pause. Stark broke it. "Anyway, you say you found a valve in the oxygen line to room No. 8." His voice was almost back to normal.

"That's right," said Susan cautiously.

"Well, I think I know what that's for. I'm chairman of the OR Committee, as you might have guessed. That valve is probably the bleed valve for getting rid of air bubbles when the system is charged up. But one way or another, I'll have someone check it and make certain. By the way, what is the name of the patient you wanted to see at the Jefferson Institute?"

"Sean Berman."

"Oh yes, I remember the case. It was just the other day. One of Spallek's. A meniscus case, as I recall. Tragedy . . . the man was about thirty. A real shame. Well, good luck. Tell me, are you off to the V.A. today?"

"No, my stomach condition will keep me in bed, at least for the morning. I'm quite sure I'll be able to get back to work tomorrow, though."

"I hope so, Susan, for your sake."

"Thank you for your time, Dr. Stark."

"Not at all, Susan."

The line disconnected and Susan hung up.

The soiled gloves fell into the wastebasket beside the sponge rack. On the rack was a group of blood-stained sponges hanging like dirty clothes on a line. A nurse passed behind Bellows and undid the string at the neck of his operating gown. Bellows tossed it into the hamper by the door and left.

It had been an uncomplicated gastrectomy, a procedure Bellows usually liked to perform. But on this particular morning Bellows's mind had been somewhere else and the double-layer closure of the stomach pouch and the small bowel had been tedious rather than enjoyable. Bellows could not stop thinking about Susan. His thoughts ran the gamut from tender concern, accompanied by remorse for the words that had driven Susan away the night before, to self-righteous pleasure in the comments he had felt justified in making. He had already gone too far, gambled too much, and it was quite apparent that Susan had no intentions of easing up on her idiotic drive in the direction of career suicide.

On the other hand, the sweetness of the evening before last was still very much in Bellows's mind. He had responded to Susan in a way that had been so natural, so fresh. He had made love with her in such a manner that orgasm had been a mere part, not a goal. There had felt something so wonderfully equal, a communion of sorts. Bellows realized that he cared for Susan very much, despite the fact that he knew so little about her, and despite the fact that she was so blasted stubborn.

Bellows dictated his operative note on the gastrectomy case

into a tape recorder with the usual medical monotone, ending each sentence with a vocalized "period." Then he went into the dressing room and began to change back to his street clothes.

Acknowledging affection for Susan put Bellows on guard. His rationality persuaded him that such feelings would diminish his objectivity and sense of perspective. He could not afford that, not now, when his career opportunities were in the balance. Since Susan had been transferred to the V.A., things had already quieted down. Stark had been civil on rounds, even to the extent of semiapologizing for his ungrounded implications concerning Bellows's association with the drugs found in locker 338.

Bellows completed dressing and walked over to the recovery room to check the post-op orders on his gastrectomy patient.

"Hey, Mark," called a loud voice from the recovery room desk. Bellows turned to see Johnston coming toward him.

"How the hell are those students of yours? I understand that the girl's a piece of ass."

Bellows didn't answer. He waved his hand in a questioning fashion. The last thing he wanted to do was get into some idiotic conversation with Johnston about Susan.

"Did your students tell you what happened at the med school this morning? It's one of the funniest stories I've heard in a long time. Some guy broke into the Anatomy Building last night. He must have been some kind of a nut because he discharged a fire extinguisher, unveiled all the first-year students' cadavers, shot up the place, got himself locked in the freezer, and then had a brawl with the bodies. He knocked a bunch of the corpses down and shot up some of them. Can you imagine?" Johnston erupted in gusts of laughter.

The effect was just the opposite on Bellows. He looked at Johnston but thought about Susan. She had told him that she had been chased again, that someone had tried to kill her. Could that have been the same man? The freezer? Susan was rapidly becoming a total mystery. Why hadn't she told him more?

"Did the guy freeze?" asked Bellows.

Johnston had to pull himself together in order to talk.

"No, at least not all of him. The police had been tipped off by an anonymous phone call in the middle of the night. They thought it was a med school prank so they didn't check it out until the morning shift came in. By the time they got there the guy was unconscious, sitting in the corner. His body temperature was ninety-two degrees, but the medical boys succeeded in thawing him out without any trouble with acidosis. I think that's pretty commendable for those assholes. The only trouble was that they waited for two hours before calling me on consult. Hey, you know what the nurses in the ICU call him?"

"I can't guess." Bellows was only half-listening.

"Ice Balls." Johnston broke down in laughter again. "I thought that was pretty clever. It's a takeoff on Hot Lips from *M*A*S*H*. What a pair, Hot Lips and Ice Balls."

"Is he going to make it?"

"Sure. I'm going to have to amputate some. At the very least he's going to lose part of his legs. How much will be determined over the next day or so. The poor bastard might even lose those ice balls."

"Did they find out anything about him?"

"What do you mean?"

"Well, his name, where he was from, you know."

"Nothing. It turned out he had some I.D. which proved to be fake. So the police are very interested. He mumbled something about Chicago. Weird!" Johnston mouthed the last word as if it were some important secret message, as he went back to the recovery room desk.

Bellows went over and checked his gastrectomy patient. Vital signs were stable. Then he checked the chart. The orders had been written by Reid, and they were fine. He thought about the man in the freezer. The story seemed so bizarre. He wondered again if it really was the man that had been chasing Susan. But how could she have locked him in the freezer? Why the hell hadn't she mentioned it? Maybe he had never given her the chance. If she had locked the man in the freezer, she was now definitely in trouble legally. Could she have been the anonymous phone caller?

Bellows examined the dressing on the patient. It was still in place and not blood-soaked. The I.V. was running well.

Then he thought about Susan again and decided that the nut in the freezer must have been the man who chased her.

And if he was, then it would be important for her to know that he was hospitalized and in critical condition.

Bellows dialed the medical school and asked to be connected to the dorm. He let Susan's phone ring twelve times before giving up. Then he called back the dorm switchboard and left a message for her to call when she came back to her room.

After that, Bellows went to lunch.

**Thursday
February 26
4:23 P.M.**

Thirty-six dollars plus tax seemed to Susan an awfully high price for the tasteless room at the Boston Motor Lodge. But at the same time it was worth it. Susan felt refreshed and rested—and safe. She had spent the time during the day rereading her notebook. All the information she had about the OR cases fit the idea of carbon monoxide poisoning. The information about the medical cases fit with the idea of succinylcholine poisoning. But still she had no motive, no rhyme or reason. The cases were too disparate.

Susan made a number of calls to the Memorial to try to learn Walters's home address, but she was unsuccessful. At one point she had called the Memorial and had Bellows paged, but she hung up before he could answer. Slowly but inexorably, Susan began to comprehend that she was at a dead end. She thought that it was probably time to go to the authorities, tell what she had learned, then take a vacation. She had a month's vacation coming to her as part of her third year and she was sure that she would be able to get permission to take the time immediately. She'd leave, get away, forget. She thought about Martinique. She liked things French, and she longed for the sun.

The doorman of the motel whistled a cab for her and she got in. She told the driver the address: 1800 South Weymouth Street, South Boston. Then she settled back.

It was stop and go down Cambridge Street, a little better on Storrow Drive, but worse on Berkeley. The cab driver took her through the nicer sections of the South End to avoid traffic. At Mass. Ave. he turned left and the surroundings deteriorated. Once into South Boston, Susan knew she was lost. The housing became monotonous, the streets badly littered. Soon the cab entered an area of warehouses, deserted factories, and dark streets. Nearly every streetlamp had a broken bulb.

When Susan alighted from the cab she found herself in an area that seemed isolated from life. Straight ahead, the only streetlight she could see emitted a beam of light from a modern hooded fixture which illuminated the door of a building, a sign, and the walk leading up to the door. The sign was fabricated in block letters of a deep azure. The sign read: "The Jefferson Institute." Below the blue letters was a brass plaque. It said: "Constructed with the Support of the Department of Health, Education and Welfare, US Government, 1974."

The Jefferson Institute was surrounded by an eight-foot-high hurricane fence. The building was set back about fifteen feet from the street. It was a strikingly modern structure surfaced with a white terrazzo conglomerate polished to a high gloss. The walls slanted inward at an angle of eighty degrees, rising in a first story of some twenty-five feet. Then there was a narrow horizontal ledge before the wall soared another twenty-five feet at the same angle. Except for the front entrance, there were no windows or doors along the entire length of the facade on the ground floor. The second story had windows but they were recessed and could not be seen from the street. Only the sharply geometric embrasures were visible and the glow of lights from within.

The building occupied a city block. In a strange way, Susan found it beautiful, though she realized that its effect was enhanced by the surrounding squalor. Susan guessed that it was the centerpiece of some urban renewal scheme. It gave the impression of a two-storey ancient Egyptian mastaba, or the base of an Aztec pyramid.

Susan walked up to the front door. Made of bronzed steel, it had no knobs, no openings of any kind. To the right of the door was a recessed microphone. As Susan stepped onto the Astroturf immediately before the door, she activated a recording which told her to give her name and the purpose of her visit. The voice was deep, reassuring, and measured.

Susan complied, although she hesitated about the purpose of the visit. She was tempted to say tourism, but she changed her mind. She wasn't feeling very jokey. So, finally, she said, "Academic purposes."

There was no answer. A rectangular red light beneath the microphone came on. Printed on the glass was the word *wait*. The light flashed green and the word changed to *proceed*. Without a sound the bronzed door glided to the right, and Susan stepped over the threshold.

Susan found herself in a stark white hall. There were no windows, no pictures, no decorations at all. The only illumination seemed to be from the floor, which was made of a milky opaque plastic material. Susan found the effect curious and futuristic; she walked ahead.

At the end of the hall, a second silent door glided into the wall, and Susan entered what appeared to be a large, ultramodern waiting room. Its far and near walls were mirrored from floor to ceiling. The two side walls were spotlessly white and totally devoid of any interruptions or decoration. The sameness was somewhat disorienting. As Susan looked at the walls, her eyes began to focus on her own vitreous floaters. She had to blink and make an effort to focus at a distance. Looking into the mirror at the end of the room had the opposite effect. Because of the opposing mirrors Susan saw the image of herself reflected to infinity.

The room was furnished with rows of molded white plastic chairs. The floor was the same as in the hall, the light from it casting strange shadows on the ceiling. Susan was about to sit down when another door slid open in the farthest mirrored wall. A tall woman entered and walked directly up to Susan. She had very short, medium brown hair. Her eyes were deeply set, and the line of her nose merged imperceptibly with her forehead. Susan was reminded of the classic features of a cameo. The woman wore a white pants suit as devoid of decoration as the walls. A pocket dosimeter peeped from her jacket. Her expression was neutral.

"Welcome to the Jefferson Institute. My name is Michelle. I will show you our facilities." Her voice was as noncommittal as her expression.

"Thank you," said Susan, trying to see through the woman's facade. "My name is Susan Wheeler. I believe you are expecting me." Susan let her eyes sweep around the room once more. "It certainly is modern. I've never seen anything quite like this."

"We have been expecting you. But before we begin I'd like to warn you that it is very warm inside. I suggest that you leave your coat here. And please leave your bag as well."

Susan took off her coat, a bit embarrassed by the wrinkled and soiled nurse's uniform she still had on. She took her notebook from her bag.

"Now then . . . I suppose that you know that the Jefferson Institute is an intensive-care hospital. In other words, we only take care of chronic intensive-care patients. Most of our patients are in some level of coma. This particular hospital was built as a pilot project with HEW funds, although the actual running of it has been delegated to the private sector. It has been very successful in freeing up beds in the acute intensive care units of the city's hospitals. In fact, since the project has been so successful, an equivalent hospital is either being built or is in the planning stages in most of the large cities of the country. Research has shown that any city or population center with a population of a million or more can economically support a hospital of this sort. . . . Excuse me, but why don't we sit down?" Michelle indicated two of the chairs.

"Thank you," said Susan, taking one of the chairs.

"Visiting the Jefferson Institute is strictly regulated because of the methodology we use to care for the patients. We have developed very new techniques here, and if people are not prepared, some may react on an emotional level. Only immediate family may visit, and only once every two weeks on a preplanned basis."

Michelle paused in her monologue, then she managed a half-smile. "I must say that your visit here is highly unusual. Normally we have a group of medical people on the second Tuesday of each month, and there is a planned program for them. But since you have come by yourself, I guess I can improvise a bit. But we do have a short film if you would like to see it."

"By all means."

"Good."

Without any sign from Michelle, the room darkened and on the wall opposite from where they were sitting, a film began to roll. Susan was intrigued. She presumed that the film was being projected through a translucent section of the wall serving as a screen.

The film itself reminded Susan of old newsreels. Its outdated technique seemed an anachronism in the modern surroundings. The first section was devoted to the concept of the intensive care hospital. The Secretary of Health, Education and Welfare was shown discussing the problem with policy planners, economists, and health care specialists. The problem of spiraling hospital costs spearheaded by the cost of long-term intensive care was illustrated by graphs and charts. The men explaining the charts were dull and uninspiring, as commonplace as the suits they wore.

"This is a terrible film," said Susan.

"I agree. Government films are all alike. You'd think that they'd try a little creativity."

The movie moved on to ground-breaking ceremonies, at which politicians smiled and joked idiotically. More graphs and charts followed, attesting to the enormous savings that had been accrued by the hospital. There were several more scenes showing how the Jefferson Institute's facilities freed the beds in the city's hospitals for the care of acute cases. Then followed a comparison of the number of nurses and other personnel needed at the Jefferson facility to the number needed in a conventional hospital for the same number of intensive care patients. The people used to illustrate this point were photographed milling about aimlessly in a parking lot. Finally, the film showed the heart of the new hospital: the huge computer, both digital and analog. It concluded by pointing out that all the functions of homeostasis were monitored and maintained by the computer. The film ended with a burst of inspirational marching music, like the finale of a war movie. The lights under the floor came on as the last image disappeared.

"I could have done without that," said Susan, smiling.

"Well, at least it emphasizes the point about the economy. That's the central concept of the institute. Now, if you'll follow me, I'll show you the principal features of the hospital."

Michelle stood up and walked toward the mirrored wall from which she had appeared. A door glided open. It shut behind them as they entered another corridor about fifty feet long. The far end of the corridor was also mirrored from floor to ceiling. As Susan passed down the hallway she noted other doors but they were all closed. None of the doors had any exposed hardware. Apparently they were automatically activated.

When they reached the far end of the corridor, a door slid open and Susan entered a familiar-looking room. It was about forty by twenty feet and looked exactly like an intensive care unit in any hospital. There were five beds and the usual assortment of gadgets, EKG screens, gas lines, etcetera. But four of the beds appeared different: each was constructed with a gap of some two feet running lengthwise. It was as if each bed were constructed of two very narrow beds with a fixed two-foot span between them. In the ceiling above the beds there were complicated tracklike mechanisms. The fifth bed, which seemed conventional, was occupied. A patient was being breathed by a small respirator. Susan was reminded of Nancy Greenly.

"This is the visiting area for the immediate families," explained Michelle. "When a family is scheduled to visit, the patient is transferred here automatically. When he is placed in one of these special beds and it is made up, the bed appears like a normal one. This patient was visited this afternoon." Michelle pointed toward the patient in the fifth bed. "We purposely did not return him to the main ward for your benefit."

Susan was confused. "You mean that bed the patient is in is the same as these other beds?"

"Exactly. And when family visits, these other beds are filled with other patients so that the area looks like a normal intensive care unit. Follow me, please."

Michelle walked the length of the room, past the patient in the bed. At the end of the room was a door, which opened silently and automatically.

Susan was amazed when she passed the fifth bed with the patient. The bed appeared exactly like a regular hospital bed.

There was no evidence that its central section, its basic support, was missing. But Susan had no time to examine the bed more closely as she followed Michelle into the next room.

The first thing Susan became aware of was the light; there was something strange about it. Then she felt the warmth and the humidity. Finally she saw the patients, and she stopped in utter astonishment. There were more than a hundred patients in the room, and all of them were completely suspended in midair about four feet from the floor. All of them were naked. Looking closely, Susan could see the wires piercing multiple points on the patients' long bones. The wires were connected to complicated metal frames and pulled taut. The patients' heads were supported by other wires from the ceiling which were attached to screw eyes in the patients' skulls. Susan had an impression of grotesque, horizontal, sleeping marionettes.

"As you can see, the patients are all suspended by wires under tension. Some visitors react strongly to this, but it has proven to be the best method of long-term care, totally preserving the skin and minimizing nursing care. Its origin was in orthopedics, where wires are passed through bones to provide traction. Burn treatment research showed the benefits to be obtained when the skin does not rest on any kind of surface. It was a natural progression to apply the concept to the care of the comatose patient."

"It is rather gruesome." Susan recalled the upsetting image of the cadavers hung in the freezer. "What is the strange lighting?"

"Oh, yes, we should put on glasses if we stay in here much longer." Michelle fetched several pairs of goggles from a table.

"There is a low-level of ultraviolet light in here. It has been found useful in controlling bacteria as well as helping to maintain the integrity of the skin." Michelle offered a set of goggles to Susan, and they both put them on.

"The temperature in here is maintained at ninety-four point five Fahrenheit, plus or minus five hundredths of a degree. The humidity is held at eight-two percent with a one percent variance. That tends to reduce patient heat loss and hence reduces the patients' caloric needs. The humidity has reduced the respiratory infection problem, which you know is critical for coma patients."

Susan was spellbound. She gingerly moved closer to one of the suspended patients. A profusion of wires perforated various long bones. The wires then passed horizontally through an aluminum frame around the patient before running up to a complicated trolley device on the ceiling. Susan looked up at the ceiling and saw that it was a maze of tracks for the trolleys. All the I.V. lines, suction tubes, and monitoring lines from the patient ascended to the trolley. Susan looked back at Michelle. "And there are no nurses?"

"I happen to be a nurse, and there are two others on duty, plus one doctor. That's quite a reasonable ratio for one hundred and thirty-one intensive care patients, wouldn't you say? You see, everything is automated. The patient's weight, blood gases, fluid balance, blood pressure, body temperature—in fact, an enormous list of variables—are being constantly scanned and compared to standards by the computer. The computer actuates solenoid valves to rectify any abnormalities or discrepancies it finds. It is far better than conventional care. A doctor tends to concern himself with isolated variables and in a static fashion. The computer is able to sample over time, hence it treats dynamically. But more important still is that the computer correlates all the variables at any given moment. It's much more like the bodies' own regulatory mechanisms."

"Modern medicine carried to the nth degree. It's incredible, really it is. It's like some science fiction setting. A machine taking care of a host of mindless people. It's almost as if these patients aren't people."

"They aren't people."

"I beg your pardon?" Susan looked up from the patient toward Michelle.

"They *were* people; now they're brain stem preparations. Modern medicine and medical technology have advanced to the point where these organisms can be kept alive, sometimes indefinitely. The result was a cost-effectiveness crisis. The law decided they had to be maintained. Technology had to advance to deal with the problem realistically. And it has. This hospital has the potential to handle up to a thousand such cases at a time."

There was something about the basic philosophy Michelle elucidated that made Susan uncomfortable. She also had a feeling that her guide had herself been very carefully indoctrinated. Susan could tell that Michelle did not question what she was saying. Nevertheless Susan did not dwell on the institute's philosophical foundations. She was overwhelmed by the place's physical aspects. She wanted to see more. She looked around the room. It was more than a hundred feet long, with a fifteen- to twenty-foot ceiling. In the ceiling the maze of tracks was bewildering.

There was another door at the far end of the room. It was closed. But it was a normal door with normal hardware. Susan decided that only the doors they had so far traversed were centrally controlled. After all, most visitors, the families, never came into the main ward.

"How many operating rooms are there here in the Jefferson Institute?" asked Susan suddenly.

"We don't have operating rooms here. This is a chronic care facility. If a patient needs acute care, he is transferred back to the referring institution."

The reply was so fast that it gave the impression of a reflex or trained response. Susan distinctly remembered seeing the ORs in the floor plans she had obtained at City Hall. They were on the second floor. Susan began to sense that Michelle was lying.

"No operating rooms?" Susan deliberately acted very surprised. "Where do they do emergency procedures, like tracheotomies?"

"Right here on the main ward or in the ICU visiting room next door. That can be set up as a minor OR if needed. But it rarely happens. As I said, this is a chronic-care hospital."

"I still would have thought that they would have included an OR."

At that moment almost directly in front of Susan, one of the patients was automatically tipped back so that his head was about six inches below his feet.

"There is a good example of the computer working," said Michelle. "The computer probably sensed a fall in the blood pressure. It put the patient into the Trendelenburg position prior to correcting the main cause for the blood pressure fall."

Susan was barely listening; she was trying to figure a way to do a little exploring on her own. She wanted to see those operating rooms indicated on the floor plans.

"One of the reasons I asked to come here was to see a

particular patient. The name is Berman, Sean Berman. Do you have any idea where he is located?"

"No, not offhand. To tell you the truth, we don't use names here for the patients. The patients are given numbers, sample 1, sample 2, etcetera. It's infinitely easier to key into the computer. In order to find Berman's number, I'll have to match the name with the computer. It takes a minute or so, that's all."

"Well, I would like to find out."

"I'll use the information terminal at the control desk. Meanwhile, you could take a look here and see if you can see him. Or you can come with me and wait in the waiting room. No guests are permitted in the control room."

"I'll wait here, thank you. There is enough of interest here to keep me occupied for a week."

"Suit yourself, but, needless to say, don't touch any of the wires or the patients under any circumstances. The whole system is very carefully balanced. The electrical resistance of your body would be picked up by the computer and an alarm would sound."

"No need to worry. I'm not about to touch anything."

"Good. I'll be right back."

Michelle removed her goggles. The door to the visiting room opened automatically and she was gone.

Michelle walked through the visitors' room and halfway down the corridor beyond it. The door to the control room opened for her. It was dimly illuminated like the control room on a nuclear submarine. A good portion of the light in the room came from the far wall, which was actually a two-way mirror permitting observation of the visitors' hall from the control room.

Two other people occupied the room when Michelle entered. Sitting in front of a large U-shaped bank of TV monitors was a guard. He was also dressed in white, and wore a wide white leather belt, a white-holstered automatic, and a two-way Sony receiver. He sat in front of a vast console with multiple switches and dials. A battery of TV monitors in front of him was scanning rooms, corridors, and doors throughout the hospital. Several screens had constant images, such as the monitors for the front door and the entry hall. Others changed as remote control video cameras scanned their areas. The guard looked up sleepily as Michelle entered.

"You left her by herself in the ward? Do you think that was wise?"

"She'll be fine. I was told to let her see what she wanted on the first floor."

Michelle walked toward a large computer terminal where the other occupant of the room, a nurse dressed like Michelle, sat watching the data displayed on the forty or more screens in front of her. Intermittently the computer's printer to her right would activate and print out information.

Michelle plopped herself down in a chair.

"Who the hell does she know to get invited here by herself?" asked the computer nurse, suppressing a yawn. "She looks like a Goddamn LPN or something. She doesn't even have a pin or a cap. And that uniform! It looks like she's been wearing it for six months."

"I haven't the slightest idea who she knows. I got a call from the director saying that she was coming and that we were to let her in and entertain her. I was to call Herr Direktor when she arrived. Do you think there's some hankypanky going on?"

The computer nurse laughed.

"Do me a favor," continued Michelle, "and punch in the name of Sean Berman. He was a Memorial referral. I need his patient number and location."

The computer nurse began to key in the information. "On our next shift, you can be the computer-sitter while I float. Playing with this machine is starting to drive me up the wall."

"Gladly. The only break in the routine of floater for the past week has been this visitor. A year ago, if someone told me I would be tending a hundred intensive-care patients myself, I'd have laughed in his face."

One of the display screens flashed: Berman, Sean. Age 33, sex male, race caucasian. Diagnosis: cerebral brain death secondary to anesthetic complications. Sample number 323 B4. STOP.

The nurse keyed Sample number 323 B4 back into the computer.

The guard at the other end of the room slouched over, watching the monitors as usual, as he had been doing for two hours since his last break, as he had been doing for almost a year. The picture of the main ward appeared on screen number 15; moving as the video camera slowly panned from one end of the huge room to the other. The dangling nude patients held no interest for the guard. He was finally accustomed to the gruesome scene. Automatically screen number 15 shifted to the intensive-care visitors' ward as its camera started to scan.

The guard sat up suddenly, looking at the screen of number 15. He reached for the manual mode switch and returned the scan to the main ward. The video camera scanned the enormous room again.

"The visitor is no longer in the main ward!" said the guard.

Michelle turned from the computer display screen and squinted to see screen number 15 of the monitor. "No? Well check the visitors' ward and the corridor. Maybe she had enough. The main ward is usually a shock for first-time visitors."

Michelle turned and looked out through the glass to the waiting room, but Susan was not there either.

The display screen on the computer flashed: Sample 323 B4 terminated. 0310 Feb. 26. Cause of death: cardiac arrest. STOP.

"Well if she came here for Berman, she's too late," said Karen without feeling.

"She's not in the visitors' ward," said the guard, activating a series of switches. "And she's not in the corridor. It's not possible."

Michelle got up from the chair, her eyes staying on screen 15 until she was at the door. "Calm down. I'll locate her." Michelle turned to the nurse at the computer. "Maybe you should try to call the director again. I think we'd better get rid of this girl."

As soon as Michelle left the main ward, Susan had removed the Xeroxed copies of the Jefferson Institute floor plans she had folded in her notebook. She oriented herself from the entrance, traced their route to the main ward, and then checked the routes for gaining access to the second floor. She saw two choices. There was a stairway from MG or an elevator from M Comp R. Susan glanced down at the key in the lower right hand corner. MG stood for morgue; M Comp R was the main computer room. Susan quickly decided that the stairs would be safer than the elevator; she thought that the computer room might well be occupied.

She walked toward the far end of the ward, where there was a conventional door, and tried the knob. It turned and Susan opened the door into the corridor beyond. It seemed to be quite dark; then she remembered the goggles. She took them off and put them in her uniform pocket. The corridor was like the others she had seen, starkly white with the illumination coming through the floor. At either end of the corridor was a large mirror, and its multiple reflections made the corridor seem infinitely long.

There were no sounds and no one in sight. Susan checked the floor plan, which indicated that the morgue and the stairs were to the right. She closed the door to the ward behind her. Moving quickly, she made her way down to a door at the end of the corridor. There were no markings on the door, but at least it too had normal hardware. Susan tried the knob; the door was unlocked.

As silently as possible, she opened the door, just a few inches at a time. She could see the tiles of the near wall. Then she began to see the upper part of a stainless steel dissecting table. A corpse lay naked on it. Susan heard some voices and a laugh, followed by the sound of a scale.

"So much for the lungs. How much should we say the heart weighed?" said one of the voices.

"Your turn to guess," laughed the other.

Nudging the door an inch more, Susan could just glimpse the head of the corpse. She squinted, then felt weak. It was Berman.

Letting the door close without a sound, Susan stood in the doorway for a few deep breaths. She felt slightly nauseated but it passed. She realized that she had very little time. The elevator.

Susan's pause in the doorway had been perfect timing. The TV scanner behind the one-way mirror finished its five-second scan as Susan stepped back into the corridor. It would resume its scan in ten seconds.

She hurried back into the main ward and reached the doorway to the computer room. Hesitantly she tried it. It too was unlocked. She opened the door about ten inches and looked into the room. To her relief, it seemed unoccupied. As she pushed the door farther she could see a fantasy of computer consoles, input-output equipment, and tape storage systems.

A movement in the far corner near to the ceiling caught Susan's eye. She recognized it immediately. It was a TV monitor camera. As its unhurried pan brought its lens toward Susan, she ducked back and closed the door. When she guessed that the camera had panned past, she whipped open the door and began to run the length of the room, to the elevator. But her timing was off; she would be spotted by the TV camera on its return sweep. Susan dived behind a computer console only halfway to her destination.

She had to work her way down the rest of the room, from console to console, trying to avoid the roving eye of the camera. Making a dash for the elevator, she pressed the button frantically. Susan could hear the machinery start up inside the shaft. The elevator was on another floor.

The TV camera reached the end of its arc and started back. Susan pressed the elevator button several times in succession.

The sound of the elevator machinery stopped, the doors quivered and then began to open. Susan glanced up at the TV camera before rolling around the edge of the elevator door, groping for the "close" button. The door closed but Susan had no idea if she had been observed or not.

The elevator was cavernous and correspondingly slow. There were only three buttons. She pressed the button for floor two and felt the machine begin to ascend. The floor plan for the second floor showed that the ORs were at the extreme opposite end of the building from the elevators. A long hall stretched from the elevators back to the OR area. Both the eighth and ninth doors to the right led into the OR complex.

When the elevator stopped and the doors opened, Susan stayed inside with her finger poised over the "door-close" button. No one in sight. The corridor was similiar to those of the first floor except that the doors were more deeply recessed. The ceilings carried tracks for the trolleys.

As the elevator doors began to close Susan plunged down the corridor, mentally checking off the number of doorways she had passed. Suddenly, in the distance, Susan saw a man driving a miniature forklift loaded with units of whole blood. He appeared to emerge from an intersecting corridor. She half-skidded, half-ran into one of the recessed doorways, crashing up against the wall, her breath coming in gasps. She listened. The sound of the machine receded. She peered into the corridor. Empty. She pushed off and reached the ninth door.

She waited until her breath returned to a semblance of normal before cracking the door and checking the room. She slipped in quickly.

She was in a dressing room. A partially smoked cigarette lay in an ashtray, its smoke curling up in the still air. An open doorway led to a bath area. Susan could hear the sound of a shower going.

Michelle reentered the control room. Her sense of ennui had disappeared. Her mouth was set, but her eyes moved incessantly. Like the guard, she was now very nervous.

"That girl has literally evaporated. She couldn't have walked out, could she?" asked Michelle.

"Impossible. There's no way the front door, or any outside door for that matter, can be opened without me activating the door release." The guard was still switching from scanner to scanner.

"I think we'd better give direction another call. This affair could get serious," said the nurse at the computer console.

"I don't understand it. We have these monitors placed in all the key areas. She's got to be in some doorway," said the guard.

"She's not in a doorway. I went all the way through to the main ward. What about the elevator?"

"That's a thought," said the guard. "If she does get upstairs there could be big trouble. I'm going to secure the building and activate all the automatic locking mechanisms on all stairway doors and electrify the perimeter fence. I'll hold the general alarm until direction is reached."

Michelle moved to a red telephone. "This is absurd, really! Totally unnecessary. Why was she allowed in by herself without a group?"

Swinging doors opened from the dressing rooms to the OR receiving area. Susan stepped into it. Here the appearance was more traditional. The lighting came from fluorescent bulbs in the ceiling alongside the omnipresent tracks for the patient trolleys. There was a faint glow that Susan remembered from the main ward, and she guessed there was an ultraviolet component to the light. The floor was of white vinyl, the walls surfaced in white ceramic tile.

The OR reception area was not large. In the center was an empty desk. There were apparently four operating rooms, two on each side, with ancillary rooms between. Susan's attention was attracted by muffled sounds from the first OR. Light coming through a small window suggested that an operation was in progress.

A dark window in the door of the adjacent ancillary room suggested that it was empty. Susan walked over, peered in, and stepped into the darkness.

This service room was dimly lit through a window of a door leading to the occupied OR.

Susan waited for her eyes to adjust to the darkness. Slowly the objects in the room took form. There was a central table supporting several large objects from which emanated a low-pitched continuous noise. Counter tops ran around the room. In the left counter top there was a large sink. Immediately to her right she could see the form of a gas sterilizer.

As quietly as possible, Susan opened the cabinet beneath the sink, and with her hands she ascertained that there would be enough room to squeeze in if necessary. She then returned to the hall door and ran her fingers along its edge until she found the knob and depressed the lock. Then she paused and listened to make sure there had been no change in the pattern of noises from the OR. Susan looked at the objects on the central table, but the light was too poor to distinguish them.

Susan trod lightly to the OR door and raised herself on tiptoe. She saw two surgeons, gowned and gloved in the usual fashion, bending over a patient. But she could see no anesthesiologist. There was no operating table. The patient was still strung up in a frame. But he was maintained on his right side; an incision gaped across his loins. The surgeons were closing, and Susan could hear their conversation with relative ease.

"I wonder where that heart's going from that previous case?"

"San Fran," said the second surgeon, running down a knot, pulling it tight. "I think it's only bringing seventy-five thousand dollars. It was a poor match, only two out of four, but it was a rush order."

"Can't win 'em all," said the first surgeon, "but this kidney is a four-tissue match, and I understand it's going for almost two hundred thousand. Besides, they might want the other one in a few days."

"Well, we don't let it go until we find a market for the heart," added the other, tying another rapid knot.

"The real problem is finding a tissue match for Dallas. The offer is a million dollars for a four-match. The kid's father is in oil."

The second surgeon whistled. "Any luck so far?"

"We found a three-tissue match scheduled for a T&A at the Memorial next Friday and . . ."

Susan's mind was desperately trying to find some alternate explanation for what she thought she was hearing, but before she could, the door from the reception hall jiggled as someone tried to open it. Susan's first impulse was to run into the other empty OR. Instead, she raced back to the sink, as she heard someone enter the lighted operating room. She squeezed herself into the cabinet under the counter, wincing at the sound of several jars that tipped over when she pulled her feet in after her. It was tight quarters; she struggled to get her arms in. She was unable to close the door completely by the time the door to the OR opened and the room lights went on. Susan held her breath.

With her head twisted sideways, and the cabinet door slightly ajar, she could see two Plexiglas structures sitting on the table. They resembled fish tanks. Then she understood the pumping noise she had heard when she entered the room. It came from two self-contained machines, battery-driven, which perfused the two Plexiglas tanks. The first contained a human heart, suspended in a fluid. It was quivering, but not beating. The other contained a human kidney, also suspended in a fluid.

Suddenly the whole nightmare was clear to Susan. Now she had a motive, a horrible motive for making patients comatose. The Jefferson Institute was a clearinghouse for black-market human organs!

Susan had little time to think. A man walked past the sink, his trousers brushing against the half-closed cabinet door. He unlocked the door to the hall, then he went over to the table. Audibly straining, he lifted the tank which contained the heart and carried it away, leaving the light on and the door ajar.

Susan's mind raced back over all the details of her investigation: the T-valve on the oxygen line, D'Ambrosio's face, the image of Nancy Greenly, and the heart in the Plexiglas container. She remembered the conversation in the morgue below, and she realized that the heart must have been Berman's. She began to feel a sense of urgency, a sense of pervading panic. The concept of this lurid affair was too overwhelming. She had to get away and, for the first time, she realized how difficult that was going to be. This was no ordinary hospital. At least some of the people running it were criminals. She had to get out and get to someone who could comprehend what was going on. Stark. She had to get to Stark. He would be able to appreciate the whole business and was powerful enough to do something about it.

Carefully Susan moved her left hand out of the cabinet onto the floor, pushing open the door as she did so. She listened. There were no noises except for the quiet whir of the pump perfusing the kidney on the table. With great effort she began to pull her right leg from the far corner of the cabinet. Then she heard footsteps in the hall. There was only a second. Her foot went back where it had been. She pulled in her arm, pushing herself into the cabinet as far as possible. The elbow of the drain from the sink above dug into her back.

The man came back into the room at a fast walk. He came between the sink and the table and kicked the cabinet door shut. The sound and compression made Susan's ears ring. She heard him strain with the second tank. Then his footsteps left the room and receded down the corridor.

Susan stayed still for another two or three minutes before she dared to move, listening. There were no footsteps, only a muffled laugh from the first OR. Susan extracted her cramped body from beneath the sink. A spray can fell out onto the floor and rolled a short distance. Susan froze. Nothing. Then she ran for the door into the unlit operating room.

She had to pause once again to allow her eyes to adjust to the darkness. Here the forms of the overhead operating lights were visible. Carefully Susan moved to the common wall with the corridor, feeling for the door handle. Once she found it, she cracked the door and looked into the scrub area immediately beyond.

At that instant a piercing alarm shattered the stillness and all the lights went on in the previously darkened room. In a panic Susan let go of the door and turning threw herself against the wall expecting an assailant.

The room was empty.

A red light was blinking on and off next to a small loudspeaker. The loudspeaker crackled: "There is an unauthorized intruder in the building. Female. She must be detained immediately. I repeat . . . there is an unauthorized individual in the building . . . detain immediately." The loudspeaker went dead. Susan sighed in relief. She left the OR and peered around the wall of the scrub area. The corridor was clear.

Two white-uniformed guards strode briskly through the main ward, oblivious to the hundred-odd human beings strung up around them. Each had a pistol in his hand. The larger of the two was listening to his Sony two-way radio. He replaced it on his belt. "I'm to take the elevator in the computer room up to two. You're to head through the morgue and down to the machinery spaces."

The two men entered the corridor beyond the ward.

"And remember, our orders are clear. If you find her and she comes along willingly, fine; if not then shoot her. But shoot her in the head. They may want the kidneys or the heart, depending on her tissue type."

The two men split. The large man walked down the corridor and entered the computer room. Methodically he checked the room, then he summoned the elevator.

Susan dashed down the OR reception area, past the first operating room. She opened the door to the dressing area but heard voices within. Without hesitation she changed her plan and turned for a door she knew must open into the main corridor. Then she spotted a large pair of scissors on the reception desk. She picked them up; they were a weapon of sorts. Then she let herself into the main corridor.

The corridor was still empty, to Susan's intense relief. She could see all the way down to the closed elevator doors at the far end. Taking a deep breath, she sped toward the elevator.

She was about halfway down the hundred-and-fifty-foot hall when the elevator arrived. Susan slowed as the doors quivered and opened. The guard stepped out and Susan stopped. Each was startled to see the other.

"All right, young lady, we'd like to talk to you downstairs." The guard's voice was not threatening. He began to advance slowly toward Susan, keeping his pistol behind his back.

Susan took a few indecisive steps backward, then she spun and raced toward the OR area. The guard pelted after her. In desperation Susan tried several doors. The first was locked; so was the second. The guard was almost on her. The handle of the third door turned and the door opened.

She rolled around the door, trying to slam it shut. But the guard gripped the edge of the door with his left hand and wedged his left foot between the door and the casing.

Susan pushed with every ounce of strength she could muster but it was hardly an even match. The guard was over two hundred pounds, and his weight and strength prevailed despite Susan's efforts. The door began to open.

Keeping her shoulder and left hand against the door, Susan gripped the scissors like a dagger. With a quick overhand stroke, she plunged the scissors into the guard's hand.

The point of the scissors struck between the knuckles of the second and third fingers. The force of the blow carried the blades between the metacarpal bones, shredding the lumbrical muscles and exiting through the back of the hand. The guard screamed in agony, letting go of the door. He staggered back into the corridor with the scissors still embedded in his hand. Holding his breath and grinding his teeth, he pulled them out. A small arterial pumper squirted blood in short pulsating arcs onto the opaque plastic floor, forming a pattern of red polkadots.

Susan slammed the door shut and locked it. She whirled to survey the room. It was a small laboratory, with a laboratory bench in the center. To the left were two desks back to back. Against the wall were several filing cabinets. At the far end was a window.

The guard in the hall recovered enough to wrap a handkerchief about his left hand and curb the spurting blood. He passed the cloth between his index and middle fingers and tied it around his wrist. He was furiously angry, as he fumbled with his passkeys. The first key would not turn in the lock. The second key he selected would not fit it. The third key also would not turn. Finally, the fourth key turned, and the lock mechanism sprang back, releasing the door. With his foot, the guard kicked the door open with such force that the knob went through the plaster wall to the right. With his pistol cocked, the guard sprang into the room, spinning around. Susan was gone. The window was open and frigid February air was streaming into the warm room. The guard ran to the window and leaned out enough to see the ledge. He returned to the room and took out his two-way radio.

"OK, I found the girl, floor two, the tissue lab. She's something. She stabbed me, but I'm OK. She went out the window onto the ledge. . . . No, I can't see her. The ledge goes around the corner. . . . No, I don't think that she would jump. Did the Dobermans get released? . . . Good. The only worry is that she might attract some attention if she gets to the front of the building. . . . OK. . . . I'll check the ledge on the other side."

The guard put his radio back on his belt, closed the window and locked it. Then he ran out of the room, clutching his wounded hand.

Thursday
February 26
5:47 P.M.

The heavy industrial-weight vinyl ceiling tile was slowly slipping from Susan's grip, and she clenched her teeth. Her hands were numb from holding it with just the tips of her fingers, forcing the tile against its metal supports on the opposite side of its six-foot expanse. She could hear the guard below talking on his two-way radio. If the tile fell, he'd find her. She closed her eyes as tightly as she could to take her mind off her fingers and her aching forearms. It was slipping. It was going to fall. The guard switched off. Then the window closed. Susan held on somehow. She didn't hear the guard exit, but the tile fell with a dull thud that jarred the whole suspended ceiling. Susan listened intently as blood rushed into her tingling fingers, painfully. There was no sound below. She let herself take a deep breath.

Susan was up in the ceiling space above the tissue lab. It was ironic that before her search of the ORs at the Memorial, Susan never knew of the existence of ceiling spaces. Now clambering up there had saved her life. Thank God for the filing cabinet on which she had stood to lift the tile.

Susan took out her floor plans and tried to examine them in the sparse light filtering up through the edges of the ceiling tiles. She found it impossible even after her eyes had adjusted. Looking around in the gloom, she noticed a rather concentrated beam of light coming from some larger fissure in the ceiling about twenty feet from her position. With the help of the upright studding marking the wall of the tissue lab and a neighboring office, Susan managed to work her way over to the light source and position herself so that she could see the plans. What she wanted to find was the main chase like the one she had seen at the Memorial. She thought that if it were big enough it would be a possible way out. But the chase was not listed in the key. However she did find a rectangular enclosure drawn next to the elevator shaft. Susan decided that it probably represented the chase she was after.

She moved along the top of the wall of the tissue lab, holding onto the upright studs until she reached the step up to the fixed ceiling of the corridor. It was made of concrete, to support the tracks for the trolleys. Once on it, the going was much easier. She moved toward the elevator shaft.

The closer she got to the elevator shaft the more difficult was her progress both because it got significantly darker and because more and more pipes, wires, and ducts converged in the direction she was heading. She had to move by feel, advancing a foot forward slowly, blindly. Several times she touched a steam pipe and it burned her. The smell of burnt flesh drifted into her nose.

In utter darkness she reached the elevator shaft and felt the vertical concrete. Rounding its corner, she followed a pipe with her hands and felt it turn down at a ninety-degree angle. Other pipes did the same. Leaning over them, she looked down into the darkness. A faint light filtered up from far below.

With her hands Susan determined the size of the chase. It was about four feet square. The wall common to the elevator shaft was concrete. She selected a pipe about two inches in diameter. Lowering herself into the chase, she put her back against the concrete wall and grabbed the pipe with both hands. Then she put her feet against other pipes and pushed back firmly against the concrete wall. In this fashion she inched herself down the chase, like a mountaineer in a chimney.

The going was not easy. Moving only inches at a time, she

tried, although not always successfully, to avoid the steam pipes, which were blistering hot. After a while she was able to distinguish the pipes in front of her. Looking into the darkness, she could see vague forms, and she realized that she had reached the ceiling space of the first floor. She was making progress and she felt a certain elation. But it was tempered by the thought that if she could use the chase to go down, someone could use it to go up. And she realized then how relatively easy it was for someone to gain access to the T-valve in the oxygen line at the Memorial.

Susan continued inching downward. Below her there was a bit more light filtering upward. There was also the progressively louder sound of electrical machinery. As she approached the basement level, Susan realized that there was no suspended ceiling below her in the basement. There would be no way to conceal herself and move laterally. She worked herself down until her eyes cleared the structural floor on the first level, then stopped her movement, wedging herself securely against the concrete to survey the scene.

The machinery room and its power plant were lit by a few work lights. The pipe Susan was using for her descent, apparently a water pipe from its feel, continued to the floor. But several other pipes, larger than the one she was holding, angled off horizontally, hanging by metal straps about four feet below the concrete slab of the building's first floor. They ran high above the machinery area.

Susan stepped onto one of these pipes. She was no acrobat, but perhaps her natural ability as a dancer helped. With her right hand and her head pressed against the solid concrete, she moved crouching along the pipe, trying not to look down.

She teetered a bit but gained confidence. Ahead she saw a wall and beyond, another ceiling space. By maintaining pressure on the ceiling above she did a tightrope walk along the pipe. Susan passed directly over the power plant and was within four feet of her goal when there was a startling flash of light very close to her, almost causing her to lose her balance. The lights had come on in the machinery room.

Susan shut her eyes, pressing her hands against the ceiling and hooking the groove of her shoes against the pipe. Beneath her a guard moved slowly around the machinery, a big flashlight in one hand, a pistol in the other.

The next fifteen minutes were probably the longest single period of time in Susan's life. She felt so exposed, with a white dress against the dark pipes and ceiling, that she could not fathom why she was not seen. The guard searched carefully, even the cabinets under the workbench. But he never looked up. Susan's arms began to tremble from the tension necessary to keep her balance secure. Then her legs followed, so that she was afraid her shoes would soon be tapping a message against the pipe. Finally the guard was satisfied and left, turning out the main lights.

Susan did not move immediately. She tried to relax, conquering her tension and incipient vertigo. She longed for the fixed ceiling about four feet away. It was so close yet so far. She moved her right foot forward about six inches, then put weight on it. Then she moved the left up to the right. Both her arms and legs pained her tremendously. She thought about just letting herself fall forward onto the ceiling but she was afraid of the noise being heard. Instead she continued in her painful caterpillar way. When she reached the ceiling, she collapsed onto her back, breathing hard and letting the blood flow back into her deprived muscles.

But she knew she could not rest for long. She had to find a way out of the building. Lying on her back, she again consulted the floor plans. There were two possible exits. One was the supply room very close to where she now was. Another was at the far end of the building, beyond a room labeled "Dp." Susan checked the key. Dp stood for dispatch.

Thinking about the man carrying the heart and the kidney from the auxiliary room between the ORs made Susan opt for the dispatch room despite the proximity of the supply room. She thought that perhaps they were planning on transporting the organs. She knew that transplant organs should be used as soon as possible.

Replacing the floor plans, Susan pulled herself to her feet. Her dress was now badly soiled and torn. She kept to the fixed ceiling over the basement corridor as she made her way in the direction of the dispatch room. The going was comparatively easy because it was not totally dark. Like the machinery space, large sections of the basement had no ceiling at all, and enough light was transmitted along Susan's path that she could move at a regular pace, avoiding the pipes and ducts with ease.

She arrived at the extreme corner of the building and guessed from another glance at the floor plans that she had reached her goal. She lay supine on the fixed corridor ceiling with her head over the dropped ceiling of the dispatch room. As carefully as she could, she lifted a tile until she could just get her fingers under its edge. With effort she pulled it up until she could just see below. The room was occupied!

Not daring to let the ceiling tile go for fear of noise, Susan watched the man below, bent over a desk, filling out a form. He was dressed in an unzipped leather coat. On the floor were two insulated cardboard boxes. They were boldly labeled: "Human Transplant Organ—This side up—Fragile—Rush."

A door which she could not see opened below. A second man appeared. It was one of the guards.

"Let's go, Mac. Let's get these things loaded and out of here. We've got work to do."

"I'm not taking nothing until the proper papers are done."

The guard left by a swinging door on the far side of the room. Susan got a glimpse of another area before the door closed. It looked like a garage.

The driver finished his forms and tossed a copy into a basket on the counter. The other copy he put into his pocket. He loaded the cartons onto a dolly and backed through the swinging doors.

Susan let the ceiling tile fall back into place. Quickly she moved over to the wall at the far end of the corridor. She could hear the noise of a truck door being shut and latched.

It was darker near the wall, and Susan ran her hand along the wall expecting to feel concrete. Instead she felt vinyl tile, oriented vertically. Susan could plainly hear a truck engine turning over. She pushed against the tile but it seemed to be securely held in place by a metal flange. The truck engine caught, coughed, and quit. The starter began to whine again.

Desperately Susan pushed against the metal flange, feeling it bend up. She repeated the maneuver in several locations. The truck engine caught again, rattled and coughed and then roared, finally sinking back to a controlled idle. Susan then heard the distinctive rumble of a massive and heavy garage door being elevated. Her fingers clawed for the top of the vinyl tile. She pulled it toward herself but it stayed firm. She raised more of the flange and pulled again. The tile came in suddenly, causing Susan to fall backward. She recovered quickly and stared through the vertical opening into an underground garage area. Directly below was a relatively large truck belching exhaust. By the entrance stood the guard, activating the overhead door switch. He was watching the door ascend.

Susan leaped into space and hit the top of the truck with her feet and hands at the same time. The noise of the impact was lost within the echo of the truck engine and the rumble of the garage door. She flattened herself spread-eagled as the truck lurched forward. She felt the inertia of her body cause her to slide backward. She tried to grip something, anything, but the top of the truck was smooth metal and her hands groped in vain. She managed to clear the garage door, but as the truck mounted the incline to the street, Susan's backward slide became more uncontrollable. Her feet actually slipped over the rear of the truck as she tried to press her hands flat against the smooth surface.

The truck reached the street and the driver braked before turning left. Susan's body then slid forward, careening counterclockwise. The frigid cold struck her. The driver picked up speed, and Susan felt a sense of helpless terror. She inched toward the cab and clamped her numb fingers over a low ventilator. Then there was a bump and Susan's body flew up, only to slam down on the metal roof a moment later. Her chin and nose hit the surface so hard that it dazed her. She was only vaguely conscious of what happened after that.

Susan became lucid rather suddenly. She lifted her head and recognized that her nose and lip were bleeding. She watched the buildings and recognized the area. It was the Haymarket. Of course, she thought, the truck was heading for Logan Airport.

The truck halted for a traffic light. Traffic was still rather heavy. Susan worked her way right up to the cab. She pulled her feet around and stood up on the roof of the cab. Then she sat down and let her feet onto the hood. At that point she lowered her head and looked through the windshield at the driver. The man was shocked and immobile, his eyes staring without believing, his hands rigidly gripping the steering wheel.

Susan slid from the hood to the fender, then leaped for the ground. She scrambled to her feet and ran between the cars toward Government Center. The driver recovered somewhat, opened his door, and shouted after her. Other angry yells and blaring horns drove him back into his cab. The light had changed. As he put the truck into gear and pulled forward, he told himself that no one would believe this story.

**Thursday
February 26
8:10 P.M.**

The tattered and flimsy nurse's uniform was little protection against the razor-sharp cold. It was seventeen degrees with a twenty-five knot north wind, making the wind chill factor somewhere around twenty below zero. Susan ran along the deserted Haymarket vegetable stalls, trying to avoid the empty cardboard boxes that were being blown across her path. The debris made her progress slow, and it reminded her of the nightmare that had started the day.

At the corner she turned left and braved the full power of the wind. She was shivering now, and her upper and lower jaws clattered against each other as if they were beating out some urgent message in Morse code. On the City Hall mall it got worse. The particular design of the Government Center area, with its curved facades and expansive mall, functioned as a wind tunnel, pushing the north wind to greater effort. Susan had to bend herself into the wind to make progress up the wide steps. To her left the remarkable modern architecture of the City Hall loomed eerily in the darkness; its stark geometric protrusions formed dark, intervening shadows, giving the whole scene an ominous air.

Susan needed a telephone. When she got to Cambridge Street there were a few other humans, bent over, faceless in the wind and the cold. Susan stopped the first pedestrian; it was a woman. The stranger's head came up, the eyes looked at Susan first with disbelief, then fright.

"I need a dime and a telephone," said Susan through her chattering teeth.

The woman pushed Susan's arm away and hurried on without looking back and without saying a single word.

Susan looked down at her nurse's uniform. It was torn, soiled, and bloodstained. Her hands were totally black. Her hair was irretrievably tangled and matted. She realized she looked like a psychotic, or at best a derelict.

Susan stopped a man and asked her question. The man backed up from Susan's appearance. He reached into his pocket and extended some change toward Susan, his eyes also revealing a mixture of incredulousness and consternation. He dropped the coins into Susan's hand as if he were afraid to touch her.

Susan took the change. It was more than the single dime she had asked for.

"I think there's a phone in the diner down on the left," said the man, looking at Susan. "Are you all right?"

"I'll be all right if I get to a phone. Thank you very much."

Susan's cold fingers had trouble wrapping around the change. Her hands were so numb that she could not even feel the coins in her palms. She ran across Cambridge Street toward the diner.

The steamy, greasy warmth of the place was a welcome relief as Susan entered. A few faces looked up from their food, and noted her strange look. But in deference to the anonymity guaranteed by a large American city, the diners returned to their fare, to keep from becoming involved.

Susan was gripped by an irrational paranoia, and her eyes went from person to person, trying to detect an enemy. The warmth brought even greater shivering. She hurried to the pay phone near the restrooms.

Her hands had great difficulty manipulating the coins, and most of them dropped to the floor before she got a dime into the slot. No one got up to help her retrieve her money. The grease-smeared tattooed counterman watched her blankly, inured to the curiosities of Boston street life.

The operator answered at the Memorial.

"I'm Dr. Wheeler and I must speak with Dr. Stark immediately. It is an emergency. Do you have his home number?"

"I'm sorry, but we cannot give out the doctor's number."

"But this is an emergency." Susan glanced around the diner, half-expecting someone to challenge her.

"I'm sorry, but we have our orders. If you want to leave your number, I'll have the doctor call."

Susan's eyes roamed around for the number.

"523-8787."

There was a click. Susan replaced the disconnected receiver. She had one dime left in her hand. She thought perhaps hot tea would help. She searched around for more change on the floor. She found a nickel. She looked in a wider area. She knew that she had had a quarter.

One of the patrons got up from the counter and sleepily walked around to use the phone. He was reaching for the receiver when Susan spotted him.

"Please. I'm expecting a call. Please don't use the phone for just a few moments." Susan stood up, beseeching the stubbly-faced man.

"Sorry, sister, got to use the phone." The man picked up the receiver and reached up to drop in his dime.

For the first time in her life, Susan lost all semblance of control or rationality.

"No!" she screamed at the top of her lungs, causing every head in the diner to snap around in her direction. To emphasize her determination, Susan clasped her two hands together, the fingers interlocking, and brought them up swiftly, hitting the man's forearms. The surprisingly fast blow knocked both the receiver and the dime from his grasp. With her hands still clasped, Susan brought them down so that the heels of her hands hit the man on the forehead and the bridge of his nose. It sent the surprised individual stumbling backward into the edge of a booth. Almost in slow motion, he sank to a sitting position, his feet outstretched. The suddenness and the fury of the attack had left him momentarily dumbfounded, and he didn't move.

Susan quickly replaced the receiver on the phone, holding onto it, closing her eyes tightly, hoping it would ring. It did. It was Stark. Susan tried to contain herself in the surroundings, but the words bubbled out of her.

"Dr. Stark, this is Susan Wheeler. I have the answers . . . all of them. It's unbelievable, really it is."

"Calm down, Susan. What do you mean you have all the answers?" Stark's voice was reassuring and calm.

"I have a motive; I have both the method and a motive."

"Susan, you're talking in riddles."

"The coma patients. They're not accidental complications. They're planned. When I was doing the chart extractions, I found out that all the victims had been tissue-typed."

Susan paused, remembering how Bellows had talked her out of attaching any significance to the tissue-typing.

"Go on, Susan," said Dr. Stark.

"Well, I didn't give it any significance. But I do now. Now that I've been to the Jefferson Institute."

Saying the name made Susan look around the diner suspiciously. Now most of the eyes in the place were directed at her. But no one moved. Susan withdrew into the alcove by the restrooms, cupping her hand over the receiver.

"I know it will sound incredible, but the Jefferson Institute is a clearinghouse for black-market transplant organs. Somehow these people get orders for organs with a specific tissue type. Then whoever runs the show reaches around in the hospitals here in Boston till they find patients with the proper type. If it's a surgical patient, they merely add a little carbon monoxide to his anesthesia. If it's a medical patient he—or she—gets a shot of succinylcholine in his I.V. The victim's upper brain is destroyed. He's a living corpse, but his organs are alive and warm and happy until they can be taken out by the butchers at the Institute."

"Susan, that's an incredible story," said Stark. He sounded stunned. "Do you think you can prove this?"

"That's one of the problems. If there is a big fuss—say the police were brought to Jefferson Institute for a look-see—they probably have a contingency plan to cover up. The place masquerades as an intensive-care hospital. Besides, both carbon monoxide and the succinylcholine are metabolized quickly in the victims' bodies, leaving no trace whatsoever. The only way to break up the organization behind these crimes is for someone like youself to convince the authorities to make a real surprise raid on the place."

"That might be an idea, Susan," said Stark. "But I'd have to hear the particulars that brought you to your fantastic conclusions. Are you in any danger now? I can come and pick you up."

"No, I'm all right," said Susan, glancing into the diner. "It would be easier if I met you somewhere. I can catch a cab."

"Fine. Meet me at my office in the Memorial. I'll leave immediately."

"I'll be there." Susan was about to hang up.

"Susan, one more thing. If what you say is true, then secrecy is tremendously important. Don't say anything to anybody until we've talked."

"Agreed. See you in a few minutes."

Replacing the receiver, Susan looked up a cab company. She used her last dime to order a cab. She gave the name Shirley Walton. They said it would take ten minutes.

Dr. Harold Stark lived in Weston, along with nine-tenths of Boston's other doctors. He had a sprawling Tudor house which also boasted a Victorian library. After speaking with Susan, he replaced the receiver on the phone on top of his desk. Then he pulled open the right-hand drawer and extracted a second phone, a phone carefully maintained and checked electronically for any additional resistance or interference. It could not be tapped without Stark's knowledge. He dialed quickly, watching the tiny oscilloscope in the drawer. It functioned normally.

In the control room of the Jefferson Institute a manicured man, slight of build, reached for the ringing red telephone.

"Wilton," yelled Stark, only partially concealing his anger, "for a whiz kid with figures and an aptitude for business, you're pretty impotent when it comes to catching young, unarmed girls in a building built like a castle. I cannot understand how you could allow this matter to get so far out of hand. I warned you about her days ago."

"Don't worry, Stark. We'll find her. She got out on the ledge but obviously has to return to the building. All the doors are sealed, and I've got ten men here now. Don't worry."

"Don't worry," snarled Stark. "Well, let me tell you something. She just called me on the phone and outlined the entire core of our program. She's already out, you ass."

"Out! Impossible!"

"Impossible. What kind of statement is that? I said she just called me. What do you think, she's using one of your phones? Christ, Wilton. Why didn't you take care of her?"

"We tried. Apparently she's eluded a very reliable hit man. The same man who took care of Walters."

"God, that was another thing. Why didn't you just dispose of him rather than stage that suicide?"

"For your benefit. You're the one that was so uptight when the drugs that old codger was hoarding were found. I mean you were the one who was so worried that it might drag in the authorities for some sort of grand investigation. We not only had to get rid of Walters but we had to associate him with his goddamn drugs."

"Well, this whole affair has made up my mind for me. I think it's time we wind down this operation. Do you understand, Wilton?"

"So the great doctor wants out, does he? At the first ripple of trouble in almost three years, you want out. You got all the money to rebuild that whole hospital of yours. You got yourself appointed Chief of Surgery. And now you want to leave us dry. Well let me tell *you* something, Stark, something that you're going to find hard to take. You are not giving orders anymore. You're going to follow them. And the first order is to get rid of this girl."

Stark found himself holding a dead connection. He slammed the phone down and replaced it in the drawer. He was trembling with rage. He had to hold himself back from smashing his own belongings. Instead he gripped the edge of the desk until his fingers turned milky white. Then his fury began to abate. Anger per se had never solved anything, Stark knew. He had to rely on his analytical powers. Wilton was right. Susan represented the first ripple of trouble in his progress in almost three years. The progress that had been made was beyond Stark's wildest dreams. It had to go on. Medical science demanded it. Susan had to be eliminated. That was certain. But it had to be done in a way so as not to cause suspicion or alarm, especially from some narrow-minded people like Harris or Nelson, who lacked the vision Stark knew he had.

Stark got up from behind his massive desk and walked along the ranks of bookshelves. He was deep in thought and he let his hand carelessly caress the gilded edges of a first-edition

Dickens. Suddenly it came to him in a moment of inspiration that brought a smile to his face.

"Beautiful . . . so appropriate," he said out loud. He laughed, his anger already forgotten.

Thursday
February 26
8:47 P.M.

Susan dashed from the cab without paying and made a bee-line for the Memorial entrance. She had no money and did not intend to get into an argument. The driver jumped out of the cab, too, shouting angrily. He caught the attention of one of the guards, but Susan was already through the entrance.

Susan had to slow to a walk in the main hall. Ahead of her she was dismayed to see Bellows, headed in the same direction. Susan worked her way up to a position directly behind him and debated with herself about catching his attention. She thought again about how he had caused her to disregard the tissue typing done on the coma patients. There was a chance that Bellows was involved. Besides, she remembered Stark's admonition to speak to no one. So when they reached the corner of the corridor, Susan let Bellows continue down toward the ER. She turned toward the Beard elevators. One was waiting, and she got on and pushed 10.

Susan's view of the hall became progressively occluded by the closing door. But at the very last minute a hand wrapped around the edge of the door, halting it. Susan stared blankly at it before the face of a guard came into view.

"I would like to have a word with you, Miss," he said, still holding the door open despite its continued attempts to close, as Susan pressed on the "door close" button.

"Please come off the elevator."

"But I'm in a terrible hurry. It's an emergency."

"The emergency room is on this floor, Miss."

Susan reluctantly complied with the guard's demands and got off the elevator. The doors closed behind her, and the car began its ascent to the tenth floor without any occupants.

"It's not that kind of emergency," pleaded Susan.

"So much of an emergency you couldn't pay your cab?" The guard's voice was a mixture of admonition and concern. Susan's appearance lent a definite credence to her plea that it was an emergency.

"Take his name and company, and I'll settle it later. Look, I'm a third-year medical student. My name is Susan Wheeler. I have no time at this moment."

"Where are you going at this hour?" The guard's tone had become almost solicitous.

"Beard 10. I'm meeting one of the doctors there. I've got to go." Susan depressed the up button.

"Who?"

"Howard Stark. You can call him."

The guard was confused, dubious. "All right. But stop by the security office on your way down."

"Of course," agreed Susan as the guard turned to go.

Just then the next elevator arrived and Susan boarded it, pushing past a few departing passengers, who looked at her disheveled appearance curiously. On the slow ride up to 10 she leaned against the car's wall gratefully.

The corridor presented a totally different environment from the one she remembered from her previous daytime visit. The typewriters were quiet. The patients gone. The floor was as still as a morgue. The thick carpet absorbed the sound of her own hesitant footsteps as she moved toward her goal and safety. The only light came from a lonely table lamp in the middle of the hall. The *New Yorker* magazine stacks which could be seen were carefully straightened. The faces on the portraits of the former Memorial surgeons were smudges of violet shadow.

Susan approached Stark's office and hesitated for a moment, composing herself. She was about to knock, but tried the door. It opened. The anteroom of Stark's secretary was dark, but the door to his private office was slightly ajar, light slanting through it. Susan pushed open the door and stepped in.

The door shut behind her that instant. Susan's overwrought psyche caused a tremendous panic reaction as she whirled to face an assailant. She had to fight to keep from screaming.

Stark was locking the door. He must have been behind her.

"Sorry for the dramatics, but I don't think we want anyone interrupting this conversation." He smiled suddenly. "Susan, you'll never know how glad I am to see you. After these experiences you told me about, I should have insisted on picking you up from where you called. But no matter, you got here safely. Do you think you were followed?"

Susan's fight reaction tapered, her heart rate reached an apogee and began to slow. She swallowed. "I don't think so, but I can't be sure."

"Come and sit down. You look like you've been through World War I." Stark touched Susan's arm, guiding her to a chair in front of his desk. "Looks like you could use a little Scotch, at the very least."

Susan felt a terrible exhaustion; mental, physical, and emotional, descend over her. She didn't respond audibly. She simply followed, her chest heaving. She sank into the chair, barely comprehending what she had been through.

"You're an amazing girl," said Stark, walking over to the small bar cabinet across the room.

"I don't think so," returned Susan, her voice reflecting her exhaustion. "I just happened to walk blindly into an amazing horror."

Stark got a bottle of Chivas Regal. He carefully poured out two drinks and brought them over to the desk. He handed one to Susan. "I think you're being too modest." Stark rounded his desk and sat down, his gaze fixed on Susan. "You're not hurt, are you?"

Susan shook her head, her hand inadvertently shaking her drink so that the ice clinked against the side of the glass. She tried to steady herself by using both hands. She took a mouthful of the comforting, fiery liquid, letting it slide down her throat between deep breaths.

"Now then, Susan. I want to make sure where we stand. Have you spoken to anyone since we talked?"

"No," said Susan taking another drink.

"Good, that's very good." Stark paused, watching Susan

sip her drink. "Does anyone besides yourself have any idea about all this?"

"No. No one." The Scotch felt delightfully warm inside Susan, and she began to feel a calmness settle over her. Her breathing began to slow to normal. She looked at Stark over her glass.

"OK, Susan, now why do you think the Jefferson Institute is a clearinghouse for transplant organs?"

"I heard them talking. I even saw the shipping cartons for the organs myself."

"But Susan, it isn't surprising to me that a hospital filled with chronic-care, comatose patients would be a source of transplant organs as the patients succumb to their disease processes."

"That might be true. But the problem is that the people behind this were the ones making at least some of those patients comatose in the first place. Besides, they were getting paid for these organs. Paid a lot of money." Susan felt her upper eyelids droop, and she raised them forcefully. She felt a torpor stealing over her. She knew she was exhausted but dragged herself straighter in the chair. She took another mouthful of the Scotch and tried not to think of D'Ambrosio. At least she felt warm.

"Susan, you are amazing. I mean, you were only in the place for a short time. How did you learn so much so quickly?"

"I had floor plans from City Hall. They showed operating rooms, and the girl who was showing me around said there were no operating rooms. So I checked them out myself. Then it was clear. Frightfully clear."

"I see. Very clever." Stark nodded his head, marveling at Susan. "And they let you leave. I would have imagined that they would have preferred that you stay." He smiled again.

"I was lucky. Extremely lucky. I left with a heart and a kidney on their way to Logan." Susan suppressed a yawn, trying to hide it from Stark. She felt tired, very tired.

"That's all very interesting, Susan, and that's probably all the information I really need. But . . . you are to be commended. Your activities over the last few days are a study in clairvoyance and perseverance. But let me ask you a few more questions. Tell me . . ." Stark put his hands together and rotated in his chair so that he could see out over the black waters of the harbor. "Tell me if you can think of any other reasons for this fantastic operation you have so cleverly exposed."

"You mean, other than money?"

"Yes, other than money."

"Well, it is a good way to get rid of someone you don't want around."

Stark laughed inappropriately, or so it seemed to Susan.

"No, I mean a real benefit. Can you think of any benefits other than financial?"

"I guess the recipients of the organs get a certain benefit, if they don't have to know how the donor organ was obtained."

"I mean a more general benefit. A benefit for society."

Susan again tried to think, but her eyes wanted to close. She straightened up again. Benefit? She looked at Stark. The meaning of the conversation was becoming diffuse, strange.

"Dr. Stark, I hardly think this is the time . . ."

"Come on, Susan. Try. You've done such a remarkable job at uncovering this thing. Try to think. It's important."

"I can't. It's such a horror that I have difficulty even considering the word *benefit*." Susan's arms began to feel heavy. She shook her head. For a second she thought she had actually fallen asleep.

"Well, then I'm surprised at you, Susan. From the intelligence that you have so amply displayed over the last couple of days, I thought that you would have been one of the few to see the other side."

"Other side?" Susan closed her eyes tightly, then opened them, hoping they would stay open.

"Exactly." Stark rotated back toward Susan, leaning forward, arms on the desk. "Sometimes there are situations where . . . what should I say . . . the common folk, if you will, cannot be depended upon to make decisions which will provide long-term benefits. The common man thinks only of his short-run needs and selfish requirements."

Stark got up and wandered over to the corner where the expansive walls of glass joined. He looked out over the great medical complex he had helped to build. Susan felt herself unable to move. She even had difficulty turning her head. She knew she was tired but she never felt so heavy, so languorous. Besides, Stark kept going in and out of focus.

"Susan," Stark said suddenly, turning around to face her again, "you must realize that medicine is on the brink of probably the biggest breakthrough in all of its long history. The discovery of anesthesia, the discovery of antibiotics . . . any of those epochal achievements will pale before the next giant step. We are about to crack the mystery of the immunological mechanisms. Soon we'll be able to transplant all human organs at will. The fear of most cancer will become a thing of the past. Degenerative disease, trauma . . . the scope is infinite.

"But such breakthroughs do not come easy, not without hard work and sacrifice. Not without a price. We need first-rate institutions, like the Memorial and its facilities. Next we need people like myself, indeed like Leonardo Da Vinci, willing to step beyond restrictive laws in order to insure progress. What if Leonardo Da Vinci had not dug up his bodies for dissection? What if Copernicus had knuckled under to the laws and dogma of the church? Where would we be today? What we need for the breakthrough to actually happen is data, hard data. Susan, you have the mind to appreciate that."

Despite the darkening cloud she felt settling over her brain, Susan began to realize what Stark was saying. She tried to get up, but she found she could not lift her arms. She strained but only succeeded in knocking the remains of her drink to the floor. The ice cubes scattered.

"You do understand what I am saying, Susan? I think you do. Our legal system is not geared to handle our needs. My God, they cannot make a decision to terminate a patient even after it is certain that his brain has turned to lifeless Jell-O. How can science proceed under a public policy handicap of that proportion?

"Now, Susan, I want you to think carefully. I know it is a little hard for you to think at this moment, but try. I want to say something to you and I want your response. You are a bright, very bright, girl. You're obviously one of the . . . what should I say? . . . *elite* sounds too much like a cliché, but you know what I mean. We need you, people like you. What I want to say is that the people who run the Jefferson Institute are on our side. Do you understand, our side?"

Stark paused, looking at Susan. She struggled to keep her eyelids above her pupils. It took all her strength.

"What do you say to that, Susan? Are you willing to dedicate that brain of yours to the good of society, science, and medicine?"

Susan's mouth formed words but they came out in a whisper. Her face was expressionless. Stark leaned forward to hear. He had to bring his head up to within inches of Susan's lips.

"Say it again, Susan. I'll be able to hear if you say it again."

Susan's mouth struggled to bring her lower lip against her upper teeth to form the first consonant. It spilled out in a whisper.

"Fuck you, you cra—" Susan's head slumped back, her mouth gaping and her respirations coming in regular deep-sounding breaths.

Stark looked at Susan's drugged body for a few moments. Susan's defiance angered him. But after a few moments of silence his emotion faded into disappointment. "Susan, we could have used that brain of yours." Stark shook his head slowly. "Well, maybe you can still be useful."

Stark turned to his phone and called the emergency room. He asked for the admitting resident.

Thursday
February 26
11:51 P.M.

The surgical residents' on-call room at the Memorial was rather minimal in its amenities. It had a bed, a hospital bed, which could be cranked into a number of interesting positions, a small desk; a TV which got two stations provided you didn't mind a double image; and a collection of torn, stained old

Penthouse magazines. Bellows was sitting at his desk, trying to read an article in the *American Journal of Surgery*, but he couldn't concentrate. His mind, particularly his conscience, was functioning in an abnormally irritating manner. It kept reminding him of Susan's appearance a few hours earlier. Bellows had seen her when she entered the Memorial. He knew she had come up behind him, and he had expected her to stop him. It had been a surprise when she didn't.

Bellows had not looked at Susan directly, but enough to see her matted hair, her bloodied and torn dress. He had felt immediate concern, but at the same time felt a definite inclination to leave well enough alone. His job at the Memorial was on the line. If Susan needed medical help, she had come to the right place. If she needed psychological support, it would have been better to call and meet him outside the hospital. But Susan had not stopped him and had not called.

Now Bellows had learned that Susan had been admitted as a patient, that Stark himself was handling her case. As the senior surgical resident on call, Bellows knew that Susan was scheduled for an appendectomy. It seemed quite a coincidence, but there it was. Stark was going to operate. At first Bellows thought he'd scrub. Then prudence told him he was far from objective about Susan and that could become a handicap in the OR. So he decided to send a junior resident and wait it out.

Bellows looked at his watch. It was almost midnight. He knew that they'd be starting Susan's appy in ten minutes or so. He tried to go back to the *Journal* article but something else bothered him. Bellows stared out of the grimy window and brooded. Then he picked up the phone and asked in which room the appy was scheduled.

"Number eight, Dr. Bellows," said the OR duty nurse.

Bellows put the phone down. Funny. Susan had told him about finding the T-valve in the oxygen line to that room, the room in which so much had gone wrong.

Bellows looked at his watch again. Suddenly he got up. He'd forgotten about getting his mid rats in the cafeteria. He was hungry. Bellows pulled on his shoes and set off for the cafeteria. But he thought about the T-valve.

He got on the elevator and pushed 1 for the cafeteria. In the middle of the descent he changed his mind and pushed 2.

What the hell, he could take a look for that T-valve on the oxygen line himself, while Susan was having her surgery. It was stupid, but he decided to do it anyway. At least it would satisfy his conscience.

A phantasmagoria of geometric images, color and motion emerged from the darkness, gradually expanding. The geometric images collided, split, and recombined into forms and shapes without meaning. Out of the confusion the image of a hand being stabbed by scissors preceded a sequence of chase. The autopsy room at the Memorial appeared with a realism that included auditory and olfactory aspects. A spiral staircase took dominance; then a corridor filled with the face of D'Ambrosio grinning in sadistic delight seemed to move closer and closer. But D'Ambrosio's face disintegrated and he fell spinning into the abyss. The corridor twisted and turned kaleidoscopically.

Susan regained her consciousness in fluctuating stages. Finally she realized that she was looking at a ceiling, the ceiling of a corridor that was moving. No, she was moving. Susan tried to move her head but it seemed to weigh a thousand pounds. She tried to move her hands. They too were unbelievably heavy, and it took all her concentration just to lift her hands up from her elbows. Susan was lying on her back, moving down a corridor. Sounds started to appear. Voices . . . but they were unintelligible. She felt someone grip her hands and push them down to her side. But she wanted to get up. She wanted to know where she was. She wanted to know what happened to her. Was she asleep? No, she'd been drugged. Suddenly Susan knew that. She fought with the effects of the drug, to try to lift herself from its grasp. Her mind began to clear. She could understand the voices.

"She's an emergency appendectomy. Apparently a hot one, too. And she's a medical student. You'd think she would have had enough sense to be seen sooner."

Another voice, deeper than the first. "I understand she had called in sick this morning to the dean's office, so obviously she knew something was wrong. Maybe she was worried about being pregnant."

"Maybe you're right. But she tested negative."

Susan's mouth tried to form words but no sounds issued

from her larynx. She found that her head could move from side to side. The drug was beginning to wear off. Then the movement stopped. Susan recognized the area. She was in the scrub room. By turning her head to the right she could see the scrub sink. A surgeon was scrubbing.

"You want one or two assistants, sir?" said one of the voices behind Susan.

The man at the scrub sink turned. He was wearing a hood and a mask. But Susan recognized him. It was Stark.

"One's enough for a simple appy. I'll have it out in twenty minutes."

"No, no," cried Susan, voicelessly. Only a bit of air hissed between her lips. Then she began to move toward the operating room. She could see the door open. She saw the number over it. Room No. 8.

The drug was wearing off. Susan could lift her head and her left arm. She saw the huge operating room lights. The glare dazzled her. She knew she had to get up . . . to run.

Strong arms gripped her waist, her ankles and head. She felt hands thrust under her, and she was lifted effortlessly onto the operating table. Susan lifted her left hand to grasp at anything. She grabbed an arm.

"Please . . . don't . . . I am . . ." the words came slowly, almost inaudibly from Susan's throat. She was trying to sit up despite the weight of her head.

A strong arm was laid across her forehead. Her head was pressed back.

"Don't worry, everything will be all right. Just take some deep breaths."

"No, no," said Susan, her voice gaining slightly in power.

But an anesthesia mask dropped over her face. She felt a sudden pain in her right arm . . . an I.V. The liquid started into her vein. No. No. She tried to shake her head from side to side but strong arms held her. She looked up and saw a masked face. The eyes looked into hers. She saw an I.V. bottle with bubbles dancing up through the fluid. She saw someone thrust a syringe into the I.V. line. The Pentothal!

"Everything will be all right. Just relax. Take a deep breath. Everything will be all right. Just relax. Take a deep breath. . . ."

The atmosphere in room eight at 12:36 A.M. that February

27 was extremely tense. The junior resident had found himself all thumbs during the case, even dropping clamps and fumbling ties. Stark's presence and reputation had been too much for the fledgling surgeon, especially after the initial rapport had evaporated.

The anesthesiologist's handwriting was even more erratic than usual as he put the finishing touches on his anesthesia record. He wanted the case to be over. The patient's sudden cardiac irregularities in the middle of the case had totally unnerved him. But even worse had been the sudden closure of the non-return valve on the wall oxygen line. In his eight years as an anesthesiologist, it was the first time that piped-in oxygen had actually failed. He had made the transition to the green emergency cylinders smoothly, and he was fairly confident there had been no change in the amount of oxygen he had been delivering. But the experience had been frightening; he knew he could have lost the patient.

"How much longer?" the anesthesiologist asked over the ether screen, putting his pen down.

Stark's eyes were wildly dancing from the clock to the door, then back to the operative field. He had taken over tying the skin sutures from the bumbling resident.

"Five minutes, tops," said Stark as he ran a knot down with his deft fingers. Stark too was nervous. That was obvious to the resident, who thought he himself must be the cause. But Stark was nervous because he knew that something was not right.

The oxygen non-return valve should not have failed. That meant that the oxygen pressure had fallen to zero in the main line. Of the operating team, only Stark knew that the patient's cardiac irregularities meant that she had received carbon monoxide with the mainline oxygen. But when that oxygen source failed, he couldn't be sure whether Susan had received enough of the deadly gas for his purposes.

And then there had been the muffled shouts which had caused the circulating nurses to check the corridor. But Stark knew that the noises came from above, from the ceiling space.

But that wasn't all. As Stark was making the next to last skin suture, his eyes caught a surge of movement in the corridor through the window of the OR door. The corridor seemed to be filled with people, and at 12:35 A.M. that was inappropriate, to say the least.

Stark placed the last skin suture and dropped the needle holder onto the instrument tray. As he picked up the ends to tie the knot, the OR door swung open, and Stark saw at least four people advance into the room. Mark Bellows was among them.

The sudden visitors wore surgical gowns, and Stark's pulse began to race as he realized that most of them had thrown their gowns over blue uniforms. A deadly silence hung in the OR. But as Stark straightened up from the operating table, he knew now that something was wrong. Something was very wrong.

Author's Note

This novel was conceived as an entertainment, but it is not science fiction. Its implications are scary because they are possible, perhaps even probable. Consider a classified advertisement that appeared in the San Gabriel (Calif.) *Tribune*, May 9, 1968, col. 4:

> NEED A TRANSPLANT?
> Man will sell any portion of body for financial remuneration to person needing an operation. Write box 1211-630, Covina.

The advertiser did not specify what organ or organs, or even whose body they were to come from.

And there have been other advertisements, many others, in various newspapers across the country. Even specific offers of the hearts from living people!

As gruesome as these ads sound, they should come as no great surprise. There are plenty of precedents for the market economy in medicine. Blood—which may be considered as an organ—is routinely bought and sold. There is a commerce in semen, which, while not an organ, is the product of an organ.

Other organs have been bought and sold. In the 1930's, a rich Italian man bought a testis from a young Neapolitan and had it transplanted into himself. (He not only wanted the product but he wanted to be a distributor as well.) In the last few years there have been episodes where families have declined to give their own kidneys to dying relatives and have sought out and paid volunteer donors. Such cases have not been common, but they have occurred.

The larger problem, the danger, arises from the simple matter of scarcity. There are thousands of people waiting for kidneys and corneas today. The reason that these two organs are particularly coveted is because they have most frequently been transplanted—successfully. Thanks to dialysis machines, potential kidney recipients (some of them . . . others are left to die because of shortages of dialysis machines, personnel, and funds) can be kept alive, but their lives are far from normal. In many situations they border on the desperate, so much so that kidney dialysis centers have reported a so-called "Holiday Syndrome." What that means is that when a holiday weekend approaches, the patients' spirits rise as they anticipate the rush of auto accidents and the victims who may supply the eagerly awaited and desperately needed organs.

The tragedy in this situation is that the solution to the problem is already within our grasp. Medical technology has advanced to the point where approximately seven percent of all cadaver kidneys are suitable for transplant (and the figure is much higher for corneas), if they are taken from the donor body within an hour of death. But instead of being put to this noble use, these organs are regularly delivered to the worms or to the fires of the crematorium because of legal mumbo jumbo whose origins lie in the dark ages of English law. For back in those times corpses came under the jurisdiction of the ecclesiastical rather than civil law. It seems inconceivable that such a legacy should limit our lives today. But it does.

However, most, if not all, states have now passed the Uniform Anatomical Gift Act. This law has helped to provide cadavers for medical schools (whose supply was already adequate), but it has not helped in rectifying the sad need for useful "live" organs for transplant purposes. An alternate approach, by which all cadaver organs would be immediately available for salvage unless the deceased or the next of kin had made prior refusal, has been proposed. But alas, the wheels of change turn agonizingly slowly, and potential recipients are allowed to die while organs are wasted in the ground. Hard questions remain to be answered: such as an acceptable definition of death, and the legal rights of an individual after death. But such difficulties should not preclude a solution to the egregiously wasteful practice of discarding valuable human resources.

The problem of organ scarcity for transplantation represents only one flagrant example of the failure of society in general and medicine in particular to anticipate the social, legal, and ethical ramifications of a technological innovation. For some inexplicable reason, society waits to the very end before creating appropriate policy to pick up the pieces and make sense out of chaos. And in the instance of transplantation, failure to recognize mounting problems and enact appropriate solutions will certainly open Pandora's box, with its countless unconscionable possibilities: the Stark *et al.* of my fiction suggest only possible, execrable aberrations.

For those readers who are interested in delving into the complex problems of organs for transplantation, I recommend two excellent articles which are delightfully illuminating, despite that fact that they appeared in law journals. This is not to cast aspersions on law journals, but rather to emphasize that the lay individual will find these articles very readable: J. Dukeminier, "Supplying Organs for Transplantation," *Michigan Law Review,* vol. 68 (April 1970), pp. 811-866; D. Sanders and J. Dukeminier, "Medical Advance and Legal Lag: Hemodialysis and Kidney Transplantation," *UCLA Law Review,* vol. 15 (1968), pp. 357-413.

For those who are interested in medical policy and its phlegmatic character, combined with some positive suggestions for future change, I recommend: J. Katz and M. Capron, *Catastrophic Diseases: Who Decides What?* Russell Sage Foundation, 1975. This is an excellent, thought-provoking book, probably years ahead of its time. Its only drawback is that not enough people in positions of power in medicine will read it.

A final word about women in medicine: I must admit that the research I did on the subject (there is not much available) caused me to alter my opinions. I now have a heightened regard for female physicians and female medical students. I recognize that their training experiences are much more difficult and stressful than those of their male counterparts. Things are getting better in this respect, but at a snail's pace. The article I found the most illuminating is: M. Notman and C. Nadelson, "Medicine: Career Conflict for Woman," *American Journal of Psychiatry,* vol. 130 (October 1973), pp. 1123-1126.

ROBIN COOK, M.D.
August, 1976